Praise for Dee Carney

"*Hunger Awakened* is a hot and steamy erotic paranormal romance. Dark and sensual, it is balanced by touches of humor and whimsy that allow for a fast paced read."
—*Smexy Books*

"Wowza. This hawt, steamy, sexy indulgence was one exciting ride from start to finish."
—*Bitten by Books* on *Hunger Aroused*

"If you are looking for sexual antics and erotic fun, look no further, *Hunger Aroused* is all these things and more. I highly recommend it."
—*Night Owl Reviews*

"I loved it and I'm sure I'm going to read it again in the near future. I stayed up until 4am finishing this one and I found myself laughing and crying at the end. If you like paranormal romance, this book is for you."
—*Harlequin Junkie* on *Hunger Awakened*

**Also available from Dee Carney
and Carina Press**

*Hunger Aroused
Taming Her Wolf*

HUNGER
AWAKENED

DEE
CARNEY

Dear Ken—
Go wild for
a while!
xoxo
D Carney

carina press®

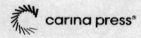

carina press®

ISBN-13: 978-0-373-00322-8

Hunger Awakened

Recycling programs
for this product may
not exist in your area.

www.CarinaPress.com

Printed in U.S.A.

Dear Reader,

I'm excited to share the second book of the Vampire Hunger series with you! Like the other two books in this series, the theme of being cured is a prominent one. Vampires, in particular, are fascinating to me because of their ability to ignore the human failing of illness. How cool would it be to never worry about getting sick?

But what happens if a vampire *were* to get sick?

Imagine being thrust into a vulnerable position where a fever can sap you of strength, where the body turns against itself after living a lifetime of never facing something so mundane before. Somehow a woman living on the fringe of society manages to ease the illness. If she has secrets of her own, though, can she be trusted?

What happens when the vampire and human fall in love...?

Please enjoy this book of my heart, and I hope you get the chance to visit the other intriguing characters in this world. Drop me a line, too, and let me know what you thought. I love to hear from readers.

Best,

Dee

HUNGER
AWAKENED

PROLOGUE

"*He'll know of you sooner or later. He might come looking for you.*"

"*Who?*"

"*What happened to the left-for-dead? He wouldn't have allowed himself to be taken.*"

"*Who? Oh, him.*" John Doe. She shrugged. "*Taken away in an ambulance not too long after the incident. What do you mean he'll know of me?*"

"*You're his kindred now. You carry something like a genetic marker that will make him aware of you.*"

What did it matter? "*So?*"

Corin walked to the accent chair by her vanity and sat. "*We live a very, very long time. Not a life of immortality as fiction would have you believe, but long enough to grow bored and restless. If he's mature, he might not care. Maybe he'll come after you just to satisfy some curiosity and merely watch from afar.*

"*Or he'll come after you because he's angry. Intentional or not, he's broken a law and there will be consequences for that. He might take that anger out on you.*"

—*Hunger Aroused*

ONE

THE ONLY REASON he noticed her was because of the depth of despair shining from deep-set blue eyes. Hunched against the side of a red brick wall, she looked a little too thin. Hungry in a way that didn't remind him of food. The poor woman might have been attractive in her day, but her pale skin seemed to have lost a little of its luster. Just like those horribly sad eyes.

Something about her intrigued him though. Almost enough to make him forget about going inside, where already the scent of the nightlife called to him. The smell of densely packed bodies. Lust. Sin. As he waffled, those enticements made up his mind for him.

He'd come to the nightclub to get laid. Period.

Bast Kent strode inside without bothering to look back, the woman and her haunted eyes forgotten within seconds.

Ignoring the seductive looks a few women gave him on the way in, he went straight to the bar, twisting in between bodies that bumped and gyrated. Touched and fondled. Danced, so they called it.

Laying a crisp hundred on the spit-shined wooden surface drew the attention of a bartender without having to open his mouth to back it up. Benjamin was always a good friend to have in a place like this. A place he didn't frequent often. There were better venues for finding willing booty. But he had his pick of slurries

in a club. And slurries were so much easier to bleed…
"Armadale. Neat."

The blonde woman tilted her chin and filled the drink order without saying a word to him. At the same time she stopped pouring with her right hand, she used her left to palm the c-note.

He slammed down the vodka, savoring the smooth burn of alcohol sliding down his throat and heating his belly. If he needed another, he'd return, but with as much adrenaline pulsing through him tonight, he wanted to get sexed up sooner rather than later. No pretending he was interested in buying anyone a drink of any kind, especially not a Goddamned cosmopolitan. Definitely no small talk about what she did for a living or what she liked to do for fun. Just one good, long fuck. In the club's restroom, in her car, her place. Whatever.

Bast searched through the writhing bodies of people on the dance floor, looking for just the right woman to bed that night. A human, preferably.

His teeth pulsed with a familiar ache, and his favorite appendage thickened at the impatient prospect of a long night of sweaty sex and decadent feeding. For whatever reason, his libido had kicked into high gear over the past couple of weeks and in this past week particularly. No matter how many times he alleviated the problem himself, he never felt relieved. So, if his own hand wasn't going to solve the problem, he might as well let a woman with legs from here to eternity solve it for him.

No, this place wasn't his scene, but it would serve the purpose. Undulating bodies moved like liquid to the beat of the blaring music. He scented their perspiration and a heady mix of alcohol and sex on the dance floor.

A subtle haze of fresh blood drifted to him from time to time and he knew he wasn't the only vampire on the hunt here. A lot of the humans were already so high or inebriated with alcohol, they were ripe for picking. Low-lying fruit on a tree.

And Bast was so hungry.

Yeah, he should give a fuck about using them, but it's why their kind existed. To keep him and his kind fed and sated. In exchange, they were kept very unaware of the turmoil that raged on around them. Bast and warriors like him kept the danger of other creatures of the night far away from their doors.

He signaled to the bartender. "Another."

The vampire nodded and went to work pouring the next one. Had to be another vampire simply because the place was too noisy for people to hear themselves think above the din, much less a few feet away.

"Hey, sweetheart. You buying?"

Bast turned to the exotic woman at his elbow. She pressed a finger into one ear and leaned close enough that he was afforded a healthy blast of her warm breath when she shouted. Some Asian ancestry ran through her genes. Bone-straight hair and distinctive eyes declared it for her. The makeup around her eyes had been plastered on, the lipstick she wore too bright, but she was pretty. And based on the way she ogled him, about to become the next notch in his bed post.

"Just out playin' the game," Bast replied. No sense in getting her hopes up for anything more. She'd either stick around or head for deeper pockets. He swallowed down the vodka chaser, already scanning the crowd for another woman in case this one didn't pan out.

"Yeah?" She edged closer, allowing her breasts to brush his torso. "What are you packing?"

Bast's lips twitched with amusement. "Enough. You interested?"

She peered past him, and her moment's inattention gave him the opportunity to notice too-large pupils. The chick was high and whatever she floated on was taking her for a nice ride. When he fed from her later, it should give him a nice momentary buzz too. The prospect of fucking her became that much sweeter.

A few weeks ago he might have felt like a shit for taking advantage of her state, but lately, he couldn't stop the craving. It had become almost unbearable. He needed to feed, and she'd do nicely.

"Today's my birthday," she said with a smile. "Why the hell not? What's your name?"

The polite thing to do would have been to at least offer a "happy birthday." At the very least, toss her a fake name to call him by. Instead, Bast took her by the hand and wound them through the throng of bodies and into the back. His gift to her would be allowing her some dignity by staying out of the restrooms, but against the wall in a dark corner proved an appealing idea.

"Always had a thing for the strong, silent type," she muttered. Sensitive hearing picked up every syllable over the rhythmic beat of music. Bast grinned to himself. He didn't have the abilities of full-born vampires, but his lineage offered him enough bennies.

The smugness faltered for a moment when he thought of what he was doing—what he was about to do.

He was going to feed, yes. But while he drank from her, another need, some primal call, demanded to be sated. The urge taunted him, and he felt an addiction to something he'd not yet partaken of. Something in the back of his mind tugged at him, whispered of caution. Ravenous Bast ignored it.

By the time they'd crossed the room, he couldn't get them away from the crowd fast enough. He swore he felt the blood race through every vein. Inside of him swelled with life, as if something within was trying like hell to get out. The urge, the gnawing in his belly, the *craving* became almost unbearable. He staggered as a wave crashed into him. Heat flared like summer in the air-conditioned room.

"Hey, you okay?"

Bast nodded, hiding a grimace behind tightened lips. "Fine. One shot too many."

Vampires didn't get inebriated off two shots of booze, and they sure as shittin' didn't get sick. Whatever this was almost had the ability to frighten him. Almost.

The woman's grip on his hand tightened, but she kept pace with his long stride, winding with him through bodies and toward their ultimate destination. He knew once he got them there, he would feel better. He would feed, and the sensation would die away.

He'd been training too hard. Ignoring his basic needs for too long. That his body finally retaliated made sense.

"Are you sure?" His companion might have been tipping toward oblivion a few minutes ago, but a new edge to her voice at once made her seem sober. "You're kind of warm."

"Warm?"

She tugged on his hand, forcing him to slow. He

caught the concern on her face when he glanced at her over his shoulder. "You might be coming down with something, sweetie. Maybe tonight's not your night for this."

Bast's eyelids felt heavy, his body sluggish. "I'm… fine," he mumbled.

Vampires don't get sick, he tried to tell himself. Then his stomach lurched, an immediate reminder that as often as he passed himself off as a full-born vampire, he was anything but.

Putting one foot in front of the other took all of his strength, but somehow he managed to stagger forward. To the dark corner. To a door. Through it.

The cool night air blasted his face, and he almost moaned in pleasure. It felt so good against his skin. He'd begun to burn up, and the night kissed away some of the hurt.

The scent of a nearby garbage bin made his stomach roll again, and this time when his stomach heaved, everything he'd consumed lately spewed forth, covering the ground until it shone crimson. All that blood, gone to waste.

The woman screamed—he still held her hand, needing it like a lifeline—before blazing heat swallowed him whole.

ALICE LOOKED TOWARD the commotion coming not far from where she crouched. She'd been peering into a crumpled white sack, hoping the grease stains on the outside meant still-edible fried food on the inside. She'd stopped near the parking lot between the two buildings in case she had to try again, if the bag's contents were rancid. In three days, she could afford to shop in a gro-

cery store, buying manager's specials on things past
their expiration date or anything a dollar or less, but
until then she had to eat. No matter where it came from.

With a mystery illness running its course, she didn't
make the assumption she'd live to see sunrise. Each day
was a gift. Seeing a new one was all she could ask for.

She almost squealed in delight when she saw the
doughnut inside a wax paper holder only had a single
bite taken from it. Two gifts for the day!

A woman screamed, and there was more noise. The
sounds of someone retching. Once upon a time she
might have thrown up herself just from the gagging
sounds, but after spending so many months tending to
Richard it took a lot to faze her now. One of the many
things she'd learned while living with a junkie brother
was how to clean up shit and vomit. Instead, Alice
clutched the bag tighter, intent on keeping her newfound delight.

But the scream caught her attention. The curiosity
of a woman's terror urged her feet forward.

Alice followed the source, intent on just seeing from
a distance why someone needed help. The staccato
clicks of heels on pavement echoed into the lot, past
cars she couldn't have afforded even in her employed
days. It was the sound of uncertain running, and she
recognized a woman's tiptoe dance in shoes meant for
little more than looking pretty.

The woman had stopped screaming and decided to
get the heck out of Dodge, it seemed. She'd left behind
someone still moaning and coughing though.

Alice edged closer.

A man elevated himself on hands and knees, swaying like a drunkard. Apropos, seeing how they were just

outside the doors of a nightclub. Alice almost turned back to more important matters, but a glint of light reflecting off something on the ground beneath him made her gasp.

"Mister?" she called softly. "You okay?"

There was no way he was okay. Even at her distance she recognized the blood pooled around him. The man tried to rise, stumbled, almost slipped in the blood. He lifted his head, looked at Alice then began to shake.

God, she didn't want to go to him. She didn't want to know if he'd been knifed or shot. It was none of her business. But then she thought of Richard, of the times he'd been brought home simply because of the kindness of strangers. This could have easily been him. Richard might have forced her out onto the streets with his backsliding ways, but he was still her brother. Whether she wanted to get involved or not, if this had been him, she would have wanted a stranger to help.

With a sigh, Alice ventured closer. "Hey, where are you hurt?"

He made a noise then dry-heaved. His mouth opened, and she grimaced, ready to watch him vomit. She tightened her stomach, mentally preparing herself for not getting sick with him. Nothing came out of either of them though, and she exhaled, relieved.

"Hey…do you have a phone? So I can call nine-one-one?"

His head lifted again, his attention coming to focus on her. Alice caught sight of his dark eyes and immediately thought it a trick of the light. They were eyes capable of seeing into tomorrow, she was sure of it.

"What's wrong with your eyes?" he asked, his voice croaking.

"*My* eyes?" Under other circumstances she might have laughed. Maybe even thought he was flirting with her.

Beads of perspiration raced down the sides of his face, the crown of his dark hair almost black in color. If she hadn't seen the clear sweat, she might have considered his head the source of all that blood.

"They're...*wrong*," he replied.

Ignoring their ridiculous conversation, she crouched right next to him. The scent of copper rushed at her, almost triggering her gag reflex. "My eyes aren't at issue here. I need to get an ambulance or the police for you. Can you wait here alone for a minute? Do you know how to press on the wound?"

"Wound?"

"Where you're bleeding from."

"I'm not bleeding." He attempted to rise again, but he'd managed to put his hand at the edge of the blood, where it slipped. "I don't think."

How much had he been drinking? He was too stoned to know he'd been shot or worse? "Why don't you tell me your name?"

"Sebastian—Bast."

Who took a perfectly good name like that and shortened it into something so ugly? Bast, indeed. "Look, Sebastian, I'm going for help." If he was talking, he seemed okay enough to leave for a minute. "Stay here." As if that might be a problem. He looked weaker than a wet kitten.

Sebastian's hand, the same one that had just been slicked down with blood, shot out and caught her arm. Alice cried out at the grip, which would surely leave behind a bruise. "No!" he said.

"No?" She tried to wrench her arm away to no avail. "You need some help. I don't think—"

Sebastian glanced up into the night sky. He scanned the stars, as if searching for something. "My car. Just to my car. I can't stay out here like this."

His paranoia catching, Alice couldn't help but look around them. "Dude, I'm not trying to get in the middle—"

"My car. That's all."

For the first time, she noticed the way her skin heated beneath his hold. "I'm going to get you there," she said slowly. "But then you need to do something about that fever and wherever you're bleeding from." No doubt his injuries explained his behavior. The blood was a mystery he was content to leave alone, and so was she. Good Samaritan duties only went so far.

If he heard her, or if he cared, she couldn't tell. Sebastian wrapped his arms around her neck and used her as leverage. Alice almost toppled over as he rose, the solid weight of him enough to drag her back down to the ground. By the time he stood, he towered over her.

Wanting to weep for her meager clothes, Alice pressed herself against him, into the wall of muscle and heft and simultaneously into his own bloodstained clothing. Beneath the overpowering scent of blood, she smelled some cross between clean linen and coconut coming directly from him. Had they been at the beach, slathered beneath sunscreen, she could understand the memories of summers by the waves he conjured, but this man was sinfully sexy and erotically dark. Nothing summery or beachy about him.

She recognized him now. The man from not even twenty minutes ago who'd stopped to look at her while on the way into the club. Now that she knew he was in serious shit or at least seriously sick, she pushed aside stirrings of attraction and focused on getting one foot in front of the other without allowing him to bring them both down.

Sebastian reached into his back pocket and retrieved a key fob. He pressed it in the general direction of a row of cars, and they made their way forward to the one that chirruped back at them. Richard's old toy collection, and the unforgettable prancing horse medallion, were the reasons she recognized the Ferrari Sebastian leaned against when they stopped.

"Help me. Inside." His voice sounded shaky again.

She realized she'd been gawking at the silver vehicle worth more than she used to make in five years combined. Maybe more than five.

Between the blood, the shakes and the car, he had to be a drug dealer or something close. *Had to be.* "I'll get you inside and then I'm gone." Her damned conscience pinged. "And you need to get on a phone. Get to a hospital."

Sebastian unfolded into the passenger's side he opened. "No hospital. Just…inside…"

"Hey Sebastian?" She shook his shoulder and unresponsive, he slumped forward. "Bast?"

Shit.

Alice looked around. Despite being outside a crowded nightclub, no one else loitered in the parking lot. An unconscious man slouched inside an insanely expensive car next to her. They were alone at night in what wouldn't be classified as the best part of town. She could leave him and hope to heaven someone with a kind heart found him before he died. Maybe he wouldn't even die; his car might be stolen with him left on the cold ground in nothing more than his shirt, but that was okay, right? He'd be alive at least.

The night had begun to chill noticeably, and she still hadn't picked a place to sleep until morning. She couldn't stay here and wait for him. Her own survival took precedence.

Alice scanned the lot again, let out a breath and studied Sebastian's profile.

Double shit.

TWO

Alice slid into the driver's side then stared at the keys in a jumbled heap next to Bast's feet. Every time she reached down to retrieve them, her insides began to quiver so badly, she gave up the thought. If she had to, she could do this. She knew how to drive. The lack of a driver's license didn't stop that from being true.

No—it was the thought of what could happen should she venture onto the road that made her tremble. The license had been taken with good cause, a fact she could grudgingly admit two years later. Still, she hadn't had a seizure in a long while, she didn't think. Hard to tell because of their subtlety. They probably weren't permanently gone, but no news was good news, right? No real hope for getting better, but she'd take "not getting worse" any day of the week.

She ran her hands over him again. A quick patdown for anything that might be dangerous—or perhaps worth hocking. Her fingers hooked inside shirt and pants pockets, but nothing surfaced. Damn it to hell, not even a dollar bill.

Alice chewed on her lip while staring out the windshield. She considered whether it would be worth trying to get into his back pocket. Bonus points for getting to cop a feel on a delectable ass, but mostly she wanted access to any wallet that might be tucked away there. Guys like him held on to thick leather wallets, the bills

inside crisp and hardly used. If she could get him leaning forward. Maybe…

She eyed his bulk. No, not by herself. She'd have
to get him out of the car. There simply wasn't enough
room inside it to maneuver. Maybe if she dropped him
off at the hospital, she could help herself to a lost-and-
found fee. Surely he wouldn't mind.

"Lincoln and Fourth."

Caught up in scheming, she'd failed to pay close
enough attention to him. His words wrangled half a
scream from her. "I thought you'd passed out."

Bast raised a limp hand. "Drive." It sounded as
if saying that one-syllable word cost him energy he
couldn't afford to relinquish. "To Lincoln and Fourth."

Trying not to think about the sticker value of the
Ferrari, she shook her head. "I don't have a license,
and I'm not supp—"

"Please…"

Whatever else he might have said withered on his
lips as Bast slumped forward again.

"Sebastian?" When he didn't respond, Alice reached
between his legs and forced her fingers to curl around
the keys. "Shit," she muttered. Her latest best friend
of a word.

She took a moment to fasten the seatbelt over his
torso, whispering a few quick prayers under her breath
as she did. His skin was like fire, almost hot enough
to make her snatch her hand away. This dude was sick
and needed some medical attention, like, yesterday. She
didn't know what was at Lincoln and Fourth—a resi-
dential area, if she recalled correctly—but that couldn't
be their destination.

Alice made a decision. If she was going to put their

lives in danger by driving them around, they would at least be heading in the right direction. Hope Haven Medical Center couldn't have been more than five or ten minutes away from here.

She looked at Sebastian one final time, taking in the long dark eyelashes, his straight nose, thin lips. The long sideburns were an interesting fashion statement, but the short, thick hair kind of went with the whole James Dean look he had going. The white silk shirt hidden beneath a black leather jacket similarly matched the tight leather pants he wore. Silver-tipped black boots rounded out the ensemble, and Alice was certain of his playboy status. Nothing about him said "cheap" either, especially not his ride.

"You'd better be worth it, pretty boy," she muttered.

The engine hummed to life, and Alice exhaled. She closed her eyes, luxuriating against the gentle vibration beneath her body and the soft cushion of the leather seat as it engulfed her. Classical music eased from the speakers, relaxing her even further. Drug dealer or not, Bast had nice taste.

Hand on the gearstick, she shifted then pulled away from the parking space. Just like riding a bike. Man, the car drove like a cloud. If she touched a pothole, damn if she could feel it. Hell, she could probably run over some roadkill, push a button a second later and car wash attendants would rain down from a helicopter to clean the tires. Rides like this didn't happen every day for sure. *Nice*.

She chanced a few glances at him during the drive, in between straining her vision for any cops who might be out and about. No matter how she tried to convince herself they wouldn't know she didn't have a license, it didn't stop her heart from thumping into her throat.

If she wanted to keep her sanity, nothing like finding something else to do to help. Even the gorgeous car couldn't ease her anxiety completely. "So, Seba—Bast," she said to his unconscious form, "how'd a guy like you end up in a place like this?" When he didn't respond, she kept talking. "Me? Just looking for some dinner. It's amazing what people throw away, especially near some of the trendier places." She kept wishing he would say something. "People like you don't worry about money or making your dollar stretch. People like me? Well, we have to count every penny."

"Why?"

Alice bit back another shriek. "Don't do that!" She chanced another look at him. No improvement in his pallor. Sweat-slickened hair clung to his forehead. "Either be conscious or unconscious, not slipping in and out. And especially give a girl some warning before you start talking out of nowhere."

Bast leaned forward, his soft groan increasing her worry about his condition. "Sorry." His eyelids looked like they might close at any moment and not lift again. "Where are we?"

Alice returned her focus to the road. "Hanover and Forty."

A pause. "Wrong direction."

"I know, but...listen, whatever you're going through, you need some medical help. I know someone who tried to handle DTs on his own once—"

"DTs?" Bast laughed, a dry hacking sound. "Lady, I'm not in DTs."

"Then what's wrong with you?"

"Hungry."

She frowned, certain she hadn't heard him correctly. "I suppose that explains the blood and the fever?"

He shifted in his seat. "Might." Bast twisted, peering into the back window. "Turn around. Go to Lincoln and Fourth."

"But—"

"Please. I'm asking you nicely. Please go to Lincoln and Fourth."

She would regret this, seriously hate herself for giving in later, but Alice slowed at the next intersection and did a quick U-turn, almost swiping a parked Toyota in the process. If Bast noticed the near miss, he didn't mention it. Her nerves however, went into overdrive.

Watching the street signs, she bit her lip, willing their destination to get here sooner rather than later. The more she thought about what she was doing, the more her stomach began to hurt. "Maybe you should keep talking. Might help keep you from passing out."

Silence stretched between them for so long, Alice thought she might have made the suggestion too late.

"Why are you watching every penny?" Bast finally asked.

"No." She smiled but fought back her embarrassment. Of all the things for him to have overheard, figured it would have been that. "I meant you should talk about you. You do the talking. Not me."

He didn't seem to like that idea. "Turn here."

Great. So neither of them would be doing any talking. Suited her just fine.

The neighborhood he'd guided her to was straight out of a magazine. One minute they were cruising a road full of businesses and retail shops, and the next they'd entered a virtual millionaire's row. Streetlamps lit the road, precisely placed in between tall oak trees and other trees she couldn't name. Even in the dark she noticed that not one of the houses had a blade of grass out of place. The sculpted topiaries must have been the envy of gardeners everywhere. Spotlights illuminated hand-tended gardens and expensive statues. Unlike in her old neighborhood, where cars were parked on cinderblocks in driveways, here the few vehicles she did see were parked in large circular drives behind scalloped fences. No chained Rottweilers or bulldogs barking their fool heads off. No burglar bars.

Alice lifted her foot from the gas, bringing the luxury sports vehicle to a more respectable crawl. "Where are we going?"

"Sixth house on the left."

Her heart sped up as she pulled into the drive he'd indicated. The car paused at the closed gate, and she was just about to turn to him when the gate slowly began to open. Some sort of sensor, perhaps? Nice.

Bast's house was down a cobbled drive, set far away from the street. The two-story home was surrounded by manicured bushes, the red bricks highlighted by decorative lighting. What she could see of the molding guaranteed someone had an eye for detail. Every one of the double-paned windows had a spotlight shining against its panes. The bushes beneath each of them had been trimmed to ankle high. Definitely someone taking precautions with safety there.

He reached for a button on the rearview mirror then pushed it. The door to an attached three-car garage lifted slowly, and Alice pointed the Ferrari into it. Two additional cars, one a late-model Benz, the other some foreign number she didn't recognize, already waited inside.

Turning off the engine once parked, she felt assaulted by the sudden silence.

Bast didn't wait for her to ask *what next?*—the words poised on her lips—before exiting the vehicle. Nor did he bother to wait for her when he entered the house through a side door, his gait unsteady.

Ingrate.

So, she could sit here and wait for an invitation not likely to be extended. She could walk back down the drive then find her way back to a homeless shelter, assuming any would have an open bed left. Or, she could just follow him in and see what happened next, satisfying her raging curiosity. Maybe even wrangle a meal out of her host, since the doughnut had gone the way of the wind a while ago. Hell, she didn't remember when she'd even lost it. Bast might consider a financial donation and if he didn't, maybe she could find one worth borrowing until she could pay him back.

She sighed.

Yeah. Like this would be a tough decision to make.

BAST COULDN'T REMEMBER the last time he'd felt like this. *Correction*. He'd never felt like this. Like something the dog threw up.

His stomach ached. A gnawing, crawling pang that started at the center and then radiated outward. From there it traveled at a snail's pace, covering his torso, then limbs. Like a creeper vine, except on the inside.

And the hunger?

Christ, every time he came to his senses, all he could focus on was that thick, sweet scent of human. His ears tuned in to the slow knocks of her heart. Each time it sped up, he had to chew on the inside of his cheek to keep from lunging after her.

He'd never been this out of control in his life. Not once in almost four hundred years.

Bringing her here was such a bad idea. The thought of letting her go, even worse. He needed sex and to be fed but was getting neither, and planned on acting like it didn't matter.

Bast snorted. Who the fuck did he think he was kidding?

The sound of footsteps on the kitchen tile pulled him out of his thoughts. He glanced back to find the human shifting from side to side. She looked ready to bolt, and that seductive heartbeat began to flutter against her ribs. Something to be said that she held her ground when he turned to face her.

"Haven't left?" He was both pleased and intrigued that she'd stayed.

"Well, yeah, um...you're still sick."

His stomach began chewing on itself again. A not-so-gentle reminder. "S'all good, but thank you. For all of it." Why had she decided to stay? Then he remembered. Something about watching her pennies. "Should I call you a cab? My treat, of course."

Dark blue eyes refused to look at him, instead moving in the direction of the appliances that never saw use. To bare yellow walls in the hallway. To sandstone tile. "You're still sick," she repeated.

"And?" Bast folded his arms over his chest.

"You shouldn't be left alone. Not until you see a doctor."

"Because..."

She looked directly at him this time. "What if you passed out again? What happens if you fall—"

"And can't get up?" he added dryly, channeling the old television commercial.

"Well, yeah." She suddenly seemed to realize he'd been teasing her with that last line. Her face went a delightful shade of pink, enough to make his teeth pulse.

"I have a feeling there's more to this."

"Okay then, what if we made a deal?" Her gaze almost made it to the height of his chin this time.

"A deal."

"I could make sure you didn't die or something in the night."

He almost grinned. If anything, the dark rejuvenated him. "That would be very kind of you."

"And in return," she continued as if she hadn't heard him, "you could let me sleep on the couch tonight."

Bad idea. Very bad idea. There was no way in heaven or hell he would ever let a human in his life. Not now. Especially not now with the unspoken rivalry between vampires and lycans threatening to erupt into violence. He had a duty to his nation and to the members he'd been sworn to protect. Letting her inside the house was damned near bad enough.

He opened his mouth, poised to tell her absolutely not. What came out instead was, "Fine."

Inwardly, Bast groaned.

"Only just for the night. I won't be a problem. Just a couch and—wait. What?"

She'd fired off word after word, barely stopping to breathe. And the persistent thrum of blood lingering just this side of his hearing did wicked things to his thinking.

He studied her face—this woman whose name he didn't even know—beneath the soft overhead light. Perhaps for the first time since they'd met.

Round blue eyes beckoned for his attention first, but then his gaze drifted to the small beauty mark just above the fleshy part of her cheek. Her small button-like nose and kewpie doll lips made her appear very young. Not much more than mid-twenties, he'd guess.

The faded gray shirt she wore made Bast frown as he took in the streaks of dark red staining it. His mind said *blood* while his memory reminded him it was his. Worn blue jeans hung loosely on her frame. A split-second's pause made him venture into imagining what she might look like outside of them.

But that wasn't right. She was a little skinny. Just shy of pretty. Too young. Definitely not his type. His type wore stilettos and designer clothes. Drove expensive cars and moved like silk, leaving behind fragrant trails of Guerlain or Shalimar in their wakes.

Still, he needed to feed. She stood right here in front of him. An untouched human. His for the taking.

"What's your name?" He stepped forward, wanting to breathe in the scent of her blood again. If he couldn't get perfume, he'd settle for the next best thing to inhale.

She stepped back. "Alice."

Bast fought the urge to step toward her again. He needed food so badly. "A place to sleep for the night is the least I can provide."

"Maybe I shouldn't…"

He could hear the doubt creeping into her voice. Reconsidering what he wanted from her in exchange, perhaps. A single woman alone in the home of a man she didn't know could lead to very bad things. What she didn't know about him could get her killed.

His stomach twisted, inciting an eruption of goose bumps across his skin. A wave of nausea collided into him, the aftereffects enough to make his hand shoot out to grasp the slate countertop or otherwise collapse. The incisors he'd managed to hide until now lengthened, pulsing with a hollow ache. Needed to pierce skin.

He doubled over, fighting to hide his need. The last bit of common sense clinging to his consciousness shouted at him to call for help. To get someone from the guard over here fast. But the intoxicating scent of blood—the human Alice—lured the thought away. Bast could only think of feeding his thirst, of satisfying the parasitic sexual lust growing in tune with his need to drink from her.

Alice rushed forward, cradling him against her body. Such a dangerous place for her to be. Their new position put his mouth so close to her neck. To her beating pulse. Bast shifted his attention. Elsewhere. Needed to focus on something else.

He took one jerky step forward, almost off-balancing them both. He must have outweighed her by upwards of sixty or seventy pounds, at least. It was cute she thought she could keep him upright if his own body decided to fail.

"Whoa, there. We need to get you off your feet," she said. "Which way to your bedroom?"

He swallowed hard. "Why are you helping me?"

She considered it for a minute, her gaze meeting his. Her shoulders lifted in a shrug. "Karma."

But he had no karma. No goodwill. All he could think of now was feeding and sex. Feeding during sex.

Taking from Alice until he'd satisfied his carnal and primal appetites. "You should go." He fought with every heartbeat to regain control of himself. Some sort of maneuver Alice used forced him to take another step. Then another. Her leverage was reminiscent of defense moves he'd taught his men. She'd done this before.

"I'll get you in bed, call someone to come over for you and then I'll go."

"But…" Even to himself he sounded weak.

"Tell me where your room is. And then who I can call."

"You should—"

"Go. You said that." She craned her neck, the subtle gesture enough to make his lips brush against her skin. "Is it down here?"

He shuddered. She smelled so good. *Christ, so good.* Maybe if he ran his tongue across her neck, the taste would be enough. He'd regain his control. One little taste. "Alice, please go. Before…"

Before he took her? No. He'd never forced himself on anyone before and he wouldn't do so tonight, no matter how insane the want made him. If he hurt one hair on her head, he'd drive a stake through his own heart afterward. That was a vow.

"You're on fire," she muttered. Her hand went to his forehead in the universal gesture mothers everywhere used to test for a fever. "Do you have a thermometer?"

"No." Black spots hovered in his sightline, and all thoughts of blood and sex crumbled.

"Hold on." Alice brought her hand around his waist again, her breast pressing into his side. His cock twitched just enough to remind Bast that perhaps not all thoughts of sex had been driven away.

"I won't hurt you." Bast tried to lift his head, now seemingly weighing a hundred pounds.

"I know you won't." A light flooded the darkened hallway they'd been traveling. "Here we go."

She'd found one of the guest bathrooms. This bath had been decorated in all white with highlights of gold reflecting from the fixtures, decorative rugs and original paintings hanging in the recesses built for that purpose. The interior designer said the gold would take away the sterility of such a stark room. He'd nodded and signed the checks.

"Sit." Alice directed him to the toilet and let gravity do its thing. She pushed the coat from his shoulders, not batting an eyelash when she slipped off his shoulder holster housing a Glock. Her fingers worked quickly, loosening buttons on his shirt. Removing his boots and then socks.

"What are you doing?"

"Cold shower slash ice bath, or hospital. Your choice. You're running too hot to suit me." Intense blue eyes peered up at him from where she kneeled on the cold floor. "Tell me you can handle the pants yourself."

Shaky legs almost buckled when he stood, but Bast managed to use the vanity for support. Alice inclined her head away when he reached for the button at his waist. He paused, considering just how well his little Florence Nightingale would appreciate or perhaps run screaming from his arousal, not yet beaten into submission. With a mental shrug, he flicked the button and then reached for the zipper.

Either the cold shower would cure what ailed him or simply make things much, *much* more interesting.

THREE

BREATHE. A NAKED man looked just like another naked man. They all had the same parts. She'd had lovers before. Hell, she'd seen Richard naked when she'd bathed him during his self-prescribed home recovery.

But when Alice looked at Bast, all thoughts of her brother fled.

How his silky shirt had hidden all that toned sinew and muscle, she'd never know. He'd felt solid, his flesh unyielding beneath her fingers where she'd gripped him, but the definition of his chest and abs belonged to someone otherworldly. Men in real life just didn't look like this. Except he was here. In real life. And oh-so-drool-worthy.

Kneeling before him, she marveled over the fine line of dark hair along his abdomen, pointing its way down into those tight leather pants. And as much as she wanted to follow the trail, she kept her gaze above his waist. Poor guy was sicker than a dog, and all she could do was fuel fantasies while ogling him? Way to be.

She studied his feet instead, noting the delicate bones. The trimmed nails. But then his foot lifted, one after the other, and black leather pooled before her. Those incredible tight pants no longer hugged his body, instead now lying on the floor.

Suddenly, all commands to herself to breathe became a foreign language she'd never learned. Heat flooded her cheeks, and without looking at herself in the mirror, Alice was sure her skin glowed red all over. Even her scalp tingled with awareness.

Casting her face even further toward the gold mat, she pointed with her finger in the general direction of the shower. "Inside." It came out as a squeak. She cleared her throat. "Can you manage on your own?"

"I think so." He took an unsteady step forward, and then another.

Alice bit her lip, fighting with herself on whether she should go to him or not. The sound of running water a moment later assuaged her conscience.

"I'm just going to sit here." Back turned. Head down. "Keep talking and let me know you're all right. I don't want the sound of you falling being my only clue you've passed out. And keep the temp cold!"

"I've never been sick before," he said over the sound of displaced water.

"Of course you have. Everyone's gotten sick at least once."

"Not me."

"Never?" Alice frowned.

"Not that I can remember."

Surely he meant as an adult. All kids got sick. "That's weird, but maybe you got some bad oysters or something."

He chuckled, mirthless and dry. "Or something, perhaps."

Getting him to speak was going to be a small chore. A long silence stretched between them before Alice found something worth poking at. "So...what kind of work do you do?"

Bast didn't respond at first, the silence making her turn toward him. "Private security."

Her brow lifted. "Private security gets you all this?"

"I've been in business a very long time. But you've got good instincts. It didn't all come from my job." He stared at her through the shower glass door, their eyes meeting, before he turned his back. Only then did Alice recognize the clarity with which she saw him. There was no steam to fog up the glass, giving her a teasing view. No rippling or fracturing to distort parts of him. What she saw was frank masculinity at its finest.

It didn't help that the shower stall could hold a football team. Hell, she'd had bedrooms smaller than inside there. Three showerheads sprayed Bast with water, flattening his thick, dark hair. A few feet behind him, bottles of bath products lined a marble seating area. Next to the seat, she noted a fourth showerhead, this one attached to a wand. Perfect for a woman who planned on shaving her legs. All of this she took in with a three-second sweep, a pathetic attempt to look at anything but the man in the middle whose presence demanded she watch him instead.

Movement grabbed her attention again, and she swung her gaze to him—above the waist still—another frown drawing down her eyebrows when he staggered. "Are you feeling any better? Or different?"

He shook his head before his body bowed. An arm wrapped around his waist, as if trying to hold his insides in place, before he swayed. Bast dropped like a stone weight, his head cracking against the tile with a sickening crash.

Alice scrambled to her feet, throwing open the

shower door and rushing to his side only seconds later. "Bast!"

Ice water stabbed her skin. How had he been able to stand it? At least five minutes of freezing torture, like the snow had melted only a nanosecond before. Her skin erupted in goose bumps right away, but she fought down a shiver.

When he moaned, his body writhing on the stone floor, she steadied him with a hand. "Hold on. Lemme check you out first." Her voice sounded shaky. "That was one hell of a fall."

"Christ, it was."

"How many fingers am I holding up?"

"Somewhere between zero and ten. I'm leaning toward two." He laughed, mirthlessly. "I don't get sick," he insisted.

Alice tried not to smile. She pushed her hands through his hair, trying to locate any sign of damage. "Yeah, well, you lying here beneath a freezing shower says otherwise. I'm surprised you didn't break something when you hit the ground."

"Too mean to die. Too mean to break. And it sure as shittin' ain't gonna happen while I'm buck naked."

This time Alice did smile, helping him to sit upright. No blood poured from his head. No particular tenderness at the site. He'd probably get one righteous goose egg, but she could live with that. Her poor, abused shirt clung to her body, but some of the red streamed from it, circling the drain before being sucked away. The secondhand jeans became an unbearable weight, turning dark beneath the saturation.

"Shit." Bast wrapped his hands around hers. "Your fingers are turning blue."

She'd started to shiver too. "That might be true, but you're still throwing off some outrageous heat. The water's practically evaporating off your skin."

He stretched above them in a graceful catlike move and turned the knob. When he pulled her to him, settling her in his lap, Alice let out a squeak of surprise. Her body curved against his, molding next to him as if they were designed for nothing—and no one—else. "I won't risk you getting hypothermia."

Curled beside the warmth of his bare skin, she almost purred in contentment. "One of us has to go. You need the cold, and I need the heat."

"You're right." His low timber sent another shiver skating over her spine. This time, the temperature of the water held zero influence over her reaction. "One of us should go." His breath felt close, his lips closer. "Which one?"

Neither of them made a move, which suited her just fine, but Bast's mouth whispered over the skin of her neck. She tried to regulate her breathing, gone erratic since stepping into the shower, but pulling her concentration away from Bast seemed an impossible task. He was insanely good-looking, built like a god, and she hadn't seen any action since George Junior left the presidency.

"You're making it difficult to think." And breathe right.

"I'm trying to make you warm."

She hiccupped a laugh. "It's working." Boy, was it working. Her heart pounded, blood racing through her veins, making her nipples and between her legs swell with arousal.

This wasn't right. She didn't know this man at all.

Just because he looked nice, drove a nice car and lived in a nice house didn't mean he was the kind of guy she should give liberties. She'd thought he might be a drug dealer; still thought it. "Just tell me you don't do anything illegal to maintain your lifestyle," she added.

"I've been a mercenary in the past." He followed his statement with the touch of his lips beneath her jaw.

"But now?" She gasped. That warm mouth, the trail of fire would consume her.

"I protect important people. Nothing illegal."

"Thank God." Later she'd think about her impulsivity. Maybe even chastise herself for it. Right now there was a very aroused male draped around her body. He might be feeling a little under the weather—okay, maybe a lot under the weather—but his readiness suggested it'd take more than illness to stop him in his tracks.

But what of the illness? What could make him sick like this? "No drugs, right?"

He held her chin. Twisted them both so his lips moved to the hollow of her throat. "None."

"Contagious diseases?"

"Never." One hand slid beneath the clinging shirt, splayed flat over her belly. "Now, shh...I need to get you warm."

"But what about you? The f—"

Bast whisked away the word *fever* when his mouth captured hers. Her eyelids fluttered closed and she knew this was wrong. Not just wrong, but nonsensical. He moved too fast, the heat flaring between them burning too hot.

Complete strangers didn't do this. Men like Bast didn't lust after nobodies like her.

The moment his tongue slipped into her mouth though, she reconsidered.

Red heat swam from him into her and she swallowed it down. Felt the burn spread through her belly and ricochet through her extremities. She fed the fire back to him, sweeping her tongue to his. But for as much as they should have gone up in smoke beneath the water's spray, Bast was gentle. Teasing.

SHE TASTED SO sweet. Like a delicacy. He treasured moving his lips over hers. Pulling into him her scent. The heat had pooled in his belly, but the moment he opened her mouth beneath his, it flared and then extinguished.

Moving his thumbs to her slender neck, he caressed the supple skin. Marveled in it. So feminine. So fragile. Alice moaned when he stroked along her beating pulse, and he heard and felt the thrum quicken.

"A kiss, sweet Alice," he murmured, his lips moving to brush next to his thumbs. Blood roared so close to the surface. The song as seductive as her moans. Stepping beneath the icy spray of the shower had done nothing to the fever boiling him alive. But being so close to feeding his hunger, reveling in the way she clutched to him, the ache became mollified somewhat.

"Sebastian…"

His cock thumped, his name never before said with such want. He licked his lips, pleasure searing him when he touched sensitive incisors with the motion. "A kiss right here. *Please*."

"Yes, kiss me. More."

She didn't know what permission she'd given him, but it couldn't be his concern right now. His need had grown frenzied. His appetite about to consume them both. Sebastian lowered his mouth to her neck, to the rapid beat lifting her skin ever so slightly, and let his nature take over.

Alice arched into him when he pierced her flesh with teeth elongated and hurting. Her whimpering moan became an orgasmic cry when he pulled. He heard the pleasure in it, felt her shudder ripple into him. His hand stroked over the soft skin of her belly, trailed to the rounded curve of her breast. Her nipple beaded beneath his fingers, and he used it to elongate her orgasm. He teased the tip, pinching it when she twisted beneath increasing pressure. And all the while he fed.

Growling into her neck kept him focused. Kept the tug at the base of his spine from turning into an all-out loss of control. His dick became steel, trapped between their bodies, throbbing in tune with the teeth sunk deeply into her flesh. He would not come like this, not from a simple feeding, but never before had blood tasted so good to him. Felt so good. Velvet on his tongue. For every tug, his mind cleared. The heat cooled. The sexual appetite hadn't abated, but he could think now. Every ounce of her blood warmed through him, healing and soothing.

He didn't want to take too much; this human deserved more than to be food, but he'd become an addict to her taste. Hearing her throaty moans, her breathy cries as she shuddered, he knew the very essence of her.

She'd become a thing he needed as his own.

Bast growled.

No. This he would not allow to happen.

Withdrawing from her when he wanted nothing more than to drink until she surrendered her life to him almost pained him as much as the hunger previously had.

But he licked over the wound, sealing it closed. He knew that when she looked at the spot, only a faint bruise would be visible. One created during the heat of the moment and understandable to her confused senses.

"Oh…my…God," she said with a shaky breath.

He held her against him, enjoying the aftershocks making her shudder in his arms. "Thank you."

"Thank me?" She laughed, sounding surprised. "I am most definitely thanking *you*. I'm almost embarrassed at how easily I did that."

"Did what?" he asked, stroking her slick hair away from her face. He wanted to see those eyes again. Wanted to kiss her lips. It made little sense, but the urge was there.

"All you did was kiss me and I…well, took to it very nicely." She twisted to look at him, her face turning bright red as soon as she did. The way she studied him gave him the sense he wasn't supposed to know the extent of her reaction. But he knew. Damn, how he loved it. "And I cannot believe I just did that. With a complete stranger. Who is sick. In his shower."

Alice pushed away from him, scrambling on her hands and knees to the other side of the stall. She rose to her feet, swaying on unsteady legs. Bast rushed to her when they gave out, catching her before she fell. He'd taken a good deal of blood from her and she would need a little while to recover.

"That was one hell of a kiss, mister. I'm a little dizzy."

She weighed next to nothing, a fact that startled him. Another minute or two and he might have taken too much, indeed. "When's the last time you had something to eat?"

"Put me down—"

With no intention of acquiescing to her demand, he stepped out of the shower, taking just enough time to turn off the running water. The mess in the bathroom could be dealt with later. The woman he wanted to deal with now.

"You helped me. Let me help you. I'm only going to take you into the guest room, so you can dry off and get into bed. I'll order a pizza for you or whatever you'd like."

"You don't have to."

"I know, but I'm going to. You have no idea what you've done for me tonight."

No, he couldn't explain how she'd saved his life. If anyone had seen him—any of the lycans, any of the guards, any other vampire—the destructive possibilities boggled his mind. The kindness of this human would not be forgotten. She'd given him food when none other could be obtained, not to mention staved off a mysterious illness that made him even more vulnerable.

"You sound much better." He felt her studying his face. "You *look* better. How do you feel?"

"Like new." Meaning it. The sun would rise in a few hours, but he had phone calls to make. Tomorrow evening, the guard would expect him to show up for part of the ongoing manhunt under way, but what if he became sick again? He had to find out what was happening to him before then. Had to.

"Your fever feels like it's broken, so I guess the shower worked."

"Yeah, I think whatever it was has passed. Maybe a twenty-four-hour bug, you know?"

She made a noncommittal noise and he wasn't sure

if he'd satisfied her curiosity. God knew he didn't have any answers.

They didn't speak any more as he carried her down the long corridor, the hardwood floor cool beneath his bare feet. At times he wondered why he'd chosen to live in such a large home, but tonight he was thankful for the extra room. She needed a place to rest. To recover.

"What do you want on your pizza?"

"Bast, I—"

"If you don't specify, I'm just going to go with everything."

The maid kept the rooms in the house ready for a guest at all times. No telling when one of his men would need a place to crash. This particular one was farthest from his bedroom. He didn't need to feed again, he didn't think, but he wasn't sure how he felt about letting her stay beneath his roof. Then again, with his sexual appetite only whetted and not sated, he wasn't sure who was more dangerous to whom.

"Everything would be fine. Thank you."

"Good. I'll make the call." He lowered her onto the bed, trying not to smirk at how she avoided eye contact with his groin. "There is some men's clothing in the drawers, extra towels in the closet. Help yourself to them. In the morning, you can take a real shower if you'd like. For now, just get some of your strength back with rest, and later, food. Okay?"

"Why are you doing this?"

He thought about the lives he'd taken in his years as a hunter. The humans he'd fed from during the heat of frenzied, anonymous sex. The ones he'd sometimes killed, whether by design or by accident. A hollow pit formed in his stomach. He replied, "Karma."

FOUR

"GRAY, I NEED you to assume leadership for a little while."

His second-in-command, Gray Thallum, got straight to the point. "How long?"

Bast pushed a hand through his hair, at once wishing he could still consistently see his reflection in a mirror. Every once in a while a trick of the light helped him do so, but now was not one of those times. "I'm really not sure. At least until tomorrow night."

"You know Cicero will string you up when he finds out."

"Yeah, well, Cicero can go fuck himself."

Gray laughed. "Easy, man. I'm just telling you what's what. The Council's getting restless, too. Do you want to tell me what's so urgent that we're not getting together for another night?"

Fuck, he was right. The vampire community's ruling body would not be pleased at all.

Bast's precarious position as Commander of the Council guard might go from shaky to nonexistent, but he couldn't see another way through it, other than to rely on Gray at least for a little while. He could be trusted with the Council's safety as well as Bast. None of the seven members of the Council would see harm with Gray in charge. The man had proven himself time and again. He wouldn't have been made first lieutenant otherwise.

Once upon a time, there hadn't been a need for the Council's guard. Hell, there hadn't been a need for the Council. But with vampire creations spiraling out of control, technology threatening to expose vampire existence and an overall lack of direction for the vampire community, the need was recognized. And organized.

A new crisis had arisen over the last few weeks. Someone—something—was killing off newly created vampires in vicious attacks obviously designed to instill fear in the entire community. When a recent threat had been directed at the Council, Bast and his men were tasked with putting an end to the menace, with extreme prejudice and expeditiousness. They had some clues, but no solid leads.

It frustrated the hell out of him. Still, it couldn't be helped. For just a single night more, he needed to stay away from his men and Council business.

Bast stuck his head into the hallway, looking down the hall to where he'd tucked Alice in for the time being. The heat burning him from the inside hadn't returned, but that didn't mean it wouldn't. For now, every passing minute without any sign of the illness was a small victory. What the hell had happened to him? More importantly, would it return? He so did not need this shit. Not now.

"It's nothing—"

Gray cut him off. "You can't tell me that. I have to tell the others something. Give a dog a bone here."

"Tell them…" He blew out a breath, a habit he'd picked up from hanging out with humans. "Tell them an expected visitor showed up and I can't shirk my duty in that regard."

"An unexpected visitor. You really want that to be the reason?" Bast could almost see Gray run a hand through his military-style cut. "Dude, if your visitor doesn't go furry the night of a full moon, they aren't going to want to hear it. Give me something better than that."

"It's not Council business," Bast replied. "It's personal. That's all I can tell you."

Gray snorted. "I hope she's worth it."

He went still for a moment, trying to decide whether to let his lieutenant in on his illness. If he told, Gray would be by his side, helping him figure out the problem, to hell with everything else. Then again, if he told and Cicero found out, Bast would be off the guard detail faster than he could spit. Some members of the Council already had their doubts about him. No fucking way was he giving them another reason. "It's not just a woman."

"But it has something to do with one."

"Sir, I can neither confirm nor deny whether there's a woman involved."

Gray laughed, not bothering to say anything further before disconnecting.

What would Gray—or better yet, Cicero—say if they saw the hold she had on him? Agreeing to let her stay with him went beyond insanity. He'd taken only enough blood to satisfy his thirst. Just barely. Tomorrow, when the sun had set, he'd need to find better sustenance. A willing partner among the humans who'd want to exchange sex for blood. What he'd done to her was just short of stealing, if not worse.

By the time the pizza had been called for and delivered, he was no closer to figuring out why he reacted to her the way he did. But the good news was that he hadn't felt any of the nausea or weakness plaguing him for the past several hours. His stomach growled its disapproval at him from time to time, but he suspected that had more to do with the quantity he'd taken than anything.

Pizza in hand, he knocked on her door, waiting for her soft voice to bid him enter before turning the knob. He then sat in one of the chairs farthest away from the bed, watching her eat. She'd finished the first slice before he decided to tackle the problem at hand.

"Alice—"

She yawned before taking another slice from the box. "You should eat too."

A smile touched his lips. "I've eaten already."

"Crap. Almost forgot to take my medication."

Frowning, Bast watched her scramble from the hold of the comforter and to a neat little pile she'd created on the bedside table. A single key, a small box of mints and some loose change were there. A few dollar bills, crinkled and damp, had been laid flat in an attempt to dry them off as well, he figured. She pried open the candy tin before fishing in its contents.

"What are those?"

Alice returned to the bed, picking up the bottle of Coke he'd added to the food order. "I told you, my medication."

"What is it for?"

"Nothing. Just prophylaxis."

"Like birth control?" A surprising wave of dismay rushed him.

She looked up sharply, her eyes wide. "What? No. Nothing like that. Just...forget it, okay?"

His emotions settled, but not altogether a good feeling. The tightening in his stomach didn't have to do with his illness this time. Pulsing in his teeth made him sharpen his focus. "This is a mistake. You shouldn't be here."

"Because I won't tell you about my medication? It's just lamotrigine and I have to take it daily. There. Happy?"

The name was unfamiliar to him, but he didn't care. He leaned forward, making sure he had her full attention. "No, this isn't about your meds. I shouldn't have said yes earlier. I was desperate and hurting and—"

"It's the middle of the night, Bast. Are you really kicking me out now?"

Fuck. Of course not. "Not now, but in the morning."

"But what if you get sick again?"

Alice rose to kneeling. The shirt she'd chosen was loose and big on her small frame, barely covering her thighs, reminding him that she wore nothing underneath. His gaze dropped to the subtle sway of unfettered breasts, and Bast had to pull his attention to safer areas. The haphazard curls of her hair had tightened into ringlets, emphasizing her youth. Her cheeks were flushed, and the lighting made her eyes brighter.

He tightened his jaw, feeling the beginning stirrings of hunger that had no right to life. "Why aren't you afraid of me? Street savvy will only take you so far."

"If you were going to do something to me, you would have tried it by now," she replied softly.

"I don't know if that statement is merely arrogant or just plain naïve."

She paled, just a fraction, enough to let him know he might be getting through to her. This was too dangerous. For both of them. "You wouldn't hurt me."

"And what makes you so sure of that?"

She shrugged a single shoulder. "Just the way you look at me."

"How do I look at you?"

Alice met his gaze. "Like that."

He didn't have to question her response. He knew what she saw. The desire. The heat. The want. No matter how he concentrated on something else or how he'd thought it had been tamed, it still remained. Forcing her away was the only way to keep her safe from him. From his world.

"I just need a place to sleep, Sebastian. Let me stay the night and I swear I won't be any trouble. I won't get in your way. I'm a simple person who's having a hard time."

Twenty different reasons for why she should leave, along with another twenty alternatives for her sleeping arrangements, flittered through his mind. For every one he almost gave voice to, his gut clenched, something inside of him tightening until his vision went hazy.

At least he could physically remove himself from her presence. The sun wouldn't rise for a few more hours, but he had to separate himself from this woman. Maybe do a little research on illnesses known to affect vampires. If the affliction was the result of the other part of his genealogy, there would be nothing for him to do but wait for it to pass. Although not a praying man usually, he gave a silent word of pleading to his god that vampirism explained everything and not his unknown heritage.

Alice must have mistaken his silence for indecision. "If you get sick again, I'll be able to help. You shouldn't be alone." Her gaze went to her hand, where she still held a slice of uneaten pizza. Quietly, she added, "Even if it's not me, it should be someone."

Bast stopped trying to argue with himself. If somehow he found the strength of will to turn her away, there was no way he would let her walk out now, alone and in the middle of the night. Even he wasn't callous enough to do that to a defenseless woman. "I keep odd hours and will be asleep most of the day tomorrow. You should leave during that time." He held her up a hand when she started to protest, rising to his feet at the same time. "Or you can stay until I'm awake and we'll talk again then. Go or stay. The choice is up to you."

DESPITE WHAT HE SAID, she had no choice. Sebastian didn't want to understand her plight, but she had nowhere else to go. For some reason he was willing to let her stay, and in her old life, she would have stormed out at the first sign he didn't want her there.

Alice sighed.

In her old life, she wouldn't have allowed a stranger to bring her home. Most definitely she would have never let a single kiss make her feel…

Her face flushed. What had he done when he'd kissed her? She'd never had such a strong reaction to anyone or anything in her life. God, she'd had lovers who'd failed to bring her to that level of pleasure during intercourse. For Sebastian, it had taken a single kiss. What would have happened if they'd gone further?

She shook off the thought. That didn't matter. What *did* matter were those last words of warning he'd given her. He'd been so serious. So ominous. And silly, desperate her forced herself into making light of the matter.

What she needed to do was come up with an escape plan. Just in case. For all she knew, morning would come without a hitch, but if she needed to make a break for it before then, then she needed a plan B, one that included procuring a baseball bat or at least a knife. She didn't have anything like that on her, but if Sebastian had crooked plans for her, she wasn't about to make it easy.

Ignoring the way her body protested leaving the comfort of the first real bed she'd slept in in weeks, Alice lowered her feet to the plush rug. Padding to the door took a small reserve of courage, but after several minutes of pressing her ear to the wood yielded not a peep from the other side, she turned the knob.

His scent was everywhere, as if he'd marked every foot of the palatial house inch by painstaking inch. Or maybe she'd just become hung up on how good he smelled. It almost distracted her from choosing a window near her guest room to unlatch. Almost.

Instead, she turned the lock slowly, breath held, praying it didn't make a sound when unbolted. He'd stopped her before she'd located his room, and if Bast hadn't gone there immediately after leaving her, he could be anywhere. Her nerves were on screaming alert, but when the tiny click did little more than puff out the sound, she released a breath.

This plan B was a little rudimentary, but in a pinch, would do nicely. Besides, there was no way in hell she was walking out of here without something she could hock for a fifty. There wasn't a whole lot she could walk away with on the sly, but everything she'd seen so far screamed opulence. It was taste and *Better Homes and Gardens* and shit-you-can't-afford all rolled into one. If he'd offered her more than a hot and cot, maybe she'd reconsider lifting something. But tomorrow, when her ass was parked on a bench somewhere, one eye open while she slept, she'd be kicking herself for being too nice.

Nice didn't keep her fed. Burying her conscience did.

Testing her luck, Alice trailed her hand along the wall as she edged further into the house, toward the direction of the kitchen to grab a knife for protection, at least.

After only a few feet, Alice stopped suddenly and took a moment to get her bearings. The hall seemed to stretch in both directions for a mile. Where was the kitchen again? To the left or... *Shit.* Damn this place for being larger than any single guy could ever need!

Glowing ahead caught her attention, and Alice inched closer to it. A muted sliver of light fell into the hallway, a beacon if ever she saw one. Venturing toward its source, she realized it was a computer monitor that lit up an office almost as well as daytime. If only it affected the corners of the room, which remained in inky blackness.

Deeper inside, her shoulder brushed against some artwork as she hugged the wall, the blunt pain a reminder she shouldn't be here. A little nagging voice directed her to exit the room, exit the house and go back to her own world. But another little voice, one more demanding and a hell of a lot more curious, insisted a quick look at the screen would ease her suspicions about Sebastian. For instance, if she just found run-of-the-mill software programs running, even just a simple Internet site for porn, she could dismiss him as just another red-blooded male. If, however, she discovered something a little more nefarious, her next decision—namely, leaving—would be justified.

It almost physically pained her to abandon her search for a weapon, but she comforted herself with the knowledge that it was only temporary. One quick look, and she'd get back on task.

Swallowing past a dry throat, she moved toward the computer, putting an unsteady hand on the mouse as soon as she nudged the desk.

"Wow," she said softly before she could recall the sound. She knew diagrams like this, learning them almost before she'd learned to read. But the extent of detail which had gone into the family tree diagram on the screen before her would have made any museum curator proud. His lineage went on for *generations*. Nothing like she'd ever seen before. Her mother's research had been impressive, but what was before her made their family line look like what they taught children in elementary school biology.

Back when things were good, when they'd been a whole, functional family, she and Mom spent hours on the weekends working on their own tree. Even after she'd died, Alice had been loath to stop the research. Ultimately, her homelessness forced it to end. She missed it.

She continued to study the display, only then noticing the missing information. "What about over here?" she mused aloud, noting that merely one half of Sebastian's tree had been completed. He sat as a lone box in a sea of wiggles, dashes and lines.

"It's still a work in progress."

Swinging her body in the direction of his low voice, Alice shrieked. "Fuck!"

A dark shadow moved, and it took her eyes a second to adjust. Sebastian stood from a wing-backed chair placed in one of the corners, a half-empty glass dangling from his fingers. His movement was slow, yet at the same time reminded her of a predator. "Is that a request?"

"Wh-what?" She racked her brain, trying to understand, before her own last remark came back to her. "Oh."

The same little voice she should have listened to earlier gave her a triumphant *told you so*, but Alice stood her ground as he approached. Her fingers folded around the computer mouse, intent on using it to her advantage if he stepped too close. Not quite the baseball bat she longed for, but that was the price she paid for morbid curiosity.

He came closer than she would have liked but didn't act threatening. Not yet, anyway. The scent of liquor hovered around him, although nothing in his manner suggested he was inebriated. "Couldn't sleep?" he asked.

The subtle aroma of liquor coming from his breath sent a shiver through her spine. "It's hard to sleep in a new place sometimes."

"So you decided to pass the night by snooping? Or perhaps stealing?" There was a slight hint of amusement in his voice.

Her face went hot. *Did he know*? "I'm not a thief."

"So you've told me." Sebastian pulled the glass to his mouth, the ice cubes within tinkling as they collided with each other. He swallowed the remainder of liquid before setting the glass down. "Yet here you are, wandering the halls, after I've asked you to lock yourself in."

Technically, she *had* locked herself in. It just hadn't lasted that long. A not-so-smart decision in retrospect.

His height forced her to tilt her face up if she wanted to meet his gaze. His close proximity forced her to swallow again.

"I'm not afraid of you." The trembling in her voice didn't aid the lie. "I wouldn't still be here if I was."

In the dark, she couldn't be certain, but she swore something flickered in Sebastian's eyes. Before she had a chance to further scrutinize her finding, he leaned closer, planting his hands on either side of her. With the desk at her back, Alice had no place to turn. No direction to look for safe harbor, but at him.

Sebastian kept his face just above hers, his body heat conspiring to confuse her. She breathed in his scent, his air, and fought to keep previously dormant hormones under submission. Then he lowered his head before his lips brushed hers in a barely there caress, and all plans to act aloof went out the window.

"With a heart beating that fast," he said, meeting her mouth again with a soft touch, "if it's not fear, then it must be…*excitement.*"

FIVE

IF ANYONE ELSE would have discovered his pet project, he would have been enraged. Even now he wondered at why he was letting his dick do the talking instead of his brain. Then again, every time Alice came near him, blood went free-falling from his head to another area further south, in a rush.

Instead of working on one of a million things that required his attention, he'd chosen to sit in the dark, brooding over the woman who lured him as if a siren. At first glance, he'd thought she didn't have what it took to capture his attention, but for every second he spent with her, the more that belief faded.

He wanted her so badly every bone in his body ached, every muscle tensed with fragile restraint. When he told her to be afraid of him, he meant it. Hundreds of years of discipline turned into a jumbled mess when he touched her. And when he kissed her, like now? Forget it.

These innocent, stolen meetings of his lips and hers were supposed to help him remember himself. To remember she was a stranger, a human, someone who shouldn't stir his emotions. Instead, all they did was make him forget himself in her taste. Her feel. The way she clung to his shirt as if afraid he would disappear. God, how he understood that desperation.

Bast tore himself away from her mouth. "You truly are fearless."

Heightened vision saw her face cloud over. "No, not really." She sighed. "Things just couldn't get much worse, is all."

"What are you running from?"

She hesitated before replying, "Everything."

"Except me, a complete stranger. Who others might caution you to run from."

"Get over yourself. Since I've met you, you've been under the weather." She released the mouse, as if forgetting she'd held it in the first place. Not like the little gadget would have done her any good should he have wanted to hurt her, but he liked seeing her grab it. She wasn't as careless about her safety as he'd first thought. Alice widened her stance, putting both hands on her hips. The frown she gave him rivaled the best mother's around the world. "Besides, if you were really going to do something, you would have done it by now."

A fair point. Maybe his control was better than he gave it credit.

"Now," she continued, turning away from him, "tell me about this genealogy chart and why one half is so bare. I'm pretty good with these things."

Licking his lips, removing the last trace of her taste, helped settle his roiling emotions. Moving his focus to the chart soothed the remainder.

He normally didn't share this little project with anyone. Not even his men. For some reason, Alice's reaction to it intrigued him. What could it hurt to show her?

The screen saver had kicked in, so Bast hit one of the keys. He turned his shoulder, blocking her view when he typed in the password, which allowed modifications to be made on the document. Together they stared at the complex diagram, which grieved him every time he tried to put it to rights.

"This side is my mother's line," he said carefully. "I can trace them back to the Middle Ages."

"But your dates are wrong."

He ignored her, pretending not to notice that some members of the family—specifically a handful close to his own generation—had unusually long lives. "In some places I worked from supposition and rumors passed through oral storytelling. I know the entire thing can't be one hundred percent perfect, but I think it's pretty damned close."

"But your paternal line? You don't have that?"

Bast shook his head, unclenching his jaw at the same time. "No. I only knew my mother. I've spent a long time going through documents and files trying to locate him, but I only come up blank." Whoever the man was, he'd done a damned good job of covering his tracks. The only reason Sebastian suspected he might have been preternatural was because of the extent to which he'd disappeared from the face of the earth. He doubted any human could be that thorough.

She leaned in closer to the screen, tracing a finger along one of the lines. "You made a mistake here. This person's on two different branches, unless…" Alice started muttering to herself. "No, not the same person. A mistake. I think if you…yeah. She needs to be on this line, not that one."

He'd worked with painstaking precision on the chart. "Show me."

"Here." She made a face. "And here."

"Son of a bitch," he said with a low growl. "I don't know which one is correct. *Fuck*. I'll have to——"

"You could hire me to do it."

"What?"

Her words picked up speed, her enthusiasm growing. "Let me do this for you. Like a personal assistant or something. My mother worked on these in her spare time, and I know how to do the research. Let me——"

"No."

"But Bast, it's a win-win. For room and board. You've got this huge house——"

"No, I'm sorry. I won't let you work on this."

"But why not?"

He shook his head again, regret washing over him that he couldn't share even this tiny snippet of his life with someone. Especially not a human. "Not this."

"Wait, wait. Before you make a decision, just think. I've spent more than ten years working on my family's genealogy charts. It took me less than two minutes to find not one, but two mistakes on yours. I'm not here looking for skeletons in the closet. Whatever secrets I find will go to the grave with me. I'm just looking for a way to not end up on the street tomorrow. That's all."

"I don't know you and you don't know me. Yet you want that level of trust?"

"*Yes*. I'm worth it. Give me a chance to prove it to you. Anything I find, anything at all, remains between you and me. I don't have anyone else to tell, I swear it."

"You swear a lot."

"'Cause you keep putting me in situations that require it. Come on, Bast. What do you say?"

At some point he'd stopped believing she would be leaving in the morning. If he was wrong and she happened to slip out while he slept, he would deal with it later, but with everything within him, he knew he'd have a very difficult time letting her go. He didn't question the why of it, not yet, but allowed his gut instinct, which had never steered him wrong before, to be his guiding light.

"No," he said, still questioning the decision. Because he wanted this too. To be able to share this burden with someone else. Someone who'd shown him a little compassion. "While I appreciate your enthusiasm, this isn't for you. I owe you a debt and *will* repay you."

Her eyes flashed when she turned to him, a smile pushing her cheeks. "So I can stay tonight, right? And maybe beyond tonight?"

"Just one night." He tried to keep his voice stern. Somehow not betray his own growing excitement. "One guaranteed night, but the next day…we'll see."

She launched herself at him with an impressive speed only a vampire could admire. Prepared for the attack, he opened his arms, letting her fall into them. The thoughts that raced through his mind when their bodies collided would have made a hedonist blush.

In the darkness of the room, the flickering white light from the monitor highlighted her in a breathtaking glow, the smile on her face brightening her face simultaneously. Her expression faltered for just an instant, as if she realized the faux pas of moving into such an intimate position. Bast tightened his arms around her though, letting primal instinct have its way.

"You are very tempting," he said, his voice thick and strained. "I still don't know if this is a good idea."

"It doesn't have to be a good idea. I need a place to stay and you need a nurse. That's me. Kind of."

"So I just became your boss? Kind of?"

Alice's lips broadened into a mischievous smile. "Absolutely."

"Is that so?"

"Oh, yeah." Her gaze went to his chin, almost searing in its intensity. After a coy glance, she pushed away from him. Her fingers trailed over a letter opener he'd left on the desk, and something about the way she caressed the metal was both seductive and arousing. What he wouldn't give to have her touch him again like that. She didn't seem to notice his scrutiny of her, adding, "I mean, I don't have any formal training or anything, but what could go wrong?"

He snorted. "That fills me with loads of confidence." Bast folded his arms over his chest, at once confused and amused. "Why am I agreeing to it again?"

"I don't see anyone else around, so I guess you're stuck with me."

No, he wasn't, but damn if he could stop himself from behaving otherwise. "You're so Goddamned innocent. What if I'm trying to take advantage of you?"

"Nah, I don't believe that. If you're not still sick, you're at least recovering. You wouldn't want to drain the last of your strength on frivolous activities."

He choked out a laugh. "Frivolous activities?"

She began backing away, one sure step behind the other. Her mood had buoyed, and he supposed having a place to stay for one more night had something to do with it.

Bast stalked after her, matching her pace. Slow. Methodical. A cat after his mouse. "You're forgetting one thing, Alice."

"Oh? What's that?"

"It'll take a lot more than two or three hours of frivolous activities to drain the last of my strength. Don't forget, I…"

Her breath quickened, and he watched the color in her face brighten.

"Don't."

He smelled her arousal now. Might have been the game quickening her breath; might have been his presence causing her eyes to dilate. Either way, he reveled in the signs that she was turned on.

"Get."

Alice squeaked when she bumped into a wall. Instead of fleeing for safety, she flattered against it. Her breasts heaved beneath the force of her quickened breaths. Her once-damp hair had dried into a small crown of frizz, the tips framing her face. She sucked in her bottom lip to chew on it, and he had a sudden flash of remembrance. As if they'd done this before.

"You don't get…?" she asked softly.

He mentally shook off the sensation then crossed the few feet between them, blocking any retreat she might have had. "Sick."

OH, WOW. ALICE'S heart threatened to kick its way out, the excitement of the moment more than she'd faced in a year. Bast was so damned good-looking!

Her fingers crept over the tight terrain of his abdomen, the ridges and valleys of definition worth memorizing. His T-shirt clung to his body as well, jealously guarding a vision of near masculine perfection. But she'd already seen it. Even now, she slipped her eyes closed in order to recall the memory.

His kiss was possessive, laying claim to her lips as

if he explored them every day of his life. Even the grip tightening around her waist was meant to ensure she submitted to being owned.

In another time, in another life, she would have relished it. Today, Alice had to wrench her mind away from drugging kisses and seductive holds. She ignored the feel of a man pressed tightly against her body, the evidence of his arousal burgeoning against her stomach. The days of being able to appreciate being a woman were long gone.

The way her stomach churned now was in response to his kiss. Not because she kissed him while plotting to steal his possessions.

And maybe if she told herself that enough times, she might actually start to believe it.

She'd gained a little of his trust and entrance to his home for the time being. Just a few more minutes—with another tiny sliver of trust erected—and she'd start to evaluate how to make gains from this situation. She had to. He had all of this, and she had nothing more than the clothes on her back. She hated this life, but she hated starving even more.

The moment she had the chance to repay him, she would. Either that or donate money to charity in his name. Ten years ago, if someone had asked her if she'd ever steal from someone, she would have scoffed indignantly. Knowing she'd never call herself a thief.

Ten years was a long time ago though. Since then, she'd eaten out of garbage dumpsters, had to sleep beneath overpasses and went days without showering or brushing her teeth. Just because she could work the system a little better now, snagging spots at homeless shelters and burying her pride long enough to accept hand-outs, didn't mean she couldn't use the extra money when it surrounded her on all sides. Like it did now.

Pushing away from Bast took a little more effort than it should have and she didn't know if it was the man or what he represented that she clung to more. "Whoa," she said after blowing out a breath. The man knew how to kiss. For sure.

His eyes were dark with promise. "You okay?"

The way her heart fluttered did not inspire confidence, but she nodded. Time to get him to show off. If she prodded just the right way, he'd want to display his wealth. That's what men like him did. Women like her took advantage.

"It's a little overwhelming."

Bast frowned. "It?"

"You. Your home. Everything. It's been great." A quick glance to the side. Bashful. "Thank you."

By stepping away, he took a little of the oxygen with him. "Come on. Let me give you a quick tour."

"In case I stay more than a night?"

He hesitated before grinning. "So you don't accidentally set off the alarm."

By the end of the tour, her sense of direction remained challenged and yet she stood very impressed. His house echoed the owner: tasteful in an understated manner. A man's home. She couldn't help notice the lack of family pictures, or even pictures of Bast himself. There was nothing in the place that spoke of personalization. That the house belonged to him. It could have been anyone's place of residence, and she would have been none the wiser.

Alice cleared her throat. "You have a lovely home." So many nice things. Things she would never be able to afford on her own, not in this lifetime or another. "I'm surprised you live here by yourself."

She'd taken note of every electronic device, which ones were portable. Estimated street value for some. It was almost a shame a woman with expensive taste in jewelry didn't live here. Despite the prep work, without being left alone and handed some sort of map, it would be difficult to relieve Bast of some of his possessions. It wouldn't stop her from trying to get something small. Something her conscience wouldn't beat on her too badly about.

His insurance would cover the losses, no matter what she took. One day, when she was back on her feet, she'd mail him back the money, she reminded herself. That thought soothed some of her guilt. Just some though.

He paused before speaking, his attention drifting toward the front door just down the hall. A slight tilt of his head followed. "I live a hard life. Long hours, even longer—"

Ascending and descending chimes surrounded them from all sides. The sound of a doorbell, intrusive yet soothing. Despite herself, Alice started at the noise.

After a quick glance at his watch, Bast grumbled, "Stay here."

She wasn't wearing a watch, but it had to be somewhere around three or four in the morning. Who the hell was showing up at this man's place at this time of the night? He didn't seem particularly surprised. More annoyed.

He said he wasn't a drug dealer, nor did he do anything illegal for a living.

Right.

Well, at least that made her feel a little better about

lifting any valuables he'd happen to leave lying around. His ill-begotten gains would become hers. Unfortunately, during her recon, she hadn't noticed much that would be easily removed. The letter opener. Maybe some of the silverware. Maybe he left some cash in his bedroom, the one place she hadn't failed to notice they hadn't gone.

Would the visitor be there long enough to serve as a distraction? She could hear Bast's voice and that of some other man not too far away. As tempting as it was to peek around the corner just to see the other individual, it was more tempting to shuffle back to the office, if she could find it quickly, and have another look at the bric-a-brac. Torn, unable to decide between waiting or going, she held her breath and listened hard.

"If not tonight, when?" the man asked. His voice had risen, and she couldn't tell if he was closer or just plain angry. There was an edge to his words that put her own nerves on notice.

"Things have come up." Sebastian's tone, on the other hand, remained even-keeled. He was patient, as if explaining the concept of calculus to a child.

"Things? What kind of things could have come up which make you forget your duty to the Council and the community?" Louder now. "If this responsibility is more than you can bear, step down, Bast. There are at least another dozen men who would happily take up the task, and at least half of them deserve it more than you."

Whoa. Alice froze in place, all plans for leaving vanished. Sebastian might not be a drug dealer, but whatever position he held must have been in a precarious place. And she thought things had already gotten interesting tonight.

"Is that a challenge, Cicero?" There was a level of calm menace in his words. "Any time you want to challenge me for leadership, you only have to say the word." His voice dropped lower. "Go ahead. Say it."

God, she wanted just a teeny peek at this guy. Anyone stupid enough to want to take on Sebastian on purpose must have balls the size of Africa.

Fortunately for her, she didn't. She'd stay tucked away and out of the path of two heated males. Maybe figure out if his bedroom was the third doorway on the left or the second one on the right. Had she been in either? Damn, she couldn't remember.

Their voices dropped, deflating her growing curiosity, and Alice took that as her sign. With as much stealth she could muster, she backed into the hallway.

She counted darkened doorways, sorting through her memory to identify where each one led. A few she recalled; some she couldn't. Something told her she'd been down most of them though.

Doing an about-face, she peered in the other direction and almost cursed. If she was right—and she was pretty certain about it—Bast's mystery bedroom lay this way. Wouldn't matter if she could get there without passing the main hallway, where Bast and his friend were convening. But she couldn't. Not without being seen if one or both men faced this way.

Okay, so do a little recon. Figure out if she could sneak by and then make a decision from there. That ought to work.

Coming to a crouch with painstaking slowness, Alice prodded herself to dart her head out, eyes trained toward the direction of their voices. It didn't have to last more than three seconds. Just long enough to capture their image in her brain and then decide if she could dash across the opening.

She inhaled and exhaled twice. Once more. Ignoring the riot of voices telling her this was a bad idea, Alice peered around the corner. When her gaze collided with the two men standing in the foyer, she forgot all about stealth.

Sebastian easily stood six foot two or three. There was no way he weighed less than two hundred pounds. But Cicero?

Crap. He just about towered over Sebastian and looked like he could take her benefactor down without much problem. Pitch black eyes peered out over a prominent nose and thin lips. Dark skin was sensual against a silken fall of long black hair. He was Middle Eastern in looks. Alice hadn't thought *tall*, *dark and handsome* meant much these days. But staring at him now, she reconsidered. While he didn't have the same innate magnetism as Sebastian, Cicero made her swallow in appreciation.

There were two drop-dead gorgeous men squaring off less than ten feet away. At some point during the night she must have died and gone straight to heaven. As cliché as the saying went, it explained her situation better than anything else.

Cicero turned those glittering black eyes toward her, and Alice's heart roared. He scanned her in a single visual sweep, as if he took in every detail of her face, memorizing every cell. "What do we have here?"

Stupid. Stupid. Stupid. It was supposed to be just a glance at the men. Not a full-on ogle.

His lip lifted in distaste as he turned toward Sebastian. "Is this the reason you're putting off the men for another night?"

Sebastian glared at Alice. "No, she's not the reason."

"Fuck her. Feed from her. Whatever…but do it, get rid of her and then get your fucking priorities in order. The full moon is seven nights away."

Stepping into Cicero's way, blocking him from her sight, Sebastian's body swelled with agitation. "You report to me, not the other way around. What goes on in my private time is none of your damned business."

"Except I plan on reporting your casual indifference to the Council, so it just became my business." A pause. "But I'll make you a deal. Let me feed from her too and instead of reporting you, I'll just wait for you to hang yourself with your own ineptitude. She looks sweet enough. I haven't had a pure human in some time, and it's almost worth staying quiet for a few days."

"I don't kill them," Sebastian said quietly.

This conversation had gone from zero to beyond eerie in no time flat. What were they talking about? She got the fucking part, but feeding? And killing? *Hello*! What did they mean?

"*Move*," she muttered to her paralyzed feet, willing them to take her in the direction of a back door or any other overlooked entrance. To her dismay, they failed to listen, and never had she wished for a baseball bat more than now. Damn it, why had she come this way first?

Cicero peered beyond Sebastian to lock gazes with Alice again. "That's up to you. Do we have a deal?"

SIX

As TEMPTING AN offer as it was, Bast mirthlessly chuckled. "Of course we don't have a deal." He stepped closer to his second lieutenant. "Get the fuck out of my house and don't come back unless invited. Tell the Council whatever the fuck you want. Afterward, go fuck yourself."

He could feel the stirrings of unease moving the contents of his stomach around, but Bast ignored the sensation. Of all the people he feared discovering he'd come down with an illness, Cicero Nadeem, a true Hassassin of ancient days, topped the list. He'd be the loudest and most adamant about Bast's immediate removal from the Council guard.

They hated each other as fierce rivals, but there was probably no one better suited for serving beneath him than Cicero. Even Gray didn't have all of the skills Cicero had honed over the years. In the heat of battle, Bast trusted him as much as any of his other men to guard his back against lycans and any other threat to the Council. Right now though, they weren't in battle.

Cicero snapped his gaze to meet Bast's. There was fury firmly tucked in it, but the expression on his face hadn't changed one iota. "Your warrant, *hybride*."

Hybride. Bastard. Mongrel. Impure.

He'd been called all of those names and worse. This early in the morning, with Alice staring on, he wouldn't let the slur get to him. Instead he tilted his chin toward the front door. "Gray knows my mind. I expect that you will follow him without hesitation. For the time being, see yourself out, Lieutenant."

Cicero stared past Bast one final time, a dangerous look slanted in Alice's direction before he turned on his heels. The sound of retreating footsteps and then a door closing drifted to him seconds later. Bast stayed in position, not allowing himself to move either. Not yet.

His hands shook with barely contained anger. But the longer he worked on reining in his roiling emotions, the more confusion took over. Which infuriated him the most: Cicero's intrusion or Alice's decision to ignore his warning?

Or was he simply worried about the interest she had invoked in his lieutenant?

"Sebastian?" A one-word question spoken by such a small voice.

He forced himself to take breaths like humans did. One slow, deep inhale followed by an equally lazy exhale. And then another. It took almost a full minute to apply any sort of calm to himself. At last he said, "That was only one reason why you shouldn't be here. I was an idiot for thinking this might be a good idea." It physically pained him to reach a final decision. "In the morning, gather your things and leave, Alice. This is no place for you. For now, go rest."

"But…"

"I owe you a debt of gratitude and I swear on my life I'll repay you. Good night, Alice."

Bast didn't wait for another protest, choosing instead to head for his gym. His stomach churned with every step he took away from her, but his decision had been made. She didn't try to stop him, and the disappointment over her willingness to leave in the morning became a living thing within his veins.

He stabbed the security console with the appropriate digits, barely seeing the numbers for the red haze covering his vision.

This was stupid. Just because he wanted to fuck this woman was no reason to be so distraught over her exit in the morning. He'd bedded how many dozens in his lifetime, always with the ability to walk away the next morning without a second glance.

Barefooted, he crossed the cushioned mats covering the floor and headed to the custom-built home gym squatting like a watchman in the corner. Sitting down on the padded seat, reaching for the overhead bars gave him something else to focus on.

His muscles screamed in protest as he moved, pulleys making it possible to simultaneously lift over three hundred pounds of metal. The resounding clang that resulted each time he slowly released the weight rattled his teeth, but he kept going. Kept working. Head lowered, seeing nothing but the expanse of gray on the floor, Bast pushed his body to follow his commands. He needed the control. Lived for the discipline of this moment.

No matter how his body strained though, the slow heat building in his belly made its presence known.

"Do you want to tell me why you're so angry?"

His head snapped up. First to Alice and then to the closed door. "How did you get in here?" he barked.

She stood well out of his reach. Smart woman. "For someone as security-conscious as you are, you're not very good about covering your tracks. You didn't even hear me behind you when you punched in the code. I simply had to watch. Don't you think you should tell me what just happened out there? Who was that guy, and what did he mean?"

The burn began to spread into his chest. He ignored her questions. "The second you leave this room, I'll be changing the code. Don't bother to keep it memorized." Damn, he was pissed. If any of his men had made such a rookie mistake, he'd have him reassigned off his team so fast there'd be skid marks.

Alice moved to the closest wall, her attention darting back and forth between him and the display of weapons. "You provide security for important people, and that man Cicero reports to you." He watched her take in the collection of guns, swords and knives. Most of them were older than Alice. Some he'd fashioned out of steel himself. "You kill people. I get that. My brother lives in a hard world too."

He rested his hands on his thighs, barely able to control the urge to curl his fingers into the cotton. The heat moved faster now. "You don't seem bothered by it. You continue to surprise me."

"My brother's friends once broke every finger on his left hand when he couldn't repay them right away after he'd stolen some drugs. Those were his *friends*. So far you haven't been a jerk or done anything inappropriate to me. In fact, you're kind of nice at times. I can't let a hitman or mercenary or whatever make any nevermind to me, so long as you don't come after me or mine."

"I don't deal in illegal activity, I told you."

"But you do something that's heinous enough for

me to be considered a liability. Worth killing. Doesn't sound quite legal."

He shrugged halfheartedly. "Where I'm from, it's perfectly legal. Required, in fact."

"I won't ask you where you're from then. What did Cicero mean when he talked about feeding from me though?"

Bast had to admire her courage. The way she'd switched topics so smoothly. She didn't raise her voice. Any inflection indicating her concern or arising hysteria remained absent. Neither convinced the truth from him. Bringing together the worlds of human and vampire wasn't his responsibility.

"Go get some sleep. It's been a long night."

"Stop avoiding me." She stepped closer, eyes narrowing. "You're perspiring."

"I've been working out." He'd hardly begun. And just like illness, sweating belonged in the world of humans. Still, beads of sweat began to form along his hairline. The first drip of cool moisture trickled behind his left ear.

"Why do you have to be so stubborn? Why won't you accept you need my help?"

Bast stood. "I don't need your help," he said through clenched teeth.

In fact, he thought he was burning alive. Heat weaved in and out of his body, twining through him until he swore he saw smoke rising from his flesh. Something crawled along his back in waves, like fingertips pushing from the inside. Like something struggling to get out.

The speed with which his illness swept through him seemed to increase every time he faced an attack. The first time, it had taken close to thirty minutes before he'd felt its full weight. Now? By God, it had been less than thirty minutes.

The next time...

He swayed, and Alice rushed forward. Her hand touched his skin. The instant it did, she cried out. "Your fever's back." She reached for his face, wincing as her fingers skimmed his cheek. "I think it's worse. Sebastian, *please*, we have to get you to a hospital."

"No hospitals." Four syllables had never made his mouth ache as much as those did.

"Come on, then." Alice grunted as she tried to heft his bulk. "The shower."

Sebastian took a step. Wavered. Staggered back. "Leave," he urged, his voice barely above a whisper.

"Yeah. In just a minute."

Alice didn't understand. He needed her to go.

Not because he feared what his world might do to her if they found her with him, instead fearing what he himself might do if they stayed together just another minute more.

Along with the heat—the burning, all-encompassing flare—came a ravenous hunger. If Alice didn't leave him now, he didn't know how he'd be able to handle it. His want lived inside his body, screaming for attention and demanding to be appeased.

His mouth watered from the remembrance of her taste. Not just her lips, but the dark, sweet slide of her blood against his tongue. Incisors lengthened, pulsing from the memory of puncturing her soft skin. Licking his lips didn't help. The gnawing in his belly expanded, announcing with deep rumbles the depth of his growing hunger. Bast had to taste her now.

Had to.

THE MAN WAS built like a freight train. Sebastian dropped, and Alice thanked God he'd managed to fall onto the padded seat. If he'd hit the floor, it would have been next to impossible to get him up again on her own. "It's like you eat rocks for breakfast," she muttered.

Somehow he found the strength to rise again. Her spine almost telescoped in the process of assisting him, but at least he was standing. Now they only had to tackle crossing almost the entire expanse of his house to the bathroom.

"Wh-what?"

Alice stilled, something about the slight spaciness to his answer setting her nerves on edge. She was reminded too much of her brother Richard during one of his high sprees, when she wasn't sure if she'd wake up to find most of her belongings sold to one of his friends, or discover one of the same friends groping her while she'd slept.

His body heat clung to her, causing her own body to perspire as well. How hot could a person go before permanent damage was inflicted? She needed a thermometer and a few minutes with Google. She needed help.

"Sebastian, I have to go call someone. Even that Cice—"

Oh shit.

His teeth.

His teeth were long. Like a dog's.

Like a vampire's.

She'd just meant to look into his eyes, to check to see if maybe his pupils were dilated too. If there was still sweat coming off his forehead, that should be a good sign. When she'd glanced up, the angle gave her a perfect view between his parted lips.

Who hadn't been required to read *Dracula* in high school or hadn't heard of the *Twilight* series? Even if someone had been home-schooled, the teenage pop phenomenon couldn't be ignored.

"It makes sense now." The physical perfection. Cicero's comments. Bast's wealth. Yet she couldn't bring herself to believe it. "You have hidden cameras in here? Or someone's gonna come jumping out from another room, telling me I've been punked, right?"

"Alice?" There was an unsettling gleam in his eyes, which seemed too keen at the moment.

"You don't really expect me to believe this set-up. I'll admit for a split second you got me. I was convinced that all of this was real. The nice place, the scary bad-ass at the front door. Even your teeth now. You got me good."

Sebastian's stomach made a wet, lurching sound, and he doubled over. She stepped back automatically, ready to keep her feet out of the line of fire. Vomit where he wanted, just keep her out of it, literally.

And that's when she remembered the blood outside the club. The puddle that had been beneath a man with no visible wounds. Pooled blood. She was certain of it. He'd been retching then too. Oh God, had he thrown it up?

She peered at him now, knee to the ground, his face obscured from view. One arm wrapped around his abdomen, the back of his other hand pressed against his mouth.

A sick vampire. Just her freaking luck.

Gathering every ounce of her courage, she took a tiny step closer. She had to prove to herself this wasn't real. It was some sort of not-funny joke that she'd giggle about later, because of course vampires didn't really exist. They were born out of the imaginations of authors and older brothers hell-bent on scaring the shit out of their younger siblings.

Heart pounding, breath barely squeezing past her lips, she tilted her head to the side to look at Sebastian's face again. One more look into his mouth at those teeth. They couldn't be real.

Couldn't be.

SEVEN

ALICE'S FACE HAD gone pale, blue eyes widening as she stared at him. Not stared. Studied. She saw something in his face that must have terrified her, for Alice had stopped speaking, all snark and bravado suspiciously absent.

The last time he'd fed from her had been a stolen moment. One he didn't want to repeat if he could help it.

But he didn't know if he could stop himself.

Somehow he'd managed to not give in to screaming impulse. Fuck, it hurt to even turn his gaze toward hers. "What?"

"Your teeth." She licked dry lips. "That's what he'd meant, right? This is real and I'm not being punked. And I'm not dreaming." Her voice dropped into a mutter. "But maybe I am. Passed out or something back at the club. Or maybe something fucked up had been in the doughnut…which I didn't get to taste. *Shit*."

Bast turned his head to the side and coughed up something thick, which he swallowed back down with a grimace. It would have been amusing to watch her continue to justify what she'd seen, but he was in no mood for it now. Instead he focused on where she'd been touching him. On how soothing her hands felt on his bare skin. Except now, with the wariness in her eyes, she stood too far away to be effective. "Touch me again, Alice."

Her eyebrows lifted, eyes narrowing. "Touch you? And what happens after I do that?"

Maybe some of the illness would calm down. "I won't hurt you. Not ever."

"But I don't know that... Weren't you the one trying to convince me to leave not long ago?"

Because of how much he wanted to get close to her when it shouldn't have been such an unshakable compulsion. "Please..."

She took a tiny step back, her body poised to run. He didn't have to hear her thoughts to know it would take only the slightest provocation to make her flee. "Tell me if you're a vampire first."

"Would hearing an answer from me really satisfy you?"

"Try me."

The consequences for telling her the truth weren't as terrible as they used to be. Once upon a time, any vampire caught divulging the secrets of the preternatural world would be exterminated, along with the human who'd been told. And anyone the human might have been in contact with. Neither friends nor family would have been spared.

Now, with the preternatural and the human worlds colliding with such frequency, it was becoming more and more difficult to keep them separated. The Council, in its wisdom, agreed to allow a revealing under extenuating circumstances, and only those of a certain privilege had the means with which to do so. When the Council discovered Bast's breach—and they *would* discover it—the fine would cost him an outrageous sum of money. True, he'd amassed an obscene wealth over the years, but that didn't mean he wanted to part with two and a half million dollars when a lie could spare it.

"No," he said. "I'm not what you think."

Alice folded her arms across her chest. "Explain the teeth then."

"Later." His stomach rolled again. He couldn't see himself, but if he could, he imagined his face had managed to turn a shade of green not found in the natural color spectrum.

Alice's pale-faced expression touched panic. "Not a chance. Tell me now or I walk. And just so you know how serious I am about that, consider the fact that I don't have a place to sleep tonight. When I leave here, I'm heading for the closest bridge or safest park. Sometimes cars in a tow truck lot are kept unlocked and if I'm lucky, I'll be able to snag a few hours of sleep before the lot opens. The pizza? Was the first time I'd had restaurant food not taken from a trash bin first in months. Bottom line is if I leave your place right now, know it's for a *very* good reason. There is nothing waiting for me out there. Absolutely nothing."

"When are you going to tell me about yourself?" he asked. Curiosity raged through him, and so did another type of anger. He had to hear more about this woman and why she was in such a desperate place. And here he was being a jerk about it. A couple of million dollars was pocket change to him. Not the difference between sleeping in a bed or sleeping on a park bench.

"Tell me about you and those teeth first."

The edges of Bast's vision went white and then faded to black over the course of seconds. His entire being burned from the inside, deep in his belly, turning into a cauldron of heat. It was as if he'd swallowed a ball of fire that pulsed inside him, needing an escape route. It pushed at his flesh, tendrils of feelers racing through his veins. Panicked and desperate in its need for release.

Bast groaned in part fear, part pain. He could deal with the stabbing sensations, like little needlepoints covering every inch of his skin, searing each place they touched. And he could even deal with appearing weak in front of Alice, as much as that sucked. But it was the unknown, the realization he had no idea what this all meant, nor how to fix it—assuming it could be fixed—that practically paralyzed him.

"Yes," he admitted at last. He'd pay the damned fine. Whatever it took.

Alice squinted at him. "Yes to what?"

"Goddamn it, yes, I'm a vampire." Bast snarled, his face contorting. He lifted his lips over his teeth, giving her the best possible view. Even if she hadn't wanted to see, he probably would have done it anyway. They were so fucking sensitive now, they too pulsed, sending rhythmic pounding into his head. "Now what are you going to do?"

He couldn't admit he needed her. That he would burn alive without her. Bast didn't know how and he didn't know why, but for some reason, Alice was the solution to this current problem.

For two heartbeats, she did nothing. Still studying him, Alice took a deep breath. And then another…right before turning tail and hauling ass toward the exit.

Bast swore and took off after her. She'd just managed to get her hand on the knob, pulling the door toward her before he launched himself forward. His palm slammed into the metal, forcing the door shut again. It crashed closed, the resulting boom cutting through the air, shattering what had been a perfect silence.

He could smell her fear as he towered over her. She stood tense, her back to him. He didn't want this. Not like this.

Bast gently stroked his hands over her arms, trying to regain what had been happening between them. His stomach tightened in agitation, his vision swimming. The crawling-pushing sensation at his back climbed into existence, spreading with alarming swiftness.

Just a little more time. Please.

"Swear you won't hurt me," she said meekly, breath whispering against the dark metal.

"I swear."

She turned to face him, blue eyes round with apprehension. "How do I know that you mean it?"

He gritted his teeth, wincing as they punctured the inside of his mouth. Bast straightened his spine, wobbling as he kneeled on a single knee. He looked the human in the eyes as he placed a fist over his heart. "My lady, I do swear to you my everlasting allegiance. I swear that in every matter, your life remains before my own. I swear that I am yours in protection and in loyalty, no matter the circumstance. And I s-swear that you may receive this pledge with the utmost confidence, assured I would rather have my tongue cut from my mouth, my eyes blinded and my body burned 'til only ashes remain should I ever break it…I…I—"

The world wavered then went bluish-black.

Bast awoke to the sensation of soft lips caressing his own. He was lying flat on his back, arms by his sides. His eyelids fluttered, threatening to shut again, but he pushed them open wider with some effort. Damn it, had he passed out?

It took a moment for everything to come rushing back. To figure out why he inhaled the scent of soap and rain as tendrils of dark curls obscured a woman's face from his view.

Alice.

This woman slipped her tongue between his lips with delicate precision, kissing him tentatively. Sensual nips. Exciting him to full arousal. Her hand cupped his chin, holding him in place as her mouth tasted him. He remained still, fearing if he moved, she would stop. As relaxed as his tense body could manage, Bast followed the progress of his illness melting away. It was such sweet relief, every inch slowly leaving him. As if she pulled the heat roasting him from the inside with her very kiss. He didn't understand it, nor did it make any sense, but Bast reveled in the sensation. When he was well he would search for a reason for this easement, but for right now, he would enjoy its soothing comfort.

Alice squeaked when he could take no more and threaded his fingers into her hair. She attempted to pull away, but Bast held her in place. Enjoying the taste of her. The scent. His cock betrayed his excitement, swelling with prurient intent.

He'd spoken with truth when he pledged his loyalty to her. They were old words from a time in his past, but the sentiment behind the allegiance proclaimed today remained the same. He would not harm her, nor allow her to be harmed while in his presence.

He also wanted her more than he wanted his next heartbeat. "Why did you stay?"

"I don't know," she murmured. Alice managed to

pull away just enough to speak, making him want her all the more. The way her lips brushed his made his balls tighten. "I guess I'm going to trust you."

"I'll never hurt you." Nor would he take her blood without her willing permission again. The familiar gnawing in his belly signaled his hunger, but he would not succumb to it so easily.

Alice's hand slid to her neck, covering the pulsing rhythm of her carotid. It was a subtle move, almost so casual he could believe she didn't realize she'd done it. Her gaze snapped to his. "In the bathroom earlier… you—you had bitten me, right? That's what I felt when I…when I…"

"When you climaxed, yes." Bast released his grip, allowing her the freedom to flee, which he knew she must have desperately wanted. He sat up, another pang of hunger stabbing him in the belly. "I fed from you while making sure you wouldn't know that I had. It's how we've managed to stay alive as a species. If feeding was painful or traumatic, humans would hunt us down to the last one."

"So it always feels that way?" she asked quietly.

"No." He stifled the urge to wrap her hand in his. "But for you, I would have it no other way."

"And you need that now, don't you? To feed from me."

Bast paused, unsure of what to tell her. How to tell her. "Normally, I can go days without feeding. What I took from you, while not a full meal, should keep me satisfied for a while. Normally. For some reason I don't know about or understand, I am as starved as if I'd gone days without feeding."

"Does that mean yes or no?"

"Yes," he replied. "Yes, I need to feed from you. Or if not you, I must leave and find sustenance. I'm not sure how long I could go on without nourishment. When I told you earlier I don't get sick, I meant it. This fever is completely foreign to me."

Alice sat back on her haunches, watching him. There was no way to tell what kinds of thoughts were rushing through that brain of hers. Whether she was more afraid now than before. Whether she wanted to run straight for the front door and never return. Whether she was looking for a way to exterminate him now and rid the world of a would-be menace.

"Am I being naïve in trusting you?" she asked.

It didn't matter whether the question was directed toward him or a general musing aloud. "You're not. I gave you my word, and I will hold to it. But you can either decide you trust me or decide I'm not worthy of it. What you do now is totally up to you." There were consequences to her knowledge and he'd undertaken a new responsibility, but it was a burden undertaken willingly.

Her hand lowered, moving away from hiding the area of her neck he coveted. Mouth watering, Bast waited for the permission he desperately needed.

There was a brief nod from Alice, a quick jerk of her chin, and he crawled cautiously toward her. Not intending to frighten, hopefully settling some of her apprehension instead.

Alice rose to her knees, facing him, and Bast heard the fluttering of her heartbeat. The way it raced. He wanted to rest his hand against her chest, to feel its frantic movement as he drank from her. But because this gift was so precious, he chose not to revel in it but to give her trust in him the respect it was due.

His gaze went to that beautiful pulse, the place where her flesh rose and fell in rapid succession. The place where he would kiss. "Just a little bit, princess," he whispered. It was a promise.

She trembled as his arms wrapped around her, but Alice turned her face away, allowing him access. Her chest rose and fell during each shuddering breath, and his cock stirred at the feel of her breasts pressed against him. By the time he bit down, blood immediately flooding his mouth, he was rock hard.

Alice gasped, her hands tightening on his shoulders. A soft whimper escaped her mouth, the motion sending more of the sweet blood he'd been craving as he nursed the wound. The cry that came upon its heels was less surprised, however, and more seductive in nature. Bast pulled again, and Alice released a sound so innocent yet so carnal, he was at a loss as to whether to continue the pleasure she was feeling or to end it before he gave in to its lure.

She writhed in his arms, her pelvis brushing against his straining erection. The fervor in her movement, the way she dug her fingertips into his muscles, was not lost to him. Bast wanted to keep her there enthralled, in the place where she shuddered. He could scent her arousal and imagined their naked bodies coming together the next time he drank from her. And there would be a next time.

And maybe when that time came, he would be buried deep inside her cunt. Her slick walls grasping onto his cock every time he pushed inside of her and then withdrew. If this sensation of feeding from her—taking her life's blood—was this passionate, this all-consuming now, it would only be that much more glorious when he took her as a man, not just as a vampire.

Alice cried out, and he glanced into her face to watch the way it twisted as she came again. From between closed lids, tears leaked and ran down the sides of her face. She looked as otherworldly as he felt in that moment. Beautiful and serene. When she went limp, becoming a dead weight, his wonder hastened into heart-rending concern.

"Alice?" Christ, he almost forgot to lick the wound closed. Heart kicking, Bast tended to the puncture wounds, studying her composure in the meanwhile. "Alice, are you with me?"

He could still hear her heartbeat, ticking a little too rapidly. She breathed easy, some of the bliss still set into her features. So, not dead. And while certain he hadn't taken too much blood from her, apparently it had been more than her body could deal with.

Shit. He was an unthinking, unfeeling asshole. Hadn't she said she lived a meager life, barely scraping by? If she was malnourished, which was most likely the case, feeding him twice in one night would have been a strain.

"Fuck," he muttered. How long ago had it been that he vowed to protect her? Ten, maybe fifteen minutes ago.

Annoyed with himself, Bast hoisted her slight body into his arms, stood and then carried her toward the guest room. He toyed with the idea of removing her sweatpants but wrestled his libido into submission and decided to leave them on. Instead, he tucked her beneath the sheets, rolling back the comforter out of her way.

She was safe in his home—in one of his beds—where he could keep watch over her as the sun rose and the day lazily went by. His own eyelids were heavy, demanding sleep. His internal clock screamed at him to rest. Tonight had been trying, both physically and mentally. Time to refresh. The hunger had been sated.

As he partially draped his body over hers, he assured himself it was for the protection of both of them that he kept her so close.

Not because he wanted her to stay.

EIGHT

"*If it breathes, it can bleed!*" *a human screamed.* "*If it can bleed, it can* die!"

The lone steed dancing upon spindly legs, eyes wide with terror, paid little attention to its rider's declaration. Glistening with sweat, its sides heaved as it darted between blazing bushes and trees dripping sparks and fire onto dried leaves below.

Aurak RithRagoth dove forward, dark wings folded back, streamlining a perfect body made for cutting through cross breezes, and ended up bypassing the horse and its quarry. Sparing them.

For the time being.

His clawed fingers hooked in, the rage of having witnessed the aftermath of destruction vibrating not just through his wings, but through the enormous bulk of muscle and sinew. It propelled him through the sky, urged him to take action. To give voice to the voiceless.

There had been voices, not so long ago. No more, though.

Quiet now. Destroyed without mercy or pity. Put to permanent night before a single sunrise had been glimpsed.

So many eggs smashed by the humans. Killed before they could grow fully into the powerful creatures they would be. How many hundreds? Their nests hunted systematically. Even the shells that hadn't been brutally crushed had been cracked, their stone-hard casings displaying zig-zagging shadowed patterns.

Marbled fields of oceanic blues, honeycombed reds, kaleidoscope grays and the precious, rare blacks speckled with lethal spider web designs. All gone.

Their guardians had been lethargic in their duties. Complacent.

Danger hadn't existed for their kind in so long. Not danger from other creatures with two legs, nor even four. Famine. Disease, maybe.

But now...

He blinked away the shimmering blur in his eyes, tears turning to ice as they dripped down scale-covered cheeks. So different from the curls of smoke drifting from his nostrils and the flames he called forth to set ablaze the frightened humans and their belongings.

For every one of his decimated kind, he planned on taking one of the evolved monkeys in the most vicious balance of justice he could deliver.

Did the humans have any idea—any idea at all—what they'd done?

His kind was mostly elderly now. So old, they'd forgotten what it had been like when they'd ruled the skies. When they'd lived as savages, killing indiscriminately. Fighting each other over the tiniest bauble in the name of greed.

Even the adolescents, those just emerging into adulthood, were a few hundred years old. For such a long time there had been no viable births. The ones which had managed to live through incubation sometimes hatched deformed. Oftentimes simply too weak to survive.

He'd come to the humans to learn of their ways. Their success at survival. He'd wanted to offer them secrets. Treasures. Anything at all to assure that another generation of his race would arise.

"They will disappoint you," his closest friend, Murh ThraxJhar, had cautioned. "Go beyond them. To the others."

"The others? The ones who drink blood and shun the sun? Or the ones who bay at the moon, you're considering perhaps. Or what of the ones who live in the trees, or the oceans?" Disbelief and disdain had bloomed within his blood. A droplet of fire fell from his mouth, thick and caustic. Even his words had felt bitter. "Breed with those…aberrations? Never."

So he'd gone to the humans. He'd been betrayed. The flags of war raised.

Now, as he watched one of them run screaming from an enclosure burning in a brilliant orange, he regretted having spoken too soon about an alliance he refused to forge. In the end, it had been done.

The fire's scent caressed him, enfolding him in its embrace like a lover. He took it within him, agitated senses settling into a calm, helping to loosen the memories of before from his mind. Aurak rode the scent's current to the little domicile he'd set up for the female thing—the vampire—aiding his quest now.

It was no aggravation for him to shift. To make himself look like one of them. She would not have accepted him into her body otherwise. A small concession.

He discarded his current task of gliding through the night and instilling general mayhem among the populace to check on her progress. To see the culmination of centuries of brawn and power of his kind deteriorate into something resembling her and her clan.

It didn't take long to get to her location for he kept her close to him, trusting neither her nor the others like her from interrupting his loose plans.

When he walked into the hut, the bitter pungency of blood flooded him. From the doorway, he studied her thin frame dispassionately. Sweat flowed from her skin and dampened her dark hair such that he no longer saw the curls and twists, which had captivated him from the first. Instead, her hair clung to her already pale face… even more appallingly white now as she strained.

Interesting that men were not permitted to be a part of this process. He, of course, would not be denied to witness the birth of evolution.

The woman grunted again, a long, low groan as she worked hard to push the new life form from her body. More of the coppery scent of blood swirled past him, making his lip snarl in derision. He tried to view the process without inserting his head or his heart, but really, this way of bringing about new life disgusted and fascinated him. So unlike his kind. He longed for the beauty of an egg, the patterns soothing to the eye and designed for easy visibility from the sky.

This…this way. Carrying a fetus in the body…

He shuddered.

His gaze went to the guardians stationed around the room. Four of them for one woman and the infant she carried. If news had breached the humans, other vampires or even the werewolves of this union, he might have stationed more guardians. A hundred if necessary. But no. She'd come to him willingly. After three miscarriages and certainty the future of his race was at an end, she managed to hold on to this one.

He paced the room. Hating this. Hating her. The child.

A plume of smoke followed him as he covered the ground with long strides meant to jar loose the agitation settling in his old bones. He would have sought the comfort of the sky once again, but in these times of war, when his kind was hunted for sport, he recognized the wisdom in blending in. They could not retreat to caves, sleeping and waiting for the time of man to pass.

He'd done this thing. This horrible thing.

Each time he'd filled her with his seed, he did it while looking like them. Fragile skin. Hair on his arms, legs, chest and pubis. Jaw short and stubbled. This form made him feel weak and insignificant, yet he would do it a hundred more times if necessary.

The more he thought on it, the hotter the flames simmering his blood grew. Smoke plumed out of his nostrils, singing the crisp air. Something caustic bubbled in his stomach, pushing up and out, turning his insides into molten rage. Why did he ever think this would work?

A sharp scream rent the air.

Twisting toward her, grimacing at the new scent of fresh blood, he moved next to the bed and watched the child slither from between her legs. It landed on the cot in a heap of limbs and skin and fluid. It didn't move, but the woman continued to moan and writhe. He glanced into her tortured face, still uncertain as to whether he should dispose of her now or later, but decided to wait on that decision. First he wanted to see what would happen with the child.

It was a male. Still not moving. Was this the way they behaved at birth? So unlike their kind, he lamented again.

No scales. No claws. No wings. His kind—his beautiful, strong kind—thrived with life from the moment they burst through their shells.

Maybe this wasn't the way. Maybe they'd have to try and build their cities again. If raging wars meant ensuring the survival of his race, then so be it. This trial did not work. This child was an abomination. And he needed heirs. Not this.

"Toss it outside," he ordered one of the men. "It's dead."

The woman struggled to sitting, crying out at his order. "No!"

He held up a hand to halt the guardian when the man would have stepped forward despite her protest. For some reason he watched her. This woman bent, face pale, and touched the child. She brought it to her breast, stroking it. Talking to it. Aurak reared back when the thing actually began to move. The woman looked up at him. "Not dead, sire. Not dead."

Studying it, he still didn't like the fact that it didn't look like him—not Aurak's true form. Then again, it had looked dead only moments ago.

Perhaps this was a sign.

He grabbed the woman's chin and forced her to look at him. "One month," he spat. "You have one month and then we sire another one."

She quivered with fear. "Another?"

"You will breed until you can't. And then I'll find another who can."

He dropped his grip, no longer caring to touch her.

As he stormed away, the sound of the child's wailing began to fill the chamber.

Yes, it was a good sign.

NINE

ALICE WIPED SOME of the perspiration from her brow, at a loss to explain the amount of heat surrounding her. She inhaled the clean scent of sheets, a smile curving her lips as she recognized the scent of a man nestled into the fibers as well. There. The undertones of coconut, again reminding her of a warm day on a sunny beach.

Wait...

She sat up, pushing away clothing and sheets and his bulk. God, he was next to her in a bed. The last thing she remembered, she'd been giving him—her hand flew to her mouth as she remembered—she'd been feeding him blood. He'd been drinking her blood.

"Gonna be sick," she groaned before covering her mouth with a trembling hand.

"No, you aren't," Bast said gruffly. "Breathe."

Her stomach lurched, and Bast sitting upright made the bed shift. The movement did not work in her favor. Swallowing rising bile, Alice tried to focus on something else. Anything other than what they'd been doing not long ago. But she couldn't stop remembering the way his mouth had felt on her. The way her body had responded every time his tongue teased against her skin. It had been too much, yet she wanted more. She would have let him stay there, drinking from her forever, in exchange for just a few more minutes of that exquisite pleasure.

"God—" Alice whipped her head away from him as digested pizza came tumbling out of her mouth. She gripped the sides of the bed as she leaned over it, painful waves in her belly forcing the vomit to rush out undaunted. Eyes slammed shut, she waited for it to stop, but she couldn't stop thinking about Sebastian. The man who was supposed to be her temporary knight-in-shining-armor. The man who'd taken her off the streets for a single night.

He wasn't a man. He was a vampire.

She'd kissed him and she'd lusted after him. Damn it, she'd even cared for him when he'd fallen ill.

And in exchange, he'd taken her blood.

Powerful hands brushed over her forehead, and Alice idly realized he was holding her hair out of the line of fire. He waited until she stopped gagging before asking, "Better now?"

Panting, she nodded. Her face felt fevered, and she couldn't decide if it was embarrassment or nausea that caused it. "I'm so sorry about…"

"It's easy enough to clean up. I suspect I'm the reason behind you getting sick. Correct?"

"I'm so sorry," she mumbled. Too proud to admit his role in her discomfort.

"There's a bathroom right there." Bast's fingers twirled her curls, managing to twist them into a neat little package that wouldn't fall in her face. "Why don't you go freshen up, and I'll clean up out here? I need you looking and feeling better. That includes getting your stomach to settle down enough to eat. I have a proposal for you when you come back."

Every part of her felt shaky and she wondered if she'd manage to stand upright without collapsing, much less make it across the room under her own power. But it wasn't until she stood, legs quivering but not yet giving out, that she turned to him. "What about you? How are you feeling?"

With a sinewy grace, Bast rolled out of the massive king-sized bed. Alice wished she didn't notice the definition of his muscles as they moved like quicksilver. But she did.

"No sign of the illness yet." He shook his head. "Look at us. We're a match made in heaven. When one's not sick, the other is. I think you were meant to find me, Alice. Someone in the heavens wants us to be together."

Her stomach rolled at that statement, and she hurried toward the bathroom. She couldn't keep those words from echoing in her head, not bothering to sort if they were teasing or serious. Yes, she was sick, but what kind of demented god would destine her to be with someone like Bast? Then again, it was too much of a coincidence to be ignored. Granted, she took her pills religiously. While they wouldn't make her better, they should keep her from deteriorating too quickly or at all. Maybe it was her time to go, and Bast would ease her way from this world without the suffering she might normally have to endure.

It seemed plausible. Someone *did* want them together. That someone would also probably frown on her stealing from him.

Shit. Yeah, so maybe later she'd kick herself hard for letting opportunity slip through her fingers, but he'd been kind to her. He made her feel human again and not like a composition of skin and bones, taking up valuable space on the earth. When he kissed her, he made her feel like a woman. No, she wouldn't take anything from this house. Not even the lovely little letter opener, although that she'd hold on to for a little while longer. No telling if that Cicero guy would show up again, intent on getting at her.

She considered it for only a moment longer, her thoughts about her nonexistent finances disintegrating when she inspected the bathroom. If the other guest bathroom had the ability to take her breath away, this one made her practically orgasmic.

Alice walked the entire perimeter, stunned that any one person could possibly be able to afford such opulence in their home. Between the lush Oriental rug in the center of the room, where a plump recliner sat, to lighted floor tiles and the flat-screen television in the mirror, she was awed. She peered into the shower stall, separated by its own room, and couldn't locate the showerhead. Until something told her to look up.

There, in the ceiling, were dozens of perfect holes decorating the ceiling, set in a stainless steel panel. Twisting the knob in a far corner of the spacious area confirmed her suspicions. It was like watching rain fall from the sky.

Exploring must have cost her twenty minutes, and she still hadn't peered into medicine cabinets. It was all she could do to prevent herself from simply rubbing her naked body over the luxurious towels and other linens stacked so carefully in a walk-in closet.

Taking a shower and cleaning up must have taken another twenty minutes to complete, but Alice couldn't find the will to make herself go any faster. The water was at the right temperature. The towels, when wrapped around her damp body, were heated to perfection. The mirror didn't fog, and the toothpaste even had the right balance of mint.

She'd taken this kind of stuff for granted not too long ago and now, faced with the best in modern amenities, she couldn't stop taking pleasure in them. If Bast wanted her to get out any faster, he'd have to come in armed with a crowbar. Even then, he might find a serious struggle on his hands.

Slinking into the bedroom, towel wrapped around her torso, she came ready with an excuse about not being able to operate the complicated toilet poised on the tip of her tongue. Her thoughts froze as she espied Sebastian.

He stood in the corner, his face downcast, shrugging on a shirt over his glorious chest. His naked, *holy-shit-that-can't-be-real* chest. While solidly built, it was the honed definition of someone who knew how to get hours of work lifting weights to make a difference. Bast was lean, ropes of muscle lending him a razor's edge. She could have spent hours running her fingers over every single one of those lines, each displaying the beauty of man at its finest.

"Holy shit," she whispered, echoing her thoughts. The words came tumbling out, as uncouth and low-brow as her life had become. If her mother were alive to hear Alice now, she would have been spitting out soap for the next week.

He lifted his head and turned it toward her. "I thought you'd gotten lost."

Alice's mouth couldn't have been drier. She struggled to speak again. "I almost could have been." Hell, if she was going for uncouth and low-brow, might as well take it all the way. "Bast? What are you doing with all this? It's just you, right? I mean, I know you guys always seem to have a lot of money in the movies and stuff, but it's just you…"

His expression flattened. "My father left me well provided for and it's only grown over the years. When you've lived as long as I have, you get the opportunity to acquire a great many things. By now, it's simply become habit to surround myself with some of the finer things. But honestly? I don't even notice half of it anymore. Not until someone like you walks in and points it out to me."

"That's a sin, you know."

"What is?"

"To have all this beauty around you and not even realize it's there. Life is so very short for most of us, so you're supposed to take the time to appreciate what's around you. And when you can afford to live in a place as palatial as this one, and then not even notice what others steal and lie for…" She paused, at a loss for words. Finally she said, "You shouldn't be allowed to have it."

He shrugged, the crisp, white shirt like a second skin on him. "I could almost agree with you, except you're comparing apples and oranges. I'm not a human. I was born vampire. My lifespan isn't comparable to yours, and so the same rules don't apply. Incidentally, I don't find beauty in things." His eyes flashed. "Only people."

Wait. Did that mean what she thought it did? Still, she disregarded what might have been a compliment. "I'm very sad for you then. You don't get to appreciate just how precious life is. That's a shame."

"Don't feel sorry for me, Alice," he said softly. "There are better people in the world to feel sorry for."

Her fingers tightened on the plush towel, hiding her body from view. For some reason, she felt as if Bast had the ability to see beneath the material and was studying her now. He somehow saw the imperfections of her body. There weren't any scars or other obvious flaws to speak of, but standing next to him, she became so much more aware of how simple—how human—she really was.

"I would like to offer you a job," he continued. "You made a proposal earlier—"

"A *job* job? That pays money?" Her eyebrows narrowed. "I don't understand." She clutched at the towel while watching him stride to the bureau. From its surface he plucked a slender black case and returned with it. "What's that?"

He unzipped the leather case and withdrew a slick, black laptop. Based on the way he handled it, the weight seemed almost nonexistent. As with everything he owned, it looked top of the line.

"This here is especially equipped," he said while it booted up. "I'd like to pay you by the hour to go through and correct the genealogy chart. Now that you know what I am, what's listed on it might make a little more sense."

"You do? Really? Why?"

"I need to know more about who I am. Who my family is. This laptop has access to every major university database, as well as some governmental access most people couldn't pay to get into," he said. "Do what you can and see if you can get further than I did. Even adding one or two names would satisfy me. Finding more mistakes would satisfy me more."

"How much you paying, if you don't mind?"

He named a figure that made her eyes widen with surprise.

Alice sat down hard on the bed before her legs gave out. "Wow. Thank you. Any and everything I discover goes with me to the grave, right?"

"Naturally."

She reached for his hand. A tentative brush of her fingers over his followed. "Thank you," she said softly. "I know you don't know me, but I won't betray your trust."

"I think I know more about you than you think I do."

Unable to fight her curiosity, she began to see what the laptop could do. Her fingers moved over the keyboard, her eyes searching the screen. "Yeah? Like what?"

"You have at least a high school education, although I would guess even more than that. Some college, certainly. You've spent a good deal of time in libraries while growing up. You respect authority figures and have had some experience caring for an ill person."

Alice slowly looked up to find he seemed to revel in the way blood drained from her face at his declarations.

"And that's just the tip of the iceberg about what I know. You intrigue me, Alice. I can't wait to find out more."

"How could you know all that?"

"It's not difficult if one's paying attention. Your ease with a computer before. Your need to call for help last night and to take me to the hospital. The way you managed to physically move my body when men twice your size would struggle." Bast put his hand atop hers, giving it a little squeeze. "You're almost an open book, except for the things you wish to hold close to your chest.

Like your brother, for example, although even there I'm starting to understand him and your relationship to him a little better."

Waves of emotion rolled through her, and she didn't know whether to be excited or apprehensive. If he could discern all that from their brief time together, what else had he figured out?

Did he know about how sick she was? About the potential tumor slowly growing larger day by day—the one that could eventually end her life?

It was supposed to be her secret because she didn't want anyone's pity. If her own brother couldn't handle it, she would not accept it from someone who wasn't blood.

"I think I should get dressed now," Alice said to change the topic. Her voice wavered as she made the suggestion and she hoped he didn't notice any of it.

"I wish I had clothing for you," he said. "Would you prefer to wear more of what I have here, or should we shop for more appropriate attire?"

"Shopping would be nice." Clothes of her own. Clothes that fit. The very thought was enough to make her throat tighten. God, she was falling apart because someone chose to be a little nice to her, after all this time. "But wait. Where are we going?"

"I need to check on some of my clients' interests. I'd like you to come with me."

She frowned a bit. "Why?"

"Are you my nurse or aren't you?"

She weighed the question, trying to determine the hidden agenda behind his meaning. The clock in the bathroom said a full day had passed. What made him shift positions about her all of a sudden? A job, money, clothing. She didn't know what to think. These changes certainly hadn't come from the goodness of his heart, assuming vampires even had hearts.

Vampire. God, it was hard to believe she accepted their existence so easily. Then again, after everything she'd seen, there really wasn't any reason *not* to.

"Where are you going?" Alice asked, still suspicious.

"The entire trip will only take about three or four hours."

She quirked an eyebrow. "That's not what I asked you. Where are you going?"

"Charleston."

Her expression reverted back to a frown. "Charleston... Charl—wait. As in the city? In South Carolina?"

"The same."

"That isn't a three-hour trip! That's how long the drive'll take, one way."

"After we stop to get some clothes for you, one hour there, two hours of business, one hour back. If things are looking good, I might be able to cut down the business stuff to just an hour." He shrugged a single shoulder. "Like I said, three or four hours." Bast crossed the room, opening and shutting drawers. Watching him move, and especially clothe himself, was a feast for the senses.

"How is that even possible?"

Bast straightened after brushing off the tip of one gleaming black boot. A slow smile spread across his features, and damn if her belly didn't cartwheel at the sight. "Alice, how do you feel about flying?"

OKAY, SO WHEN Bast asked her about flying, she'd flashed back to old Bela Lugosi movies, where Dracula poofed into a vampire bat. It seemed a reasonable enough conclusion to reach. Getting into the Benz an hour later baffled her as to the mechanics of it all, but she sat back and enjoyed the ride.

More of the rich classical music serenaded them, keeping a comfortable silence at the level of companionable. The city was beautiful this evening, the moon providing an ethereal patina to the cars and the dark buildings they passed. She almost wished it would rain, just to add sparkling, like diamonds, to everything. It was a city she didn't recognize, not when she usually spent the time looking for hidey holes to sleep or looking over her shoulder to make sure Richard's cronies weren't looking for him. Or worse, her.

She'd been living a rough life, and it would only get rougher. If she hadn't learned the usefulness of a five-finger discount from Richard though, she couldn't imagine how bad it could really get.

"You're awfully quiet over there," Bast said. He handled the car like a dream, turning onto a road blazing with lights, despite the desolation of the area.

"Just thinking about things that I can't control."

"So then think about the things you can."

Alice liked that about him. So practical. "That's a pretty short list."

"What would you add to it?" The hum of the window's motor filled the air as the glass slowly descended. He waved a card beneath a scanner, a curious piece of electronics standing sentry before a tall chain-linked fence. Despite the brilliance of lights running parallel to the road, she couldn't imagine what could be at the end of the gravel driveway they traveled.

Bast pulled forward, and Alice kept watch of their

surroundings. She'd begun to start to trust him, but as isolated as the area kept proving to be, he could do some serious harm and no one else would be the wiser. She'd kept the letter opener as her only weapon, but maybe she'd be able to wield it well enough to defend herself if it came to that. Her trust only went so far.

"I don't need what you have," she said after a minute. "I'd just like to know where my next meal was coming from and have a safe place to sleep at night."

"Will you tell me about it? Your situation."

She sighed. "There's not much to tell. Our parents are dead, and it's just me and Richard. To make ends meet, he started dealing." Her throat tightened as she remembered the early days, when she'd been waiting tables and he'd panhandle. They'd pool their meager earnings, prioritizing which bills would be paid and which would be studiously ignored. "But the number one rule of dealing is never become a user. My brother apparently didn't know that. Things went down quickly from there."

It hurt to think about. The way their lives had down-spiraled into such destruction.

"What about you, Bast? With all that you have, is there anything you'd add to your life?"

He didn't hesitate. "Respect."

An answer she didn't anticipate. "Will you tell me about it?"

"Another time, perhaps. Time to board."

The car pulled to a stop and as he turned off the engine, Alice's mouth fell open. A plane. They were going to fly on one of those private jets, the kind that billionaires owned. He'd stopped right next to it, so there could be no doubt. "This is what you'd meant by flying?"

"Of course." He sounded genuinely baffled. "What did you think I meant?"

"I—never mind. Wow." Heat licked her cheeks as she once again thought of vampire bats before pushing the image aside.

Bast crooked a finger at an elegantly dressed, but outrageously thin man standing near the open door of the plane. Dressed in a black suit, including a black worker cap and starched white shirt, she figured him for the pilot. Pale, with bright blue eyes, he slanted a quick smile in her direction before hustling to the rear of the car.

As Alice exited, she realized he unloaded the bags of clothing Bast had been generous to purchase. Everything inside them was functional the way she needed, thank you Target. He'd wanted to go to some place with a name she couldn't pronounce, much less find anything worth a damn. That just wasn't the way she rolled, even with Sebastian.

Sebastian. She *loved* that name. So made for someone with his wealth and stature. It was elegant and refined. *Bast*, on the other hand... Alice shuddered. The shortened version mocked that same elegance.

She thought about the wistful way he'd said he wanted respect. And that conversation he'd had with the other vampire, Cicero. What was the story behind Sebastian?

"Ready?" he asked.

Startled by his nearness, lost in her own musing, she mentally sought out the comforting weight of the letter opener, tucked inside her sock. It was hidden by the brand-new jeans she wore. Not the most practical place for quick, effortless access, but it helped settle her nerves as she nodded and took his hand. Together, they walked toward the plane.

Still, as she settled into one of the leather chairs, she couldn't help but wonder, again, what she'd gotten herself into.

TEN

"WHY ARE YOU so nervous? I assure you, the pilot has been flying longer than you've been alive."

The pink tee Alice wore softened her skin tone, making her eyes appear dark as she studied him. His gaze swept over her face, descending until he found the two little bruises on her neck. Perfectly positioned. The faint blue marks turned him on.

He'd put the bite there. Her blood was his to claim. Even now, the sound of her coming as he offered the dark kiss echoed in his ears, a memory worth clinging to.

"I'm just not sure why I'm here. You don't seem sick tonight."

A fact that startled him. He'd been so focused on providing her some comfort, including more food after her unfortunate early evening, it had slipped his mind the reason he knew Alice in the first place.

He said, "You must be good for me."

She turned her face away from him, her disbelief almost palpable.

He smelled a fine layer of fear hovering over her, and it irritated him to know she still was uneasy about him. A smart woman would be cautious, but he wanted this woman to learn him. He wanted to take away her doubt.

She kept her attention on the laptop, and he surmised he'd touched some sort of nerve. But he respected her quiet request for privacy and didn't push. With the up-coming meeting happening in less than half an hour, he had more urgent matters to pursue.

He'd needed Alice to come along in case he fell ill. This was supposed to be a trust-building mission, one for a politician who might be able to sway the lycans away from the vampire populace, but that they'd requested it so close to a full moon didn't bode well. She wouldn't be coming with him into the actual meeting, but he recognized needing her close by.

On the other hand, she was a weakness. Between the lycans and his own men, if discovered, she could be used against him. Bad enough Cicero knew about her. No telling who he'd run his fucking mouth to. But if he had to choose between his men and the lycans discovering about her, certainly the warriors had earned that loyalty. Although a few of them questioned the Council's decision to make him leader, all, in the end, had earned his respect and trust.

Bast looked up as Pope left his seat to approach them. "Sir," Pope said, "we'll be landing soon. Is there anything additional you require?"

Shaking his head, Bast replied, "No, but Alice?" He waited for her to acknowledge him. "I'm going to leave you with Pope here. If you get off for any reason, stay next to the plane where he can see you. I won't be far, but don't want any of what I'm doing to touch you."

"But—"

"Stay here. Work on the chart. It won't take me long. I've already decided to cut my business down to just an hour."

She didn't look pleased, but nodded.

"Thank you. If something goes amiss, and I'm not

expecting it to, listen to Pope. He'll get you to safety. I'll be back though."

Bast studied her face one last time, visually caressing the beauty mark on her cheek, the swell of her lip, the twin marks on her neck. The heat remained at bay, but the urge to kiss her one more time, to taste her mouth swelled inside him.

"Come here," he said, his voice husky.

Something in those pretty blue eyes flashed at him, and the slow, sly grin she gave could have made the coldest heart go up in a ball of flame. "No," she whispered.

Bast stood, ignoring the downward tilt of the plane coming in for landing. Two steps took him to her side, and sensitive hearing picked up the rapid tattoo of her heart. "That's not an option. Not right now." A pause. "But if you won't come to me, I'll gladly come to you."

She lifted her face to his, and he drank in the sight of her. His teeth lengthened, a surge of need in him rising swiftly. It wasn't the hunger of a vampire that reigned, however, but that of a man.

His hands slipped so easily around her neck, and she entrusted her delicate body to his powerful strength. The skin there felt smooth. Thin. And he knew the extent of his ability to break this woman if he so chose.

Instead, Bast lowered his mouth to hers, lured by the pink fullness. The parted-lip expectation. He caressed her lips, breathing her into his lungs before capturing her with the force of his desire. Alice made a low sound, one that came deep from her throat, and Bast growled his pleasure to hear it. Their tongues twined together, taking and retreating. Teeth nipping and teasing. Finally, he didn't have to be careful she'd discover his vampire nature and let the elongated teeth scrape gently against her mouth, each sudden touch sending bolts of pleasure through him.

Bast rode the smooth descent of the plane, letting the force sway his body to and from Alice. He held on to her as if she were his last chance for living. That she clung to him with insistent hands ignited his already-rising lust.

Pulling away took the strength of titans.

"When I return," he said, breathless, need strangling him, "you and I will sit down and talk some more. For now, stay safe and wait for me."

"I will." A whisper of promise.

EVERY TIME SHE PAUSED, the seductive weight of Sebastian's parting kiss burdened her mind. A distraction she could ill afford. An hour wasn't much time to make significant changes in the genealogy chart, but she intended to make a lasting impression upon her employer.

His family history impressed the hell out of her, the dates an impossibility to her mind. That he'd lived for four hundred years baffled her and more than once she caught herself imagining what it must have been like. Hell, twenty years ago the iPod didn't exist. What about the emergence of the automobile, man's first trip to the moon and so many other wonders of technology—how did they affect Sebastian who'd have seen their rise and, sometimes, their fall?

"Ma'am, may I get you something from the galley?"

She smiled at Pope, at his quiet approach. He'd remained a silent watcher while she worked, but she felt his presence near the rear of the plane. "Thank you, no." A glance at his watch. "Se... Bast will be back any minute, right?"

"He's a little overdue actually. I expect the meeting ran long."

A sudden concern for Sebastian's health crept over her. What if he'd fallen ill again? Alice shook away the fear. If he did, he'd simply get help from his associates. They couldn't all be like Cicero.

Still...

"I think I'll go stretch my legs and wait outside." When she watched Sebastian's approach, the rising concern would dissipate. She was sure of it. "I won't leave sight of the plane."

"Would you like me to wait with you?"

"No, not necessary." For all his politeness, hanging out with someone who was probably another vampire didn't sit well with her.

"Yes, ma'am. Call if you need anything at all."

Without looking, she knew Pope watched her make her way down the aisle and to the exit. They'd landed on a well-lit runway, and climbing down the steps took no effort at all. As she reached the bottom, Alice wrapped her arms around her torso.

Only three hours north, but the cooler South Carolina temperature slapped her. Across the runway, pine trees bowed to the brisk wind pushing their tips over. And somehow the air just smelled different up here. Cleaner.

Dozens of fireflies seemed to wink into existence before changing their minds and disappearing again. With the beauty of the growing moon sharing a silvery gleam, the world looked silently beautiful. Grown so used to city life, Alice had forgotten what being out in nature could be like.

She turned to the plane, and comforted with the knowledge she could see into it—and by assumption, Pope could see out and her—she dared move a little farther away. Just a little distance. There were a few cars parked near a building, but none looked like anything Sebastian might own. She hadn't thought to watch him leave earlier and didn't know what mode of transportation he might be using. Hell, for all she knew, the vampire bat theory still might hold water.

Why hadn't he taken her to his meeting? If he was out there suffering and unable to get to her for help, she was going to be seriously pissed. Odd that she felt some sort of responsibility for him, but it remained. The fact that she wanted to spend hours in his arms, locked into one of his toe-curling kisses didn't make it hard to want to be with him.

Alice kept walking, letting nature court her senses. She glanced back, realized there was no way she couldn't be spotted from the plane and let her guard drop just a bit. Any person who approached would be visible from any direction they took. With the airplane's engines turned off, the sound of a car would be an intrusion to all this quiet.

There was no danger here. Just the imaginings of an overactive mind that whispered about vampires and what they could do to silly little girls who allowed themselves to be bitten.

When the hair began to rise on the back of her neck, she went still, however. Nothing seemed amiss, no person or thing obviously out of place. But the sense of unease remained, as if another presence had managed to sneak up on her despite her wariness. She turned toward the plane, trying not to look as frantic as she suddenly felt.

It was as if one of Richard's friends was stalking her now. She didn't have to see or hear him to know the truth of it. How she'd been found way out here didn't make sense, but she knew that feeling well.

Each step seemed to take longer than the last, none of them bringing her close enough to the plane for her comfort. Later, she might decide she'd indeed been silly. This sudden rush of panic and being stalked. With the newfound knowledge that some of the things that go bump in the night *do* exist, better silly than dead, however.

The low sound of thunder too close to have come from the sky made her stop in her tracks. Heart roaring, Alice struggled to pinpoint where it could have come from. The trees, maybe?

Not the trees.

Near the plane. Somehow the noise came too close from the sanctuary she sought. The not-thunder rumbled again, sending a riot of goose bumps across her crawling skin. Low. Menacing. All animal.

Throat drying, she stared into glowing eyes, her mind screaming at her to do only one thing. Run.

GODDAMNED LYCANS.

Bast couldn't have been any more pissed. He pressed down on the accelerator, letting the racing car carry away some of his frustration.

They'd been the ones to ask for the meeting and not one of them had the fucking balls to show. He'd waited there for the full hour, even longer, never letting his mounting impatience show in his body language. Had they discovered him in an agitated state, who knew if someone would take exception to it.

And for what? Nothing.

He'd wasted two hours, plus an upcoming additional hour of flying time to be here. Time he could have utilized researching this illness that he'd managed to somehow keep at bay for the night. Hell, even a few hours with his men would have been more useful, going over some of the latest recon or reviewing plans for the Council's foray into the public. Maybe he should have sent one of them in to meet the werewolves. Then it would have been *their* time wasted and not his.

But at least Alice waited for him now. Alice of the blue eyes and gentle nature. Whose kisses fueled him until he was consumed by her.

He hoped she had better luck with tracing his roots. So very different from the other born vampires. He'd aroused their suspicion from the moment he'd proven he could walk in the sunlight. Just like one of the vampires who had been turned—or "bred"; very unlike a born vampire. So far he hadn't found a weakness by straddling the two races, but he was still young. That his birth had been witnessed by others saved him from being exterminated as an abomination. But if he gave them one excuse—just one little error in judgment—that proved he was defective, that his birth should never have been...

The head beams of the car scanned over a large shape, drawing Bast's attention. It had been too quick to be useful, but he leaned forward, intent on trying to find it again. Whatever it was avoided the lights of the air strip, choosing instead to stalk in shadow near the plane.

Too damned close to the plane.

ELEVEN

Vampires lived with rules about human interaction. Lycans did not. He wanted to get to her now. Vampire relations with lycans were tenuous at best. If they went after her for some reason, Bast couldn't say he wouldn't let it be an impetus for shattering the reluctant relationship. Acid churned in his stomach, and with a sinking heart, Bast recognized the familiar feeling. The one that began as a slow simmer and would soon rage until it was an uncontrollable fire within him. He didn't have time for this shit.

Gunning the engine, he reveled in its roar as the car charged toward the beast. It might have been a large dog or just an oversized, run-of-the-mill wolf, but he couldn't take chances. He wanted it to flee, to get away from the plane. If it did, reacting as any normal animal would, the surging adrenaline running rampant in his veins would ease, his racing heart return to normal. But it didn't, turning to look at him, ignoring the threat of the approaching car because it knew there was something better for it than a thousand pounds of steel. It had intelligence beyond animal keenness.

This was no ordinary wolf. The car hadn't stopped before Bast jumped out, Glock in hand. Against another vampire, he'd need ash wood, but with these fuckers? A silver-tipped bullet would do the job quite well.

A burst of perspiration erupted on his brow, the heat

in his belly rising. Swirling inside him until it filled every limb. But for the first time, Bast reveled in the heat. In the power that swelled inside him.

It was the same affliction from before, yet not. This time, he didn't feel as if the conflagration would bring him down. Instead, it buoyed him.

"Alice!" His shout sounded strangled, even to his own ears. Fury twisted the sound in his throat until it was a whip against the night air.

The beast swung its ugly head toward him, lips snarling. Yellowed teeth bared. Now that he was next to it, he realized it stood the size of a small pickup.

"Sebastian." A desperate whisper. Somewhere beyond the lycan.

"Stay where you are," Bast ordered. Before he could shoot at the werewolf, he wanted to be certain of her position. Daring to take his gaze away from the brute for a split second, he peered beyond it. The blazing lights of the runway should have been enough, his vision should have helped him, but Bast had to focus to find her.

From a distance, he normally could detect distinct shapes. Distinguish between blond hair or brown. Heightened vampire vision ensured he knew if someone wore a round-neck collar or one with a vee. A person's facial characteristics could be separated from another's.

But now—somehow—as he looked for Alice, the world changed. The area became sun-brightened, light flooding it until there were no more shadows. Until he almost squinted from the harshness of it. Bast seemed to pull the light into himself, and what were once shades of gray became distinct reds and yellows. Black separated from brown.

His gaze skimmed over the lycan, noting the wire-stiff hairs. Each individual one was black at the roots, the strands blending to shades of auburn. Bands of other colors dripped down its heaving sides. On any other night, he might have studied the creature more, to try and figure out why the sunlight had come out on such a beautiful night, but right now Bast's primary concern was one female he'd pledged his life to.

The heat surrounded him. Filled him. Nourished him.

Alice's unique scent called to Bast, and between it and the steady thump of her heartbeat, he triangulated her position. There, just beyond the beast's right shoulder, eyes prettier than a field of bluebonnets peered out. Her attention darted between him and the lycan, and the moon highlighted her fear within the sea of blue.

With a steady hand, he pointed the Glock at the wolf, targeting the yellow razors of teeth. A gleaming row of ferocity. Alice shifted her head, and Bast jerked the gun up. Aiming at the slow rise and fall of a barrel-like chest, he tried to get a better shot.

"Move, princess," he muttered. Just another inch or two. Enough so the bullet wouldn't rip through the lycan's chest cavity and burrow directly into her.

Crawling forward, the werewolf snarled at Bast. It whipped its large head from Bast to Alice, then back to Bast. It stood paralyzed with indecision, seemingly wanting its original weaker prey but recognizing the danger it faced in the armed vampire.

Bast kept tracking the damned thing, waiting for the right opportunity. The wolf raised its muzzle, staring Bast down with a swirling mix of gold and brown in its feral eyes before it made a low sound in its throat. Instead of the warning Bast expected, the wolf's low keening struck him as if the very sound scraped against raw nerves.

An answering howl, fast on the heels of the lycan's whimper, shot out of the night air. Somewhere beyond the line of trees bordering the airfield. Jaw tightening, Bast waited for the next howl and the one following.

So here were the werewolves he was supposed to meet. Not quite their original chosen destination. Instead of letting him come to them, into their hold, they'd met him and his charge.

Fuck them.

Whirling quickly, he squeezed the trigger in the direction of the trees. Hoped for a distraught yelp. Wasn't surprised when he didn't get one.

He did study their bulk in the not-sunlight, still shining bright, and managed to count six before returning his attention to the threat standing between him and Alice.

"That thing touches her, and *every one* of you dies tonight," he shouted. Movement to the left. From the direction of the plane. "And I promise on my life, it won't be quick."

"I've got your back, boss," Pope yelled.

It would be a help, especially if the pilot was armed and ready as well. They were both trained soldiers, ready to defend themselves against their kind's current threat. Whether or not either man had seen action in their lives couldn't be helped, but really Bast wanted nothing more for them to point their guns in the right direction and fire. Even a single second of not having to track six lycans would help him focus on the important one. The one standing in front of Alice.

Heat licked along tense muscles. It massaged itself

into his arms, coiling around his torso until it stretched down the lengths of his thighs. When it finally bottomed out, having no place else to spread, Bast jerked upright as it rushed up his body again.

He didn't need this. Not now.

But the heat ignored his silent plea, pushing at his back as if determined to create an exit for the furnace within if he wouldn't give it a place to escape. Sweat rivulets clung to his brows, threatening to dribble into his eyes, drop by stinging drop. He blinked once. Twice. A quick toss of his head to fling the distractions away.

Movement from the trees.

"Vampire," a male voice called.

A figure approached, walking not with boldness nor stealth, but with a casual indifference that pissed off Bast. His nudity didn't bother Bast; the knowledge of what lycans could and couldn't do during a physical shift wasn't news. He just wished he'd had an opportunity to explain some of it to Alice, who couldn't be understanding any of this.

"Lower your weapon," the man continued. "We're not here to take you out. If we were, you'd be dead already."

As fucking if. His gun hand didn't waver.

"Let her come to me. Right by my side. Then we talk." He kept his eyes on Alice. "You asked for this meeting, Locke, and this is how you treat me and my guest?"

"We were detained," Locke answered. "I'd hoped to catch you up here. And it seems we have."

No one so much as twitched, which didn't fill Bast with good feelings.

"Tell your dog to move," he growled. "The woman

goes safely into the plane, and then the eight of us can figure out who's got the biggest dick."

The werewolf growled deep in its throat, a trail of saliva spilling from black lips.

Locke chuckled. "Wilde doesn't seem to like that idea. But if you insist on training your gun on him while I deliver my message, I'll allow it, as I'll be brief. That being said, she stays where she is for now."

"You don't need her."

"You're right, but I'll take whatever leverage is handed me." A tuft of hair rifled over Locke's smooth shoulders, disappearing almost as quickly as it had arisen. A sign that Locke was about to change into his furry self, maybe.

Bast chanced a quick glance at the sky, despite knowing the full moon was still a week away. Still… were the fuckers in control of their shifts? They were supposed to be. Then again, creatures of the night were supposed to be just figments of imagination.

"Make it fast," Bast ordered. Pulses of heat were making it difficult to keep the gun steady. The flesh of his back crawled over his bones, and he didn't know how much longer he could stand it.

"Like I said, my message is short. Tell the vampire Council to withdraw. We're not your enemy." The rest of his message came through his hardened stare. *But we can be.*

"So the newly transitioned we're finding butchered should be disregarded? The bite and claw marks ignored?" His stomach tightened, pain and mental anguish from the memories disgusting him. He'd seen the bodies himself.

Locke made a small gesture with his hand as he

backed away. "If we wanted war with you, it would be direct. We've seen the damage you think we've caused and I can assure you that a werewolf had nothing to do with it. Why would we? Look elsewhere for your butchers."

"Vampires have no reason to do these heinous acts," Bast spat. "It *has* to be you."

"Are you vampires really so arrogant that you think the only creatures of the night that exist are you and us? I assure you, our populations are only the tip of the iceberg."

"We might not be the only creatures that exist, but only your kind is unpredictable. The moon rises, and your beast takes over. All thinking and intelligence… gone." He snapped his fingers on his last word. It probably wasn't the most PC statement he could have made, but the minute they held Alice hostage, peacekeeping flew out the window.

Locke took a step forward, and Bast tightened his hold on the trigger. The werewolf's teeth were bared. "We don't turn into animals, and the moonrise makes us more predictable than most. You vampires have no idea what it's like to share a body with something stronger than yourself. Something more cunning. More keen. And it's not just sharing. It's combining the strength of man and wolf. It makes us formidable."

"If you say so," growled Bast, "but I'd rather be in complete control of my faculties. There's just room enough for me in this body."

"We *are* in control. We can shift at will. But you? Are you in complete control of yourself, Bast Kent? Really? You're not even like the others. I don't understand how you defend them when you are so much more than they are."

Frowning, Bast tried to wrap his thoughts around Locke's words. "What do you mean?" It came out harsher than he'd intended. Certainly filled with more curiosity than he should have shown.

Locke's next words were mired in smugness. "Wait. Are you telling me...you don't know?"

Bast swallowed hard, his jaw clamped shut against the urge to cry out against the pain enveloping him. Locke shouldn't have been able to sense his agony, but it seemed his last words might have been a jab at his condition. "Do you know what I am?" Bast asked, his voice a harsh whisper.

"Like I said, werewolves and vampires are not the only creatures of the night. We're larger in numbers, sure. Maybe even the most intelligent, but we're not alone. Something else wants us at odds, and you're foolishly falling into line. Tell the Council *it's not us*."

"Answer me," Bast said hoarsely, still with a singular focus. What did Locke know about him? Somewhere in the periphery of his mind, he heard what he'd said about werewolves not being responsible for the recent killings, but he couldn't concentrate on that. Not with pain crawling over every inch of his skin right now.

There was sudden movement in front of him.

Bast's finger squeezed the trigger before his mind caught up to the instinctual action. Locke had freed the creature from its guard, allowing it to bound away on four legs. Bast's aim was true, the shots slowing but not stopping the beast that vaulted over him.

His head tipped back, allowing him to see with deadly accuracy where the hairs split to make way for the bullets. The blossom of red within. He tried not to see the flesh beneath but failed at that task. He refused to shut his eyes against the gruesome sight. Instead, Bast focused on the rapid heartbeat of the creature, its harsh breathing and rumbling growl ricocheting through its chest.

Even as the heat flared, he saw this and knew he shouldn't have. The world was so very, very bright. Brilliant. As if the flame within leaped from his body and found home within the trees. Setting them aflame until the conflagration raged out of control.

The lycans used the harsh glare of light to their advantage, shifting into their natural forms. They left in a silent horde, taking their wounded wolf with them. The sharp tang of copper on the air was the only remembrance of their having been there in the first place.

"Good luck, *vampire*. You're going to need it," Locke called ominously, his voice dying on the night air.

Damn it. There was more Bast needed to say to them. To understand.

It would have to wait. He trembled violently, muscles tight with blinding agony.

Bast kept the gun at his side, despite the sparks of fire that surely must be welding the metal to his hand. "Alice," he said hoarsely.

He hadn't forgotten her. Never. But he needed her now. Not just the knowledge that she was safe, but at his side. His only salve against a burn that consumed him.

She came to him at a run, her body trembling when she pressed it against his. Her rainwater scent greeted him first. "Are you all right?" she asked, breathless.

He tilted her face to his. "Are you hurt? Did it touch you?"

"I'm fine, but Sebastian…your eyes." She brought a hand to his face. Paused before sliding her fingers over his skin. "You're sick again, aren't you?"

"To the plane." He kept his voice low, despite the tremors overtaking him.

Alice took a step forward, and Bast gritted his teeth, commanding his body to follow her. One jerky step after another, they tottered toward the plane. Not until they stood before the first step did Alice leave his side. Even then, she allowed him to partially drape his bulk over her as they lumbered up the stairs. From behind, it would look like he went to great lengths to protect her from possible assailants. In his heart, however, he knew he barely managed to lift one foot after another. The six or so steps might as well have been climbing Mt. Everest. Darkness hovered at the periphery of his vision, weaving in and out. He would either pass out and tumble down the stairs or struggle for the strength to keep moving forward.

They were inside, door secured and plane taxiing before Alice turned to him. "Kiss me," she demanded.

Bast's guts were churning, but he found the strength to chuckle. What he would have said next dissolved as she took charge and pressed her mouth to his.

Goddamn, she tasted good.

His tense body relaxed a little beneath her kiss and Bast allowed himself to sink into the relaxing hold of the seat. But not before pulling her down to straddle him. Alice came to him willingly, holding his face between her hands as she gave him what he needed. Her kisses sustained him, and he would not question why.

The plane climbed into the air, pulling Alice away from him, but Bast would have none of it. His fingers

threaded together behind her back, holding her still.
Letting her feel the force of his arousal for her pushing up from his pants and into the juncture between
her thighs.

Her tongue slipped in between his lips, and with it
the cooling force of her breath. It extinguished the fire
raging inside of him, and the relief was so sweet, he
could have wept from it.

"You have marked your claim on me," he said in
between nipping at her lip. Those big blue eyes of hers
fluttered open. Drowsy and seductive. "Now—please—
my turn."

TWELVE

ALICE COULD BARELY catch her breath. Not five minutes ago there was this dog—a wolf—staring her down. Then Sebastian came, and she had the letter opener, but he was sick and she had to get him better. Had to get him home...

"Oh my God," she said, her voice trembling. "This is so crazy."

His lips moved over hers. His hands holding her so very, very close. "You handled yourself like a warrior, princess." He paused, studying her eyes. "Yes. My warrior princess. I like the sound of that."

She unclenched her fingers from his shirt, wincing as the blood rushed back into them. It felt as if the sharp edge of the letter opener still cut into her hand as she gripped it tightly. If Sebastian hadn't arrived when he did, she might have had to defend herself with it. That prospect didn't frighten her as much as it probably should have. She'd been fending off attackers since her late teens. "I could feel you getting sick. I saw it. The others might not have been able to, but I knew what you were going through. What if..."

"Shh," he soothed. "It's over now, and we're both alive and well. Kiss me again. Kiss away my hurt."

Alice lowered her face to his, wanting the oblivion. Needing it. She slanted her mouth over his, opening herself to his taste. His heat. "That *thing*...what was it?"

"Nothing more than a warning." Keeping one hand on her back, he slid the other beneath her shirt. "Are you still planning on using that letter opener?" he said, chuckling.

A wince later and she uncurled her fingers, still wrapped around the smooth handle. "I was going to put it back lat—"

"I knew you had it. You're not very good at being stealthy." His fingers kept trailing fire along her belly, his mouth paralleling with a similar flame on her neck.

"Am too stealthy. You couldn't have known."

"Your walk gave you away. A little stiff-legged."

Her breath caught as Sebastian pulled the T-shirt up and over her head. He leaned forward, covering her breast with his mouth, moistening the bra as if it wasn't there. Alice found herself arching into the heat coming from him, her mind almost too caught up in his actions to process his words. She paused though when his nibbling became almost too much to bear. "You knew but didn't stop me?"

Sebastian sighed, his forehead resting against her sternum. He took a deep breath then raised his head to look her in the eyes. "I gave you carte blanche access to my home, where I am still a stranger to you. With your background, I would have been more surprised if you'd left my belongings unmolested. I don't condone your behavior, but I do understand it."

A sudden wash of shame flooded her. "I was going to steal it at first. That's inexcusable and…I'm sorry. For what it's worth, I'd decided to return it before you offered me the job. I thought you'd never know."

Sebastian gently bit her lower lip, pulling a gasp from her. "I know."

Why? It made no sense. For him to know what she was, to have figured out she would have robbed him in his sleep if given half a chance, he should have turned her out at the first suspicion. Instead, Sebastian kissed her. He took sustenance from her and allowed her to take from him.

Just her luck, right? To have a man so perfect, he would have been a Prince Charming for any other woman. To her, he'd been no more than a mark.

The realization made her heart clench.

Then again, her life didn't come with a Prince Charming. Hers came with stoners and meth addicts. With a brother who tried to sell his sister to his friends. With an illness that might kill her one day—sooner, rather than later.

Alice rocked her hips, purposely brushing against Sebastian's erection. Anything to banish the current thoughts from her mind.

"You're thinking too hard," Sebastian said. His thumb brushed beneath the curve of her breast. Back and forth, stirring her arousal.

"Kiss me again, please." Her words were a rough whisper. Full of yearning. She wanted him, the man, but she wanted for herself. Just once, she wanted…

Gentle lips brushed over hers, and the live wire short-circuited every synapse in her brain, detonating one after the other until there was no thought left. She moaned into his mouth, reveling in the heat still lingering there. Like before, he fed it to her and she consumed it greedily. Never had it been like this. The intensity, soul-grabbing.

He nibbled down the length of her neck, and each stroke of his tongue over the spot where he'd twice bitten previously sent a bolt of awareness through her. Alice's back snapped straight, pleasure and heat and greedy need making her fingers fold into the material of his shirt. When he'd drawn from her last, she'd been prepared for the pain that had never come. The first and last time he'd bitten that place, the passion he aroused in her became a living thing, a part of her and him, creating a union from them both. God help her, she wanted to feel his bite again.

Alice made quick work of the buttons of his shirt, needing to savor all that warmth beneath her hands. His skin against hers.

She raked her fingernails over his chest, pride flaring in her as he hissed in a breath. When her touch went lower, stroking over the ridge of flesh tightening his pants, the same slow inhale became ragged.

"Not here," he said in an abrasive voice.

The words managed to penetrate the haze of her mind. She kept stroking him. Memorizing the length of his promise. "Even if I want it? If I'm saying yes?"

"*Christ, Alice.* Not while we're likely to be interrupted. Or overheard." He kissed the tops of her breasts, which threatened to tumble from the confines of sensible white cotton. "This is as far as I dare."

But his fingers belied his words, rubbing the burgeoning tip of a hardening nipple.

How quickly she'd forgotten about Pope. She looked toward the front of the plane and found him studiously occupied with cleaning individual specks of dust from the galley. His ears and neck blushed a deep crimson, and for some reason, that made her smile all the more.

Alice kept that slow, sensual rock of her hips steady.

The grip of her hand on his cock sure. "What's the matter, Sebastian?" she whispered, her breath against his ear meant to be as tantalizing as her words. "Don't have a bit of exhibitionist in you?"

"You would torment the man?"

"If it meant getting closer to you? Yes." The brush with the wolf had left her shaky, yet exhilarated. Trapped behind it, there had been a moment of paralyzing fear during which she'd made a promise to herself. Each day had just become her last. After she'd spent twenty-four hours with a vampire, the past two years with seizures that left her at their mercy, and then staring at death's golden wolf eyes, she'd realized she had to start living in the now.

And here, the now was with Sebastian.

"Are you really all right?" He was serious. So serious. "I swear I'll work quickly on finding another cure for my sickness. I won't put you in danger again."

"In twenty-four hours I've done and seen more than ever."

"So you enjoy being *this* close to being eaten by a werewolf?"

The blood in her face drained in a rush. "A what?"

The smile on his face was grim. "And as much as I'd love to be with you, I think perhaps I should spend the rest of the plane ride explaining a few things about my world. The things you don't know can get you killed. It might also help with some of the research you're doing for me."

She wanted to argue. To go back to what they were doing. To experience the feelings he roused in her. Her disappointment tasted bitter, but Alice nodded. Instead of leaving though, she rested her head against his chest, and listened to the deep timber of his voice as he began to talk about his life.

"SO LET ME make sure I have this straight…"

Bast stared into her eyes, doing his damndest not to look at her lips. Every time his gaze dropped, they ended up making out like teenagers. Made explaining things a little on the slow side.

"Vampires, werewolves and other 'fictional'—" said with air quotes, "—creatures exist."

"Yes."

"Vampires and werewolves don't get along."

"Right."

"You're in charge of the people who guard the vampire leaders just in case war erupts?"

"Succinctly said, but that explanation will suffice. So, yes."

Alice narrowed her eyes. "And the reason you're telling me all this is…"

Because he found it hard to believe he'd ever let her go. Not when in little more than a day's time she'd shown him more compassion than he'd seen in his lifetime. His sluggish heart beat a little faster, something akin to fear fueling a surge of adrenaline every time he thought about her leaving for good. "Part of it is to ensure your safety while you're under my employ. The other part is to help you in your genealogy research."

She wiggled a little in his lap, teasing the longest-held erection he'd had in years. Damn, he didn't remember as a teenager being able to sustain one like this. With the creamy curve of her breasts just beneath his view and the heat of her cunt resting so close to him, he didn't know what to wish for more to end the sweet misery.

"You're killing me," he grumbled.

"Am I too heavy for you?" she asked, the smile on her face drippy sweet. Alice tilted her hips forward, and the contact electrified him.

"Ask me again after I start feeding you properly. For now, don't even think about moving."

"You encounter those things a lot? The werewolves?"

"More now than we used to, but rarely resulting in bloodshed. Once upon a time the vampire kept to his community, and the werewolf kept to his. Now that it's becoming more difficult to keep our existences away from humans, we're finding we need to occupy the same places. We're almost like animals on the verge of extinction struggling to survive in the twenty-first century. Human population growth, steel enclosures, technology...all of it threatens to expose us."

She shook her head. "That doesn't make any sense. How can you be on the verge of extinction when according to the movies, you guys are supposedly superior?"

She said the latter with such distaste, he found himself smiling. "We live for such a long time that the Council has seen to it that we don't overpopulate. No new vampires without their consent. Face it, you're food. And if we run out of food..." He shrugged. This probably wasn't the most appealing of topics for her.

Alice didn't seem to focus on being relegated to nothing more than a cheeseburger. Her gaze became a little vacant. He studied that look. "So if someone, a human, was sick," she said softly, "it needn't be a death sentence. The person could be fixed. You could make him—or her—a vampire, right?" Her face canted away from his.

"*I* can't." He almost choked on the words.

She peered at him. Cautious. "What do you mean?"

His throat tightening, Bast considered how much to tell her about this thorn in his side. "I'm…" He struggled to find the right word. One that wouldn't break him to say. "Flawed."

The fingertips that caressed his jaw were gentle. Soothing. "Sebastian?"

"It's doubtful I'd be able to turn someone and even if I did, if they'd survive it. The Council would never approve any attempts to find out."

"But if you didn't ask first? If you just tried it?"

"Both that person and I would be executed." He watched a riot of goose bumps cover her skin. And there was a curious flickering in her expression. As if shutters had closed behind her eyes. "Never mind. It's not worth even talking about," he continued. "The plane's coming in for a landing. Unless you plan on walking out like that, maybe you should put your shirt back on."

He didn't know why, but he had a feeling the woman who climbed down from his lap moved now as she struggled against a heavy weight. She turned back around suddenly. "If you had a good reason, might you try? To make someone a vampire."

After a moment's pause, he shook his head. "No. There isn't reason enough to risk the wrath of the Council. They're ruthless in their pursuit of those who break our laws. There's a team of us whose sole mission is their protection. There's also a team of men and women whose sole purpose is to punish law breakers."

"Execute them, you mean."

"When appropriate, yes."

Alice took a step forward, relentless in her persistence. The plane began to tilt, but she rode its descent as if on a surfboard. "But there must be ways around those laws. Reasons why an individual might be allowed to live."

Bast pushed a hand through his hair. Why was she so dogged in her questioning? Didn't he make it clear? Even if he *wanted* to turn someone—even her—he simply *couldn't*. The Council and its controversial measures aside, he simply didn't have the physiology. His blood couldn't initiate the process.

Hybride.

"Maybe. Perhaps they could be convinced. There was a rumor about a woman who'd supposedly received a stay of execution about a year ago. Rumor, though." He trailed off, trying to remember the details just out of his recollection. Supposedly the woman had been marked for execution but then ended up being mated to the vampire sent to eliminate her instead. The stories surrounding them both were fantastical and difficult to believe.

"Would you think about it then? Maybe consider trying it in the future or at least some way around the Council's rule?"

"For you?"

She nodded, not looking him in the eyes. His heart clenched.

"You wouldn't want this life," he said quietly. They could be lovers for as long as she was willing to stay with him. But as mates…it was an impossible scenario. "It's not easy and not even remotely glamorous. Books make it seem romantic and erotic. I promise you, it's not."

"Don't make a decision yet. Please. Just…just think about it."

His gaze narrowed. "Is there something you're not telling me? Some reason why you want me to consider it? I can promise you so many, many things, but this is beyond me. I'm an officer of the Council. I am bound by blood and by oath to uphold their laws. Even the ones I don't agree with."

Alice crossed the aisle to her seat at last, only dropping into it after shrugging on the T-shirt. She continued to avoid his gaze as she worked on getting the seat buckle secured around her waist. "It's not important." She looked up, her lips curved into a smile, but he saw the force she used to plaster it there. Immediately, Bast also noticed the dark circles beneath her eyes and the fatigue making her body limp. "I think I'm just looking for an escape, is all."

He wanted her hands in his at this moment. To hold. To provide comfort. "I wish I could do that for you. I really do. The best I can provide is a temporary reprieve from what you once knew. When we get home, I'm going to tuck you in for a nap because you look exhausted. When you wake up though…"

Her expression changed, a wry grin slowly blooming. "Yes?"

"I promise you sexual oblivion."

THIRTEEN

BAST LISTENED AT the door until the rhythm of her breathing changed. After his promise, she tried to argue her way out of being sent to bed, but it only made Bast smile. She'd been yawning through most of the car ride home from the airport, her lids half-drooped. Even the fast food he'd bought for her had barely been consumed because of the way she nodded off after finishing only half. It almost pained him to wake her to make sure she finished, but she needed the pounds and the fuel.

When they met, it would be after her body was energized and ready for his advance. Once he began loving her—and he would take her more than once—there would be no stopping him. He knew her spirit was willing, but he needed her flesh in the same state. It would be hell enough restraining himself from hurting her because of his superior strength.

No, they would wait, and the experience would be that much better for it.

As he turned away and headed toward the back of the house, he pondered his decision. Just over a day ago, Alice had been nothing more than a homeless waif whose existence he overlooked without passion or mercy. Yet not only had she discovered him vulnerable, she'd selflessly cared for him as well. Even after she discovered what he was. Did he feel a sense of obligation toward her? Yes. But there was something more there. Not just the obligation of returning a favor, but also a lethargic kind of attraction.

Lethargic, hell. What compelled him toward her was nothing short of full-frontal assault.

He changed direction to go to the kitchen. There was a disquiet within him and perhaps a good old-fashioned snack of cookies and milk would help calm what ailed him. Of course, it didn't take a psychiatrist to tell him that the munchies had little to do with food or even blood.

"What's gotten into you?" he muttered to himself as he stood at the large butcher block island. When was the last time a woman—damn it, especially a human—made him feel this way?

There was a full sleeve of Chips Ahoy sitting in the pantry, untouched, but Bast knew he could plow through a dozen of them and that achy craving wouldn't be sated. His elongated teeth hummed, his brain supplying him with the sensual memory of tasting Alice in the throes of her passion. Christ, he wanted another taste of her again. Just as she'd been. Her skin flushed, her lips parted. Shuddering and moaning...

"Fuck," he snarled.

A quick turn of his head provided him with what might be some way to kill time. And perhaps the cold would kill the swelling in his cock. Without thought or pause, Bast strode outdoors, discarding his clothing and allowing them to land wherever. When he dove into the pool, the pristine water swallowed his nude body.

The water parted for him seamlessly and he stayed beneath its depths, at once relieved by the cool spread surrounding him. As he'd needed, his muscles involuntarily pulled in, an instinctual effort to keep his vital organs warm.

After the first lap of butterfly strokes, he could still hear Alice's soft moans when they kissed. By the tenth lap, his still fingers tingled with the urge to touch her soft breasts again. On the fortieth lap, his memories had dulled to just that of her taste. Somewhere around seventy, his body begging for relief, he'd lost himself to the rhythm of arms rising and falling. Chest lifting and descending. Legs kicking and straightening.

He flipped onto his back, letting the water carry him. Gliding through the cool water and thinking about nothing. Fatigue kept him wrapped in its embrace, and Bast was grateful for it. Just a few minutes' reprieve was all he needed. There were a million things he needed to do, another billion tasks he needed to follow up on, but right now he relished this peace.

Only the tug of his body's internal clock, set to the sun's rise and fall, nudged him to the pool's edge. Bast hefted himself out of the water, sitting on the cold concrete for a full minute before rising. The swim had been perfect.

His gaze sought out the east, daring to peek at the change coming over the horizon. Pain, sharp and swift, immediately stabbed him in the eyes.

"Jes—" An artificial breath, one made from habit and not necessity, ripped out of his mouth. What the fuck?

Squinting, Bast peeked at the horizon again, bracing against an impact he shouldn't have felt. The sun usually meant certain death for born vampires; for blood vampires it was rarely fatal. His half-born self had never before felt the sun's sting, but he preferred the night anyway. Right now though…what the hell was going on?

Fingers curling into fists helped him focus. There was pain, to be certain. Indescribable. Breath-stealing.

Mushrooming misery started in his eyes, spreading through his limbs. His gut joined in the attack, the raging fury not to be contained. The illness he'd forgotten, the illness he'd chosen to ignore, was back. And the fucker had brought friends.

Bast staggered toward the back door, his mind wrenched in two directions. Some part of him begged him to find Alice. To cower in her comfort. Another part of him though, a deeper, darker part, assured him if he ran to the human for help, neither would survive it. This was something he had to face on his own. A part of him he had to combat and win.

The taste of sulfur swelled in the back of his throat, and some memory whispered that he remembered this taste. He swallowed reflexively several times, trying to push it away yet savoring the flavor simultaneously. It was acrid. Beautiful. Familiar.

The moment passed and heat wrapped around his neck. It swelled, bloomed and then spread until he couldn't imagine a single hair having survived.

One knee buckled under a new weight of agony and Bast went down. His palm slammed against the concrete, keeping him from collapsing altogether. He let the wet cold be a place to focus. His thoughts had gone wild, rendering decision-making almost impossible.

Pain. Sulfur. Fire. Misery. Heat.

His muscles pulsed, even his back now crawling with sensation. Perspiration rolled down his face in fat droplets, the slight cool so pleasure-inducing, he willed the rest of his body to sweat. Anything—anything at all—to help him.

He balled one hand into a fist, the other fingertips pressing into concrete. Much longer and there'd be five perfect indentations on his patio. Like he needed a memento of this thing that had claimed him.

Growling, he pushed up. Demanded his body to heed the command to rise. There was a split second of victory, when he was certain he could move without collapsing again. But as he looked toward the back door, figuring it would only take half a dozen steps to make it inside, his vision narrowed and pain exploded down his back.

Bast screamed, unable to hold back the cry of being tortured by a body that was no longer under his control.

The odor of sulfur, thick and viscous, seemed to weep out of him. His mouth. The pores of his skin.

Every part of him was hypersensitive again. Almost as if he could feel each individual cell mutating. Changing. Becoming something new. Something different.

His insides began to claw. Push toward the surface. His skin was a barrier that would be barrier no more if he couldn't stop it now. There would be nothing left of the vampire in minutes. Maybe seconds.

Bast cut his eyes to the door again. His hope, his lifeline fast asleep in a bedroom within. Taking one step seemed an impossibility. Getting to Alice simply unimaginable.

He swore he heard the crackle of flames then and the only thing he could do was scream.

GROGGY, ALICE SAT up, pushing away both covers and the blanket of fatigue still hovering over her. Sebastian had insisted transitioning to a nocturnal schedule would be difficult at first. Frequent napping would be expected. Still, he'd made a promise before tucking her in, and she damned well wanted to cash in on it.

Already her body tingled with anticipation, knowing that being with the vampire, having his body over hers—in hers—would be exquisite.

A year ago she could have never imagined the past twenty-four hours. Driving an insanely expensive car. Having full run of a mini-mansion. Being aboard a private plane. And the vampire thing…wow.

She hadn't met just a vampire either. There was the whole werewolf matter she had to wrap her mind around as well. A new world existed outside of her reality and slowly, she would be getting to know it. What other creatures…

Her mind was blown with possibilities.

Sebastian's family tree. Jeez, she'd been so focused on the fact that he was a vampire that it had never crossed her mind to consider more otherworldly creatures. What else existed out there that might explain the branch he'd spent years trying to grasp? He wanted so badly to be a vampire. With near-manic eagerness driving his every decision, was it possible that he'd somehow bypassed the obvious?

Alice swung her legs over the edge of the bed, letting out a little shriek as toes met cold floor. It took only a minute to grab some clothes and head to the guest bathroom to freshen up. She had an idea to explore, but she also had a gorgeous man to meet too.

Once done, a quick circuit of the large house proved Sebastian wasn't anywhere to be found. Her heart sank with each empty room she encountered, but something within her felt reassured he wouldn't leave her alone. It wasn't until she'd gone into the kitchen to snag an apple that she peered into the dark wilds of his backyard.

Her gaze immediately went to the form swimming with an exotic beauty in the center of the pool. From this distance, she could discern the way Sebastian's muscles rippled as he swam. He was doing some sort of complicated maneuver that seemed as natural to him as breathing. The water barely had a chance to dribble down the smooth expanse of his skin before he dipped beneath its depths again. She could have gazed upon him for hours, mesmerized by this definition of masculinity, while crunching on the apple. Instead, she let her sights move beyond the pool—still so very aware of Sebastian at its center—and took in the copse of trees surrounding the perimeter of concrete. They were lined well beyond the pool yet somehow didn't clash with it. Whoever had designed the landscaping knew how to weave nature into the background seamlessly.

Alice moved forward, lured by the beauty of the night, intent on holding Sebastian to his promise. But as she moved closer to the door, the pale light of the moon became its own beacon. As quickly, the reason for finding the vampire in the first place became of renewed importance. For with the moon's bold face, she remembered the existence of werewolves.

When she met him for their tryst, maybe she could bring some little piece of hope about his existence. It was impetus enough to wait just a few minutes longer to touch Sebastian again. To kiss him. The glide of his fingertips a pleasure of its own…

Damn. Better get going now or have hormones make a different type of decision altogether.

She turned on her heels and headed to the laptop in Sebastian's office. Google wouldn't boot up fast enough for her, and she drummed her fingers against the wooden desk. As she waited, she ran through a list of otherworldly creatures, trying to pinpoint one capable of being Sebastian's forebear.

After typing in a search term, the first result came courtesy of Wikipedia. The list of supernatural creatures was surprisingly small and unusable. She quickly dismissed ghosts, demonic possession, witches and extraterrestrials. Trying "preternatural," "paranormal" and "supernatural" in the search engine proved equally useless. It wasn't until she stumbled upon an entry for "mythical creatures" that she struck gold. "Here we go," she exclaimed.

The more she read, however, the less elated she became.

Some of the creatures were common enough: banshee, centaur, dragon, elf, gremlin. Some of the others had to be someone's idea of a bad joke. Hibagon? Magnathorax? "Phooka" had probably been named by some thirteen-year-old who'd giggled the entire time he'd been writing it down.

Going through and researching every single one was going to take time. And of course, that was the biggest problem she faced. How much time would Sebastian allow her with him? Surely there would come a turning point when he got tired of her presence, or when he found someone more desirable or more suited to his lifestyle. God, she didn't even want to think about if she grew sicker. When she could no longer care for herself. The affluent vampire seemed unlikely to be at an invalid's bedside. And that's what she would be, no doubt about it.

The doctors offered her only uncertainty, unable to pinpoint the reason for her seizures in the first place. Her illness almost as mysterious as Bast's. They leaned toward believing it was a brain tumor too small to be detected, but it could have been some metabolic disorder lab tests hadn't yet detected or possibly just a malformed brain. She had a feeling she could meet with a dozen different doctors and walk away with a dozen different reasons. None of them felt confident in suggesting she'd live a long life without a definite diagnosis.

She neither had the money nor the patience for their poking and prodding. Preventing the seizures with anticonvulsants seemed the best course for now. Too bad the cost ate every bit of her meager income provided by the government. Every bit.

But thinking about that was for another day. Right now, she had a sick vampire who needed her help. While still able, he would be her focus. Just because Richard felt he no longer needed her didn't mean no one did. Sebastian appeared to want her around. Maybe even needed her a tiny amount. She would be there for him.

Fingers poised over the keyboard, she began her search. Maybe by the time he finished his swim, she could at least have crossed a few creatures off the list. First stop? Phooka.

Alice sighed. Over half a million hits for that word alone. There had to be a better way to narrow down the search.

Frustrated, she pushed a hand through her hair and forced her mind to use some sort of logic to help her out. Eyes closed, she tried to come up with some distinguishing marks or maybe distinct personality trait she'd seen displayed in him.

She snapped her fingers as she happened on one. Sebastian's eyes had a habit of changing. At least twice they'd become almost pearlescent. The next time, she'd have to see if she could get a closer look or maybe borrow a cell phone to capture the image. What did a Phooka's eyes look like? She leaned closer to the monitor, selecting the image link, which would supply the information she needed.

As an agonized scream rent the air, the hair on the back of Alice's neck stood ramrod straight.

"Sebastian," she whispered.

Fueled with concern, she rushed from the room and headed for the pool. He'd made it through a good six hours without getting sick. She'd thought, assumed, he was getting better. How naïve.

A second scream. Her heart pounded. Chills rippled over her spine.

She didn't know enough about him. How to get in contact with help if he needed it. Did she take him to a hospital, where they might discover he was a vampire?

No. He'd avoided the hospital before for a reason. Whatever help he needed would have to come from her. No choice for it.

Alice flew through the back door. "Sebastian! Bast!" She scanned the pool's interior, searching desperately to see if he might still be in the water. Heaven forbid he lay unmoving at the bottom of the pool. "Talk to me!" she screamed.

The pool was illuminated, the bottom clearly visible. No matter how hard she looked, however, she couldn't find him within. She didn't know whether to be more thankful or fearful of that.

"Sebastian," she called again, ears straining for the tiniest sound. He'd passed out previously and maybe was unconscious now. She had to find him. If the fever raged as before, unchecked and at precarious levels, the chances of him surviving it slimmed to almost none.

At once Alice realized that the air was thick, making it difficult to breathe. A forest fire at a distance, perhaps, sending smoke into the backyard. Not just smoke though. The scent of hard-boiled eggs clogged her nose too.

Her head swiveled toward a sound. Crinkling, like cellophane. It wasn't the light crackle of something paper-thin though. This was heavy. A sluggish weight.

"Bast?" she whispered, moving gingerly toward the noise. What if it wasn't him? What if one of those werewolves or something like it had come for him, and he was unable to help himself?

She'd gotten rid of the little letter opener too soon but didn't dare return to the kitchen to brandish a knife. No weapon in hand, but she *would* scream like a raving lunatic if it came down to that. Then again, it hadn't done him much good, had it? *Shit*.

She crept forward, heart thumping.

A moan. A new sound, like a kite. No––a sail. The loud, indignant snap of material being shoved by the wind.

She moved forward even slower. "Bast." Desperate.

In a dark corner, a place the moon seemed to have shunned, something—someone—flopped. Graceless, inelegant movement of limbs and torso, uncoordinated and nothing like what she expected from Bast. Damn it, he was hurt, and badly.

Dropping into a crouch, she searched for broken bones, fever, trembling. Any signal of what had claimed him.

His skin was hot. So feverish. Worse than she'd ever encountered. A viscous fluid covered her hand as she lifted it away, and Alice's stomach turned. Blood?

Holding out her arm, angling it toward what little light shone, she squinted at her palm. Instead of red, this was clear. Thick, almost mucus-like. Her hands dropped to her pants, to quickly wipe away the gunk making her gorge rise.

Her stomach rolled again, but she returned her focus to Sebastian. Somehow he'd found a blanket of some sort to wrap around his body. The zig-zagging patterns on it twisted as he struggled to rise from beneath its depths.

"Let me help," she murmured, already reaching for the coverlet. She lifted the material, a thick leather, and a scream clawed its way through her throat.

This wasn't a blanket. It was flexible. Moving. Alive. And dear God…attached to Sebastian.

He turned his face toward her, his eyes different and captivating. Dark with agony and confusion.

Sebastian shifted, and every vein in her body chilled. Her heart pounded, kicking its way out of her chest.

Not a blanket.

Wings.

FOURTEEN

ANOTHER SCREAM BUBBLED, ready to burst, yet terror held Alice immobile. Jesus *God*, what was this? "Sebastian?" It came out in a harsh, grating whisper barely capable of carrying sound. Every hair stood against the back of her neck, goose bumps rioting on her forearms.

"What's happening to me?" he croaked.

"Let me help you," she repeated, voice trembling. Alice crouched over him, ignoring every howling instinct to run. To leave him and his world behind and go back to her own. "Can you stand?"

She'd thought his eyes had gone from beautiful to incomparable, but words failed her at trying to categorize them right now. They were a crystalline blue, while silver and pearl swirled through its sea. His pupils had elongated, the darkness a slice that seemed out of place.

"I'm *wrong*." Sebastian's voice contained raw emotion. "This…" His wings repositioned.

Jesus. He had wings.

"I know. We'll figure out what's going on." She spoke with a false confidence that she clung to. "How are you feeling otherwise? Any pain? Faintness?"

He rose to his feet without her assistance, and the stomach that contracted painfully before released just a fraction. She wanted to inspect his back, to study his new appendages, but if he was on the brink of destruction, that had to be their priority.

As she stood next to him, all of her senses became hyperaware. While her stomach might have been put at ease, the rest of her body went taut at the looming presence of Sebastian in this new form. He had always been gorgeous, no doubt. The transformation, however, had given him a new strength. More definition. A devastating beauty.

The sharp angles of his face became slashes of bone and shadow. When he'd spoken, the teeth he kept well hidden were longer. More lethal looking.

And those dangerous eyes. They gave her delightful shivers.

"I hurt everywhere." His gaze was disconcerting. "And nowhere. I'm hungry too."

Alice took a slow step closer, keeping her hands outstretched and nonthreatening. Not like she could ever do him any harm, but the underlying skittishness in Bast needed reassuring. "Let me take a look at you," she said. "Maybe I can help a little."

"You think it's wise?"

She smiled. Not only was he still nude, he was sporting an impressive erection. "I'll take my chances."

He remained rooted, indecision spread across his expression. "I don't know who I am anymore. What I am."

"You are still the man who protected me from a blood-thirsty vampire and a dangerous werewolf. I believe you are the man who vowed to protect me from any and all dangers. You're also the man who kisses me until I can't think straight anymore." She paused, licking her lips. "Finally, you're the man who promised me sexual oblivion. Remember that?"

It probably wasn't appropriate to bring up his promise, but it was hard to think straight with the sign of his arousal so blatant.

"Like this? You would have me still?"

Alice took another step forward. She wrapped her arms around him, astonished by his new definition. Cautiously turned on. "You've got wings now, honey. It's kind of hot."

That seemed to startle a chuckle out of him.

"Let's check you out and make sure you're okay. We'll take it one step at a time after that."

"Fine." A curt nod. "How's my temp?"

"Just under combustible. Pain?"

"Tolerable. Notice any blood?"

"No, just this stuff on your wings. Mucus of some kind."

Sebastian sighed. "This just gets better and better. Not only do I have wings, I've got snotty wings."

She ignored the dry humor. "What about your hunger?" She looked up in time to catch the clenching of his jaw.

"I can't keep drinking from you, Alice. I'm taking more than you can regenerate. Your fatigue isn't just from going nocturnal. You need time to recover from blood loss. I'll need to find someone else to supply me."

That thought sent a rush of liquid anger erupting through Alice. The idea of Sebastian putting his mouth on someone else, bringing the woman immeasurable pleasure, filled her with a bold jealousy.

She shook her head, clearing the senseless emotion. "One thing at a time, as we agreed. The fever has to go."

"Ideas?"

"Just as before. Kiss me."

He peered down at her, his gaze narrowing. His

focus intense. This close to him, she could see those pretty blue eyes slowly begin to shift. Ocean blue becoming a brilliant jade.

"Your eyes," she whispered.

Sebastian set his jaw, his body tightly drawn. He placed a warm hand beneath her chin, tilting her face toward his. "You're always saying that to me. You need a new line," he teased.

What Alice might have said next melted when he lowered his mouth to hers.

This could never get old. The way his lips whispered over hers. The warmth that spread over her, as if allowing every bone in her body to dissolve so that she could mold herself to him. Incredibly strong Sebastian was there to hold her, to make sure their bodies fit so very, very well together.

Unlike his other kisses, not only heat greeted her. There was also the subtle undertone of smokiness. She slid her tongue into his mouth, tentatively touched it to his. Sebastian made a low noise and pulled her closer, deepening their connection. His mouth opened wider against hers, and she breathed in his scent. His taste.

The press of his erection against her belly was a sensual distraction. Her hands rested against the firm walls of his chest, but as his arm squeezed her closer, the urge to slide them down past the muscled planes of his abdomen teased her mind.

Sebastian nipped at her bottom lip, the sting bringing her back to this kiss. He fed her his heat, the warmth spreading through her.

She sipped at his lips, growing bolder. "I think you're feeling better," she muttered against his lips.

The sound of flapping wings filled the night air, a

gentle reminder of the current situation. She reached around his back, gently sliding her hand over the small of his back. Up until she met the base of his wing. Sebastian gave a small shudder, and Alice smiled.

He pulled away almost immediately, anguish in his next words. "How can you touch me like this? Why aren't you scared?"

She *was* scared. Not of him, not when he could kiss and touch her like this. She was scared of what this meant for him and his future.

A response teetered on the tip of her tongue, but then she paused. This wasn't about *her* fear. It was about his. She turned her face away from Sebastian, exposing her jugular. "You said you were hungry. Drink if you think it'll help."

His grip tightened. "You're not ready."

"That's not important. I'm food, remember? Take what you want."

Strong hands dropped to her shoulders, holding her at a distance. His eyes blazed red. "Is that what you think? That I see you as nothing more than fucking *food*?"

"Isn't that what you told me, Sebastian? Humans are food. I'm just a human. You're a vampire who's hungry. And you know what? You're not even that. You're something more. Something bigger and stronger than what I met yesterday. Hell, your eyes haven't stayed the same color for more than five minutes at a time."

Those wings twitched irritably. "You are more than that to me and you know it. Human or not. My eyes, what I am, can't be helped."

"Then what of the things you've promised me? Did you mean them?"

"Of course."

"That you would protect me…did you mean that as well?"

"Yes."

She poked him in the shoulder. "Then why should I be scared of you?"

The world spun as Sebastian turned her around so quickly she almost didn't recognize what had happened. His breath was hot against her ear when he whispered harsh words. "Just because I will protect you with my life doesn't mean I can't or won't hurt you. Even accidentally." His mouth traveled the back of her ear, brushing over the skin of her neck. Hot kisses touching down in unpredictable patterns. "Hurt can sometimes be so wonderful, you don't realize it's slowly killing you."

His teeth scraped over her flesh, the sensation finding a nerve that went straight to her sex. And it hurt so good. The pulse of her body. The craving.

He stood flush against her, his erection nestled in the curve of her ass. Hands strong enough to inflict damage worked with delicate precision to rip a gap in her shirt, the ragged line going between her breasts.

"Bast," she gasped. It was both admonition and encouragement.

"Did you feel the slice of my nail against your skin?"

He'd begun to peel away the shirt from her body, letting it fall until nothing blocked his skin from hers but the brisk night air. Her nipples beaded to hard tips. Alice swallowed, then nodded. "Yes."

His nails, sharper than she remembered them, slid down her back. A tug of movement at her waist made her draw in a sharp breath. "I am dangerous," he murmured.

The loose-fitting pants fell to the ground after a quick tug. She felt movement behind her, heard the sound of his bulk drop closer to the ground. "A fire burns in my veins from here—" he ran the edge of his nails up the length of her calves then thighs, stopping beneath the curve of her buttocks, "—and the burning is excruciating here." He stood behind her again, the hot length of him like a brand. His hands spanned her back, holding her in the same location his wings now resided on his anatomy.

Despite the low, growled words, Alice didn't remember to be scared. She was too excited, exhilaration moving beneath her skin. Her heart pounded wildly, but it wasn't from fear. It was too hard to stay afraid when it came to Sebastian, the vampire.

"I can smell you, Alice, your readiness. I no longer know who I am, what I might become. But you still want me." The last words were hushed. Almost reverent.

She turned on her heel. Cautious and slowly. When she met him eye to eye again, she saw they'd returned to the pearlescent blue and silver. "You won't hurt me." Her hand went to his jaw. Stroked the tightness. "And if you do, it'll be because I asked you to."

Sebastian's lips crashed down on hers, and this time he didn't restrain himself. His tongue stroked into her mouth, teasing her. The hand that cupped her naked breast did it with the same possession his mouth claimed. She might not be able to scent his arousal, but every action spoke of his readiness too.

"Please," she moaned. "Inside. To your bed."

His lips moved over hers. Insistent. "I won't change your mind, will I?"

"Nope." Said with a small shake of her head. She took a step back, immediately missing the warmth of his body and the shadow of his wings, which acted as a canopy for them both. Her clothes lay in tatters on the ground. "Life's too short," she said softly, almost to herself. "Live in the now."

Sebastian followed her, dipping his head to kiss her over and over as she backed away from his amorous pursuit. It became a game of sorts. For every step she took, he stole a minute of blinding pleasure with a simple kiss.

"Are you sure you want me, Sebastian?" She kissed him hard. Another step took her over the threshold.

He growled low. "You have to ask?"

Her teasing had struck home. Licking her lips snapped his attention to her face, while at the same time Alice brushed a hand over the head of his cock. The grip tightened, sliding down his length before stroking up and over the head again. The vampire sucked in a breath, despite previously telling her they didn't breathe, and she giggled.

She leaned toward him, her face coming so very close to his…before pivoting at a run and rushing toward his bedroom, perhaps the only room she hadn't yet been in.

He let out a sound, a roar that should have been frightening but only fueled her amusement. And desire.

For a split second she wondered if he would stay behind, but the sounds coming from behind her gave him away. His tread seemed awkward, less sure than it had been only an hour earlier. A quick glance over her shoulder proved the wings unbalanced him. She would have gone to assist if she believed he'd accept the help.

Instead, she kept her eyes toward his bedroom, her steps seeming to take too long to complete. As she finally crossed its threshold, Alice pushed down the only material Sebastian had left on her body. There was an audible hiss from behind her as panties hit carpeted floor.

She turned to watch his approach. To revel in his masculinity.

The look on his face was of stark desire. He was striking and imposing. He'd managed to lift his wings from the floor, holding them aloft. She knew they weren't the down-feathered type depicted on angels, but his wings were like the man. Formidable. Compelling.

A part of her wanted to explore his change more closely right now. To find its solution, if one was to be had. But whether they discovered the cause for this mutation now or an hour from now didn't seem the difference between life and death. Still, she couldn't help her indecision.

"Bast," she called softly. "Are you…can you…"

He stood in the doorway, almost blocking all light coming in from behind. The result was an ethereal halo, surrounding him and highlighting the newly formed wings. "Yesterday, I didn't have this." His expression tightened as one wing ruffled. She could tell it took effort for him to control his new appendage. "By tomorrow I might be dead. Or I might be a god. No matter what's intended for me, no universe could be so cruel as to deny me this time with you. Because neither of us knows what's going to happen, I'm not going to waste another second on wondering. Afterward, yes. But not right now."

Alice knew otherwise, but she bit her lip. The distant future for her was bleak, his merely uncertain. At this moment though, the immediate future seemed almost carved in stone. And she had to agree with him. They could either waste time or they could appreciate each other.

Decision held firmly in her mind, she waited for him to come to her.

With every step forward he took, she took another back. A waltz between partners who did not touch. Did not speak. Yet understood the rhythm of the dance.

Sebastian approached the bed, his face intensely serious. Alice held her breath, her heart swelling with so much emotion for him. She didn't know this man fully yet, but what she did know made her ache with longing for him.

For once in her miserable life, something very good was on the cusp of dawning. Head tilted toward his, lips parted, she waited for his mouth to claim hers. Outside world, be damned.

FIFTEEN

HE WOULD NEVER be able to get enough of her taste. His heart damn near did double-time every time he dipped his tongue into her mouth. And Christ, to feel the softness of her skin against his made his balls tighten with anticipation.

Bast wanted to touch her everywhere. To taste every little place. To find the secret spots that made her gasp or shudder. He wanted to come inside her. Mark her. Claim her. The worst of it was that he wanted to do all of these things at once.

Instead, Bast took his time. He caressed the shell of her ear, his fingers trailing down to the lobe. The pulse in her neck jumped delicately as he found its beat beneath slowly roaming fingertips. Alice turned into him, perhaps even unconsciously, as they kissed, giving him unspoken approval to learn her body. The faintest remnant from the last time he'd bitten her remained, and just the sight coaxed a low groan from him.

"You still wear my mark," he murmured, lips brushing her goose-bumped skin.

She touched the bruise. "Yes, I feel it sometimes."

Bast ran his hands over her shoulders, memorizing the curve. He brought his hands together at the dip in her lower neck, then slid further down. Alice inhaled deeply, her breasts and dark nipples rising to greet him. She gasped, a sweet, pretty sound, as his thumbs stroked over their tips. "Sensitive?" he asked.

Her smile rivaled the stars in its beauty. "There too."

Alice opened her mouth, letting him delve inside as he teased those twin points. The sound she made was pure eroticism. Wrapping her arms around him, she stepped closer, their bodies molding together so well. Every one of her soft places pressed exquisitely where he was hard.

He could smell her body's perfume, her readiness to be taken by him, but Bast refused to rush this. It would be near rapture to take her as she hovered on the edge of orgasm. In all his years of living, he knew this time with her would wash away the memory of his past.

His back still ached, the weight of his wings something he couldn't forget. He'd almost been torn in his decision to focus on Alice instead of his change but in the end decided, what good would it have done him? It was only a matter of time before the Council discovered his affliction. At worst, they would destroy him; at best, shun him.

No…he would fight that good fight later. Just one hour was all he asked. Now, he wanted to lose himself with the human. His human. Alice.

He lowered her body to the bed as his lips traced over the heat of her skin. Bast inhaled deeply, taking in her rainwater scent as he came within millimeters of touching her. It was with slow, precise skill he didn't allow himself to touch her, instead watching and finding extreme joy in hearing the hitches in her unsteady breathing.

She gave him silent encouragement, her fingers grazing over the skin of his face, stroking over a jaw that felt aflame from her touch. His eyes had become sensitive since his transformation, everything around him sun-brightened. With heightened vision, he watched the tremble in her hands, the way her throat bobbed as she swallowed. The way her nostrils flared as she tried to regulate her breathing. He caught every subtle change, every diminutive sign of her arousal.

Alice licked her lips, and Bast's own thirst became evident. He said hoarsely, "What you do to me…"

He lowered his mouth to the tip of her breast, closing over the hardened nipple. She cried out as he teased the point with his tongue, every taste of her a feast for his senses.

"Sebastian…" His name whispered from her lips was nothing short of worship. That wasn't how it would be between them, though. He would give everything of himself to the woman who'd pulled him from the edge of madness time and time again.

He fit himself between the cradle of her thighs, so very, very tempted to push his cock deep inside her. To fill her until there was little doubt that he was part of her. Instead, Bast crossed to her other breast, loving it with the same force.

His fingers moved languidly over the curve of her belly, and he memorized the way she felt beneath fingertips sensitive to every part of her now. When he brushed the fine hair covering her mound, his dick hardened impossibly more. Even his new wings trembled with excitement.

The reminder of his change yanked him from a sexual haze. Bast clenched his jaw, fighting for control of his body. He tried to distract himself. "I would stop if you asked me, Alice. It would kill me but I would stop."

She lifted her head and gifted him with a wry smile. "Stop, and I'll be the one to kill you."

Bast laughed, his heart no longer pounding in expectation of her refusal, but in jubilant freedom. Warm moisture greeted him when his fingers moved down a fraction, confirming that she indeed still wanted him. Alice's legs parted wider, her hips tilting. She gave herself to him willingly, her body language encouraging his touch.

His wings folded behind him, finally tucking out of his way, and Bast dropped to the floor. From his kneeling position, the glistening folds of her pussy drew his attention. Nothing else in the room mattered but this woman and the pleasure he could bring her.

He leaned forward, his intent clear. The moment his mouth covered her lower lips, he let his eyelids flutter closed. Her taste was almost muted at first, warm and silken, but not nearly enough. Bast pushed his tongue into her body, lapping at the piquant tang.

His heart thudded loudly, almost as if it danced in his ears. He could have drowned beneath the sound if he weren't so focused on tasting the most intimate part of her.

Above him, Alice didn't seem to know whether she wanted to close her legs around his head or to widen them. Her body writhed beneath the way he kissed her, the rise and fall of her hips available to him only peripherally. No, what he focused on, what he wanted to study, was the way her belly undulated, the way the tips of her breasts peaked and then fell as she fought to breathe. The way her hands pushed into his hair, grasping his skull closer, made him growl low in his throat.

"Oh God!" Her whisper erupted into a cry and her cunt contracted wonderfully against his mouth.

She gasped for air and, with a wicked swell of pride, Bast decided to allow her the luxury. He lifted up, gaze taking in every erotic inch of her from his current position. "Sorry...am I not doing it right?" he asked. Knowing damn well he was.

"I've changed my mind. You're going to kill me," she complained. Her eyes were unfocused, her breathy statement almost unintelligible.

He ran his lips over the sensitive skin of her thighs. Alice twisted beneath his scorching touch, almost as if he branded her with his mouth, a moan spilling from her in approval.

"Would it be such a horrible way to die?"

Alice opened her arms, and Bast crawled toward her, his tongue skimming along the silky length of her stomach. When he reached her breasts, he placed a lingering kiss on each one before moving to the object of his intent.

"Not at all," she whispered. Her arms wrapped around him, pulling him closer. Holding him as they kissed.

His lips touched down again and again, breathing in the scent of her all the while. Her taste. Her.

Pleasure rippled down his spine, spreading through his wings. He felt splendid. Languid. A sense of rightness almost overwhelming him.

He wondered if this is how it was meant to be between men and women. If soulless murderers like the warriors he'd chosen to become even knew feeling like this was possible. Of course women were there to be worshipped bodily, but surely not for this precise weaving that interlaced him with her. It went beyond lust and wanton need.

It humbled him how much he'd come to feel for Alice.

HER HEART SWELLED for him. The man. The vampire. The mystery he'd become.

Bast had climbed into a soul driving on empty, lost in self-pity and without a future. She'd been living hour to hour, not even day to day. Without Richard to care for, she'd wondered if caring for herself was worth the time and effort. Yet something within must have known what was coming. It must have known there were men like Sebastian out in the real world. She only had to wait for just a little while longer. Take her pills just one more day. Do everything in her power to just be. Not to give in. And her reward would come in a package of brawn and beauty and strength.

And here he was. Kissing her. Touching her. Perhaps even caring for her.

It was too much. Too soon. What they were doing, this tentative introduction to a real relationship, made promises she'd never be able to keep. For her sanity and for his, she would have to maintain a distance. They could be lovers—would be—but no matter how close he tried to get to her, she would remember to take a deep breath and a step back.

Yet… The here and now. That was her mantra.

Sebastian's hands slid down her breasts, stopping just long enough to send a spark of pleasure with a single flick of his thumb over nipples so tight they almost hurt. Her spine arched of its own volition, her hips rocking to hold him even closer. To lure him.

Her lips parted, ready to urge him to put her out of this misery of sensation zipping beneath her skin. She tightened her fingers on his strong forearms. Studied him from behind a dreamy gaze. "*Yes.*"

His lips curved into a mischievous grin. "I think I like you like this." That decadent mouth brushed over hers then nuzzled her chin. "So wet. So...mine."

"Oh?" Alice wasn't so far gone that the arrogance of his words flew past her. "Who's more ready?" she asked, hand sliding between them. She wrapped it around the spongy tip of his cock, gently squeezing as she did. As she expected, Sebastian's hips involuntarily lowered, the rest of his body taut and on the verge of trembling.

His eyes went brilliant. Feral.

There was a sudden snap of his wings, a dark canopy spread wide to blanket their bodies. Hands that were devout in their exploration became possessive. Sharp sensation scraped over her breast, the tips of his fingers now honed to a fine edge. Alice almost looked down, the alteration to his anatomy not unnoticed, but Sebastian pushed one thigh higher, baring her wide open to him. He gripped beneath her hip, tilting her pelvis toward him.

The sudden scent of smoke saturated her senses, and Sebastian's low growl sent a wild burst of exhilaration through her. Alice opened her mouth to question the change or maybe to talk down the primal compulsion, but the bittersweet push of his body into hers captured her words.

"My God," she moaned, holding on to his shoulders. The bands of muscle became an anchor, keeping her from drowning beneath a torrential pleasure. Her eyes slipped closed as he filled her. Completed her.

Breath stuttered out of a chest rapidly rising and falling. Her heartbeat pounded wildly.

By the time he'd seated himself fully within her, every part of Alice's body seemed hyperaware. His groin pressed against her clit, sending ecstasy bursting out of the sensitive nub. The tension humming beneath his muscles felt alive beneath her fingers. The heat of his gaze as Sebastian gazed down on her could set her aflame. And when he started to rock, the rhythmic push-pull of his body entering and leaving hers, Alice came undone.

Sebastian held her tightly as they fucked, his mouth raining kisses down on hers. She tasted the smoky-sweetness of his breath. He teased her with warm, sweet murmurings and a ravenous hunger that threatened to consume her. The contrast of sound, of sensation, of taste, of smells; it was both heaven and hell. A thing she craved.

A powerful rush filled her veins and Alice screamed as an orgasm buried her beneath its weight. Her body tightened, muscles locked and no longer under her control. It came out of nowhere, blinding her. Binding her to him. It spurred Sebastian, and he drove into her faster. Again and again.

"This is how I've needed you," Sebastian murmured. His hot breath caressed her ear as he whispered. "Beneath me. Trembling. I belong here."

"Yes!" she gasped, eyes rolling back. Lost. So lost to the way he felt inside her.

"You've saved me. Now, let me save you."

"God, Sebastian…please…"

"This is how we were meant to be."

"S——" His name almost slipped from her mouth again, but then there was a delicate stroke of his finger on her clit and the world brightened with luminescent starbursts. Alice's back arched, her hips rolling. Chasing his touch.

She pulled him closer, tight nipples brushing against him. They were connected from chest to groin, his length blanketing her beneath warmth. Her fingers brushed against his wings, causing the rhythmic thrust of Sebastian's body to falter briefly before he resumed again.

He was so sensitive there, and she reveled in it. Fighting her way through the fog holding her trapped, she sought where the wings sprouted from his back. Feather-light caresses made Sebastian cry out. She looked up in time to see the strain of his body, the way his eyes clenched shut.

Already another wave was building beneath her belly. Spreading through her, an ebb and flow that would overtake her soon. When it had nowhere else to go, it would devastate her, she knew. But not before she took him with her. "Join me this time, Bast. With me," she whispered hurriedly. "*Please…*"

His wings folded behind him, tucked almost out of sight. The delicate rub of his fingers on her clit began to circle faster, sending shooting bolts through Alice, little trembling spasms resounding through her limbs in response. She writhed beneath him, her body simultaneously needing more, yet shying away from too much.

God, she was close again. So very close…

There was a sudden shift in the atmosphere surrounding them, a pulse of something powerful. Heat bloomed from Sebastian's flesh, cocooning her in its shelter. He made a low noise in his throat, and Alice watched his muscles swell, the cords of his neck strain. His jaw tightened, his teeth audibly clenching together. A final thrust pushed him deeper into Alice—a breath-taking moment—and Sebastian threw back his head with a roar.

Alice trembled as he released inside her. Her cunt contracted around him, pulling his offering. The air was thick with the scent of their sex, the warmth of their actions, and she gasped through her shuddering.

His weight dropped down on her, and Alice wrapped her arms around his back, holding him in place. Sebastian's mass comforted her, and she cherished holding him like this for a few moments.

Together, they came down from their high. When at last he lifted his head to look at her, his emerald eyes looked drowsy. "Words fail me," he said softly.

Alice smiled...before it faltered. She looked closely at his face, past the perspiration beading along his forehead. The red flush of his cheeks was to be expected. What gave her pause wasn't the debauched expression or the lazy grin of satisfaction pushing at his lips.

All of those things she expected.

What gave her pause, instead, were the small plumes of smoke coming from his nose.

SIXTEEN

"You're on fire. Literally!"

Before her outburst, Alice looked so very satisfied, a fact that thrilled Bast down through his toes. Reluctantly he pulled out of her before a traitorous body insisted on it. Then again, based on the semi-hardness of his cock, maybe not.

"What do you mean, I'm on fire?" He kissed the tip of her nose.

She waved a hand next to his face. "Smoke. Do you see it?"

Panel lighting around the floorboards of the bedroom provided what little light they used to see by. Blackout curtains hung against the windows in thick layers, blocking out the morning sun. The way he was feeling, he was pretty certain the sun hadn't gotten very far in its rise, but it was enough to keep him in the dark comfort of this room. The dim lighting proved to be a good thing now, though. Beneath fluorescent brightness, he might have missed the small rings of smoke Alice pointed to with a surprisingly steady hand.

Bast rolled to his side, enjoying the view as he did. Alice's breathing hadn't quite returned to normal. Her breasts rose and fell in quick succession, baiting him to take one in his mouth again. God, he almost could. Even now his dick stirred, willing to resume his call to action. If only she wouldn't use that delectable pink tongue to wet her lips. There. Just like that...

He focused. Nodded in response to her original question. "At the end, just as I was finishing, I felt something." He tried to bring back the sensation. The rush. "Power."

A pause. "Yeah, it's called coming."

Bast snorted out a laugh. "*As* I was coming, smart ass." He let the mirth settle before continuing. "It was kind of like when I'm sick. There was something burning in me, like fire, pushing to get out."

"You think that's where the smoke is coming from?"

"I'm almost certain of it. I don't see it anywhere else and as hot as that was, the bed's not on fire. It's more of this fucking mystery that I can't seem to solve."

Alice turned to face him, her hand coming to rest on his chest. "When you researched your family, tell me how you went about it."

Bast closed his eyes, remembering the early days. "You're a child of the modern world, so you might not understand what it was like for me. In the beginning, I only had verbal reports. Word from my mother's side of the family giving me little snippets of memories about my father. I don't even know if they were ever really married. They weren't together very long, maybe a hundred years or so——"

"A hundred years? Wait...what?"

He looked at her. "I was born a vampire to a vampire. We live very long lives. A hundred years of marriage is nothing and considered a failed one."

She reached for his hand, threading her fingers with his.

"The fact they didn't succeed," he continued, "was

a reiteration that they should have never been together in the first place. That I managed to be conceived during that time, more salt on a festering wound. So, what family would tell me of him came couched in between little digs at him as a person, regrets over their marriage, condemnation of me. It wasn't until the proliferation of the Internet that I could really research our family well. Of course, by then, his trail had gone cold."

"And your mother? She must have been able to tell you something."

Suddenly bruises to his heart that he hadn't felt in a long time resurfaced. "Nothing. And I haven't seen her in person in at least two hundred years. Letters once in a while, mostly to let me know she's still alive, but we don't have the best of relationships. I was an asshole to her in the last few months before I left her household. I did a lot of idiot things and said much that I regret. I'm waiting for her to forgive me."

"Christ. I thought I had some messed-up family dynamics. You're just as bad as me." Alice squeezed his hand.

He recognized the sympathy, the camaraderie in her tone. "Until now I could ignore that I don't know everything." A lie told before he could recall it. "But obviously this situation has become more dire."

"I came to ask you earlier if you'd searched beyond vampires and werewolves for him." Her voice softened. "If you'd looked closely at your new characteristics for a clue to your lineage."

Bast shook his head. "Until a few days ago, I didn't have much to go on. Everything about me says I'm vampire…except the few things that say I'm not, like my ability to withstand the sun. I've tried asking her for help, to help me understand, but she's frustratingly elusive. Something about my father having to keep his origins known to as few people as possible. Don't know what the fuck I'm supposed to do with that." It angered him beyond measure that neither of his parents was willing to help him. Isn't that what they were supposed to do? Look out for their progeny and help him become something bigger and better than they'd ever been?

"All right, well, let's put together what we do know. You've got wings." He could hear the smile in her voice. "Damn, those things are sexy."

His gaze flew to hers, which was focused just behind him. It took effort, but he managed to extend the right wing, allowing her the opportunity to study it closer. "I don't know what it says about you that you think they're sexy, princess."

"It says I have good taste. Now..." She shook her head as if coming out of a daze. "We need to itemize the other things. Like the heat."

Bast's wing snapped into place. "It's more than heat. Just short of combustion, almost."

"Where there's smoke, there's fire," she muttered. "What does it mean though? Wings, fire, heat, smoke... wings, fire, heat... Shit. Off to Google. Let me go grab the laptop. I'll be right back."

She rolled away and off the bed, darting out of the room before he could stretch out his hand to restrain her, or at least delay her parting. If he inhaled deeply, he could still smell her rainwater scent on the sheets and on his skin. Places where she'd touched him as they'd fucked tingled, almost as if she was some kind of live wire. His mouth still bore the taste of her.

He rolled into the spot where she'd been lying, absorbing some of the residual warmth. Finding an odd comfort in it.

No, not so odd. Every time he touched or kissed her, the immediate relief that poured through him bordered on miraculous.

"You know what's funny?" Alice asked, walking back into the room. She fumbled with the latch to the laptop, opening it wide as she sat on the bed again. Although Bast heard her speak, he was more focused on the sway of her soft breasts and the teasing view of the vee between her legs she managed to give him while getting comfortable.

"What's that?" Nothing could stop him for reaching for her thigh to gently trail his fingers over the velvet texture.

"That you call me 'princess.' It's what my mom used to call me."

"Should I stop then?"

"No," she replied, shaking her head. "It's just funny to me that you chose it. She got me hooked on genealogy because she said we were descended from royalty. That somewhere along the line, I'm technically a princess. Like, my great, great, great times sixty grandmother was a real princess.

"She wanted Richard to be just as interested, but he didn't have the research bug, I guess. I like looking facts up and learning new things, you know? If my life was different, I might…"

The chimes of the system boot-up sounded, and Alice turned her attention to it. She became glued to the image on the screen.

"You might?" he prompted.

She looked up. "What? Oh…I dunno. I guess I might

have become a librarian or something. Hell, maybe even a lawyer. But my life took me in a different direction."

"I like the place life took you for purely selfish reasons. I know it's been shitty, but if things had gone differently, I would have never met you. We wouldn't be here together right now. Selfish, but I can't help it." Because damn it, he liked her. Really, *really* liked her. With more time, it wouldn't be hard to imagine that like shifting into something more.

Alice must have sensed something deeper behind his words because a flicker of fear crossed her features. "Sebastian…you and me, about that…there are things you should know about me."

GOD, DID SHE have to tell him? Life was so damned unfair. Why did she have to go meet some amazing guy, this creature who couldn't have come out of her wildest or most erotic dreams, and tell him that there wouldn't be a future between them?

The doctors called her seizures "idiopathic." Probably Latin for "no idea." The tests couldn't explain why she went into mild states where she lost time or stared into space for a half a minute or less, unable to explain what had just happened. The men in white coats didn't know if the seizures would get better or worse. But just to be on the safe side, they were betting on worse. She held on to a sliver of hope that something malignant didn't proliferate within her, that the seizures were caused by some bad wiring. God, she hoped so.

They were happening more frequently, despite taking the anticonvulsants religiously. If she had the money—hell, if she had a lot of things—she'd go back and see about getting more tests. Maybe try to figure out if idiopathic had turned in to something *pathic*, but it was bad enough convincing her doc to see her just once a year so he could refill her prescription with a good conscience.

A week ago, Alice hadn't given the future a second thought. Not one for herself. Not until… She looked at Sebastian, at the clear innocence on his face. Not innocent in deed, especially not after the amazing sex they'd just shared, but his naiveté about her. Was it fair to drag him into her problems, especially when he had so many of his own?

"Alice?" he queried, his voice soft.

"It's nothing," she said, her voice a little shaky. Not today. Not now. She wouldn't ruin what had been an almost perfect sunrise by telling him what little she knew about her illness. It wasn't like the seizures could be cured. Only possibly prevented or monitored if one happened to occur anyway. "I…I'm often restless after sex. You'll get used to it. In fact, this is probably a good way to let go of some of that energy." She moved her focus between him and the laptop, pulling up Google as soon as the browser was ready. Her fingers flew over the keys as she spoke. "We said wings, fire, heat, smo— no, not smoke for this. Maybe add in supernatural."

"Wait. Are you telling me that I didn't tire you out? Even a little?" Sebastian genuinely sounded confused.

She'd hit Enter, but his tone pulled her attention from the screen. "Nothing personal, dude. I just get kind of fidgety afterward. It doesn't mean anything."

"Of course it means something. You're hitting me in my male pride here. I've never left a woman unsatisfied."

Alice leaned forward, coming so close to Sebastian's face that when she spoke next, her lips brushed his. "Does it look like I'm unsatisfied?" After she lowered her mouth, intentionally leaving him with a kiss that left *her* breathless, she pulled back just far enough to stare into his eyes. "I'm just trying to be polite by giving you a break, and then I want more. Not unsatisfied, lover. Greedy."

Sebastian pushed his hands into her hair. "Fuck being polite," he muttered before branding another kiss on her lips.

She giggled against his mouth before it melted into a moan. He was already hard, his readiness pressing against her thigh while he stretched Alice against the bed. Their fingers twined as their tongues danced, and the feelings he'd stirred within her came rushing back to life, never having expired truly in the first place.

He did things with his tongue that made her forget herself. There was little to do but succumb to his touch. His tenderness. His attention.

If the outside world disappeared right now, she would stay here with him, so very replete and unwilling to give a second thought to everyone and everything else.

Alice parted her legs, making room for Sebastian to cover her body with his. Sizzling kisses burned against the skin of her jaw and then down her neck. She tilted her face away from his, allowing the burn to consume her.

It was instinct that guided her to arch into him, to let her fingers crawl over his back. To touch and learn his sensitive areas. Reveling in the ones that caused him to inhale sharply.

"Once wasn't enough, huh?" she asked, barely above a whisper.

"I can't explain how you make me feel when you touch me. When I'm inside you. It's like…" Sebastian shook his head, apparently at a loss for words.

He pushed into her, the stretch of sensitive tissue a delicious sort of burn. Alice took a long, deep breath, trying to ignore how sore he'd made her when she smelled the same thing as before coming from him. The familiar aroma of a smoldering fire, woodsy yet pleasant, filled her nose and she turned to him, breathing in this new iteration of the scent coming from his skin.

She held on to him as he rocked his body, filling her so completely before leaving her empty for far too long. A pause that stole her breath. With each slow return, a low moan rumbled to life. Whether it began with her or him, she couldn't tell.

It was difficult to remember the sad state of her life when he loved her body so well. That for them both, tomorrow was a gift and not a guarantee.

He lowered his head to her neck, nipping lightly at the skin. "A kiss?"

The way he nuzzled against her, breathing her in, she knew what permission he sought. A kiss so dark and sweet as to be addictive. One only a vampire lover could deliver.

Alice nodded. "Yes…"

Her cunt spasmed around him greedily when Sebastian didn't hesitate, but plunged wickedly sharp teeth into her flesh. A cry tumbled from her lips and her eyes filled with tears, but the pain felt so good. So right. She couldn't stop the sounds of extreme pleasure from spilling out of her as he drank. Coupled with his comforting weight on top of her, and the way his pelvis brushed against her swollen clit, she began a swift ascent.

She moaned his name. It was a sound of encouragement. Of need.

He pulled harder, and Alice had to clench her eyes shut against a wave of rapture sweeping over her. A second pull, and she was soaring.

The sweep of his tongue came too quickly. She'd wanted him to keep drinking from her, to keep taking. Her hands flexed and fisted, grabbing uselessly at the bliss surrounding and filling her body. Her seemingly boneless body quivered, shockwaves of orgasm holding her hostage. It was addictive, this way of being connected to him. He said his illness eased away from him whenever he took from her like this, but to Alice, every part of her body tingled with awareness. The sensitivity almost bordered on painful, yet she couldn't stop herself from wanting.

"More," she pleaded. Eyes squeezed shut, body shuddering.

"Shh," he cooed. A feather-light kiss touched her lips. "Later. This isn't the only way to make you feel good. I promise."

As if to put weight behind his words, his hand slipped between their bodies. The tender touch of his thumb on her clit almost overwhelmed her. The sensation was electric. And, she wanted more. "Yes, oh God, please…"

Alice tilted her head back, indenting the pillow behind her as another orgasm rushed through her veins, turbulent and swift.

She couldn't think. Couldn't speak. Words climbed into her mind and fell away, meaningless. There was nothing for her to do but succumb.

Sebastian pushed his face into the crook of her neck,

his moist lips like a heated torch on her skin. It touched the place where he'd bitten, the breathy caress igniting sensation through her again. She heard his soft grunts, the low muttered words of desire and pleasure. He drove into her harder and faster than he had previously, and the burning soreness of her cunt surrendered, becoming as needful as her lust.

She opened her eyes, immediately staring into an ocean of green so clear and distinct, it rivaled the world's most beautiful emerald. Her heart clenched, the beat following ever frantic and wild. "What have you done to me?" she whispered.

There was feeling beneath that beating heart. Emotion. She didn't have to search for it.

"Alice…" Sebastian kissed her long and deep, the connection between them so strong she almost feared it. But then she felt the first shudder of his body, the sudden clenching of muscles wire-tight. His fingers threaded with hers, tightening around them as another shudder overtook him. The growl that permeated the air on its heels sent goose bumps rising in a contagion on her skin, but satisfaction sank deeply as he emptied inside of her.

With a heart pounding so insistently she could have counted the individual knocks, Alice held on to Sebastian as he slowed the instinctual rhythm. Until he stopped moving altogether.

He seemed to part reluctantly, pulling her in close next to him when she would have given him his space. Tucked against the warmth of his skin, she knew comfort and a feeling of being needed. As her eyes fluttered, fatigue seducing her into slumber, her eyes found the laptop screen, tumbled on its side during their activity. There, on the search results page, she thought she glimpsed repeating words, "angel" being the first. Sebastian draped his arm over her chest, covering both breasts jealously, also shattering any belief he might actually be related to one of the divine beings.

She was so damned tired and would look at it closer later, but as heavy lids insisted on having their way, she thought she saw another familiar word.

Demon.

SEVENTEEN

"...FORTY-THREE...FORTY-FOUR...FORTY-FIVE!"

A sharp scream rent the air, a little girl's cry of pain coming from a young man of nineteen. He tripped over his own legs in his haste to remove himself from harm's way. Tucked next to his belly, the damaged arm smoked, the skin crackling beneath the weight of newly formed blisters. Jacob's face twisted in agony, but he grinned. "Forty-five seconds in the direct sunlight. Let's see who among you can best that."

Sebastian met the eyes of the others, and knew they were all silently wishing someone else would step up and test his hand.

In a hundred years or so, with more exposure to the sun, such a short period of time in its natural light wouldn't mean much. But right now, for every second their fragile skin spent beneath the sun, the quicker they would burn. It was also a rite of passage. To prove worthy to be named as one of the privileged, each would test his manhood. That, or travel to the wilds of a newly discovered land called America.

"You next, Edmund? Or will it be Sebastian?"

"This is childish," Edmund protested. Not five minutes ago, he'd been jeering on Jacob to test his mettle. One look at the latter man's disfigured fingers, fused together from damage, seemed to have tempered his lust.

"Take your turn or step aside, Edmund," Sebastian

drawled. He didn't want to feel the sun's burn anymore than his companion, but there would be no satisfaction until everyone did the deed. He didn't like the rite of passage, but he accepted it.

"What's the rush? Need to get back to rutting your mother?"

He'd heard enough of the taunts about his mother— and lack of a father—to let them roll off him by now. "No, a sapphire-eyed, raven-haired vixen needs my attention…"

Edmund scowled at the description of his sister. Sebastian smirked.

"Get on with it, both of you." Jacob spoke between clenched teeth, but his arm no longer smoldered. The angry red flush covering his face diminished to a healthy pink. A few minutes more, and the burn would be nothing but a memory. He plucked the pocket watch from Edmund's vest before winding it. "The hour grows late," Jacob continued. "At the ready."

Sebastian silently swore, but pushed up the sleeve of his linen shirt. The material scraped against the coarse hair covering his arm, pulling on some of them due to his haste. His expression remained impassive. These little acts of fortitude were childish, but expected among the vampire elite. If there was any chance—any at all— that he and his mother were to be pushed higher than their current stations because of a little pain, he would go through with it. This or any of a million other tortures they could put him through. She deserved it.

He and Edmund stepped forward. A quick glance into the other man's face proved a pallor gone unnaturally white. Sebastian stood straighter at the sight, unwilling to let the young men surrounding him see the least bit of trepidation in his own face or stance. Thank the old gods they couldn't hear the way his insides trembled. Undoubtedly, this was going to hurt like hell.

Ignoring them watching with gleeful anticipation, he clenched his teeth and stared into the beam of light. The starkness of it drew his attention, the glare so innocent-seeming. Amazing that such a little thing could inflict such damage.

"Ready," Sebastian said to Jacob. Beside him, Edmund echoed the same.

"Now!" shouted Jacob.

Closing his eyes, Sebastian thrust his arm forward and into the beam, prepared for the worst.

"One...two..."

The knocks of his heart matched the cadence of Jacob's counting, but Sebastian paid it little attention. Instead, he opened his eyes and studied the skin of his forearm.

Surprisingly, the warmth there wasn't anything like he expected. While true that he felt its caress, the agony he expected didn't ignite. Instead, his arm faintly glowed with awareness. He studied it, as if it hadn't been attached to him for the past twenty years. As if it were a newfound toy, a puzzlement meant to be solved.

"Fourteen...fifteen..."

Sebastian glanced into Edmund's face, then frowned. Already his friend pulled his teeth back, baring them against pain. Jacob watched him too, fascination spread across his features. The others edged forward as a crowd, similar to what Sebastian had done when it hadn't been his turn beneath the sunlight. He understood their morbid curiosity too well.

"Twenty-nine...thirty..."

Edmund's arm had begun to flush pink, every passing second encouraging the color to deepen. Before his eyes, Sebastian focused on the long, curling hair on his arm that began to draw in, withering as if a fine plant deprived of water. Edmund struggled with keeping his hand beneath the sunlight, his arm jerking in his body's reflex to protect itself. His mind, probably overwrought with the need for the acceptance of his peers, kept the arm in place.

"Remarkable! Forty-seven...forty-eight..."

Sebastian's gaze slid to his own arm. And his heart kicked so, so hard.

There was a sudden shout before Edmund yanked himself away from the sunlight, stumbling over his feet in his haste. His face was scrunched in pain, tears leaking from his eyes. He panted heavily, his blistering arm crossed over his chest.

Sebastian looked again into the beam shining on his own skin. Self-preservation told Sebastian to step back. To pretend to the others.

But his preoccupation held him enthralled. He monitored the progress of his arm, its appeal unwavering to him.

"What is this?" Jacob whispered.

All eyes turned to Sebastian, and he suddenly wished he'd listened to his gut. "I'm a year older," he said. "I've been exposed longer."

Jacob held up the pocket watch. "One minute, one... two..."

They all stared at his arm. The supple skin still intact. The healthy glow steady in its color. It did not smolder.

There was no damage whatsoever.

"Ten…eleven…twelve…" Jacob droned on in a low voice.

"What is this?" Edmund echoed. His voice wavered, and Sebastian didn't know if pain or amazement trembled it.

He didn't know how long they stood there, waiting and watching for the slightest indication that the sun did damage to his arm. "I thought you were full-born?" Jacob asked.

"I am."

"I've never heard of a full-born who could withstand sunlight. There has to be a mistake."

Sebastian wouldn't accept that. Couldn't. There were already enough rumors and speculation about him and his mother. Once word got out about this…

"My birth was witnessed and documented," Sebastian said aloud, more of an affirmation for himself than the others. They were slowly distancing themselves from him now, whether they realized it or not. "I was born a vampire, just like all of you."

"Not like us," Edmund replied. "The sun would have destroyed your skin if you were anything like us."

Sebastian pulled his arm from the sun's beam. At least two minutes, maybe three had passed by now. His skin was as intact as it was before being introduced to the potentially lethal rays. Folding his hand into a fist took no effort at all. One by one, the fingers curled in, the skin stretching across his knuckles. The sun might as well have been water for all the damage it had done.

Was there something about himself he didn't know? Did this have something to do with his father?

"You're not like one of us," Edmund sneered. A hard look filled his eyes. "How far back can you trace your *bloodline...oh, beg pardon. You can't." He took a step forward, careful to avoid the sunlight. "So you're not even just a bastard. You're probably a half-breed in addition. What sorts of creature is your mother willing to fuck, Sebastian of Kent?"*

Sebastian didn't think. Unlike Edmund, he didn't bother to avoid the sliver of light, instead launching himself at the dark-haired man. The other young men began to cheer them on as fists flew, intense blows landing on belly, back and jaw. Sebastian felt the crunch of Edmund's ribs snap beneath a punch, while pain exploded in his groin from a well-placed kick.

As Sebastian grunted, then rolled, blocking a punch aimed for his ear, the last of Edmund's words echoed over and over in his mind.

Who was he?

EIGHTEEN

"FUCK!" BAST BOLTED UPRIGHT, the flash of pain so bright, it flared behind his previously closed lids. By the time he'd figured out what happened—no, he wasn't even certain of that—the pain had vanished. As quickly as it had risen.

A delicate hand rubbed a small circle on his lower back. "You okay?"

He turned to face Alice. His lover. His friend. Her voice was whiskey-rough from their slumber. Very sexy.

"Sorry, didn't mean to wake you." He leaned over and kissed a greeting on her lips.

"Is it the heat again? Do you need to feed?"

Always so quick to put him first, despite his insistence she couldn't sustain him at the current pace. There was no way her mortal heart could tolerate the drain on its system. "No, not hungry." He stretched his torso, pulling out the kinks. Elongating his spine. "For a second there, I'd felt like…shit. *Shit.*"

She struggled to a sitting position as Bast threw back the comforter and stumbled from the bed. "Okay, so you felt like shit?" she prodded.

He staggered in a wide circle, needing a mirror. He needed to see himself, what he looked like right now. Except damn it, he couldn't use a mirror properly. *Not enough reflection, idiot.* "My back…the wings…"

The moment his discovery became evident to Alice

couldn't have been pronounced more clearly. Her eyes went wide as her gaze dropped behind him. Blood drained from her face, leaving her gaping lips a shock of pink against pale skin. One hand covered her mouth before its twin topped it in sympathy. "Where did they go? What happened?"

Bast shook his head. Stunned. Elated. "I dunno. I just felt this *pop*, and they were gone."

"Oh my God. What does that mean? Are you getting better?"

"I…I don't know. Maybe. God, maybe." Mind still reeling, he stopped pacing the room.

Thoughts crashed in on him from all sides, bombarding him with a variety of ideas, plans, dreams. It was way too soon to know for certain, of course, but what if the heat didn't come back and he was free of illness once again? Able to resume a normal vampire life. Maybe it really had been his body's way of letting him know he'd been pushing himself too hard. Going too long without feeding. It made sense now that a supernatural body retaliated in a supernatural way.

If that were true, why then with wings?

Bast shook his head again, clearing the intrusive question. The answer was simple enough in any event. The wings had been some throwback to early evolutionary times of the vampire or something. Had to be.

He refused to listen to the little voice of reason that suspected that his ordeal wasn't really over. That his explanation didn't hold water.

"I'm not sure what started it, but I could hug whatever stopped it," he muttered. The pacing resumed, while his mind came up with scenarios and conclusions, tossing out one after the other. None of them sticking.

She said, "I'm so hap—"

He turned in her direction and watched those pretty blue eyes looking beyond him, her face a study in concentration. Her lips opened and closed as if on the verge of speaking, but no sounds issued. She blinked a few times, lost in her thoughts perhaps.

Bast started to speak, amused by the unusual display of spaciness, but instead chose to study her a little further, lured by the sensual presentation. The ribbons of hair he loved to twine his fingers through spoked in different directions, tattling about a night of passionate lovemaking. As did the miniscule bruises on her neck.

His gaze dipped to view her naked breasts and he realized they hadn't escaped from his ardor either, little purple circles evidence of his fulfillment. A swift fury churned in his belly at the thought that he'd managed to damage her, even if unintentionally. She deserved more than that. So much more.

He moved toward the bed. "I'm sorry for what I did to you."

She blinked twice. "What?"

"The marks." With his chin, he indicated the bruising. "I was too rough."

The smile she gave him took its time in becoming, but once blossomed, was a sight to behold. "Not even a little bit, Sebastian."

"But—"

"Take a look at your sides. I don't think you escaped unscathed. Let's call it even, huh?"

He looked to where she pointed. Rows of scratches decorated his rib cage in precise places, some of them snaking around his side and going to his back. "Wildcat," he said with a grin.

She'd marked him with her nails. Damn, that was sexy as all hell. His cock stirred, and it didn't fail to miss her notice.

Alice laughed, her cheeks flushing a deep crimson. "Again? God, you're insatiable!"

Bast stalked closer to her and then climbed onto the bed. Power raced through his veins, more potent than anything he'd ever experienced. "If you'll have me," he said huskily.

She would. Without a doubt in his mind, he knew she would.

Alice ran a hand through those untamed curls before leaning into the mountain of pillows behind her. The look in her eyes was welcoming, the slight part of her lips beckoning. She crooked a finger at him, and Bast answered the call.

This time, she cried out as soon as he entered her, so Bast kept his pace slow and easy. Gentle. She clung to him, arms wrapped tightly around his body. He breathed in her scent and the scent of their union, for the first time realizing this act was not jumbled with the desires of his illness, but emerged directly from the man. And when he could no longer hold off and succumbed to a natural conclusion, feeling her cunt clench and her entire body tremble beneath him, it was with the man's heart he celebrated.

Afterward, they lay side by side, hands clasped. "I have to go to work. As much as I want to, I can't stay here with you another night," he said. "It's bad enough I haven't contacted my men. One more night, and I'll be crucified."

"Go ahead if you need to. I'll probably sleep a little while longer and then get back to the genealogy chart.

I'm definitely not used to a third-shift existence yet." She stretched and turned to face him. "And you're sure you're okay, right? One hundred percent?"

Bast took inventory. "I feel fine. No heat in a while. Wings are gone. I guess it was some kind of genetic aberration I'll need to tuck away for future. Other vampires can't get sick, but this one can. No more ignoring my hunger because it's inconvenient. Bottom line is I need to take care of myself."

"I just want to be sure. I can't help but be worried about you."

"I appreciate it, but I can't stop. Not even for an illness. This pause is more than I should have ever dared. Either I go out tonight and come back fine, or I go out and meet my end. Regardless, I have to go."

"Okay."

Her voice was too timid, and Bast heard the subtle undertone of anguish beneath it. "Hey, look at me. I have no intention of dying tonight. None. I'll be back, and you'll be here waiting for me."

She raised her gaze. "I'll be here."

It wasn't enough to hear her say it, but it would have to do. Bast headed for the shower and prepared himself to meet the men.

For a split second it crossed his mind to find a way to stay, but then reality thumped him on the side of the head. No matter how badly he wanted to, he was sworn to the Council. To its ultimate safety, above his own.

But if he was a detriment to them, didn't that constitute a reason to withdraw himself? He growled in response. There were worse threats to the Council than one sick vampire.

By the time he exited, Alice was buried beneath the comforter, already fast asleep. The faint circles beneath her eyes testified to a long day of restlessness, a lot of which had to do with him. Fucking her again this evening hadn't been in his plans, but the compulsion rode him and he'd given in. Quite willingly. Still, he needed to remain mindful of her fragility.

From the solitude of the kitchen, he called Gray. "What's on the agenda?"

"The Council's on the move tonight," Gray replied. Straight to the point as always. "They're attending some political event, a fundraiser for their cause or some shit."

"All of them?" Bast barked. That went against the first protocol, which required the men and the women of the Council never all to be gathered in the same place, at the same time. On the most recent occasion where that had occurred, there had been threats to individual lives. Bast was determined to never have it happen again, especially on his watch.

"No, Sierra is behaving and staying behind. Our biggest problem is how Gage wants security handled."

"And how is that?"

Gray blew out a breath. "We're to be a non-presence, modeled after the humans' security. In the background and hardly visible. No one is to know we're there."

"How the fuck are we gonna do that?" Bast thought hard. Most of the six members of the team were built like linebackers. All muscle and for most of them, a generous height. They'd been chosen partly because of intimidating looks, not for their ability to blend in.

"The plan for now is to pretty ourselves up and hope we're not asked to leave. If we are, we'll only retreat as far as the outside of the building, monitoring any and all who go in. Gage handed over a guest list and we ran background checks. Almost everyone seems okay."

"Almost everyone?" Bast raised an eyebrow.

"Yeah. A celebrity couple who's attending tend to bring not exactly trouble, but at least some attention wherever they go. Nothing we can't handle, but it puts me on alert. The old guard might be an issue if they've gotten wind of the party."

"Damn it." He hated the thought of having to defend themselves against their kind, but the old guard vampires didn't want anything to do with the newly formed Council and its rules. "Is the couple old enough to be old guard?"

"He is. Not his wife. But there's some kind of agreement there anyway. They're not our problem. What gets me hot is the insecurity of the entire situation. One werewolf gets word of the event—that the guard isn't allowed near the delegation—and it's over before it began."

Bast closed his eyes. "Let me think about it. I'll figure out a way to keep things intact. Give me an hour and I'll join you."

"We can't do our jobs if they won't let us," Gray grumbled, then hung up.

Thinking about the limitations being placed on them, Bast returned to his bedroom for a different set of clothing. He hadn't needed to get dolled up for the muckety-mucks in some time, but he owned a few things that would be suitable.

He stood before the closet, hand on the knob before releasing it as if scalded. Balling the same hand into a fist, he turned and looked toward the hallway. His thoughts focused on Alice.

And then he had an idea.

BREATHING DEEPLY DIDN'T help with the anxiety ratcheting up Alice's heart rate as she sat next to Sebastian in the Ferrari. She was going to be the *only* human in a room full of vampires. The only one.

"No one will touch you. No one will dare come near you." Sebastian kept providing reassurances, but she didn't know if they were making her feel better or worse. "You're with me, and I won't let anything happen. Not a single hair misplaced on your head. I promise."

"It's not that I don't trust you..." Even her voice wavered.

"I will be by your side the entire time, along with my team. Six of the vampires' finest warriors at your disposal."

Her fingers flicked the red tassels on her thigh, another reminder of how dramatically short the dress he'd chosen lay on her. For heaven's sake, the thing was backless and the cleavage went almost to her belly button. Along with a pair of heels she could barely totter in, he'd managed to turn her into a streamline of woman. All legs. A single teardrop diamond hung from a slender silver chain, stopping at the juncture between her breasts, drawing attention there. Similar diamond studs glittered in her ears.

He'd walked into the boutique, had a quiet conversation with a saleswoman who scrutinized Alice from a distance with her head cocked. She'd withdrawn for a few minutes and came back with three selections.

Without consulting Alice, Bast had chosen one and then had ushered her into a dressing room to get changed.

So yeah, not only the sole human in the room, she was dressed to kill. Even if she wanted to run off and hide in a corner, fat chance it would actually be allowed to happen. The barely there thing yelled *look at me*! at the top of its lungs.

"Tell me about the peo—vampires who'll be there." A little knowledge would go a long way.

"All politicians, all very old. None of them will be interested in you. No offense," he added quickly. "They gather like this every once in a while to parade their ages and their wealth to each other. It's very tedious and underwhelming to someone who doesn't give a shit. Underneath, alliances are being made and deals are being struck. It's subtle yet overdone at the same time."

They turned into a driveway, and Alice pulled her attention away from him to study the place. The gray building surrounding by box hedges probably wouldn't have stood out to the average passerby. At least, not until one noticed the wrought-iron fencing surrounding the lot or the multitude of security cameras mounted on the building's corners. All of the windows were tinted, casting a reflection of the outside world but not allowing anyone on the outside to see in. Hell, she couldn't even tell if it was occupied because of the dearth of lighting that should have at least hinted at occupants inside.

Sebastian waited at the gate before it opened quietly. And ominously. She was about to comment on being let in without having to go through some sort of checkpoint when she noticed another camera mounted on a tree beside the entrance. The sudden creepy feeling of being watched by some all-seeing eye prickled her skin. He drove to an underground garage, the downward slope not helping the butterflies looping in her stomach any.

"So what's my cover story supposed to be?" she asked to start him talking again and hopefully rid herself of the sensation.

"I'm still thinking about it," he replied. "Some sort of liaison between humans and vampires, I'm guessing. Someone important enough to be worthy of a vampire guard."

She fell back against the seat, closing her eyes. "This is crazy."

"I know," he said softly. "If you don't want to do it, I'll understand."

Alice thought about it for a second before facing him. "It's important to you, so I'll do my best. But you've gotta know how scared shitless I am."

He reached for her hand and pulled it to his mouth. The kiss he placed on it was as tender as a cloud. "You will never be out of my sight. At worst, I'll never be more than three steps away from you. I promise you that."

"And these men of yours. Anything like that Cicero guy?"

Sebastian had the decency to wince. "He's one of them. Let's go inside and meet the others. They're not like him."

"Then what's his deal?"

"He and I...we have issues. But in a fight, he's someone I'd want on my side."

"Tell me the people on the Council aren't like him either."

"Well...I wouldn't say that exactly."

Great. The first time she'd met another vampire,

and his first instinct had been to bite her. And now that same vampire was supposed to be one of the ones who'd be watching over her in a nest full of them?

"And you can trust him?" she asked incredulously, not bothering to wait for him to help her out of the car, despite the stilts he'd placed her on. Sebastian hustled to her side and offered an arm, which she took. No sense in ending up with a broken ankle—or two—just to prove a point. "Do you recall that he wanted to feed from me the first time he saw me? And if your half of the conversation was any indication, perhaps kill me?"

"But he didn't, because I would never let him. This isn't much different. He reports to me, and I have complete faith in every single one of my men." They walked along a narrow corridor from the car to a nondescript gray door. "Look up for a sec."

She followed his gaze to the camera peering down on them, forcing herself not to visibly react. Based on everything else she'd seen so far, there was no reason for this to be a surprise. He'd glanced toward the eye and then splayed a hand against a flat gunmetal gray box next to the door. Something clicked, and he pulled on the knob. When the door swung his way, Alice placed a mental bet that it had been locked tight seconds before. Between the visual confirmation, along with a finger or palm print of some kind, he'd been allowed in. The complexity of it all amazed her.

"But it's not just him this time," she said, blowing out a breath. "There will be others there. Peop—vampires who might not care what you have to say about the matter. Can you stop them all?"

He stopped so suddenly, she almost wobbled off balance. Sebastian whirled her into his embrace and, straight out of the movies, tilted her entire body back until she could do nothing but fall into his hold and stare into fathomless eyes. The world around them tumbled away as she listened to the smooth rhythm of her heart. Her breathing was easy. Steady.

His gaze did a slow crawl from her face, down the skin of her neck and between her breasts before returning at an equally glacial pace. There wasn't an ounce of strain on his face or in the way he held her. Seconds passed—maybe even a full minute. Never, not once, did she think he couldn't hold her there for another hundred years if determined to do so.

"Do you trust me?" he asked, his voice almost a whisper.

"With my life." The response came without hesitation and she knew it to be true.

His mouth lowered to hers, brushing an achingly sweet kiss across her lips. Every muscle in her body relaxed, becoming almost languid. Somehow she managed to drag heavy hands to his lapels and grasp them. Lifting her head to his took a strength she didn't know she possessed. But when her lips met his again, she kissed him with a new hunger.

"Our fearless leader returns at long last. With food."

Unable to stop herself, Alice stiffened at the familiar voice of the vampire who'd wanted to kill her.

Cicero.

NINETEEN

BAST NIPPED AT Alice's bottom lip once. A gentle reminder. He was here and would not let anything happen to her.

Not ever.

He pulled her upright, loving the look of complete adoration mixed with a bit of drunk satisfaction in her expression. Yeah, Cicero had probably messed with her head by stepping in when he had, but Bast wasn't about to let that go. "Lieutenant," he growled in warning. He did not want to hear his shit. Especially not about Alice, and definitely not in front of her. The men would be given an explanation for this breach of security, despite Bast not owing them one, but in his own time. Not theirs.

Cicero folded his arms across a brick wall of a chest. "You brought a *human* here? Do you—"

Rage and righteous indignation propelled Bast forward, the momentum barely allowing him to register that the other members of his team had also approached. Goddamn, he was sick of the man's constant needling and insubordination. Only one of them could be in charge, and it sure as hell wasn't going to be the Hassassin. *Enough.* The hand that pushed Cicero against the wall had enough force to punch through skin to land on bone.

His lieutenant fared better though. Bast clamped

onto his neck with jaws capable of crushing the vampire's windpipe. His teeth punctured the skin there, blood squirting into his mouth almost immediately.

The battle-seasoned warrior knew better than to struggle. Any movement would have done nothing more than encourage Bast to rip out his throat. It wouldn't kill him, but it would hurt like holy hell. The healing process even more painful and excruciatingly slow. Whether or not he'd recover his voice, questionable.

Bast drank from the spilling wound on pure instinct alone, the taste coming nowhere close to the sweetness Alice provided him. Cicero vibrated with returned anger but smartly stayed stock still.

Bast wasn't the oldest vampire by a long shot. Of course, he wasn't even a full-born vampire like the others. Hell, he wasn't the most lethal of the men. But he'd been chosen to lead them—*him*—and he had no problem reinforcing to any of them why that decision had been made. No one but fucking Cicero ever seemed to need a reminder.

At last he pulled away, stepping away from the direct spray of blood once the pressure had been removed. If Cicero wanted the wound healed, he could ask one of the others to lick it over. Bast didn't give a shit if he bled out. "Let that be the last time," he told Cicero in a low voice. "The last fucking time."

For some reason Bast couldn't be bothered to explore, Cicero was almost fanatical about staying with the guard. If he was going to voice his displeasure again, Bast wouldn't be the one to hear it. That alone kept Bast from taking his life and being done with it.

He turned his full attention back to his lover by outstretching a hand. "Come here, baby. Let me introduce you to the team." Once the pale, trembling woman stood at his side, he made his intentions clear to the others. She held his hand tightly, and he returned the hold, knowing how insane this must have all seemed to her. To him, it was just another day. "Alice is under my protection."

Gray's eyes contained a mix of curiosity and admiration, but he gave a curt nod. There was no attempt to touch her, even with a friendly handshake, and Bast mentally thanked the vampire's insightfulness. "And if you are under his protection, you are under mine. Gray Thallum, at your service."

One by one, the other three members introduced themselves. Drew and the twins, Kemp and Conell. Dressed in tuxedos, none of them managed to hide the innate thug that made most people—vampire and human alike—instinctually fearful. Despite what others might think, he trusted every one of them, including Cicero, with his life…and now with Alice's.

"She's our way in, gentlemen, so it's crucial that we not only keep an eye on the Council, but our human ward as well. They won't object to the six of us if we say we're not there for them, but for her."

Drew nodded. He was not only a sharp thinker, his quick mind made him an excellent strategist. "I think their biggest issue is appearing weak before one another. On top of that, if we're hovering around all of them, it also looks like they don't quite trust each other."

"We're not trying to exacerbate either of those beliefs. With that in mind, it should be a nice, quiet night. We're not expecting trouble." A confirmation look directed at Gray, who nodded his agreement. "Excellent. You ready?" Bast snapped at Cicero. Kemp had tended to his wound, and they were both now checking his shirt for blood splatters.

Cicero returned a glare. "Yeah." His voice was raspy. Good. It would be a perfect reminder for a while.

"Let's move. Three vehicles. Drew, with me." He would have loved to have confided in Gray some of the shit that had gone down over the last few days, but now was not the place nor the time. First protocol held true not only for the Council, but also for their guardians. Both leaders avoided being in the same place at the same time too often.

No further words were needed as they moved en masse to a fleet of black Escalades. He helped Alice into the backseat of one before joining Drew up front. She didn't seem as discomforted as before, which gave him one less thing to worry about.

For some reason, ever since arriving here, a strange feeling began gnawing at him. Nothing like the illness, but definitely a sense of something…wrong. No. That wasn't it. Something different. It didn't hurt, but the presence was there. It knocked at him from the inside. A reminder of something he couldn't quite place.

Whatever the feeling, its origins were physical. A new iteration on the illness he'd just gotten over, perhaps? He couldn't be sure. It felt like two heartbeats. His and another echoing right on its heels.

Fucking great. Just what he needed. Another new twist on something he couldn't get under control.

"Alice," he grumbled, "any movement on the chart?"

"I'm still running that search we talked about."

To think they'd tossed around the idea that he was some sort of demon offspring. Not like he'd ever heard of any existing, but he could see the connection. Alice had flat-out refused to believe, despite the evidence. *"You're not evil,"* she'd insisted.

Guess that depended on her definition of evil. Didn't matter anymore, though. When his wings had disappeared, so had her theory, in his mind. Still, she wanted to keep searching for other creatures who might bear the same similarities, just in case. It wasn't like he hadn't already spent two hundred years searching, so if she spent even twenty with her theory, it wouldn't hurt any. All it could do was help, so he'd gone along with the idea.

"I might have something new for you. Be alert, okay?" He wouldn't discuss the illness in front of Drew but knew she understood him when there was a small squeeze to his left shoulder.

The closer they got to their destination, the more Bast wished she'd continue to touch him. His head pounded, the sensation issuing down his spinal column and radiating through his shoulders. It was a dull, achy feeling, almost too light to be considered true pain. The persistent knock of two heartbeats, one behind the other—the unnatural sensation made his chest ache.

"Boss?" Drew said in that gentle voice of his. "We got a cover yet?"

"Still working." Rubbing his chest, he glanced out the window, trying to come up with something that Alice could handle. That the Council would buy. If worse came to worst, he could always shove her in the restroom and have her wait there until everyone was ready to depart.

As soon as the thought finished forming, he tossed it out. She might go along willingly at first, but she'd unscrew his balls later for the mistreatment.

Damn it, if his head wasn't feeling so fuzzy…

He turned to Alice. "How good are you at genealogy, really?"

"Very. I spent hours researching with my mother. For years."

"So to someone who doesn't know much about it, you'd sound like an expert?"

Her mouth turned down at the corners slightly. "Sure."

"And if someone *did* know a lot about it, how would you appear to them?"

"More than an amateur, less than an expert, probably. Even then, I can pretty much hold my own."

Bast studied her again. At the vision she made. Her curls had been piled high on her head, silken strands cascading down her elegant neck in random places. It drew attention to the twin marks of her neck, a distinct signal to the other vampires that she belonged to someone of their kind.

The only makeup on her face was a light layering of lipstick. Just enough to make her lips glisten and her eyes appear an even more rich blue. That intense gaze peered back at him now, so warmly.

They looked at one another, and Bast wondered—just for a split second—if the thing happening between them went further than he'd originally intended. Than he'd imagined.

What would it be like to have someone around all the time? Someone who saw his flaws and didn't run, but actually embraced him instead?

Alice sat lost in thought again. She blinked in rapid succession, not saying a word. Her throat worked at swallowing several times, and Bast hoped he didn't ask too much of her. Her hand opened and closed in her lap, but those eyes remained focused on him.

It wouldn't be terrible to imagine looking into them for a long time to come.

Of course, that would never happen. It just wasn't in the universe's plan for someone like her to be with him for a lifetime. He would have to be grateful for the little time together the universe had bestowed upon them.

"Well," he said after a while. He'd faced front again, using the street lights racing by as a place to focus his turbulent mind. It took effort to shake off the emotion flooding him. The one that had no right to life. "I think then we have our cover."

Drew turned the wheel effortlessly and glanced at him. "Yeah?"

"I'll call the others and let them know. Alice, I'm thinking your knowledge is about to come in very handy." There was no response from the backseat, so he turned to her with a smile. "You with me, princess?"

She shook her head as if dazed. Probably back there doing all sorts of charting in her head or something. "I'm sorry, what?"

"I'm giving you a promotion."

THEY WERE ALONE again, the Escalade's motor still running although it was parked next to the other two. She didn't have to study the empty lot too hard to know their group was the first to arrive. That didn't help the churning sensation in her belly any either.

Despite overhearing Sebastian's half of the conversation to his men, she still wasn't quite sure she understood. And his instructions didn't clear the confusion any better. "You don't have to do anything but be yourself. They'll spot a lie before it's out of your mouth, and that does neither of us any good."

Drew left a few minutes ago to help the others, but Sebastian had stayed behind, keeping his earlier promise.

"So you want me to talk *genealogy*?"

"Only if asked, and knowing this group and the way they like to show off to each other, they're going to love you and do plenty of asking. You're going to be a dream come true..."

He lifted his head, his gaze darting to the entrance of Pomodoro di Oro, which had been shut down for the night in order to cater to its auspicious guests. Who knew vampires had a thing for Italian food? She could have laughed at that. Then again, maybe it was all that marinara sauce that appealed to them, with the color being the same as their favorite nourishment and all. "I can't believe I'm agreeing to do this. What else do I need to know here? What happens if they don't believe me? I feel like I'm flying blind."

"All right, slow down and take a deep breath." He paused as she tried to rein in her nerves. "Now, don't think. Start with one question. Ask me the first thing that comes to your mind."

"Who is the Council that they need to be guarded?"

Her question raised his brow. "Not they. It. We're not here for the individuals. They have their own private security for that. My men protect the group. The idea. The symbol...the Council. Not the Council members. Does that make sense?"

Alice's head hurt. "No."

"It's a new concept for us." She figured he meant the vampire populace. "One ruling body to keep us from being hunted, from warring over territory, from trying to take over. There are thousands over the world. Way too many people to be governed by one person, so some of the younger vampires came up with this. It didn't happen overnight, but eventually it was an idea most could agree upon. But there are those who want nothing to do with the Council, preferring the old ways. So we guard the Council, to ensure that any threat to it is immediately squashed."

"So wait, are you saying that even if one of the actual members was a threat to the group…"

"He or she would be sacrificed for the greater good. Yes."

"Whoa." Talk about hardcore.

"I'm telling you this so that you understand that if you go in there with your intentions centered on the group, and not the individuals, you'll support us being there with you. And when they all find out why you're there, there isn't a single one of them who won't be curious."

She dropped her face in a hand, covering her eyes. After a deep breath, she said, "All right. Tell me again who I'm dealing with."

By the time Sebastian finished, an hour had passed, and Alice's head was buzzing. She stared down at her short, blunt nails, noticing the distinct lack of professional care. Odd that her natural nails didn't bother her before. Dolled up now next to Sebastian, about to face men and women who could buy and sell her, she couldn't help but notice how different she would be to them.

Where was Richard now? He probably couldn't ever imagine that his older sister sat in a car worth more than the rundown two-bedroom he shared with his crack-head friends, nor that the cost of her dress could have bought them groceries for a few months.

Hell, she'd stopped trying to figure out what she could lift for quick resale from Sebastian from the first day she'd met him. If she thought hard enough about it, within hours of meeting him, he'd stopped being a walking dollar sign.

It seemed like a lifetime ago that she'd been eating out of garbage bins, cursing violently if their lids had been locked tight against people like her. Homeless. Desperate.

A sense of shame, not pride like she expected, washed over her at the thought of walking into a room where people—vampires—had no clue about the struggles of humans around them. She would not only pretend to be like them, Alice would have to dust off creaky manners and long-gone charm in order not to be an embarrassment to the man who'd brought her here. The pressure was excruciating.

"Hey," Sebastian called softly. "You're going to do fine. Relax."

She cut her eyes to him. "You a mind-reader now?"

"No, but I can detect the change of your scent. It's wild now. Not like before."

"Wait…" Her eyes narrowed. "You can *smell* my emotions?"

His grin didn't put her shock at ease. "Something like that."

Alice's stomach did a barrel roll. "You're not help-ing. Not even a little bit."

"Come on, let's go. I think anticipation of the event is making it a lot worse than it'll ever be."

Blowing out a breath, she nodded. Still, as she waited for Sebastian to exit and then come to her side of the vehicle, she couldn't help but visualize what others saw if they'd happened to turn right now—a tall, brooding man built like a badass intent on intimidating anything or anyone in his way opened the backdoor to a luxury vehicle. A woman who'd missed one too many meals stepped out in heels and couture. Before both feet were on the ground, a five-man contingent of even more bad-asses surrounded her and Bast.

The men paid her little attention; instead, their focus trained on their surroundings. None spoke, but hell, she'd probably not want to know what was on their minds anyway. They moved with quiet efficiency, jaws clenched, hands deceptively loose. She knew better. Bast had already warned her they would be armed to the teeth.

Seriously. Don't let the tuxedos and stiff collars be deceiving, or end up at the business end of a gun or a stake.

Butterflies still spiraled in her belly, but Alice straightened her back and did her best to look the part of someone important. One glance at her trembling hands would immediately squelch that image, so thank God for a small clutch she clung to.

The small group hovered at the entrance as Kemp—maybe it was Conell?—spoke in low tones with a steely eyed man. Her guards tightened their formation around her, acting as a single unit, to the point she could have questioned her own value if she didn't know better. Bast covered her hand with his own warm one, and Alice let loose a breath she didn't realize she'd been holding.

"Easy," he said softly.

She glanced up at him, needing someplace to focus, a question poised on her lips. But the tension stretched across his features made her forget what she was about to say. "Bast?"

A sense of dread filled her, because she recognized the expression of forced concentration. He was in pain again.

"Don't worry." His brow unfurrowed. "It's not the same."

"But something is wrong," she replied quietly, knowing damn well the other men at her side could hear. It couldn't be helped.

"Wrong isn't the right word." They began to move forward as a single unit, squeezing in pairs through the doorway. "I just have this feeling."

"Heat?"

"No. Not like that. It's...I don't know how to explain it. Like I'm being pulled almost. Weird." At his sides, his hands went into fists, knuckles cracking with the movement. "Kind of like static electricity, but it's zipping around my inside. I swear I feel two heartbeats. If I hold still long enough, my heart is doing double-time."

"It's racing?"

"No." He shook his head. "One right after the other."

"Boss." Drew edged closer to his side. "You know what that is, right? And even better, you know it's not possible. At least, it shouldn't be, unless there's something you need to tell us."

"What's not possible?" Alice asked. "I don't understand."

"I did nothing wrong. Nothing. Not even in a drunken fit." The confusion and outright anger on his face held Alice captivated. He looked like a man just given notice he'd been fired from a job of thirty years. Or maybe it was the expression of a teenager who'd been informed that in nine months, he'd be a father. To Alice he said, "There's another vampire here."

Well, obviously. "Okay?"

"I mean, one that's connected to me."

"I still don't understand. How's he connected to you?"

"That's just it. I'm not sure how."

"Start from the beginning." His gaze kept darting from her face to something behind her, his entire manner as close to frantic as she'd ever seen on the normally stoic man.

His expression straightened. "I'll explain it later. This isn't the time."

She weaved her fingers with his, trying to grab his attention. "Don't shut me out now."

He only shook his head. "It can't be up for discussion this second, Alice. This…it's wrong. I can't say anything else about it now other than it's wrong. It has to be."

But what was the matter? She got that he didn't want the others to know he'd been sick, but right now they seemed to know more than she did. Something about being vampire. Something he wasn't allowed to tell her—or did he flat-out just *not* want to tell her?

Drew slanted a sympathetic glance her way, but when he turned to face forward, his expression straightening, she followed his example.

A very lean man, with salt and pepper hair and a hawklike nose, made his way toward them. A woman in a pretty black dress hovered a few steps to his right side. A glass of something sparkly was gripped between her elegant, unadorned fingers. Before he'd stopped moving, coming to rest right before Drew, he held out his hand. Without hesitation or the slightest clumsiness, the woman deposited the glass. Almost as if this practiced move had been done thousands of times before.

He should have looked out of place amid a sea of tuxedos and formal wear, but the brown pinstriped suit that would have seemed gauche on anyone else seemed determined to show off his sense of greater style. The manicured nails and flashy watch accentuated the picture perfectly.

"Sebastian." He spoke with confidence, but without airs. "This is a closed meeting. I believe your lovely companion would enjoy her dining experience elsewhere."

"Councilman Renner, I'd like to introduce you to Alice Bowman. She's a genealogist...with a proposal."

"Pleased to meet you," she murmured in response, not bothering to hold out a hand. She wasn't sure he would have taken it.

Shrewd brown eyes studied her in a head-to-toe sweep. "What would you plan on mapping, Ms. Bowman?"

His directness almost made her forget herself. Alice shook off the disquiet and repeated the words she'd rehearsed with Sebastian not long ago. "Why, the Council, of course."

"She would offer herself as the Council's historian, if the Council would agree to it," Sebastian added.

Councilman Renner pivoted on his heel while bringing the glass to his mouth for a delicate sip. "Hmm... yes. We'll have to see about that. Why don't you come in and tell us all about it."

Her heart pounded.

TWENTY

BAST GRITTED HIS TEETH, trying to stay focused on the conversation in front of him. No matter how he tried though, all he could do was continue to concentrate on the double-time *thump thump* knocking against his ribs.

God, was it going to stop? First the illness without explanation, and now this unbreakable pull, tugging at him with a strength that almost made him shove everything else from his thoughts.

Others had talked about the sensation, about the double heartbeat and its significance. It usually meant a link had been formed with another vampire. The link between sire and issue. Somehow, a vampire in the vicinity was physiologically attached to him. His father, perhaps? Maybe now that Bast needed him the most, he was somewhere close by.

The thought churned some deep emotion in Bast, making him feel much younger than his years. Fucking great timing. Maybe it simply meant that all this time with Alice had him thinking about his father too much. No good would come of it.

The double heartbeat meant nothing. He couldn't allow it to mean anything.

The men fanned out around Bast, Alice and Councilman Renner, allowing the three to stroll through the hallway leading to the dining area without hindrance and allowing him to focus. Bast was happy to move himself just behind Alice's left, the way Councilman Renner's ever-present assistant kept to his right.

He needed to keep his attention on her right now. On the people of the Council.

"So I understand," Alice said, "that the Council is only a few hundred years old."

"I won't bother to ask the source of your information," Renner responded dryly.

"Of course it's true that I'm not one of you, but I think my skill set could prove useful to your group. Imagine, if you will, having the family lines of the members to draw upon to demonstrate the history of power occupying those seven seats. Don't you think it would provide a message to those who still question its legitimacy?"

Bast kept his face impassive, although he was seriously impressed with the start of her presentation. He'd only had to plant the half-baked idea in her mind and she'd crafted it until the idea enticed even him.

He took the opportunity to study their surroundings when the conversation took a turn. Something about coats of arms and hiring a painter. Nothing he needed to know about. Renner seemed captivated by what Alice had to say, the man's tension evaporating as the minutes passed.

Bast wished he could say the same. As hard as he tried to not allow his mind to drift, a knot of muscle formed at the base of his skull, tugging wickedly at his head. The pull being created by something—or someone—near him kept growing stronger, as much as he tried to ignore it. The double thump pounded with greater insistence. He felt compelled to face his feet toward one of the side rooms and just follow. Way to get dead.

He couldn't help himself from looking. Trying to see past shadows and darkness and perhaps get a glimpse of someone within.

Gray stepped into his sightline, obscuring any chance of catching a glimpse of the magnet. "Under control?" he asked softly.

For a second Bast hesitated, almost ready to shake his head 'no.' Damn it, he was sick of this shit. Tired of feeling like he'd been dragged behind a pickup. Worn down to his bones. Maybe he needed to confide in Gray, if only to make sure the Council vampires remained protected. If he wasn't at the top of his game, Bast just couldn't be effective at doing his job.

Then Alice laughed.

A coiled spring of tension unfurled deep inside Bast, reacting solely to the sound of joy coming from the woman next to him. He released a slow breath, pure habit, letting ease wash over him. The annoying tug still wrapped tight around his center, but knowing that she stood next to him, ready to claim and save him, made it that much more bearable.

Before turning to see what had tickled her, he did another scan of the room. Familiar faces greeted him, the remaining members of the Council gathered in groups of two or three. Other vampires surrounded them, some secluded in their own little cliques, while vampire staff served food. Keeping the crisp white uniforms of the latter group that amazing gleam of white must have been hell on the laundry bill, but that wasn't his problem. He tagged one of the servers as a little too flam-

boyant before his gaze lifted and then collided into
eerily black eyes.

The man with the boxer's jaw and classic Grecian
nose was a legend among those vampires who fought
the good fight. Corin Gerulaitis, former gladiator and
current vampire exterminator, stood over six feet tall
and looked every bit the death dealer. Clothing wouldn't
have hidden his dark aura and apparently he'd thought
so too, choosing to dress in gray slacks, a black T-shirt
and a duster. The latter item caught Bast's attention
the most. He skimmed its surface, looking for telltale
bulges, and found them. Stakes. Designed for vampire
execution. He probably had a few other items hidden
beneath the duster, but just knowing they were in the
same room as the Council made Bast's blood run cold.

"Our celebrities," Gray said almost beneath his
breath, having caught on to the threat in the room.

"Where's the wife? Rose or something…" Bast whispered back. He glanced at Alice, who seemed deep in
thought while still continuing an animated conversation with Renner.

Bast was curious to see the woman who'd somehow
managed to make the executioner not only disregard his
order to kill her, but ended up mated to him instead. According to rumor, she'd defied the Council mandate just
by being alive, until the couple had convinced—maybe
coerced—the Council to rescind the command. It was
something never before done. Not done again since.

"Jasmine," Gray corrected. "Over there."

He followed Gray's direction and when he finally
spotted her, the force of the double heartbeat almost
punched through his chest. Bast released an anguished
sound, unable to bite back the surprise and recognition.

She stared back at him, blood draining from her face in a rush. Jasmine was petite, the roundness of her very pregnant belly almost comical. But Bast saw the way she swayed when she looked at him, and thankfully she grasped her husband's arm for support.

"Oh God...*shit*." Bast felt a tremor hurtle through his veins and every muscle, the shock of seeing his very first blood issue keeping him rooted to the spot. Physiology didn't lie. "What. The. *Hell*."

The executioner pulled his wife close to his body, his mouth moving frantically near her ear. Despite acute hearing, at this distance Bast had no idea what they were going on about. No doubt, it had loads to do with him. The connection between them.

"Excuse us, Councilman," Bast said to Renner. Later, he'd do damage control on interrupting the man mid-sentence, but for now, he grabbed Alice's hand and hastened her toward Jasmine Gerulaitis.

The woman he'd sired. Somehow. She was his vampire progeny. His.

"What's going on?" Alice sounded breathless beside him, but he couldn't stop looking at the other woman. The consequences of having an unauthorized bloodborne were huge. Astronomical.

Bast's mind whirled with questions and more questions. *How the fuck had he sired someone*? How had she survived? Transition was a miserable experience to live through without a sire's care. *Jesus Christ.* This had to be the reason she'd been ordered for execution.

The insistent tugging he'd been feeling all evening. The feeling of unrest and unease, which had been with him since they'd arrived, had been trying to tell him something. His bloodborne. *His.* An impossibility, an unfathomable feat, stood in the same room with him, ready to be claimed.

"Sebastian?" Alice's concern stabbed him.

"The pregnant woman," he said between gritted teeth. "She's mine." He felt her hesitate, her grip on his hand slipping free. "Not like that, Alice...there's only you like that. The woman...I don't know how and I don't know when, but she is my creation."

He struggled with his next words because they made no sense. He wasn't full-born. Turning someone was supposed to be *impossible*. The word kept tumbling over and over in his thoughts.

Just fucking impossible.

"She's...I made her a vampire," he finally forced out. There was an audible gasp beside him, echoing his sentiments almost perfectly. "This is bad, princess. Really bad. I have to find out more."

They didn't speak again until they'd woven through numerous bodies. Most were indulging in alcoholic beverages, while others dipped crunchy bits of fried calamari in marinara or chewed on rolled eggplant stuffed with cheese. He'd planned on allowing everyone to enjoy the restaurant's offerings, but the night hadn't even begun and it had swung a left down a one-way street, hurtling in the wrong damned direction.

The only thing on his mind right now was this woman. His bloodborne.

His disciplined men kept Bast and Alice in the center of a circle of protection, while still giving them some freedom to move through the others. Gray stayed the closest, and for that Bast was grateful. He'd need sound advice in this matter.

"You're the man who was shot that night," Jasmine

Gerulaitis said when they were close enough. "You're the reason I'm here."

Bast studied her face, trying to recall it from memory. He'd been shot a dozen times or more, but try though he might, he couldn't place her. What history did they share?

Her husband, a hulking brute of a man, stepped forward and put his body in between Bast and his wife's. Corin's arm was hidden inside his duster, the look in his eyes a mix of rage and contempt. "You have no idea what you did, and it's the first of three reasons why you're not dead by me right now."

Bast kept his gaze trained on his tucked hand, looking for any sudden movement, while his instincts went on screaming alert. "I don't give a fuck who you think are, Council executioner or not. Don't threaten me. I promise that you're not good enough to take me down, so I suggest you put that hand where I can see it." He didn't bother to mention the five men who surrounded them.

Corin tensed. "Bring it."

WIDE-EYED, ALICE WHIPPED her attention from Sebastian to the man and back again. Time out and wait a minute. What was happening here, and should she duck and cover?

"Corin, sweetheart?" Alice had almost forgotten about the woman standing just behind the man threatening Sebastian. She looked adorable dressed in a sleeveless purple dress, with some sort of drape over one shoulder. Her skin gave off the kind of glow only pregnant women could ever achieve. "Honey, I've gotta pee. You're going to have to hold off on any killings until I get back, 'kay?"

The change in Corin's face was immediate and dramatic. Everything about his look softened, love shining from him with such loudness it almost seemed a private moment between the two. "As you wish," he murmured. He looked to Sebastian. "If you would allow me to finish what I'd started to say... This woman and our child are the other two reasons I would never harm you. Thank you."

"But I don't understand. How did this happen?" Sebastian asked. "You have no idea..."

Corin laughed. It looked both unusual and intensely interesting on him. "Let me escort Jasmine to the restroom and when I return, you and I will have a long talk. And don't worry, unless you decide to tell others about this, her origin stays with us."

"Oh, good Lord." Jasmine rolled her eyes. "I think I can handle going to the bathroom by myself. Been doing it that way for a long time."

"Not until I check it out, *mellita*." His sharp gaze went to Alice. She shrank internally from the scrutiny. "Too many whack jobs getting too close to you. Both vampire and human."

Sebastian tightened his hold on her hand. "Alice is with me."

"And you trust her?" Corin asked.

"With my life." He sounded so grave, Alice could have gone wobbly kneed from his declaration. Something was shifting between them. Something that would have to be explored later. "Is there a problem?"

"According to some fanatics, my wife has no sire. They have made our lives very interesting with their twisted devotion. They worship her as some type of goddess, her mysterious turning proof that a new age of vampirism is upon is. Some of them have been a little too enthusiastic, wanting to drink from her or her from them. And once we were no longer able to hide her pregnancy, they've become even more zealous. I don't dare leave her side."

"Corin, unless you want me to leave a yellow trail behind me, can we move, please? This kid of yours is line dancing on my bladder."

Another one of those looks of pride mixed with admiration shined from his resulting smile. "Of course."

"Alice, you look like you could use a break from all the testosterone flooding the room for a minute too," Jasmine said with her own pretty smile following. "Care to come with? Perhaps I'll be allowed to pee in peace with a female escort."

Alice found herself drawn in by her calm demeanor and easygoing manner. "Sure."

"After I check out the restroom," Corin amended. He turned to Alice, his face hardening again. She could see why the other woman was attracted to him, but his intensity sent a shiver of fear through Alice. "Are you carrying?"

"My purse?"

His jaw tensed. "Weapons of any kind."

Sebastian stepped forward. "We are her weapons."

Corin glanced at Sebastian before visually locating each member of his team, all of whom stood unspeaking. None of them ate or drank. A dead giveaway to anyone who was observant that they didn't quite belong. "Fine," he said.

His reconnaissance only took a few minutes, by the

end of which Jasmine was bouncing from foot to foot. "You have any children?" she asked Alice when they were finally left alone to use the posh room.

"No," Alice called to the closed stall door. "I'm not sure I'm the mother type, you know? Maybe one day, but not yet." She paused, but then decided to push forward. "Is it true that Sebastian made you a vampire?"

"It is. First one to be made without direct contact, or so I'm told. The whole thing of it was an ordeal, but it's how Corin and I met. You said his name is Sebastian?"

"Yes." Alice listened with rapt attention.

"The one and only time I ever met him, I was his nurse and he was a GSW dumped outside my clinic."

"GSW?"

"Sorry, old habits. Gunshot wound victim." The toilet flushed, and the sound gave Alice a brief moment to reflect on the fact that Bast had been in mortal danger at some point recently. She knew he had a dangerous job, but it never really occurred to her just how dangerous. "Anyway, I accidentally got stuck with a needle that had been contaminated with his blood. Sebastian supplied the enzyme necessary to make me into a vampire, and Corin did the rest."

"So this wasn't an authorized turning? I thought it had to be approved first."

Jasmine laughed lightly. "Definitely not authorized. Corin and I almost didn't make it out of the whole thing alive."

Alice stood before a sink, looking into the mirror. Her heart pounded wildly, the implications of what Jasmine was telling her almost too difficult to comprehend. Despite his illness, despite everything he'd been told, Sebastian *did* have the ability to create a new vampire. He was less mystery creature and more vampire than he realized. He could return to the life he was living before, his mind intact.

It also made her realize that she no longer harbored fantasies of becoming a vampire herself, instead content with simply being with him. It was selfish to ask him to take her on for God only knew how long just because she didn't want to die. If Sebastian wanted a lifetime with her, it would be because he loved her. Not because of pity. She'd come to care for him too much to have it any other way.

Her vision blurred for a split second. Then, blinking, she cleared the stinging in her eyes, not really sure how long she'd been lost in thought.

"You with me again?" Jasmine asked gently from beside her.

"Sorry?" She turned to face Jasmine, noting the concern in her eyes.

"I know you don't know me from Adam, but I'm a registered nurse and you left me there for just over two minutes. Do you remember what happened?"

Alice's hands began to shake, fear causing bile to churn in her stomach. Two minutes? That was longer than any of her other previous seizure events. The absence seizures made her stare off into space for usually less than thirty seconds or so. Someone not paying attention, unaware that she was seizing, would be none the wiser. She wasn't always aware of them herself.

"Oh my God," she gasped. Her brain was deteriorating. How quickly, she had no idea. She whirled, facing Jasmine head on. "Are you sure of the time?"

"When I realized what was happening, I started timing. Honestly, it was probably closer to three minutes. How long have you been having seizures?"

"You can't tell him," she said quickly. "*Please*. Sebastian has his own issues right now, and you cannot tell him."

"Honey, it's not my place. I don't know either of you and even if I was your healthcare provider, I wouldn't betray your confidence."

"Thank you—"

"*But* I must strongly advise that you tell him. I'd stepped behind you in case you went tonic-clonic, but I knew what was happening. If you two are an item, he needs to know just so he can be prepared. This is your health you're messing with. What does your doctor say?"

"I don't have one," she muttered. At once, embarrassment for her situation, her inability to take care of herself slapped Alice in the face.

"I can help you find a neurologist, if you'd like."

"Can't afford it."

"But your vampire can, I bet. All the more reason to tell him what's going on."

"Please, Jasmine. I don't have any friends. Be one for me and don't tell him."

Jasmine exhaled loudly, throwing her hands in the air. "I already said I wouldn't, and I mean it. Will you at least take my number and call me from time to time so I know you're doing okay?"

She nodded, albeit reluctantly. "I'd like that."

"Alrighty then. Let me jot it down quickly before Corin comes busting down the doors. I love that man, but becoming a father-to-be has turned him into a bear."

Alice had no sooner tucked the little slip of paper

inside her purse when someone from inside the restaurant screamed. It was followed by several booms of noise and the simultaneous crash of glass.

"What the hell?" Jasmine muttered. She'd rushed to the exit before Alice had a chance to stop her.

"If something happens to you, your husband will be coming after me," Alice said when she caught up to her at the door. "I'll peek, but you stay behind me."

The heat from Jasmine's body pressed against Alice as they moved into the doorway together. Alice felt a surge of protectiveness toward the pregnant woman she didn't have to explain. Her exuberance, her devotion to her husband and her eagerness to friend Alice after only knowing her a few minutes marked her as someone worth getting to know. Whatever was happening in the restaurant, she'd do her best to see her safely returned to Corin.

They crept out of the bathroom but immediately ran into Cicero. Alice's heart clenched when he moved to shelter her. "Don't come any further," he said urgently. "Stay behind me."

She didn't trust him as far as she could see him, but Sebastian had assured her that even he would look out for her best interests that night. Besides, with his big ass blocking the way, she couldn't see past him or the crowd forming a perimeter.

Her relief was short-lived when Corin squeezed through to join Jasmine's side. "Jasmine, to me." He sounded calm and in control, yet an undercurrent of quiet panic rippled through his tone. "This has nothing to do with us, and I want you away from this."

"What's wrong? What's going on?" Alice tried to

peer past Cicero, but he kept her almost cocooned by his body.

He looked into her eyes. "Bast…he's shifted."

"Shifted?"

"There's little hope for him from the Council's interest," Corin said. "If I hadn't seen it for myself, I wouldn't believe it. But my first priority is my family and I must get them away from the shit storm brewing. I can provide protection for you for a short while, if you'd like. Until things calm down. I would do no less for the friend of my wife's sire. Let his men see this to its end."

"Its end? *Bast*!" She didn't like the finality of Corin's words.

"If you value your life, come with us. Now."

"No!" She pushed at Cicero's shoulder, silently begging the solid wall to move just a fraction.

Jasmine tried where her husband failed. "Alice, come with us for now. Whatever's happening, let it settle. Corin won't wait for you."

She turned to her new friend, hoping she understood. "I have to get to him. I won't leave. Not without Sebastian."

Jasmine returned a brief nod and held out her hand for Corin. Together they pushed through the crowd, away from what was obviously the center of attention, without another word. Alice wished them well, certain she would meet them again. For now though, she had to get to her man.

Alice met Cicero's glare and made one more attempt. The world seemed to slow as she ran toward him and, in a move from the early days with Richard when things were still good, feinted right before ducking left. She pretended she carried a pigskin and was on her way to a touchdown.

For a split second, it seemed the warrior fell for it. Then a viselike grip went around her waist, just as she thought she'd ducked under his flailing arm.

"No!" she screamed.

Cicero hauled her back against his front, ignoring the way she pedaled against the air. Kicked at him, fingers scrabbling against his forearms, anything to make him let go.

Her feet hit the ground at the same instant she finally caught sight of what held the crowd enthralled. The reason why Corin felt it necessary to protect his wife and their child by fleeing. Her heart threatened to kick its way out of her chest, but surprise soon gave way to despair as she stared at Sebastian.

Alice gulped down another scream, this one fueled by terror.

Bast stood shirtless in the center of the room, what once had been an elegant coat and pristine starched shirt now in tatters at his feet. The change thrust upon him was both sensual and beautiful. Covered in black scales that formed a neat collar around his neck, his torso and arms now glittered with them as well. A ridge of spiny protrusions sprouted from his shoulders and traveled along his triceps, culminating in clawlike structures at his elbows. Even from this distance, she could tell his eyes glowed red as they scanned the room.

Possibly worst of all, his Goddamned wings were back, now larger and more menacing than they'd ever been.

TWENTY-ONE

HER SKIN CRAWLED with warning, but Alice refused to immediately give in to the stark terror of seeing him so different. So changed. Despite every instinct demanding she throw herself into the crowd and become lost in its depths, she battled with herself to remain calm and still until the stronger part of her won.

The gentle flap of spread wings echoed in the silent room, the mild breeze it created caressing her face. Anguish filled every part of his transformed features. The sight twisted her emotions until she didn't know which one should reign.

"Sebastian?" Did he recognize her?

Dark red eyes shifted to meet hers. Lips that had been pulled back, baring wicked-looking teeth, slowly lowered. The rumbling growl vibrating his throat softened into nonexistence. Sebastian tilted that elongated head to the side, as if trying to discern who she was and why she spoke to him. After an eternity, beneath the questioning gaze, she detected the man she'd come to know. Her vampire was determined to be seen.

"I see you," she whispered. Alice refocused her attention on the only thing blocking her from going to the beast. "Cicero, *please*. I can help him!"

"No one can help Bast." He struggled to hold her against him, but Alice was not going to give up without a fight.

The men who lived and died for the same cause beneath his command, the men who called themselves allies, surrounded Sebastian on all sides. All had guns drawn. They didn't appear ready to gun him down, not just yet, but their protectiveness over the Council could not be questioned.

She stopped struggling, swallowing down fear for her lover, and tried to speak calmly to one of his greatest rivals. "He's not a threat to anyone like this. Sebastian's hurting really badly right now, I promise. Let me go to him and help. I've done it before."

"My duty is to protect the Council. Not him."

"Then let me take him away. Let me go and I'll get him to leave without a fuss. But I can't help if you keep me here." Alice thought she felt a little hesitation, the slightest give in the tension of his arms. Perhaps a little uncertainty on his part, so she pressed on. "Protecting the Council should mean getting them away from him. Which is easier? To move one man, or to move seven people with their staff and companions?"

God, please see the logic in her argument. Sebastian looked so lost and alone while he lifted one hand to his face. The claws that had replaced his long, graceful fingers flexed and unfurled, as if he tested whether the things truly were extensions of his own body. If her own fear both of and for him was ratcheted so high, she couldn't imagine what he must have been feeling.

An interminable stretch of silence passed, during which Cicero seemed to be weighing the consequences of her words. If Bast was worth the aggravation. What was the best course of action for all of them.

"If he makes one wrong move toward any of the Council, I *will* kill him. Go." Cicero's arms dropped, the pain of his previous grip still sending ripples of sensation over her arms.

Stunned, Alice couldn't find the commands to get her feet to move just yet. She was certain he would change his mind and pull her away before she could take one step forward. When one foot landed in front of the other, and then repeated without interference, she quickly flushed away all thoughts of Cicero to see to Sebastian.

The sudden parch in her throat made swallowing difficult, so she chose not to verbally excuse herself through bodies she pushed roughly past. Face it, most of them wanted to move in the opposite direction of where she headed anyway.

"Do you know me?" she called, her voice box silently screaming in agony. A swift headache tapped at her temples, probably Morse code for *do not do this, stupid*.

He lifted his head, and Alice bit back a gasp. The scarlet-hued eyes she could deal with. Even the new swirling decoration of scales could be ignored. Something about the way his face had elongated, twisting his masculine jaw into something more reptilian, brought tears to her eyes.

"Baby, it's me," she said softly, heart breaking all the while. Regardless of what he looked like, the creature—the man—was still Sebastian. She would not abandon him now.

The look in his eyes—so much confusion—stole her breath. Blood raced through her veins as she moved closer to him without saying another word. She didn't need to speak to this tormented giant, not when her actions could express so very much.

When they stood face-to-face, almost close enough

to touch, she opened her trembling arms to embrace him. Apprehension flittered through Sebastian's eyes, echoing the sensation swimming within her. What would those scales feel like beneath her fingers?

Once, Richard had taken her to a friend's house where an albino python resided. On a dare, she'd petted the thing, expecting to meet slime and ick but instead finding cool sleekness. Something told her Sebastian's scales would be like the snake's and her tentative fear of touching him would be unfounded. It helped settle frayed nerves a fraction.

His mouth dropped open and agonized sound grated out of his throat. It made her heated blood run cold almost immediately and she reconsidered her stance. How much of him was still in there? How much of his intelligence and passion? Was the man she'd started to develop deep feelings for even aware that she accepted him in all iterations, including this one? Her heart no longer simply pounded. It quivered with indecision.

She took a cautious step forward, and panic bloomed on Sebastian's face. He flicked his gaze beyond her to where the crowd watched, before it bounced back to her again. His body began to tremble, and Alice's heart broke all over again at the sight.

"I won't hurt you," she whispered. "Not ever. Let me hold you, Sebastian."

He made another one of those agonized screeching noises and despite every instinct flaring, each one demanding she cover her ears and flee, she held her ground. Sebastian twisted, trying to avoid her, but Alice twisted with him, ensuring that when he stepped forward, it would always be toward her.

It was quite possible that her trust in him was misguided or warped by her feelings, but it was a chance she was willing to take.

Her arms felt as if weighed down with the worries of the world when she opened them wide again. Before Sebastian could do anything more to avoid her, Alice pressed her body against his and tucked him into her grasp. The cool scales brushed against her skin, her eyes closing at the sensation. She'd been right. He was so very solid but not scary at all.

He flapped his wings frantically at first, not quite struggling to get away, but his displeasure so very evident in their rustling. At last, when he must have realized she wasn't going anywhere, he settled. His chest expanded and fell against her, the heat of his breath warming the skin of her neck.

Gray called to her, his voice low and urgent. "Can you get him to go with you outside?"

Alice nodded. "I think so." To Sebastian, beneath the hearing of everyone surrounding them, she said, "I'm here with you, sweetheart. Nothing can make me turn my back. Nothing will get me to leave. The way I trust in you, for a little while trust in me. I'll take care of you, I promise." As she spoke, she took a tentative step forward, at once relieved when he allowed himself to be led. With every step, her own fear seeped away.

The remains of his pants clung to his legs as they walked, but she held no illusion that they wouldn't crumble around him before long. He'd grown in size everywhere, and the clothing just couldn't stand up to the change. By the time they stood before the Escalade that Kemp—or was it Connell?—had brought to the front, Alice had a very healthy view of scales that ran across his lower abdomen and covered the tops of his thighs. She didn't dare look between his legs…she just couldn't.

Arm outstretched, beckoning him, Alice backed into the open door of the vehicle. Drew already sat in the driver's seat, the anxiety on his face probably mirroring her own. It didn't help that a crowd hovered at Sebastian's back, watching their progress. Fortunately, the twins and Cicero formed a barrier between him and the mass of people too stupid to run, or maybe too scared to.

Her heart thundered as she crouched in one of the backseats, waiting for Sebastian to come inside. What they would do with him once away from everyone's prying eyes was something they'd have to figure out later. Right now, she focused on the terrifying premonition that he'd turn and attack the very people he'd been sworn to protect. And if it came to that, he wouldn't survive the retaliation.

Sebastian put one foot on the inner console, and Alice held her breath. His hand brushed over a headrest before he paused. The once-blank expression on his face tightened, a frown growing in its place.

"Hey, honey," she called. "What's wrong?"

The groove between his brows deepened as his gaze darted between Alice and the interior of the car. His entire body stiffened, and she felt him start to withdraw before he actually started backing out.

"Fuck, what's he doing?" Drew whispered.

"Sebastian? Bast?"

He stared at his hand, curling those horrible claws in before stretching them again. His gaze shot to Alice then swept over the car's interior.

"I don't think he wants to come inside here," Alice

whispered back. Did he think it was too small to
hold his bulk, maybe? Admittedly, it would be a tight
squeeze, but he would fit. "Come on, Bast. Come inside with me."

A low growl rippled from Sebastian before he withdrew completely, obviously intending not to comply.

"Damn it!" Drew shouted.

Sebastian roared at Drew while flapping his wings,
which sent one of the other vampires behind him
sprawling. He didn't seem to notice the ruckus he'd
just caused, instead darting around the back of the car.
His wings trailed behind him, twitching with agitation,
as if they didn't understand why he hadn't taken flight
instead of using his less-powerful legs.

Then he did the most amazing thing.

Alice swore his wings bulged right before dropping,
as if suddenly weighted with iron. She clung backward
to the backseat, cautiously excited, as Sebastian lowered himself to one knee. Head raised, eyes on her, he
took a single breath—his chest expanding and then
letting go—and simply sprang from the ground and
into the air.

The change on his face, the utter shock and realization that he could fly, that he could do this, was just
short of astonishing. He released a sound of triumph.
Of familiarity. And God, how Alice's heart reacted to
his cry.

"Follow him," Alice cried to Drew. He didn't hesitate, and the car lurched forward. Not before Alice stuck
her head out of the window, calling to her man. "Home,
baby. Head home!"

A smile curved her lips as she watched, certain he
flew for sanctuary. His wings unfurled against the night

air, black on black, with only the stars above him for company. She crouched, then craned her neck to follow him, noting with some trepidation that he didn't quite have this new ability fully under control. Bast yawed a few times, the effort to move his wings with the currents a foreign skill he was set on mastering. The wings didn't flap, so much as glide, across the sky, propelling him forward.

"I know what he reminds me of," Drew said.

Alice turned just enough to catch the way he also crouched as he drove, his attention shifting between the side view mirror and the road ahead of them. "He's beautiful," Alice replied.

"I would have expected a lot more bulk though. And a tail, definitely," he muttered.

"Do you know what this is? Why he's changing like this?" All this time, he'd shunned help from his men. Had Sebastian excluded the very people who could help him?

Drew ducked to look in the mirror again before meeting Alice's eyes in the rearview. He chewed on his bottom lip, tearing away a thin strip of skin. It was disgusting and unexpected, but at the same time, a move she understood from a friend troubled over the latest happenings.

"Don't hold back if you know something, Drew." She had a feeling he fought loyalty to Sebastian over whether or not he should divulge his knowledge. "He's been sick and if the result is this…I only want to help. I care for him a great deal." Maybe more than that.

"Look at him," he demanded. "Can you not see it?"

"I see a vampire now covered in scales and flying

like a bird. I don't know what it is you people can or cannot do, so give a dog a bone here, huh?"

"It's the size of him that concerns me more than anything. He's easily seven or eight feet tall right now. If he gets bigger, I'm right. I have to be right." They were mutterings of a contemplative person, not part of a conversation.

"What are you right about? *Shit*. Wait. Do you see him?" Her fingers dug into the leather, the supple material yielding beneath her blunt nails. Alice searched the brackish sky, trying to locate his silhouette in between overhanging tree limbs and the simple clumsy trap of the car. She hoped like hell Drew was an excellent driver, because she forewent the safety belt in order to slide to the other side of the vehicle. No matter where she looked though, she couldn't find Sebastian. "Did we lose him? Speed up! We can't lose him."

"No worries," Drew said, but she felt the car accelerate anyway. "We know where he's going. Besides, he's not likely to let you out of his sight for too long. Not sure what hold you have over him."

It was more question than statement, but Alice ignored it. What went on between her and Bast was none of Drew's business until and unless Bast said it was.

"My God, he *is* beautiful," she repeated as she found him again. No other words could describe the grace of his form as it glided through the night air. He'd found his stride, his wings shifting subtly, quietly and with gentle finesse. She marveled that something his size could make it look so effortless, but if she hadn't known better, she could have sworn Sebastian had been flying every day of his life.

His head turned from side to side, taking in the area

ahead of him in a methodical visual sweep. Always the warrior, he seemed to be assessing the area for any danger. He blended in with the night sky, only reappearing when backdropped by a contingency of stars or the bright moon. She would have loved to be lying in a field of grass, just gazing up at him as he made the sky his home.

There was a dull squeeze inside her chest as she realized this Sebastian really didn't frighten her as he probably should. That she was mesmerized and possibly intoxicated by the otherworldly beauty of the man. But he wasn't a man anymore, was he? He was a dream, scary and breathtaking and wonderful in all his majesty.

"How much has he told you about his problems?" Drew asked.

Alice pulled her thoughts back to the interior of the car. Half turning to address him, she said, "I'm trying to help him find his father or whatever might explain what this is."

"He's spent so much time and energy trying to prove to himself that he's born vampire that he refuses to see what's in front of him."

"And what's that?"

"That there is a world larger than ours out there. That despite what we tell ourselves, vampires aren't the crowning glory of evolution. We don't overrun the population because we can't. We depend on others as much as they often depend on us. And as much as we assure ourselves that other creatures of the night are lesser and not worthy of our notice, we are ignoring part of who we are. Where we belong. Does that make sense?"

Drew had her full attention now. Keeping her gaze toward where Sebastian flew ensured she didn't lose sight of him. "You know more about his past than you've told him it sounds like."

"No, not at all. I just refuse to believe that with the existence of vampires and werewolves, there can be *nothing* else out there like us. It doesn't make logical sense."

"I'd tried doing a Google search and there were thousands of creatures to research, including hundreds I'd never even heard of. How are you supposed to weed out the ones that could possibly be true from the ones a bunch of fiction writers cobbled together?" Alice hadn't even gotten around to elements of mythology, much less covered the usual suspects. There'd been no time to do a decent search, despite Sebastian's every attempt to make sure she had the resources she needed. "I could spend the next twenty years searching and not be sure I'd stumbled onto the right thing."

"Look at him," Drew replied reverently. The hum of the engine created a hush that demanded an almost piety. The white-noise quiet encouraged her to follow his command.

His tone captured and held her attention for a few seconds, but Alice ignored the lure to watch Sebastian once again. Frustrated, she shook her head when whatever seemed apparent to Drew didn't make itself clear to her. "What should I be seeing?"

"I could be wrong," he said slowly, "but have you ever seen a creature like that with wings? Imagine something a lot bulkier than Bast, and add a long tail. But everything else is the same. The claws. The scales. Most importantly, the wings."

She studied Sebastian, trying to find the elusive something Drew hinted at but seemed quite willing to let her stumble upon without assistance. Her eyes blurred and in the fuzzy lines, she thought maybe… No. Alice shook her head. "I don't—"

Drew watched her in the rearview mirror. "Look again. And think back to fairy tales, where white knights saved damsels in distress. Use your imagination."

There was a subtle undertone of humor in his voice, despite the humorless situation. Still, Alice found her lips curving slightly, a thread of hope weaving through her. If Drew could be lighthearted in this dire moment, just maybe it wasn't as bad as her instinct cautioned.

Alice tilted her head as she tried to make the imaginary changes to Bast that Drew had suggested. His words became a path of clues for her to follow. *A tail. White knights. Damsels in distress.* What did they all have in common?

Oh, shit.

She sat up straighter, her fingers digging into the seat again. Her mind supplied the necessary changes and…*oh, shit.*

"Drew?"

He chuckled, although she couldn't tell if there was any humor in it. "You see it now?"

She thought back to the first Google search she'd done on supernatural beings. The way she'd had to narrow down her search term with words that described the changes overtaking Sebastian. God, she'd been so focused on the overwhelming number of returns that she hadn't once focused on the results that had repeated themselves. The smoke coming from his nose. The wings on his back. Now, the reptilian elongation of his face. It was so obvious and stupid in hindsight.

Downright embarrassing that it had taken another person to even point it out to her. Some kind of researcher she'd make.

"My beautiful Sebastian," she murmured. "How on God's green earth are you a double creature of fantasy? One part vampire. One part dragon."

TWENTY-TWO

THEY LOST SIGHT of him by the time they exited the car. Drew had parked beyond the gates of Sebastian's home. She was out of the car, eyes toward the sky, within seconds of stopping.

"I'm going to call the others and get them over here," Drew said as they walked toward the house. Like her, he scanned their surroundings, looking for a sign of their friend.

"No." Alice's heart tripped at the thought. The last thing he wanted or needed was condemnation from those people.

Drew's face was fixed in a grim frown. "I admire your loyalty to him, but it's done already. They know."

Stomach churning, Alice nodded. "I know they do, but what if...he wouldn't want that?"

"Either they come here to help or they stay away, not wanting to be associated with him. Regardless, it will let us know immediately where their loyalties lie, right?"

It made logical sense, but she had to look out for Sebastian's best interests when he couldn't. She had to. "I understand what you're saying, but you saw them back there. None of them looked anxious to help him out when he needed it most. What happens if they get here and decide the best course of action is to put him down like some rabid dog, without trying to even help him first? Are you willing to take that chance?"

His lips thinned. "No, I guess not. But if things take a wrong turn, I'm calling. Deal?"

She considered arguing but didn't see the point. It wouldn't come to that, not if she had anything to do with it.

Alice nodded.

By unspoken agreement, they walked the perimeter of the house, choosing to save the inside for last. Alice couldn't say why, but she was certain Sebastian remained outdoors, especially if his reaction to getting inside the car had been a predictor of his behavior. She slipped off heels designed for looking good, but not being practical, to make their search easier.

The soft glow of decorative lighting marked the path around his home, strategically placed floodlights helping them discern bushes and trees. The grass yielded beneath her steps without a sound, the dew settled upon its surface providing a muting cushion.

She realized as they searched how her life had somehow come full circle. It couldn't have been more than a few years since the last time she'd searched for Richard like this after one of his fugues. Only in those times, she'd been in and out of crack houses and homeless shelters. Calls to the local ER left for last, not wanting to invite even more trouble to a troubling situation. The police wouldn't and couldn't be of help. She had to help herself.

"It'll be difficult to agree to calling them, Drew. Not if I don't believe they're going to help."

He stopped walking, and Alice felt the heat of his gaze on her back. She refused to stop to humor this conversation though. "Who are you to make decisions on his behalf?" he asked. Despite the words, his tone remained steady and unaccusing.

They were in the back, near the pool. She immediately shifted her attention to the place she'd found Sebastian before. Although the corner was dark, a shiver coursed through her as she thought she recognized his shape. She pulled her gaze away from him to address Drew, hoping he'd understand. "He means a lot to me," she said softly, weighing the truth of the statement. Still not quite sure how much he'd come to mean.

Bold steps carried her to where indeed Sebastian crouched. She hadn't waited for Drew's reply, not caring if he understood nor needing his approval. Her feelings for Sebastian were true. His wealth didn't matter; neither did his illness or the fact that he was a vampire or a dragon. All she asked for was a little more time with him.

She slowed within a few feet of Sebastian. Her gaze went to his hands and then face, searching for signs of change. The wings folded behind his back still seemed the same, but maybe the lesser signs had diminished somewhat.

"He looks the same," whispered Drew, echoing her disappointing thoughts.

"Last time it was several hours before his wings disappeared," she whispered back. Her arms broke out in goose bumps as she remembered the session of lovemaking that had preceded his reversion to normal.

"Last time?"

"Yeah. This isn't the first time and I doubt it will be the last. We'd hoped it wouldn't happen again, but..." She left off the rest. Sebastian's men couldn't help. *She* probably didn't help much. But for now, Drew could allow them some measure of privacy by letting Sebastian recover in peace.

"He's my friend as well as my commander. I won't make the decision to bring others into this lightly, okay?"

She paused, but then nodded. "Yeah, okay."

Ignoring him again after that didn't take much effort. It wasn't that she didn't value his willingness to watch over them both should the need arise and in truth, she felt comforted by the ability to share this burden with someone else, but Alice figured it was her and Sebastian against the world. They'd handle whatever was thrown their way together.

She kneeled beside him and almost drew back when she realized his eyes were open and watching her movements. They'd reverted to a brilliant black, shiny from the moonlight and perhaps infused with a swirling pearl. There was intelligence behind the eyes studying her so intently. Knowledge that didn't belong to beast alone, but must have come from the man.

Alice made herself as comfortable as possible, stretching out on the damp grass in front of him. Resting her head on one arm, she settled in to wait. "You'd wanted to know," she said after a few minutes, "what brought me to this place. Why I live the way I do. Why don't I tell you about it now?"

Whether or not he understood what she said or if he'd remember later on didn't matter. She wanted him to feel comforted by her nearness. Ignoring Drew's presence, not caring if he listened, she focused on Sebastian.

"My brother and I were thick as thieves. We did everything together. So when our parents died, it made sense that we looked out for each other. But a nineteen-year-old isn't set out to be a good parental substitute, you know? He wasn't very good in school and barely graduated. I'd only just graduated." Alice blew out a breath. "Money was hard to come by. *Hard*. So to make ends meet, he started dealing. Things were okay for a while there."

She paused, her throat thickening. There had been so much hope for their futures at that point of their lives.

"Then because things were so bad—I mean, eating-once-a-day bad unless he stole it—I guess he started using. One day he was sullen and the next, he was happy again. Like everything was the way it used to be. His happiness was infectious. I didn't get it. I had no idea, but Bast, I was living high with him. Things were going to be all right. We were going to survive.

"I should have known that since it was too good to be true, it wouldn't last long. Money he owed was short. Then it wasn't turned in at all. His friends..." Alice choked out a harsh laugh. "They started dropping by. Then touching me." Her voice dropped to a whisper. "Then hitting me."

Her hand came to her face, swiping quickly at tears tracking over her cheeks. Somehow she'd forgotten how miserable things had become. How impossible. It wouldn't have been long before Richard's friends had started demanding payment from her in other ways. She wasn't naïve enough to think that once they'd finished using her bodily, they wouldn't turn her out on the street corners to earn even more money for them. If she put up a struggle, chemical means would be employed to keep her in line.

"I left before it got worse. Richard and I didn't speak

for months. Then one day he found me, barely making it, but making it. How do you turn down your older brother when he says, 'let's start over'? He's not dealing or using anymore, he says. And because you need to believe him, because you *must* have already hit rock bottom, you let him back into your world.

"The first time he'd only just come off using. I won't gross you out with the details, but he ended up in the ER that time. So here comes this vicious cycle. Me leaving. Him swearing it would never happen again. Him dealing and using.

"Then one day, by the most miraculous damned luck ever, I got a job as a receptionist in a small office. Decent money. I could buy things. Got a tiny apartment I didn't have to share. But if it's too good to be true, again…I got sick. This time it was me who went running back to Richard. And when my sickness took all of my hard-earned money, and later started dipping into some of his funds, he kicked me out." Alice laughed, the bitterness of it burning her throat. "I get by now on a miniscule bit of disability, but it's nowhere near enough to support me and my illness. So I live like this. I lived that way until you found me.

"I think I'm telling you all this to say that if I can survive everything I went through with Richard, with going hungry, with living on the street…then dealing with a vampire dragon is a walk in the park."

It was, too. It might explain why she never felt true fear around him or why she could lie before him now, ready to come to his aid if he needed it.

She stretched her arm forward, bringing her hand closer to his face. He tensed, as if ready to spring away if she tried to touch him, but it wasn't what she wanted right now. He could take her hand if he felt compelled or simply lie beside her in the knowledge that she was nearby.

When he moved again, Alice's breath caught. Although he crawled toward her with exaggerated patience, she didn't know what it meant. Drew hissed out a sound from nearby, but Alice kept her eyes on Sebastian. He wasn't growling or doing anything threatening, so she just kept watching.

What she didn't expect was for him to come to a stop when he fully covered her and then tuck her beneath his arm. The heat his body threw off could have cooked a chicken, but she remained still. He rested his cheek over hers, his touch surprisingly light. One of his wings blanketed the area in front of them, blocking her view. His breathing evened out, a gentle pace that put her further at ease.

It had been a long night for everyone involved, hadn't it?

Drew would just have to find someplace of his own to get comfortable, but for now, Alice followed Sebastian's lead. Closing her eyes, she went to sleep.

"WAKE UP, PRINCESS."

The words were a whisper next to her ear, so close she felt his lips tickle over her skin. Alice groaned softly, stretching her limbs at the same time.

She turned into the heat of his body, taking comfort in it. He was naked and aroused, seemingly a common state of being for Sebastian. His thighs parted slightly to allow a leg to slip in between his. She walked her fingers over his chest, memorizing all over again the definition of muscles and the light spread of hair.

She kept her eyes closed but responded to his nearness by gliding her lips over his skin. And it was skin
she felt. Not the scales she'd last seen on him.

Sebastian's mouth moved over the ridge of her hair,
delicately nuzzling her and sending more goose bumps
scattering across her skin. His teeth nipped at the shell
of her ear before grasping the lobe. His tongue dragged
along the sensitive area, dipping and teasing.

A moan tumbled from Alice's mouth, responding
to Sebastian and coming so, so easily. And when his
mouth moved lower, gently biting along her neck, she
involuntarily turned toward him, seeking more. His
bite became more feral, marking her as if he would
stake a claim. The possessiveness of the move turned
her on that much more, and Alice let out a small whimper of need.

The sound of a man clearing his throat snapped Alice
to attention, her entire body tensing.

"As much as I love hearing a lady being pleasured, in
this case, it's probably best I'm not witness to it. Right,
Bast?" Drew drawled the other man's name.

She opened her eyes to find herself looking directly
into Bast's dark eyes. Not the eyes of a dragon, but those
of the vampire. "You're back," she said on a breath.

"Never went anywhere."

She twisted, seeking Drew out, but Bast's wing kept
her covered and out of his view. Her joy at finding that
he'd reverted diminished slightly at the realization that
he hadn't returned completely to normal, but she'd take
this over nothing any day of the week. It didn't stop
her from leaning forward to capture his mouth with
hers either.

Bast issued a low growl, a sound of wanton desire,

as he plunged his tongue into her mouth. He not just kissed her, but devoured her mouth, taking and giving until she was breathless. "You stayed with me," he murmured against her lips when he finally broke the kiss.

"Of course. Did you really expect differently?"

"I could have hurt you. Or some of the Council, for that matter. I should have been put down."

"Like a diseased animal? Is that what you think of yourself?" She started to shove away from him, disgusted. Hurting for him as well.

Sebastian grabbed her wrists, yanking her toward him. His eyes flashed, a dangerous swirl of red creeping into them before fading. "What I think is that..." He paused, seemingly at a loss for words. So unlike the warrior she'd spent the past few days with. "I think that I wouldn't see you harmed for all the world. If it means putting me down to ensure it, then I wouldn't have it any other way."

"You stupid, noble man," she grumbled.

"You don't mean that. I've got wings. Sexy, remember?" His eyebrows waggled up and down, much to Alice's grudging amusement. His lips twisted in a smirk and then came down on hers again. The flare of passion he aroused in her arose so suddenly, she released another soft whimper.

"Just because I can't see you doesn't mean I can't hear you. Also? The sun is about to roast me whole. Can we all at least go inside now?" Drew, on the other hand, didn't sound the least bit amused. Or aroused.

"He's not protected from the sun like I am," Sebastian said almost at a whisper. Louder, he added, "and the idiot would probably burn to a crisp rather than leave us here in privacy."

His wing dropped, and Alice squinted against the blanket of dawning light covering them. She turned onto her back to find Drew actually stood facing away from where they lay. Not the lecher he'd implied after all. She studied him intently, wondering why he didn't get out of the sun's rays before it was too late. She didn't quite know how the whole thing worked, but didn't it make sense for him to *run*?

"You get inside before my woman thinks you're a spark away from going up in smoke," Sebastian said, echoing her thoughts. Sebastian squeezed her closer, and together they watched Drew turn and go inside.

"He's not really hurt from the sun, is he?"

He grunted. "No, he wouldn't really burn up just like that." He snapped his fingers for emphasis. "For a vampire, the reality of being burned is very gradual, very prolonged and very painful. Thankfully, we have several minutes of burning before serious damage is done. Mother Nature is a little kind, even to us odd creatures."

It was good news. She needed every ally possible when it came to helping Sebastian. Even now, she tensed while remembering the evening before and the way the Council members had stared at him. At the horror on their faces that one of their own had become this *thing*. She wasn't naïve enough to believe there wouldn't be consequences for becoming a danger to the very people he'd been obligated to protect. "About last night…"

"How bad was it?" he asked softly. "I can only remember snippets, and what's there is behind a fog."

Alice took a deep breath and thought about what to tell him. How to tell him. There would be no sugarcoating that it was quite possible he'd lost the faith of the people he knew. "I…"

Drew appeared at the back door. He looked troubled, anxious. "Bast," he said slowly. "I just received a phone call. A message for you."

The timing was too perfect, and Alice just knew his announcement would be about the Council. What had those pompous, overpampered vampires done now?

Drew shook his head. "I'm sorry. You've been relieved of duty and are commanded to report to the Council this evening, an hour past sunset. It sounds like they want your head."

TWENTY-THREE

WHILE ALICE AVAILED herself of the facilities, Bast stayed with Drew in the living room. He'd taken the time to retrieve a comfortable pair of jeans but kept his feet bare. The wings made it impossible to don a shirt.

He slipped his eyes closed, allowing what Drew told him to digest. The summary of what had happened in the night. Worse, the phone call he'd received this morning. All because he'd not been himself.

There were fleeting images in his mind, the echoing screams of men and women bouncing in his ears, but every time he tried to focus on a detail, it eluded his grasp. But he remembered the flying. The exhilaration as wind glided over his skin and swirled around him. He'd forgotten what it felt like…

Wait.

Forgotten? How could he have forgotten something he'd never known? Yet he remembered something else too. Not just a memory he'd had to retrieve, but a sense of purpose. Of being.

"I was a dragon," he said, the words sounding right. "I flew and…I was a dragon. And you know what else, Drew? More important than all of that, I think I've found my mate."

Drew's head jerked up, not surprisingly. "Alice… she's worth it?"

"And more." He couldn't even find the right words

to express how much she'd come to mean to him. "I'll ask her later when we're alone, but I think I want to be with her for the rest of my life. No—I know I do. I'll go to the Council and ask for permission to turn her."

It was a scary and wonderful thought. A realization that the person he wanted to spend a few hundred years with was this close to forevermore being his. They would exist as vampires together until time saw fit to cease their lives…another six or seven hundred years from now.

"They may not approve," Drew said, his voice somber.

"They will." He had to think positively. Had to. "When I prove that I'm not a threat, they'll have no reason not to. And if they demand I resign my post…" Adrenaline surged through him at the thought. "If they want me to leave, I will."

"Goddamn," Drew whispered. He looked up, blue eyes shining. A grin splitting his face. "I'm happy for you. What a fucking day, huh? You've discovered your heritage after years of searching. You've become the talk of the vampire community. You're on your way to getting hitched."

"And I was a dragon!" Bast shouted.

Alice returned, wearing an oversized T-shirt and shorts. Wet hair dripping. Skin pink from hot water use. She smiled, almost beaming. "You were. And you were beautiful."

Bast took a moment to steady his mind and keep weak legs from collapsing altogether. *Dragon*. Of all the creatures he'd researched, hoping to find the one that bore his ancestor, that one had never crossed his thoughts. Not even a flicker of an idea in his imagination. The heat, the smoke, the wings. It all made sense now.

He remembered the words Locke the werewolf had told him, that he was something more than just vampire. That had meant so little before. Now a new world had opened up before him, one his mother might have known would visit upon him one day but still remained silent about. If she would see him, perhaps he'd pay her a visit in the future and try to mend their broken past. The thing that had come between them had been obliterated.

He still wanted to seek out his father and trace the bloodline, to know who he was and how he'd come to breed with a vampire, but just having the knowledge he'd been seeking for so very, very long settled a restlessness inside of Bast. He knew who he was. What he was. He could explain to anyone who wanted to know why he didn't have all of the vampire traits, but selective ones.

And fucking A, he could shift!

"I have a lot to think about," Bast said. He wanted to find the right way and time to approach Alice about becoming a vampire. And he would do it right. A big fucking diamond ring. Down on one knee. The whole shebang. "A lot to do. And the Council wants to see me because they think I'm a little different now? They knew that." A growl rumbled in his throat.

The tiles beneath his feet were eaten up by his long strides as he paced the room. The weight of Drew and Alice's stares tracked his movement. They were probably wrung out from stress and worry, especially Alice, but he couldn't stop now. Not when he'd just discovered this vital part of himself.

"They don't know what to think about you," Drew responded. "No one knew what you were going to do last night. If you were going to hurt anyone. If we had to hurt you."

Bast checked his watch. "I have a little over twelve hours to research who I am and what this all means. Less than a day to gather what intel I can to convince the Council I'm not a threat to them."

"I'll help you." Alice stood near the overstocked bar area.

"But you shouldn't have to. I've served them faithfully all this time, and that they would turn me away so easily is an insult. Over a hundred years of searching, and they would turn my triumph into a reason to be afraid of me?"

When others had doubted the Council could exist, a cohesive body of men and women whose sole purpose was the advancement of the vampire nation, Bast had stood beside them. He'd been one of the ones to insist upon a guardianship, to ensure that everyone surrounding them knew their importance. He'd been one of their fiercest advocates for a very long time. Had he really placed a blind trust in them so erroneously?

"Your best bet is to make them see that you're not a threat. What can you do about those wings of yours? You have to admit they're intimidating." Drew would stand beside him, at least. Bast would have expected nothing less from his friend.

"Sexy," Alice corrected.

Bast smiled, despite himself. "Stand back. Let me see what's what."

He waited until they were on the other side of the living room, far enough away that should something go wrong, they'd be in a good position to protect themselves. Not like he had any idea what could go wrong, but he just didn't know how this thing would work.

Alice must have felt the same way, for her hand rested on top of Drew's arm. He could imagine the pressure she applied as she waited anxiously for whatever would happen next. It was a stance of nervousness, as if she needed the anchor to keep her from doing something impetuous.

Bast waited for a twinge of jealousy to announce itself, but when his gaze met her face, only admiration filled him. She probably wasn't even aware of her hold. Instead, Alice returned Bast's focused look with something very similar to…wonder? Pride? Love, maybe?

God, he hoped it was the latter. He didn't have to think too hard or too long to know he was there as well.

"You are so beautiful," he told her. There was much more to be said. Things he wanted her to understand, but this declaration made its way to his lips first. "Alice, thank you for…" For helping him search for the lines of his lineage. For staying by his side when things started going downhill. For choosing to be with him even now when things were at their worst. "Everything. Whatever happens, I won't ever forget what you've done for me. And I vow that I'll repay you one day. Somehow."

He took a deep breath, mostly for show. He rolled his head over his shoulders, using the motion to help him pinpoint the pull of muscle where wings met back. It took more effort than he realized to concentrate on just that singular area. He'd been spending so much time trying to get the entire wing to move, he'd never thought about the individual components.

But he recalled the conversation with Locke and

his werewolves now. They implied they could shift at will and not just with the call of the moon. Bast had no idea what instigated his own shift, but if he was like the werewolves, he should be able to turn by thinking about it as well.

He tensed, gritted his teeth and focused. His eyes closed, and Bast willed his wings out of existence, temporarily. They shuddered and then…

Nothing.

"Fuck," he grumbled.

"Try again," Alice said softly. "They've gone away on their own before. Something must trigger it. A thought or an emotion, perhaps."

She was right, of course. The morning after they'd had sex for the first time, his wings had just vanished on their own. "What were we doing when they disappeared before? Do you remember?"

Her face lit up in a brilliant scarlet. "We were sleeping." An eyebrow lifted as if to dare him to say otherwise.

He frowned. "But we *were* sleeping. I'd woken up because I felt the change."

"So something must have triggered the change then," Drew said. He turned to Alice. "What about before that, right before you went to sleep? What were you—oh. Never mind."

The look mowing him down should have shriveled Drew's balls. Bast laughed. It took a moment for the amusement to subside, but then he thought about it. "You know, Alice, every time I'm feeling ill, it's you who pulls me out of it. It started with your blood. Then all it took was a kiss."

She pushed away from Drew, leaving him behind

like a fading dream. Her steps were slow and seductive as she sauntered forward. "Is that your way of asking for another?"

Bast moved toward her, a new appetite growing. "I wouldn't turn it down. Not ever."

"You two are worse than a couple of horny teenagers. I'm going to find a Snickers. Call me when it's over." He was still grumbling as he walked into the hallway leading to the kitchen.

"I shouldn't encourage you," she murmured when he pulled her closer, seconds after the room cleared. "But those wings…"

"I know. Sexy." He grinned before lowering his lips to hers.

Could he possibly ever get tired of this? Of tasting this woman and inhaling her rainwater scent? Of threading his fingers through a mass of tangles and curls, holding her close to him as he plunged his tongue into the sweet taste of her mouth?

She let out this amazing sound, one that called to him. It was part whimper, part moan. A beacon for his lust. And when she held him tighter, pressing her soft breasts against him, holding him as if her world began and ended with him, it was a love for her that responded.

There was a brief moment when her hand caressed the muscle where back met wing, but at the realization, a flare of pain rippled over him. As quickly as it had arisen, it faded. His balance shifted, and Bast almost stumbled, taking Alice with him. How quickly he'd grown accustomed to the wings' weight. Now that they were gone again, his body worked to remember life without them.

She drew back, immediately noticing the change. "How did you do it?"

"Later," he mumbled and ravaged her lips again. He had an idea of what just happened, but it would hold. To hell with the Council and their summons. Right now, he needed her.

Greedy hands slipped beneath her tee, pushing up until skin met skin. He couldn't get over the delicate softness beneath his palms. The way her skin rippled with goose bumps in waves of feminine delight. His thumbs stole higher, brushing against the curve of her bare breasts.

"Drew," she gasped. A question of the warrior's location and potential intrusion.

"Will not bother us," Bast confidently reassured. "I just…I just need to be inside you."

She looked into his eyes with compassionate understanding. As if she knew the fierce ache in the center of his chest as he touched her now. The way his cock strained against denim. The call of his nature and his masculinity.

Alice placed delicate kisses along his chest, the ache turning into a wonderful tightening of want as he pulled her shirt off. Her nipples were already tight beads, tipped upward, and made his mouth water. She released a soft sigh as he lowered his head to the first one, pulling it into his mouth on a groan. His tongue flicked the hardening tip, teeth nibbling. Tasting her.

A burst of the cleanness of soap filled the back of his throat. Becoming all he breathed. He inhaled deeply, wanting more of her to fill him. It wasn't enough to flick his thumb over the other nipple, teasing it to a point. A compulsion rode him. One that demanded he fill her with his cock, cover and protect her with his body, fill her with his seed.

He had to mark her. Claim her. Declare that she was his and forever would be. Christ, even his teeth elongated and pulsed with blatant sexual need.

A groan rumbled from his throat, his hand dropping to slide between her stomach and the shorts hindering him from his prize. His sweet, sweet Alice helped him. A quick flick of a button, the dry rasp of a zipper and his fingertips met moist heat.

"I love how quickly you're ready for me," he whispered. Pushing her backward, he knew he had to satisfy part of his urge as best he could. Alice's legs hit the leather couch, and Bast gently encouraged her to sit at its edge.

Her breath sucked in as he kneeled before her, a supplicant at a goddess's throne. It took only a moment to peel the shorts away from her long legs. And then his worship began.

Alice cried out as his lips met her cunt. He tasted her with quick strokes of his tongue. Teasing laps. She pushed her fingers into his hair, twining them around the short strands. The space between her thighs widened as she pressed his mouth closer to her.

It was with great pleasure he dipped into her channel, pulling the pungent moisture. He kissed her intimately, tasting the exquisite secret of her body. A low growl issued from him, all encouragement, as her hips rocked beneath his efforts.

"Sebastian!" An ecstatic cry.

Her clit stood proud and erect, swollen with her desire. With the most gentle of touches, he swiped his tongue over it. Alice's thighs tightened as her pelvis lifted, feeding him more of that precious gift. His tongue continued to circle the nub, her cries coming faster and faster. When he suckled on it, the slightest press of his teeth on the excited nerve endings, Alice released a breathy moan.

He listened to the way she bit off her release, holding it behind clenched teeth as he continued to love her body. That she could suppress that sound she made when well loved told him too well that her mind wasn't completely with him, but lingered on other worries. Drew, maybe. Him, perhaps. Regardless, her distraction did not satisfy him.

Alice lifted one leg from his shoulder. "Oh, my..."

Bast shoved his shoulder into its previous position. "Again," he ordered.

"I don't...I can't..."

"You can." He lowered his head. "And will."

Tracing the femoral artery with his nose, Bast followed its path by sliding his tongue along its seductive trail. His teeth lengthened, the lure of her blood almost impossible to resist. With precise care, he let her feel the evidence of the dual way in which he wanted her, scraping against flesh until a pink wale had been left behind.

She hissed in a breath, followed by a quiet moan. This time when he approached her cunt, Bast blew out a slow breath against her sensitive tissue. Alice squirmed, but her legs parted even wider. His dick almost exploded at the sight.

"So wet. So pink," he murmured before his head dipped. He swept his tongue into her opening, taking in the pungent-sweet taste. Alice's hips rolled, a low groan riding the same wave. She pushed a hand into his hair, then the other, fingers twisting in and grasping tightly. Holding his head in place as if daring him to leave her replete.

He took his time learning her. Listening to the change in her breathing. For each hitch as she gasped. He lived for the way she gripped him close, panting out his name on more of those breathy sighs.

A low quiver was his first sign. The rhythmic clenching of her cunt teasing his tongue. He moved his mouth higher, finding the swollen nub of her clit. Pulling gently on it sent more quivers through her legs. The more intensely he worried it, the more forceful the tremors until she was biting her lower lip. Moaning. Then calling out his name.

"Again," he encouraged. His cock leaked, the urge to come with her almost overwhelming.

"*Oh God*, Sebas—" Alice threw her head back, her legs closing around his head. Then she released a cry of pure, unleashed rapture.

Grinning self-satisfaction, Bast gently licked her pussy, feasting on her juices. He waited for the little shockwaves to subside, slowly moving away from her sensitive areas to kiss along her thighs. His heart thundered with pride, excitement and the thrill of discovering that he wanted to be here, like this, with this woman for a very long time.

Forever.

TWENTY-FOUR

ALICE OPENED HER EYES, willing the room not to spin. Breathless, exhilarated, she couldn't be certain her legs would work anymore. Hell, any part of her anatomy. Everything tingled, super-sensitized. She blew out a breath, managed to lift her heavy head. Intense eyes stared up at her and she marveled at him.

"Wow," she said softly.

Sebastian kissed her lower belly, still tingling with sensation. "Did that work for you?"

Her brief nod halted mid-stride. Squinting, she said, "Your eyes are back."

He smiled. "They never left."

"You know what I mean," she replied, her lips fighting the urge to lift at the corners. "They're no longer dragon eyes. They're plain again."

Blinking as if the realization had actually struck home, his brow furrowed. A soft snort of disbelief blew out of his lips a moment later. "You're right. My vision is a lot more acute when I shift and it's not like that anymore. When I'm a dragon, I can see *everything*."

A shiver trickled over her skin. A dragon. Her man— no, wait. That wasn't right. She couldn't think of him in those terms. It bordered on permanence. God knew nothing about her life had ever been or would ever be permanent. Even her existence.

A nip at her thigh snagged her attention. "Ouch!"

"What were you thinking just then?"

Alice shifted her gaze away from him, moving to the entranceway, where Drew could be entering at any moment. "Why hasn't he returned?"

She felt Sebastian's displeasure at her avoidance of his question. Relief calmed her when his reply followed her train of thought. "Because he is my man and very loyal. He also knows what we're doing in here."

"How...*how*? Oh dear God..."

Sebastian's mouth quirked as if he fought to hide a smile. "You're not the quietest lover, princess. I think just about everyone in the tri-state area knows what we're doing."

"If you'd quit doing that thing...with your tongue." Damn, a hot flash just about sizzled her just thinking back on it.

"You mean this?"

Alice squealed. Her hand flew to his head before he could put that talented mouth on her sensitive body. "Wait! Wait!" It came out as another squeal, quickly followed by giggling.

He took pity on her and with one arm curled beneath her legs, situated her over the couch's length. Kind of disappointing, really. She'd enjoyed gazing down on him as he kneeled at her feet.

But when he shucked off his jeans, proud erection jutting forth, she forgot all about that.

Sebastian didn't disappoint by leaving her alone. He crawled over her, forcing the narrow strip of couch to hold them both, not stopping until his pelvis rested in the cradle of her thighs. With every inhale, her breasts touched his chest before retreating again, each fan of her breath caressing the skin of his face as they lay together.

"I would stay with you like this," Sebastian said. All trace of humor had fled, his words now weighed down with a seriousness that made her heart clench.

It would be so, so easy to misunderstand his meaning. To think he wanted more sex, that he hadn't yet found his release. But the way he studied her face, the gentleness behind his regard, betrayed the lie she wanted to clutch. As much as he'd come to mean to her, it still frightened her that they were both speeding along this course. What would happen if something went wrong for either of them? Would they survive the devastation?

Sebastian traced along her skin with a hand, watching the rise of goose bumps left in its wake. He followed a pale blue vein on her arm before sliding to the swell of her breast. Ignoring the swollen peak of her nipple, he moved his touch higher until Alice tilted her head again, melting into the sensation. The pulse in her neck beat rapidly and she felt the weight of his stare there.

Grasping her chin until she followed its tug, until they locked gazes again, he said, "You give to me so willingly, Alice. I don't understand you and your ability to be here with me, but I want m——"

"Shh." She lifted a finger to his lips, pressing gently until they stopped moving.

She couldn't bear to hear what he had to say. If he asked for a future together, if he even hinted that he wanted to spend more time with her, it would break her heart to pretend she hadn't heard. She was getting sicker, despite every hope otherwise. She remembered what Jasmine, her new friend, had said about the seizure she'd had. There'd been a few more like it since then. None under his watchful gaze, thank God. She feared for subtle signs that they were getting worse. Like how on occasion her head swam for a few minutes afterward. It couldn't be a good sign.

The time they had together existed right here. Right now. It was too possible that tomorrow might never come.

"What is that you won't tell me?" he asked quietly.

Alice hesitated. He'd given her an opening. An opportunity to bare all. To finally let someone else help her carry the burden of a mystery illness she worried over every single day.

"That I'm surprised I'm here with you. That I'm very glad that I am," she lied, heart thumping madly. She wanted to tell him the truth, but to what point? They'd known each other only a few days, despite a level of intimacy that had gone beyond her wildest dreams. No matter how she felt, it wouldn't have been right.

Sebastian studied her eyes and she noted the way light reflected off the darkness in his. Long lashes curled outward, lending a softness to his gaze that she'd come to adore. "Does it have to do with your brother?"

Startled, she shook her head. "No. It's nothing, really."

"I'm your friend, Alice. You can tell me any—"

Her mouth met his in a furious rush to stop whatever else he might say. Alice kissed him hard, her blood simmering at the realization that they *were* just friends. Anything more was asking for too much.

Unpleasant thoughts fell away as Sebastian's mouth opened over hers. He moved with languid ease, taking control.

Sebastian elevated himself above her with the same casual ease, lending just enough of his weight that she could not forget a very virile, very male body draped over hers. His cock, so hot and so hard, pressed against her abdomen. She stretched her hand between them to grasp its length. And despite every bit of knowledge about him and his desire for her, grasping it sent a shiver of ultimate delight skipping down her spine. As if he couldn't help himself, he began to slowly pump his hips, resulting in a cascade of warm velvety skin sliding against her palm.

"I don't know what I want more," he said, voice whiskey-rough. "To see myself spill into your hands or to feel your cunt wrapped around me."

Alice squeezed him. "Why choose? Do both."

His stomach jerked as he laughed. "Tempting."

Instead though, Sebastian pulled back and she lost her hold. A bittersweet loss. There was much power to be had in holding a man so intimately.

But when Sebastian nudged her thighs apart, lowering himself so that his cock rested at the entrance to her body, she almost shuddered from the decadence of it.

She exhaled slowly as he pushed inside her, the delicious stretch a hedonistic twist of pleasure and pain, one she would gladly endure for him again and again. His head was down, focusing on where he impaled her, and Alice fought to keep her eyes open, to watch the wash of pleasure overcome his features. She soon lost though, too wrapped up in the way Sebastian felt as he filled her to completion.

A low moan rumbled from her throat, nothing on earth strong enough to hold it back. Her fingers seized the cushions beneath her, needing something to hold on to lest she lose herself to the blinding pleasure. Mouth dry, she panted out breaths as he moved so, so slowly. Still he kept filling her.

Alice's hips tilted toward Sebastian, sexual instinct craving and demanding more. Her chest hurt from the way her heart kicked, a slave to the excitement of joining with him, her lover.

"Look at me," he murmured.

Her eyes fluttered open, meeting his heated gaze. There was a tenderness in the way his attention stayed on her, no matter what she wanted to tell herself. Vampire or not, he wasn't immune to the swell of emotions moving between them. She knew her heart. She knew his as well.

"Sebastian…" Her breath caught, sensation overwhelming her as he seated himself fully.

"Don't stop me this time. Don't run away from me. You and me…this. For whatever reason, we're meant to be together, Alice, and I like it. I want it."

Oh, God, so did she, but it didn't matter, did it? This—all of it—was out of her control. Yet she couldn't bring herself to tell him. Not now. "Me too," she said instead.

"Good." A new serenity spelled on his face, Sebastian lowered his mouth to hers and kissed her as tenderly as a butterfly's touch.

Neither of them said the word, but when he began to move inside her, Alice knew it was love that drove him. Resigned, unable to ignore it, she let it reign.

She listened to her own uneven breathing as he rode her body. To the way blood rushed through her ears, a sound of waves against a shore. Moans fell from her lips, encouragement for the things he made her feel and want.

Sebastian made love to her with a skillful touch. His mouth met and caressed hers. Trailed heat across her chin and neck. Lower.

Rough fingers stroked casually over sensitive nipples, his lips soon nibbling on their peaks moments later. He was everywhere. Touching. Kissing. Arousing. He filled her both inside and out, covering her in a blanket of warmth and gentleness.

She squeezed her eyes shut, such wonderful sensation leaving her drowsy-drunk. And she was an addict to the way he made her feel. She wanted more. Needed it. Would have done anything asked of her for more. Yet it was all she could do to endure it now. To not shatter into a million replete fragments.

Soon the first ripple eased out from her belly, warming her extremities and heating her face. A whimper spilled out as a second ripple formed. Sebastian drove into her still so very, very slowly, but he seemed to swell inside of her at the sound. Ragged breathing turned to panting gasps as more ripples formed, each one more powerful than the last.

So much sensation. Pleasure.

The ripples were no longer distinguishable, each one coming behind the other so quickly that she could scarcely catch her breath in time before being bombarded. With each ripple, goose bumps stroked along her skin. Alice's hands flew to his forearms, holding onto him for strength. She needed the tether.

"Oh God," she cried. It would soon be too much.

Sebastian nuzzled the skin of her neck. "I've got you."

He increased his pace, his cock filling her so completely she wasn't sure that they hadn't always been one. He was a part of her and perhaps forever would be. He touched her not only physically, but had grasped a hold of her heart. She could deny it all she wanted, fight the pull that kept them together, balk that the universe would make them see heaven only to eventually yank it away. None of that mattered as she began to soar. What *did* matter was knowing that it was so very right. That nothing could ever take away this moment from her. That she would remember and cherish it for always.

"That's my girl," Sebastian whispered.

Her cunt began to flutter, rhythmic pulls signaling the loss of control. She stroked over her neck with fingers that didn't seem her own. "*Please*." It came out desperate. Needy.

Sebastian visually traced the pulse of her neck before lowering his mouth. She barely felt the puncture, but the first draw of her blood made the world crash in around her. Alice screamed as she came, everything going shiny-bright before her muscles locked. Her entire being stiffened, useless to do anything beyond feel such intense, amazing bliss.

Sebastian's low groans were far away and disembodied. He was close too, pushing himself into her with increasing speed. With an urgency to beat some sort of race against time.

Alice soared, knowing the way her life seemed to pour out of the two new wounds in her neck. The rest of her exploded outward, leaving her helpless to his sexual onslaught. She lived in her moment. Propelled there by an amazing man.

He growled against her neck before his tongue

swiped at the bite. Her grip on him tightened with the first pulse of his release. Sebastian called out her name, his teeth scraping against her flesh as he clenched his eyes shut. He was pulled under, his body's demands more than he had the ability to fight.

It was over too quickly. His hips stopped moving. Damp heat filled her between her legs. But she held on to him.

For long moments they lay together, joined where he still remained erect inside of her. Alice's sweat-moistened skin craved cool air. Her lungs burned with the need for oxygen. The way her heart pumped hard and fast, she wondered dazedly if it would recover.

Too soon though, Alice felt the lull of fatigue pulling at her. She was just plain dog tired, from being loved and probably from the stress of the night before. There was a gorgeous man draped across her body, his warmth as soothing as any comforter. If he wasn't careful, she'd fall asleep beneath him. Not that doing so would hurt his ego any.

"That was...amazing," she said softly. Finding the strength to stroke his hair bordered on miraculous.

He lifted his head, perspiration cooling on her skin as soon as he did. After a quick kiss on the lips, Sebastian frowned. "You're exhausted."

"I'd love to deny it, but I am," she replied.

"I forget that you're still new to this lifestyle. You should have said something to me before..."

Before they'd had sex. "And miss out on that? No way, buddy. That was definitely worth getting up early for."

He chuckled, grimacing a moment later when Alice groaned. He slowly extricated himself. The area be-

tween her thighs pulsed from overuse, a sure sign she'd
be feeling their actions even hours from now.

She went airborne seconds after Sebastian stood.
"Hey!" She squealed, then wrapped an arm around his
neck. Being carried by him, the ground seemed ominously far away. "I can walk, you know."

But hell, it felt good to be held and pampered like
this.

He snorted.

"What's that mean?"

"It means you don't just look tired, you sound it too.
Your words are starting to slur." His stride was smooth
and even as they left behind the kitchen and crossed
through a second living room. "Don't allow me to take
advantage of you like this again."

"If by taking advantage, you mean having crazy
good sex, you most certainly will take advantage of
me. And often."

"You stubborn woman. I can do so much more than
you'll ever be able to. Seriously, don't let me forget
how fragile you are. When I'm holding you like this,
it's easy to remember, but when I'm lost inside you, I'm
truly lost." He shook his head, as if the memory of their
coupling was too much for him to process.

He pushed open the door to his bedroom with a foot
before Alice realized where they were. *His bedroom*. It
couldn't belong to anyone else.

A large king-sized bed rested in the middle of the
room, perfectly made with crisp white sheets that were
covered with a pale green comforter, which was also
draped with a brown decorative throw. The latter item
perfectly matched the leather headboard, dotted with
bronze rivets. There couldn't have been less than six

pillows on the bed, four of them probably for show, based on the way their colors went along splendidly. The leather footrest seemed big enough to hold the extras when they weren't in use.

Next to the bed, a wide band of earth-toned bricks went from floor to ceiling in precise patterns, only broken in the very middle to house a fireplace. Before its maw, a cream-colored rug stretched across the floor. At its edge, a leather recliner and ottoman guarded more decorative pillows. A stack of books had been piled next to the plush seating area.

Effortlessly, Bast walked to the bed and rested her in the middle of it, right between all those fluffy pillows. His clean coconut scent immediately wafted up, and she had to wonder what kind of detergent he used. The bed itself though felt like heaven stitched together. She almost moaned but bit it back when he pulled the comforter up over her body.

"Sleep now," he said. That same tenderness from before came back and with an embracing coziness.

"What about youu?" This time she heard the slur he'd accused her of before. Also, a new slowness to her speech.

"I have the Council to deal with. Gray and I will be working up a strategy for making sure things don't completely fall to shit. Get some rest for now. I'll be in as soon as I'm able."

"You've had…one hell…of a…night." Even saying that took some effort. She'd never been this fatigued from an hour of loving before, but it was a small sacrifice.

"Yeah, I'm tired, but I need to sort this out. It won't

take longer than an hour or so. I'll be in to join you before you know it. Promise."

"Okay, but—"

Sebastian suddenly blurred then became two distinct
persons sitting next to her. Alice blinked the apparition
away, startled when it dissipated only to form again.
She blinked harder, putting more effort into squeezing her eyes shut.

"Alice?"

She focused on his frown, but even that seemed to
happen in slow motion. She moved through invisible
molasses as she opened her mouth to tell him she was
okay, but just tired. The room went brilliant in those
moments, right behind Bast's head. It lit him up in the
sweetest ray of sunshine.

"Yyyourrgglowwing," she managed to drag out.
Worse slurring than before.

Sebastian's face became deadly serious. He leaned
closer to clasp her hands. "Alice, what's wrong? Talk
to me."

"Glowww..."

He called her name again, she thought. Couldn't
tell. His voice floated away before her ears managed
to grasp the sound. It didn't matter anyway.

All she knew was the brilliant light, a beautiful glow,
filling the room.

And then she knew nothing at all.

TWENTY-FIVE

A VERY DISTINCT BEAT, rhythmic in its evenness, aroused her first. The sound was annoyingly loud, as if it beeped next to her ear, and Alice had a hard time figuring why anyone in his right mind would use it as an alarm.

She'd fallen asleep, but God, it was hard to think straight coming out of it. Must have been one hell of a nap.

The sheets had been pulled high up on her chest, tucked in with a firm hand. The cotton was clean but lacked a distinct smell. No. That wasn't quite right. Obviously clean, the sheets smelled bland. Kind of disappointing, really. And the pillow beneath her head? Not nearly comfortable. In fact, she could use another one to stop being so damned flat.

"Awake?"

Sebastian's gentle voice made her smile. "Yeah, but still tired," she replied before his tone made her replay the one-word question. He said it with care, but there was a simmering anger beneath it. Or was that her imagination? Alice pushed open her eyelids to look at him. "Oh God!"

Her heart hammered as she took in Sebastian first, and then their surroundings. The stark walls. The crucifix with a white board beneath announcing, *Hello, Your nurse today is Cathy.* A tall metal pole loomed over the bed, holding a clear bag filled with fluid. Tubing ran from the bag, snaking over the bed to abruptly end at a mish-mash of tape bunched on the back of her hand.

"I'm in a hospital?" she asked, tamping down the rising panic.

"Hope Haven."

"Why? What happened?"

"How many times did I watch you stare off into space? How many times were you having an absence seizure, and I didn't know it? I watched you deteriorate and had no idea." He glanced toward the closed door, as if hoping to be rescued from this conversation. But her warrior, true to form, tackled the problem with aplomb. "You had another seizure. This one was grand mal."

Oh God. Her breathing picked up as panic pushed past a barrier and began to squeeze her lungs, holding them within an iron grip. All of her seizures to date had been very minor in the scheme of things. Absence seizures that made her lose usually only up to a minute of time. Not one that fully wracked her entire body such that she had the potential to accidentally hurt herself.

"Why didn't you tell me you were sick?" he asked. It was back—the low simmer of anger and, more so, disappointment.

"I...it..." She struggled to find the right answer. One that wouldn't hurt him more than he appeared to have been. "They don't know why I have seizures. I've never had a grand mal before, I swear."

"Never mind," he said sharply. Sebastian visibly went still, as if collecting himself, then tried again. "Your doctor says you haven't kept your appointments."

"I couldn't afford to go. I kept taking my meds and hoped for the best."

"*Hoped for the best*? Did you think that would be

enough? Why didn't you tell me you needed to see a doctor? I would have given you whatever money you needed." He began to pace the small room as his anger hit full, rolling boil. "If you'd been keeping your appointments, you would have continued to have MRIs and whatever other tests you'd needed."

"When should have I asked you for a few hundred dollars? The day I found you sick and barely hanging on? The day I tried to steal from you? When?"

"Fuck, Alice! I can't believe you kept something like this from me. Did you think I wouldn't understand? I would have helped you."

"You can't help me," she cried. "Didn't the doctor tell you? No amount of doctor's visits or money or anything can help! It is what it is. I didn't think it would get worse." Hoped it wouldn't.

"You didn't trust me enough to tell me. After everything we've been through, you couldn't tell me." He sat on the bed's edge, head tilted toward his chest, dejection weighing him down. "Is this why you wanted to be turned? To escape this?"

Tears almost blinded her from seeing his face, but Alice nodded.

"Damn it, I'm so angry with you I can't think straight. You didn't trust to tell me anything at all. If I had known…" His voice lowered again, the words coming from him almost strangled. "The hospital staff trusted me more than you though. They say you have a tumor. Not previously detected. That's what's been causing the seizures." A thunderous heartbeat passed. "One MRI. That's all that it would have taken. Now, it's too late."

"Why is it too late?" She thought she knew the answer. Back when she'd been to a neurologist regularly, he'd laid odds on the causes of her seizures, which ones could be corrected and which ones couldn't.

"Inoperable," he replied hoarsely.

Something inside her collapsed, the truth of her situation taking away any possible future. Until now, she could hope that she wouldn't get sicker. That maybe the seizures would just miraculously stop on their own. Perhaps unrealistic, but a hope nonetheless. Now she knew better. Now she had to face reality.

Alice took a moment to digest the news, realizing that perhaps she'd been prepared for this eventuality all this time. While it hurt and saddened her, she'd done the denial and anger thing. She'd been depressed, and no amount of praying had fixed any of her problems. There wasn't much left to do.

She waited for the unshed tears to dry up and searched the room, letting the enormity of her diagnosis settle. At last her gaze landed on the vampire standing over her.

Sebastian didn't belong here. The designer shirt and flawless jeans might have seemed casual, but his hundred-dollar haircut upheld the image that his clothing alone could pay the groceries for a family of four for a week. The white blanket beneath him had small holes in some places, loops of threads unraveling in others. Beyond him on the wall were dots of patch jobs, a white that didn't match the dingy white paint. His world was so different from hers and now, as she tried to explain being mortal, it couldn't have been more apparent.

"I've only just found you," he said quietly. "I never got the chance to tell you that I…I wanted to turn you, if you would have me."

Alice sat up straighter, grateful when her head didn't swim. "What did you just say?"

He turned his face toward her. "I was going to ask if you would consider staying with me. As a vampire."

Not that he loved her. Not that he wanted to spend the rest of his life with her. Not marriage.

No. He wanted her to *stay* with him. As his lover, maybe. Nurse. Historian. But not his love.

And that realization hurt like hell.

A week ago, she would have jumped at the chance— jumped!—to be healed. Now...it didn't feel quite the same. Not to have experienced what she had over the past few days without a guarantee of more. She didn't know anymore if she could handle going back to her old life. To a life without a man like Sebastian. Without Sebastian.

"I don't need your pity." It took everything within her to keep her voice even. "Once upon a time, I could have used your money. But it's too late for that now."

"It's not too late. I've amassed millions of dollars in my lifetime, and you cannot tell me that it can't buy your health back."

"That's exactly what I am telling you."

"And it's not my pity." He barreled forward. "I owe you my life. Without you...I don't know what would have happened to me if someone else had found me at the club. I don't know if anyone else would have stayed with me as I grew into my dragon self."

But it still wasn't love he found with her. Damn him. Was it fair to want it from him so soon after they'd met? Probably not. She couldn't help her feelings though.

"I'm not giving up, Alice, and don't you fucking dare consider giving up. I won't...not without you."

She blew out a shaky breath, letting silence referee. He was hurt, and she understood that. Arguing about it would help neither of them. Maybe one day—after she was gone—maybe he'd understand why she'd not told him. Right now, shock made him want to fight for her because that's what men like him did. They warred against the things that wronged them, not stopping until they emerged victorious.

What a sucker punch. Bast would turn her because his honor dictated it, but she'd almost be right back to where she was before she'd met him. Alone and without a future, other than the one she begged or stole for herself. If he wasn't going to be a part of her life after she became a vampire, would it even be worth it?

Of course, the other option meant certain death.

"Wait a minute," she said, brow furrowed. "What time is it? Have you met with the Council yet?"

"Drew went to make my excuses for last night."

"Last night?" Her gaze moved to the clock on the wall. A little after two. "Is it after two in the morning?"

"Yes."

"You shouldn't have missed it. You should have gone and left me here." Why would he jeopardize himself like that? From what she'd gathered, the vampires of the Council would not be happy that he'd ignored a summons.

"They don't matter to me. You're more important to me than they are. I won't leave you like this."

"Don't be...foolish."

"Foolish? Why aren't you taking this seriously? You're a sick woman, Alice."

She pursed her lips. "I've been sick a long time. Long before I met you."

"I really don't think you understand yet." Sebastian rose. He looked tired as he leaned forward and placed his lips against her forehead. The kiss was chaste and sweet. With a finger, he touched the skin of her cheek. The concern and warmness in his eyes was almost strong enough to make her stomach churn. "Your doctor says you have just one more in you, princess."

"One more what?"

"They're afraid that if you have one more grand mal seizure, that it might not stop. And it'll probably be enough to kill you."

BAST LEFT A PALE, visibly shaken Alice in the hospital room to step outside while a nurse tended to her. He'd almost gotten violent at the woman's insistence that he leave. Were it not for Alice's pleading look, his insistence upon staying might have turned physical. Didn't give a fuck where they were. He'd take her to see his own physicians if necessary. He still would be, in fact. For now, for her, he'd behave.

He scanned the hallway of the hospital, pissed beyond all hell he even stood there. At this time of night, hardly anyone stirred. Just some janitor mopping the floors, placing yellow hazard signs wherever a wet spot remained. He figured in the daytime, nurses in cutesy scrubs strolled the halls, some carrying charts. A few with syringes or medicine cups in their hands. Doctors probably walked from room to room with a stethoscope hanging about their necks, lab jackets starched into perfect submission.

Right now though, the caustic scent of death and illness surrounded him, and his stomach rolled. Even if he'd been desperate enough to seek food here, most likely it would be tainted with medicines designed to keep the weak living just another day longer.

Alice. His Alice was one of them.

Seeing her fragile body wracked with uncontrollable rigid movements had almost broken him. The sheer helplessness of having to watch while Drew called for medical assistance left him practically rooted to the spot. He hadn't known what else to do. How to help her. How to stop it. And once here, her body finally at ease, he thought the worst over. Then the doctor had taken one look at her medical records and told him that she'd been suffering the seizures for more than a year now, and his anger had grown to immeasurable.

Why hadn't she trusted him to know? With everything they'd been through, he hadn't thought he'd needed to say the words out loud. He thought his actions spoke well enough on his behalf. He loved her. Didn't she realize it? Until this disaster, he'd thought she might have felt the same.

The phone in his hand chirruped and without looking at the display, he hit a button and barked into the receiver. "Drew, tell them—"

There was a pause on the other end. "Sebastian Kent?"

A voice he didn't recognize. He frowned. "Yeah."

"This is Corin Gerulaitis. My wife would like to speak with your woman."

It took him a second to place the clipped manner of speech with the name. He wasn't surprised the vampire executioner had managed to get ahold of his number, because that's what that type did. They hunted vampires down by all necessary means. What did bother him was the phone call intended for Alice. No way was he letting her speak with a lethal member of the community without knowing a good reason why. "She's unavailable."

"Your loss." The phone clicked.

He scanned the display and couldn't fucking believe it. Corin had disconnected.

About to tuck it away, the phone chirruped once again. The same number was calling. He hit a button. "Change your mind?"

"Sebastian?" A pretty feminine voice. "This is Jasmine…please forgive my husband. He can be a little cautious at times. How is Alice doing? May I please talk to her?"

Something in him softened upon hearing her speak. He remembered the pretty woman well into pregnancy. That alone said something about her. A lot of vampire females chose never to become pregnant. The ones who did usually yearned for motherhood beyond blood. It spoke volumes of their characters.

He remembered Alice saying something about making a new friend in Jasmine. He turned toward the hospital room, willing to allow them a chance to reconnect. "Alice is very sick right now and could probably stand to hear from you." There was a sharp intake of breath, a sign that she hadn't yet lost the habit of breathing. "For that reason, I'll ask that you keep the call brief."

"I'm so sorry… Of course."

There were dark circles beneath Alice's eyes when he entered, her skin pale and gaunt. She watched him with wariness, as if unsure why he'd returned. He held out the phone. "Jasmine Gerulaitis."

Aw Christ, his heart thumped at the way her face brightened as she took it from him. "Hi, Jasmine…"

There was a lengthy amount of reassurance from Alice, letting her friend know that yes, she was sick, but no, it wasn't anything major and yes, Bast was taking good care of her. Satisfied it indeed was the true conversation of friends, Bast crossed to the other side of the room and sat in a cold, plastic chair. His eyes burned with fatigue, but there were so many things he needed to do. He needed to research whether Alice could be cured solely by being turned, which he thought she could. One never knew though. If she needed to have the tumor removed first, there were doctors to be researched. Hospitals to contact.

He fucking had more money than God, and damn it, all of it would work for him when he needed it the most. Nothing less would be acceptable.

"How do you know this?" Alice's question came out shaky. Too much distress in it.

He looked up sharply, every protective cell in his body poised for action. Bast stood, ready to put a halt to the phone call. When she held out a hand, his hackles lowered a fraction. He remained standing though, another four or five minutes, as she listened—not speaking much—before disconnecting.

"What was that about?" Not the conversation. The reason she looked distraught.

When she looked at him now though, there was surprise and joy there. "She knows of another like you, and he says you're going through the equivalent of puberty." Alice laughed. "This is *normal* for dragons."

Bast didn't know what to tackle first. His mind whirled with questions, while his knees threatened to buckle. Dropping into the plastic seat, ignoring its loud protest, he stared, dumbfounded. "How...how can she know? Who does she know?"

"She wouldn't tell me other than to say it's a friend of theirs. Another dragon."

"But..." He. A male. Could they be related? His father, maybe?

"I'm supposed to tell you that he'll come to you when the time's right, but for now, he is watching. Be patient. He knows about you. And baby, you're not alone!" Alice laughed, a tear streaking down one cheek. She cupped a hand over her mouth, but her grin pushed her cheeks high.

It was quite possible his head might explode from overload. A dragon going through puberty. What kind of universe did he live in that it would be so sadistic as to make dragons go through puberty? "Oh, my God. I don't even know what to ask first."

She held out her hands in mock surrender. "Don't ask me. Honestly, she didn't say much other than to provide some reassurance. There are a couple of websites she wants me to give to you for reference. She's going to text them to you. Get me your laptop, and I can work from here looking them up. This is so exciting!"

For a brief moment, he'd almost forgotten where they were and why they were here. "You," he said somberly, "will do no such thing. That info can go to Drew, who will look it up." Bast went to her, hating the disappointment he saw now. The bed creaked as he sat down. "Your only job is to get well. To let me help you do that. I need you to spend a little time considering my offer to become one of us. If it's not something you can do..." He'd spend the rest of her life trying to convince her to change her mind. "Then at least we need to prepare for whatever medical procedures can reverse your condition. Agreed?"

The glare she beamed him with should have made his balls detach and run for cover. "Why are you doing this?"

Frustrated, hopeful, worried, Bast leaned forward until his forehead touched hers. He inhaled her scent, pulling it deep into his lungs. He closed his eyes and tried to think of the best way to make her understand. Voice low, he said, "I need you. Not because I'm sick. Not because I'm a dragon. I need you because you see me. You've never feared me. You've never looked down on me. You accept me with all of my flaws and even then, you don't want anything from me. And I know that you don't need me very much, but Alice—"

"What?" she interrupted. He opened his eyes. Saw into her startled ones. "Is that what you think?"

He pulled back slightly. Just a little, afraid that any distance between them now would somehow become permanent. "How could you possibly need me for anything? I have nothing to offer you."

She kissed him quickly. "You silly, arrogant man. Of course you do. Do you remember the woman you met not long ago? The one who was running scared with no purpose and no direction? The one who'd just as soon steal from you as smile at you? She's gone now. You did that, Sebastian. But I won't become a vampire, not because of that." She grabbed his arm when he tried to pull away, halting him. "Not even because I'm scared as hell. I need a better reason than that to commit myself to your kind of life."

Throat tight, he tried to come up with something to give her. His money meant nothing to her. The sex, as phenomenal as it had been, certainly wasn't reason enough. Friendship might get her to at least think about it. Maybe… God, he really didn't have much to offer, did he? With a sigh, he said, "I guess the only reason I have is my love."

This time, she added more distance. "You love me?" she whispered.

Something about her caution made his heavy heart begin to pound. "I do. I love you very much. Enough to want to spend the rest of my life with you. To want you as my mate." Here came the hard part. The moment before the rejection he always seemed to face. From his mother. His friends. The community. "Do you think maybe you could love me one day?"

"I think I can." She pressed her lips to his. Held them there for three heart-stopping beats before pulling away again. She added in another whisper, "I think I already do."

"Thank you, God…" His mouth crashed down on hers again and he kissed her. Kissed her with every bit of his love. With all of the admiration and feeling he had for her.

They could do this together. They would get through it.

"Sebastian Kent."

Startled, Bast whirled, free hand reaching for a gun that wasn't there. He'd left it with Drew upon entering the hospital and passing through its metal detectors. Hope Haven would not allow gang members to finish the jobs they'd started.

The man standing in the doorway had hard eyes. Dark and close together, beneath a brooding brow. They flicked from him to Alice. Back to him. To the win-

dow. To him. The studious attention of someone aware
of his surroundings at all time. His nose was just small
enough to not be considered bulbous, yet was large
enough to detract from the rest of his face. Especially
with those thin lips and nonexistent chin.

He was probably a little shorter than Bast, but the
way the black shirt stretched across his shoulders suggested some time monitoring his physique. A gray
blazer and black slacks rounded out his ensemble. He
stood deceptively relaxed, but Bast recognized the
tensed muscles of someone ready to move. Most of
all, it was the bulge beneath the blazer that caught and
held Bast's attention as he stood, blocking the man's
sight from Alice.

"What do you want with me, executioner?" Bast
asked quietly.

The man couldn't be anyone else. The scent of vampire was all over him, overpowered by the stinging assault of ash wood. The only type of wood that could
mortally wound a vampire. The tool of the executioner's trade.

"You've been summoned before the Council. Will
you please come with me?"

TWENTY-SIX

AN EXECUTIONER? HERE? This world of Sebastian's got crazier by the minute.

"I can't leave her. I won't," Sebastian replied.

The man peered past Sebastian, who'd turned just a fraction. Just enough to let him glimpse her in bed. Alice didn't like the way he dismissed her with perusal that couldn't have taken more than two seconds. "*You* were summoned. No one else."

"She's my intended. My mate. I won't leave without her."

The man did a second perusal. "Has it been sanctioned?"

Gotta love the way they talked about her as if she didn't exist. Except with the guy's lifeless tone and the way her pulse raced, she had a feeling this was one for the boys.

"I've not made the request yet."

The executioner's left eye narrowed a fraction. Had she not been staring at him, she might have missed it. "I understand your dilemma, but I'm afraid I don't face the problem you do. I've been directed to bring you with me. I won't stop you from bringing your intended, if you want her to serve witness to what transpires—"

"She's sick."

The executioner continued, ignoring the interruption as if it never happened. "—when you stand before the

Council. As for what they plan for you, it's none of my business. Only know that it's possible you will not walk away from judgment. If you bring your intended, you potentially subject her to being witness to your end."

"I won't allow her to leave that bed."

"Then she won't be coming with you. Wise choice." He tilted a hand toward the door in invitation to precede him.

"I don't think you understand. If she doesn't leave, I don't leave." Sebastian stood deceptively still, but Alice knew better. There would be at least one gun beneath his blazer. Maybe a stake or two tucked behind his back. "I'll stand before the Council, but on my terms. Not theirs."

From behind, Alice watched two long tendrils of smoke drift away from both sides of Sebastian's face.

So not good. Not good at all.

The executioner slid his hand beneath his own blazer, not even making an attempt at being subtle. A vein in his forehead throbbed forcefully, as if about to burst through the thin veil of skin covering it. "My name is Anteaus Stavrou. You may have heard of me?"

A jerk of the head from Sebastian.

"My dog isn't in this fight. I am only a messenger. However, if you test me, *dragon*—yeah, I've been told what you can do—then I will use lethal force as expected of me."

Alice had heard enough. "That won't be necessary Mr. Stavrou. Sebastian's going with you and he won't put up any resistance. His loyalty to the Council far exceeds any loyalty he has to me."

The look Sebastian turned on her could've straightened every curly hair on her body. His jaw went rigid, but he managed to squeeze out, "Not. Happening."

Antaeus looked amused. As much as someone whose facial expressions didn't vary from *I'd just as soon knife you as smile at you* could look amused.

Alice sighed. "Would you please excuse us for a moment, Mr. Stavrou? Apparently my intended and I need to talk."

His gaze flickered from Alice to Sebastian and back again. It then darted to the window next to her bed. She studied it too, realizing there was no obvious way to open the glass without breaking it. He must have been satisfied that Sebastian wouldn't try to escape through it because he gave a curt nod. The room still tingled with his energy once he'd left.

"What the fuck do you think you're doing?" Sebastian barked as he whirled on her.

She stared back at him.

"Well?"

Silence.

"Alice, now is not the time…"

"Let's agree that's the last time you'll speak to me like that," she said softly and with purpose.

He stormed up to her side. "Then we'll agree that's the last time you'll make a decision for me like that one. You actually expect me to abandon you in this place? You are *my mate*. Mine to watch over."

She folded her arms over her chest. "Not yet, I'm not."

"What?" Sebastian leaned closer. "What did you just say?"

A deep breath. "I'm not your mate. Not yet. And if there's to be any chance that I will be, you'll set aside this grizzly bear rudeness you've got going on and talk to me. Voice lowered. Calmly."

Sebastian seemed to realize then that he'd been yelling. More plumes of smoke rose from his nostrils, the scent of a burned-out match almost overtaking the small room. He visibly shuddered before closing his eyes. She waited for him to collect himself and a temper she feared had been borne out of concern. Still…

"I won't leave you," he whispered.

Alice glanced at the equipment surrounding her. "And I won't let you ignore the Council's request, nor deal with that hulk out there unnecessarily. So it looks like I'm going with you."

He looked defeated. "Until I can get approval to turn you, I need you to stay well, Alice. We don't know when the next seizure might be. If the people here can help you through it, you need to stay here."

She considered his words for a moment but then came up with a conclusion of her own. "The final seizure is coming, whether I'm in the hospital or out of it. If my brain's gonna turn to mush because of one, no amount of doctors or nurses surrounding me is going to be able to help. Think about it. At best, they'll be able to revive my body, put me on a feeding tube or something, and then you get to watch me slowly rot over the next forty or fifty years. Think you can handle that? I gotta tell you, from where I'm sitting it doesn't sound very appealing. If I have my way, I won't meet my end like that. Besides, we don't even know when it might happen. For all we know, I'll be fine for the next twenty years and then one day while I'm watching TV, it'll come then. I've spent the past two years waiting to get here, hospitalized with no future ahead of me. Then

I met you." Alice looked at him through shimmering vision. "I don't want to just exist anymore, Sebastian. I want to live whatever time I have left to the fullest. Without regret. I refuse to do it from a hospital bed. Can you understand that?"

"I wish I was as certain as you. I wish I didn't have this weight here." He thumped a fist against his chest. "This thing that tells me that I have to do anything and everything in my power to keep you safe. Especially when I don't know how to do it. Every instinct is screaming at me to keep you surrounded by people who know what to do and how to take care of you. But then the pain tells me that no one will or can care for you better than I will or can. I'm torn on what to do."

"Trust me," Alice insisted. "Trust yourself. Trust that we weren't brought together, only to be broken apart so soon afterward. There's a plan for you and me. Trust it."

Sebastian tilted his face toward the ceiling, indecision almost visible in the air surrounding him. She would win this discussion whether he realized it or not, but it would be so much simpler for everyone involved if he came to the decision himself. Alice knew what she was asking of him. How hard it would be to just allow fate to guide their courses. But fate was what brought her to him in the first place. She couldn't be wrong that they were meant to be together.

"What happens if I'm wrong?" There was so much anguish in his words. A despair she didn't think possible to come from one person. "What happens if I take you from here and you...you leave me?"

Alice sat up straighter. "Then I leave behind a man who is stronger than he thinks. Certainly stronger than anyone else dared dream. One who will endure, no matter how hard it might seem in the beginning." Her voice lowered. "But for now, let's believe you and I have a chance. Let's go, sweetheart."

Sebastian stared at nothing, his eyes glazed over. Lost in thought, perhaps. When his phone sang a soft tune, she wasn't certain he'd even heard it. By rote though, his hand found the device. He flipped it over a second later, scanned the screen, and Alice watched his face crumple.

"What?" She couldn't keep the alarm from ringing through. "What is it?"

His brow furrowed before he closed his eyes. He opened them again and in the dark depths she found a decisiveness that hadn't been there only moments ago. "That was Drew."

"Yes? What did he want?"

"He wanted to let me know that the Council has it out for me. They've pretty much already decided my fate, which means that nothing I say or do will ever convince them to allow me to turn you." A thunderous cloud of emotion covered his face. "We're getting out of here."

GOD, HE DIDN'T know what they would do or where they would go, but he would not and could not accept that the Council had deserted him. Not now. Not over this.

"What about Stavrou?"

As if he'd heard his name, the executioner tapped against the door, opening it before he'd done knocking. "Has a decision been reached?" he asked, his tone insinuating he didn't care one way or the other. The time for talking and hesitating reached its end.

It physically pained him to say the words, but Bast replied, "She's coming with us."

He had to admit that Antaeus remained patient while they notified the nurse on duty, who then insisted Alice's doctor be notified. Truth be told, he kind of hoped the man would come in and insist that Alice stay, giving Bast just a little bit of ammunition to perhaps rehash the argument. Instead, while the physician wanted to continue to monitor Alice, he agreed with her in not being able to predict when the next seizure might occur.

Technically, the nurse explained as she unhooked IVs and helped Alice get ready, all they'd be doing is running additional tests if she stayed, which might or might not be useful. There was no way to be sure. All that, and Alice might never have another seizure again. However, she wanted Alice's promise to see a neurologist and an oncologist within a week. While Alice might have placated her by agreeing, Bast would be certain she kept her word.

When she'd been dressed in clothing he'd had the foresight to bring, he took one look at her wan face and almost rescinded his decision right then. But when he realized that if she stayed behind, there was a possibility he wouldn't be allowed to come back to her, he reluctantly retrained his mind.

"Are you sure you're okay?" he asked Alice. He'd insisted on rolling her wheelchair downstairs himself; however, a bored-looking aide trailed behind him. Antaeus followed not far behind all three.

"A little tired, but I'll make it."

"Don't push yourself, you hear me?" He meant every word yet couldn't help scanning their surroundings. Nothing but patient rooms seemed to flank them on both sides. Some doors were propped open, eerily dark inside. Others resonated with faint beeps and clicks, the sounds of equipment hard at work on saving lives. Most of the patient rooms had been left closed, allowing their visitors to rest comfortably in the late night.

Bast looked for some way out and pledged that making her leave the chair was a very last resort. Still, he had to leave that option there. With Antaeus so closely on their heels, they'd get one shot and one shot only.

How had his life come to this point? Walking the green mile with a vampire executioner at his back. While Bast was a warrior, the executioners specialized in taking down vampires. Bast realized he'd spent so long doing his service with a gun that trying to defend himself against a blade and stake would be clumsy at best. If he made it out of this, he'd refocus his skills.

Alice reached across her shoulder and placed a hand on his. Roiling emotions eased back a fraction. She was worth it.

The elevator ride down was filled with a soft rendition of "My Heart Will Go On" and he had to wonder who in hell had programmed the thing. Still, better than the ominous silence of four bodies with little in common. Also, it helped drown the doubt screaming at him that there simply wasn't enough time to plan an escape. Once they hit the ground floor, Antaeus would take over, ensuring Bast headed for the Council's transportation.

Think, goddamn it. Think!

His hands tightened around the wheelchair's handles when he pushed Alice out of the elevator all too soon. The foursome strolled down a long corridor lined with pictures of important older men done in acrylic paints. Doorways led to offices, which had been shut down for the day. Administration, patient relations and a few others. None of which would be useful, seeing how they seemed to house empty desks and chairs and not much else.

He didn't have much choice in the matter. He'd have to take Antaeus on. With hardly anyone around to witness an altercation, now seemed as good a time as any.

As they approached the automatic glass doors, he tried to peer beyond the bright lights of the entrance to see if he could spot any people lingering, maybe catching a smoke break where they could. There didn't appear to be any parked cars in the circular drive. No one hung out near the columns on either side of the doors. The darkness of night took over from there.

Sliding a hand to Alice's shoulder, he squeezed it gently. *Be ready to move*, it said. He wanted to add *don't linger if you can help it*. No matter what she heard and no matter how things looked, she needed to not interfere. Her safety meant more than anything else right now. If things didn't end the way they wanted, Gray and the others would see to her wellbeing. It was a grim prediction, but one forced on them.

The wheels of the chair whirred ominously, so Bast slid his hands back on the rails. He tightened his jaw and got ready to push her forward. As soon as they cleared the entranceway he'd attempt his assault. Only a few more feet…

Bast jerked his head toward the sound of tires coming at them. Fast. Headlights announced the car's approach with equal animosity. A white car, something large and loud, hurtled toward them.

"What the fuck?" he muttered before having to

yank the wheelchair back. He kept backing up until the wheelchair sat in the doorway once again, not willing to trust the skill of a drunkard. Had to be someone throwing back forties or snorting the good stuff. The car took the circular drive at a breakneck speed, going at least sixty in a *driveway* before screeching to a halt in front of them. It hadn't stopped moving before the driver's side door swung open and a young man, couldn't have been more than twenty or so, jumped from the vehicle.

"We need a doctor! Are you a doctor?" His wide gaze flew past Bast and Alice to land on the people behind them.

The aide spoke up. "Dude, the ER's on the other side—"

"My friend's been hurt, and we need a doctor." His voice hovered right on the verge of hysteria, teetering back and forth between high-pitched panic and unreasonable calm.

Over his shoulder, Bast watched someone push open the passenger door. One sneakered foot landed on the ground before the other followed suit. Another young man stood, his face tortured and sweaty. He lurched toward them, arm folded across his middle inadequately covering a growing red stain.

"Princess," Bast murmured. The guy needed the wheelchair more than she did. Beyond the abdominal wound, the man's skin was shiny-looking and paper pale. Blood seeped down the front of his blue jeans, creeping toward his knees as if on a slow death march.

Alice reached for his hand, and Bast helped her to rise. His gaze darted from the injured man to her. He watched her carefully. Any sign she couldn't stand without assistance, any sign they needed to turn around and he'd drag her back inside, kicking and screaming, if necessary. Fuck the injured guy.

Although her legs wavered for longer than he would have liked, Alice found her balance and took a few tentative steps. She tilted her head to him, gifted him with an amazing smile, then moved to the side. Everyone else moved en masse.

Bast realized at once what kind of clusterfuck they were in. The injured man didn't have the strength to make it to the wheelchair, his friend kept trying to shove past the aide to get inside and the aide tried to maneuver around him and the wheelchair to get to the outside. Best of all, the jostling crush of bodies blocked him and Alice from Antaeus.

"Go," he urged, barely above a whisper. The man had begun to sob openly, and Bast prayed to the universe that it was enough to drown his command to Alice. If Antaeus heard him before she could take at least a few steps, witnesses to the resulting carnage could not be helped.

Her gaze snapped to meet his, then a subtle tilt of the chin followed.

Bast did his best to remain still as she sidled away, inch by slow inch. An achingly subtle crawl away from them. *Please let Antaeus keep his focus on the man. Not on her.*

He swore he could hear his heart speed up, pounding against his ribs and telling anyone and everyone within a five-mile radius about his state of agitation, but Antaeus had little choice but to focus on the crowd in front of him. Her movement might be caught out of the corner of his eye or simply because he'd turned his attention to her at the wrong time.

Still sobbing, the man leaned forward, hands flailing as he tried to collapse into the waiting chair. Bast managed to step to the side at the same moment and somehow, the wheelchair decided to simultaneously teeter on one large wheel. The man slipped and a thick, wet sound belched into the air. He began to scream, a high-pitched, spine-curling keen of pain, and Bast sharply turned his head away from the sight of organs and other matter that bulged from the now gaping wound.

"Go!" he shouted at her, already starting to run in Alice's direction. It came out as a boom of noise, drawing Antaeus's attention. Didn't matter though. Antaeus was waylaid by the hospital employee, the injured man and his friend trying to shove the wheelchair back inside. Between the screaming, blood and gore, all of them moved in clunky uncoordinated starts and stops. None in sync. All three, hell, maybe even Antaeus himself, panicked by the sudden turn of events.

Bast couldn't be bothered to linger to watch the outcome though. By the time he reached Alice's side, he pulled her into his arms and took off at a dead run. Destination to be determined.

Forefront on his mind was getting away.

And then turning Alice into a vampire.

TWENTY-SEVEN

BAST OPENED HIS EYES, almost jerking upright before remembering where they were. Alice's breathing, bordering on snoring, drifted from beside him. Arm draped across her middle, even in the exhausted coma they'd fallen into, he had to know she was physically there. With him. Always.

The motel clerk hadn't batted an eye when they'd stumbled in just before dawn. He'd taken one look at the couple, made Bast sign here, here and here and fork over a couple hundred dollars when a credit card was not about to happen. With a Council executioner on their tail, Bast wasn't about to make it *that* easy for the guy. Get real.

Stopping to rest while on the move might not have been something he would have normally done, but Alice was running on empty. He hadn't fed or slept in more than a day, either. If they'd kept going, he would have made a mistake. And they just didn't have time for that. Not now. Not when things had reached this level of chaos and uncertainty. Even now it pained him to gently rub her shoulder, arousing her to wakefulness.

"Wake up, princess."

Her mumbled words colored the air blue.

"I know you're tired," Bast soothed. "But we're not safe here." Not like he knew where they would be safe.

"Eight hours," she groaned. "That's all I want! We

can't have been here more than three or four hours yet. Can't we sleep a little bit longer?"

Almost six hours had passed, actually. Way more than he should have spared. "Not yet. Not here. I promise you'll get to rest, but we have some things to do first."

Alice struggled to sitting, hair plastered to one side of her face. "Christ, like what?"

Bast sat up too, allowing his hands to drape between his thighs. Face cast down, he searched for the courage to say the right words to her. An eternity of self-doubt passed, only to be overtaken by a rush of pride and possessive love. He tilted his face toward hers, taking a moment to brush away those sticky strands of hair. Faint purple lines circled beneath her eyes, but he didn't find any hint of annoyance lingering in them. "You need to decide what you want. You have to know for certain."

"I don't understand."

"I want you with me for always. As my lover. My mate. My wife." What little sleep lingered in her expression wiped away with a blink. Something within her gaze softened, and it made his heart swell.

Confusion made her frown slightly. "But the Council, I thought they have to—"

"Fuck the Council, Alice. If you'll have me, and please God have me, agree to be with me for the rest of our lives…I am begging you for your most precious gift. For the gift of yourself. I swear to you that I'll cherish it always. Trade in your human life to become part of a stronger yet equally flawed family. In return, I will love you with everything I have and with everything I am. I will be yours until you tire of me."

She touched his arm. "I could never tire of you."

Bast shook his head. "You could. And that's why I need you to be sure. Take your time and think about this. You might be thinking that death is scary and something you don't want to face in the near future, but hundreds of years from now, you might regret not being able to leave this body so easily." He'd already explained to her that vampires were not immortal, but even he admitted that some days it didn't feel that way. Some days, when he was tired and blood-starved, it felt as if he'd lived one day too long. He'd spare her that lamentation if possible. "And like you know, we'll be doing this without Council approval. When they discover your creation, and they will, we'll have little choice. We will be hunted and always on the move. Always looking over our shoulders. Always facing the possibility of being executed."

He ran out of words. The only ones he could conjure now spoke of danger and death. Of the harsh existence ahead of them. Bet those authors who wrote about vampires and their exotic sex lives wouldn't know what to make of the last part of his speech. But he had to tell her. Had to warn her. For all he knew, maybe even within days of turning her, they'd be facing Antaeus and his stakes.

"I'm scared." A shaky declaration said after a lengthy pause.

"I'd be more scared if you weren't."

"Will it hurt?"

His fingers curled around hers. "Not if I can help it. Do you want me to explain how it works?"

"Based on the way you're looking at me, I don't think I want to know in advance."

He hesitated. There would be one tough part. Something she would not conceive of on her own. "I can't help you choose what to do. You have to decide if you want to become a vampire with me. You decide if you want to hear the details of how it works. Any question I'll answer as honestly as I can. If you can't decide now, then that's okay too."

"It's not going to be pleasant, is it? The turning part."

"Certain parts aren't, no. Whether I tell you now or you just wait and see, I need to know that I'll have your complete and absolute trust in what happens."

No hesitation this time. "Of course," she said with a smile.

It fell away when Bast hardened his expression. "*Complete*, Alice. I need to know you'll come out on the other side, with the understanding that I did exactly what needed to be done."

"You want this so badly. What happens if I disappoint you? What happens when you grow tired of *me*? I'm nobody special, but you want to spend the rest of your life with me anyway. I hog the covers at night and can only cook, like, three things. Only two of those well. I have no fashion sense and don't know how to be all high-falutin' like you around your high-profile friends. Can you really be happy with someone so simple?"

"If the next hundred years are anywhere close to the past week, then yes. And hell yes."

Alice studied him with a disbelieving gaze while nibbling on her thumbnail. Neither spoke.

In another time, he would have spent months, years if necessary, wooing her right. Slowly coaxing her and loving her until she loved him equally in return. If things were different...

"Yes."

"Are you sure? One hundred percent, sure?"

"Yes, I am your friend and your lover. And yes, I want also to be your wife for now and always. As a vampire, if that's what it'll take. And that's what it'll take, because I don't know how much longer this old body of mine will hold out. So yes, Sebastian. Do whatever needs to be done." She released an unsteady laugh. "But make it quick before I lose my nerve, okay?"

Bast nodded, hastily reviewing every step in his head. The last one he skipped for now, not knowing how he wanted to tackle it. He slid off the bed. "Remove your clothing," he ordered.

Swinging her legs off the bed as well, she replied, "I thought you were turning me into a vampire."

"There are some very enjoyable aspects to being turned. You'll see." An unrepentant grin followed.

Alice giggled while rolling her eyes.

When she lifted the shirt to reveal a flat, bare belly, Bast was immediately distracted from what he was about to do. Difficult to take his attention away from the woman who revealed a purple bra, all covered in lace and frilly things. The cut-out pattern teased him with blush-colored hints of her nipple, but no matter how long he lingered, they didn't divulge the full secret. She leaned forward to push down the jeans from her hips, which made her breasts spill into the cups of all that purple, filling them completely. Standing upright disintegrated the effect, but the view of her stepping out of pooled denim stretched to her full height, hips and breasts covered in pretty lace was heart-stopping.

Christ, yes.

She reached behind her and a moment later, the bra

no longer fit her in a snug hold. Instead, the material gaped before fluttering to the ground altogether. Rounded breasts, nipples already tightening, incited a rush of blood through Bast's veins. By the time her fingers hooked into the straps of lace on her hips and pushed them down long legs, his cock had swollen to almost full mast. Licking his lips barely helped the dearth of moisture on them as his gaze swept over her nudity, taking in every exquisite inch of skin, including the down-covered juncture between her thighs.

"On the bed," he whispered, throat drying.

He forced himself to remember that she was sick and had been hospitalized only hours earlier. His lust would have to wait. Still...

When she seemed comfortable, Bast crawled over her. Elevated on his forearms, he kept his weight from smothering her but reveled in the bounce of heat between their bodies. There was so much trust held in her deep blue eyes, it was almost enough to make him change his mind. To not subject her to what might be a mistake.

But no. The mistake would have been to not spend eternity together when it was possible. So Bast kissed her. It would be the last kiss she experienced as a human. One that gave her a final chance to cling to her old life and reject him.

Alice's fingers pushed into his hair, her other hand lighting on his jaw to hold him in place as she returned the kiss. Their tongues stroked and tangled, their passion rising. She breathed heavily into his mouth, her body arching beneath his, touching breast to breast. Her teeth nipped at his bottom lip and the sharp pain aroused him that much more. As she spread those creamy thighs, inviting him to thrust into the warmth of her pussy, he almost came undone.

Instead he focused. Hands stroking over her body, inciting her reaction to him. He wanted this to be something special for her. A time she treasured and remembered forever as being worth every second of hurt he would inflict on her.

His mouth moved from her lips, spreading kisses over her chin and then down her throat. The jumping pulse beneath her skin raced a little harder, a little faster as his mouth approached. He could smell the scent of her readiness and it inflamed him with the same eagerness her blood did. Incisors aching in painful anticipation lengthened even further.

She tensed a split second before his teeth punctured her jugular.

So very, very sweet.

The taste of her blood so precious and delicious, Bast opened his mouth and pulled harder. Alice moaned, twisting beneath him, rubbing against his swollen cock. He rocked his pelvis against her, brushing against her clit. Always pulling more of her precious gift into his throat. Tasting her. Loving her. Alice shuddered, crying out as an orgasm left her trembling beneath him.

Quickly, Bast pulled away from his source and bit into his own wrist. Before Alice could protest or even figure out his intent, he pushed the new wound onto her mouth. He sunk his teeth into her again as quickly as he'd left. She bucked, seating him further in the cradle of her thighs, but then almost immediately she relaxed. He waited for perhaps too long, but *there*, felt the swipe of her tongue over the puncture. A few more seconds passed before a little pressure from her mouth tightened over his wrist.

Her lips were stained by the time he took his hand from her. There was a green tint to her face, but she'd ingested his blood. All it took was a little bit. Licking the wound closed took him only a second.

Very good. Now came the hard part.

"Trust me, Alice," he said. "I love you." With deliberate slowness, he placed the same hand over her mouth and nose. Eyes meeting hers, he applied pressure until he felt her body stiffen. And then he squeezed a little tighter.

She was so brave, his Alice, as realization sunk in. He knew the moment she understood his intent to control her breathing from the way the fear crept into her face. She tried to hide it and might have from any other person. From him she could hide nothing.

For the first thirty seconds or so—an eternity by whatever measurement he used—Alice remained still. Another ten seconds, and he could feel her begin to pull away. Each time, she brought herself back under forced control, but Bast imagined her lungs were beginning to question why they weren't receiving a new exchange of air. By the minute mark, he could see her fingers clenching the bedsheets. She lasted another twenty seconds or so before her legs began to thrash.

"I love you…hold on…" His reassurances didn't calm the frantic clawing that followed, grappling at his forearms, nails scraping his skin. Her hands wrapped around his wrists, pulling with a force he didn't think she possessed, certain to leave bruises. He understood her body's desperate attempt to breathe. The will to live overrode any other natural instinct.

Full body weight pressing down on her, he did his best to keep her from hurting him or herself. God, he wanted to look away, to not witness the moment her life ceased to be. Instead, he kept his gaze trained on hers. "Don't fight it, baby… Almost over."

She didn't listen to his words. He didn't know if she could even hear him. Alice's body twisted and writhed, her legs kicking at his. She repeatedly threw her head back, trying to dislodge his grip, but Bast held on, knowing that if he stopped, they'd only have to go through it all over again.

His heart lurched when a final flash of pain-confusion-relief flooded Alice's features. Her eyes looked at his, understanding and accusation mingling within them, before her gaze shifted beyond him. They glazed over, seeing everything and nothing. He kept that mutinous hand in place another heart-rending minute more before lifting it.

Head lowered to her chest, he waited for a beat to announce she hadn't left him. When none came, no matter how hard he strained, Bast pushed aside the despair and lay next to her. He fought every internal demon and some he didn't know that existed—every self-doubt and recrimination, every bit of worry about himself as a man, a vampire and now a dragon—and prepared to wait.

It was done.

TWENTY-EIGHT

"BUT AN INHERITANCE *from whom?" Sebastian cried. "I don't understand the secrecy and whispering. Why won't you tell me about him? How did he acquire all of this? I am a bastard and you are a whore, and those words are truer because you hide* him *from all of us."*

Aurora Kent kept her gaze on the table, her long, elegant fingers sifting through the gemstones. Her hand remained steady as it drifted through the diamonds, rubies, emeralds and other various stones, some as large as her palm. Others the size of her fingernail.

She separated two brilliant blue stones from the piles. With a slight tremor beneath her words, she said, "Now tell me, of these two, which should be sold and why?"

Her clipped British accent used to soothe him as a child, but now with so many unanswered questions lying between them, Sebastian viewed it as another way to classify their differences. Other than their hair color and an existence based on blood, he was nothing like his mother.

Sebastian stalked toward her and leaned into her space, using his presence to demand she look up and acknowledge him. For God's sake, just once, he wanted her to treat him like the man he'd become and allow him to face the whisperings of the vampire community with pride, instead of resigned shame. To his frustra-

tion, she made him learn about finance, gemstones and a multitude of other tasks and things that couldn't possibly help him. Not when all of this belonged to him.

Yes, the gemstones fascinated him. Something about their brilliance and resilience made his heart thunder. He loved to play in their colors, their shininess singing to him as he gloried in the riches spread before him. They had more wealth than either would ever be able to spend, thanks to an absent father who bequeathed the fortune to them. A father he had never known and might not ever know if she insisted on keeping her silence.

With a swell of anger and frustration, Sebastian swept the stones off the table, their delicate clinks surrounding them like raindrops from a new rain.

Ezra Smythe, his mother's butler, lover, friend and guardian, stepped forward and soundlessly began to retrieve each one. Sebastian's sharp gaze went to the man crouched at his feet, and a snarl lifted his lips. The silver-haired man wasn't vampire, nor could Sebastian determine his origin in all the years the trio had lived together. Another damned mystery that neither would resolve.

Aurora didn't seem to harbor any feelings for Ezra, yet neither hid the fact that they coupled often. On occasion, her cries at being pleasured could be heard echoing through the halls. During those times, Sebastian would quietly leave the house and wander the estate grounds, regardless of the hour of night or the season.

He would never deny her a chance at companionship, especially considering the length of their vampiric lives, but this flaunting behavior only fueled the whispering. Couldn't she at least strive for some discretion?

Not allow servants and visitors alike to witness the un-ladylike inclinations.

Their enigmatic relationship haunted Sebastian. Often.

For what must have been the hundredth time in his life, he shouted at Aurora, "Is it him? Is Ezra my sire?"

She jumped to her feet, and the flash of fire burning in her eyes singed his heart. "Why must you know? Why must you question me time and time again?" Aurora's incisors were bared, her pale face ever more fierce because of it. "I will never speak of him to you. Never. Not to you, not under threat of torture, not under the weight of love. Your father is my secret and burden to carry until I leave this earth."

"So you embrace what is said about me? You?" Sebastian's throat was tight with emotion. He hated this. His life. This not knowing. With forced reserve, he said, "I called you a whore, and you didn't flinch. I'm not so strong."

"You are that strong." Her own voice softened. Aurora lifted her hand to his chin and held it beneath a firm grip. "He expected nothing less from you and he knew your potential. I've never met a more powerful man than your father. It is not a taunt to be called his son, Sebastian, but praise. You are his glory. I know this for a fact. He left you all of this because you are his legacy and one day, you will grow into it and realize it to be true."

"When?" He shuddered because he needed to hear the words again. He both resented and clung to the words that brought him closer to a man he'd never known. Any little snippet.

"I don't know when. You...you will have to be pa-

tient. *Learn your lessons. Grow your father's legacy and be his pride."*

Sebastian slowly sat. "The smaller topaz would fetch more than the larger one."

A small smile curved Aurora's lips, the sudden change in topic handled with elegant smoothness. "Why?" she asked softly.

"Because the larger one is flawed with inclusions. The smaller one is more pure."

"Very good, my son."

She frustrated him to hell and back, but Sebastian loved her. With reluctant admiration, he watched her dip in a small curtsey before turning to leave.

"There is a reason beyond stubbornness that forces her to keep your father's secret."

Sebastian turned to Ezra, who on every other occasion would be trailing behind his mother. That he stayed behind for even a moment spoke volumes. "What do you know of it?"

He shrugged. "Less than her. More than you."

Sebastian's eyes narrowed. "Keep talking."

"Your father appointed me to be your mother's... companion. And it is all I will say of him and the matter, other than to advise that if you really want to know more about him, you'll have to seek him out on your own. Without her assistance."

Gripping the chair's arms kept Sebastian from jumping out of it to throttle Ezra. He wouldn't think of touching a single hair on his mother's head, but this man? He owed him nothing.

His incisors lengthened in agitation.

"I am also your advisor," Ezra continued. "At your

father's people's request. You would do well to consider what I'm saying."

"Why not just tell me what I want to know?"

"Because I would be dead within days. There is a reason for ignorance. Trust this... You will know one day who you are."

Ezra's chin dipped ever so slightly. A blink on Sebastian's part might have hidden it. Yet he somehow caught the motion, and something about it made him aware. Sebastian waited, studying Ezra's face, trying to discern why the movement meant anything, if it did. But then Ezra's eyebrow lifted a fraction, almost infinitesimally, and he swore the man's dark eyes hid amusement.

Confused, Sebastian raised a hand in assent as the man, once a warrior, gave him a full nod before turning to depart.

His gaze slid to the gemstones and with a sigh, Sebastian began to gather them closer. They were only a small portion of their collection, but he wouldn't leave them out for others to pocket. His father had at least seen to their comfort...

Sebastian sat up straight, the gems forgotten.

Dear God.

Ezra had said he would be dead within days. Within days. Did that mean...? The way Ezra had looked at him had to have been a hint. Something for Sebastian to grasp if he was clever enough to understand.

His hands began to shake as understanding continued to bloom.

His father. It had to mean... The man, or at the very least the people of his clan, were still alive.

Sebastian only had to find them.

TWENTY-NINE

ALICE OPENED HER EYES, prepared to scream. Her last memory pinged around her mind, rising up and out in horrific vividness. But she was aware, so she couldn't be dead, right? No. She knew who she was. Where she was started to come back to her, too. The most important thing right now was a new realization. She was alive, and God, she needed.

Needed.

She hurt and needed, and everything swelled large and uncontrolled beneath her skin. Something within demanded and craved, and she didn't know how to handle it. What to do. She just knew this *need*, this rage inside her pushing to get out. To claim. To be claimed.

Alice twisted on the bed, moaning.

She almost melted into the mattress at the first touch of someone's hand—a masculine hand—that had slipped between her legs. "I've got you, princess. I'll take care of you always," the male said.

Not just a male. Her male. Sebastian.

She moaned again, eyes rolling in the back of her head as he began to slowly rub her clit, his palm grinding against her with just the oh-so-right pressure. She allowed need to drift into something more pleasurable. The pain, the ache, soothed away with each circular motion.

"For the next three days, this will be my pleasure. My duty to you. To stop what's hurting," he said softly.

"*Please*..."

"You're on your way to becoming one of us. This is the process. Let it happen."

Even the soft sheets beneath her scratched at sensitive skin, as if made of sandpaper. She couldn't get comfortable. Throat parched, gums hurting, the effort to talk or whimper a sound seemed too much of an effort. Yet she couldn't stop the moaning each time Sebastian touched her there. In the place that sent ringlets of rapturous relief echoing through her every vein.

He continued to speak softly, his voice another source of comfort. "To become one of us, the heart has to stop. But so long as you've tasted our blood recently, it will grow in your system, growing and taking over. Part of the discomfort you're feeling now is the body's way of absorbing the changes. Endorphins help to ease some of the shock."

"Three days?" God, she couldn't stand it. She wouldn't be able to live through it. Not like this. Not in this misery.

"It will ease over the three days, I promise you. Today will be the worst, and I'll get you through it. Hold on to me, Alice, and I'll be what you need."

She could do that. She would.

A cry came tumbling from her lips, the sound overridden by the crank of the air conditioner generator kicking in. The low rumble coughed a few times before settling into a hum. By then, Alice had her hand over Sebastian's, guiding him blindly, seeking more of his talented touch. Each time he pressed against the swollen bundle of nerves, she gasped, the sensual ecstasy of it enough to take her over a ledge. She climbed higher and higher, and blindly, Alice went to that place. Here, she didn't ache, and the hurt translated into something else. Something she desired.

Sebastian pushed a long finger inside her cunt. Alice's eyes snapped open. A second finger joined the first, the stretch making her stomach flutter. His thumb brushed over her clit, and the combination shattered her. Alice came, trembling. Sensation blanketed her beneath sparks of feeling, which tumbled through her, taking every thought and every breath.

Any reprieve she might have gained by a lover who eased away from ecstasy's grasp dissolved as Bast instead impaled her with a single thrust. His cock filled her in a way his fingers never could have, touching some sweet spot that made her cry out his name. It was too much and exactly what she needed, all at once.

She reveled in the feel of his muscles bunching and contracting beneath her fingers, and she held him. With hypersensitive flesh yearning for touch, she pressed her body to his. They came together. Kissing. Tongues stroking.

Her breath pushed out her lungs, hoarse cries finding life in between her quest to connect with him at the most basic level. Loving him with everything she had within her. It was rushed and hot and passionate, some unnamed urgency driving her—driving him— and they responded. They clung to each other, and the desperation with which she tried to become part of him made her afraid. But the fear was squelched, soul-robbing pleasure demanding to be first and always. When Alice came again, shuddering, eyes squeezed shut, she reveled in his long groan as he soon followed behind.

Sebastian collapsed on top of her a moment later, his weight a tolerable burden. But it was several minutes before she could get her panting breath to ease. For a heartbeat gone rampant to resume its normal, lazy pace. Sweat trickled down her sides and created a layer between their bodies. A large part of her didn't think the heat they'd generated came solely from their act. She almost felt like it was something generated from the inside.

"Are we dead?" she asked, half-jokingly. The other half not quite certain.

He lifted his head a fraction. "A few more rounds like that, and we might be."

"So that's what it means to become a vampire, huh?"

"Oh, you don't know the half of it. Things haven't even gotten good yet."

"*That* wasn't good? I don't think I'm going to survive this."

Bast pressed a kiss to her cheek, groaned, but withdrew enough to roll to his side. "You'll survive it. And we'll both enjoy every second of it. You'll love so much about this life. I'm going to give you so many, many things. Anything you want. Anything you need."

"You and me. That's all I need." She touched his forearm, loving that she could even make the statement to him and mean it with everything in her heart.

"Good. And as much as I'd love to lay here with you, wiling the day away, if you think you're up to it, we also need to get out of here. We're going to have to stay on the move and out of the Council's radar if we hope to have a chance. I've been thinking about it, and maybe in a week or so, you can contact Jasmine Gerulaitis and ask about how they outran the Council. Maybe her husband'll even share something that'll keep us alive a little while longer."

It wouldn't be a hardship to contact her friend again. With any luck, it was a friendship that would continue to flourish. She'd never had a girlfriend she could confide in before and now, with all the changes she was undergoing, having a sort of mentor would go a long way.

Sebastian pulled her hand to his mouth. Kissed it. "Another thirty minutes is all we can spare. You want the shower first?"

Since leaving the hospital, she'd been feeling a little run down. Now, even after that marathon sex, she felt a bit…rejuvenated. "Sure. If you're good, maybe you'll wrangle an invitation out of me to join in while I'm there. Too bad we only have thirty minutes."

He grinned. "I could work with that."

"You are—"

The door crashed open, a piece of the security chain popping off and flying across the room at lethal speed. The noise was a shotgun blast in what had been almost near-perfect silence. Shards of wood from the broken door scattered across the cheap carpeting of the motel room and for some reason, the little bits grabbed her attention. When she lifted her sight to the person responsible, a weight plummeted in Alice's stomach.

They'd run out of time anyway. Antaeus Stavrou had already found them.

BAST LEAPED FROM the bed, yanking Alice behind him. He met the executioner's cold stare, almost daring the man to make one wrong step in Alice's direction. He'd most likely die trying to defend her, but there was no way in hell that he'd allow the man to lay one tainted finger on his woman.

How the fuck did he find them so quickly? He asked the executioner, barely stifling a growl beneath every syllable.

Antaeus replied, "You were careless."

He stepped inside the doorway and removed a broad brimmed, black hat. Equally dark shades went into the cap after he'd stepped into the shadow of the darkened room. Bast studied the large human standing outside the doorway, figuring there was probably at least another one of him guarding the only exit. Antaeus was smart enough to bring back up this time. While Alice could still stand hours in the sun, she would have been hindered by it. Smart executioner didn't want to take the chance that the couple would make another escape attempt, because they would have. Now, they'd have to spend a little more time thinking about their next move.

Antaeus nodded at the door and the human leaned in, grabbed the knob and tried to leer at Alice. Bast took a single threatening step forward, letting the man see the *do-not-fuck-with-what-is-mine* in his eyes. The human's lip crimped in arrogant defiance but he backed out, closing the door behind him.

Bast turned, grabbed the sheet from the bed and took his time draping it over Alice. "We'll be fine," he said softly. She looked up at him, hope and trust set into her features. She nodded, and he couldn't stop himself from pressing a quick kiss on her lips. "Do you still want a shower?"

"But—" Her attention darted to Antaeus and back.

"He's not taking us anywhere yet," he replied a little

louder. "The Council does not travel in daylight. Go on. I'll be waiting for you."

Bast waited until the bathroom door closed before going to the bed. He draped an old worn throw over his lap and stared down Antaeus as he sat across from him. "So, care to tell me how you found us?"

His mouth kicked up at the corners. "Why not? It doesn't matter now." With an exaggerated glance, he searched the room. "Where's your cell phone?"

"My cell…oh, *fuck me*." How could he have been so stupid and so careless? Sure, it'd been smart not to use his credit cards, easily traceable for the lowliest of hackers. Everyone knew cell phones came with a built-in tracking device, only deactivated by removing the phone's battery. He'd been so concerned about Alice's safety, about her health, the thought that he should toss the device hadn't crossed his mind. Not once.

"I'll admit that I thought you'd left it in some inconvenient place, using it as a red herring, but a single phone call verified the couple checking into the motel at such an odd hour. And when I came here about half an hour ago and caught wind of that scent…" He let out a low whistle of approval. "So tempting when they're transitioning, aren't they?"

Something deep in Bast twisted in understanding. Even now, he could smell Alice on the other side of the bathroom door. It was something all newly turned vampires underwent. A subtle shift in their anatomy that announced their newborn status. The sweet, beckoning fragrance of cinnamon designed to lure more mature vampires to them.

"Will you allow me to help her until we stand before the Council?"

Antaeus tilted his head in consideration. "If you'll agree not to attempt to escape, I'll allow it. You know I won't kill her before she's been tried. But you...I do not have to be so kind to you."

He expected nothing less from the executioner. Bast replied, "Leave her alone, and I'll go before the Council with you."

This conversation eased his fear somewhat. If Antaeus forced Alice to undergo transition without assistance, or if he'd decided on helping her sexual needs himself, Bast didn't think he'd have the strength to stop himself from attacking him outright. Alice was his mate in every way. Before, he thought he'd be willing to do just about anything for her. Now, he'd walk through flames knowing that death waited him on the other side, without so much as blinking.

"You realize that no matter what the Council decrees for you, it won't end well for her?" Antaeus asked with a low voice.

Bast couldn't bring himself to verbally respond. He nodded.

When the Council was faced with the evidence of a newly created vampire, one made without their sanction, she would be sentenced to death. Antaeus, or some other executioner, would be ordered to extinguish her life painlessly, but immediately after a decision had been made and she'd fully transitioned.

For that reason, Antaeus should have also made him promise not to attempt a break-out for Alice. Because he would get her away from this mess. That was a promise.

As if beckoned, she came out of the bathroom, a cloud of heat and steam surrounding her. The bite mark on her neck glowed brighter than the rest of her pink skin, and from the sight alone Bast could have taken her again if not for their audience. As it was, she moved timidly, not sparing a glance in Antaeus's direction. Her attention went to the floor of the room, where her discarded clothing lay, a tale of their own. When she picked up something purple, Bast grunted out a noise. "Just the shirt. I need you to stay available to me, okay?" Her scrubbed flesh burned brighter as a blush spread across her cheeks and melted down her neck. He smiled, trying to lighten the somber atmosphere. "What? Don't tell me that you don't have a bit of exhibitionist in you."

She returned a grudging smile. "You're such a man. Sorry, but threesomes aren't my thing."

"That's what you say now."

Her eyes shot to Antaeus and back. Her voice dropped to a whisper. "You've had a threesome before?"

"I'm almost four hundred. There's *lots* of things I've done before." He waggled his eyebrows.

Alice slipped the shirt on, letting it fall over the towel wrapped around her frame. "I don't think I even want to know. And now that you have me, I don't care how old you get to be, I doubt there will be any more threesomes in your future. Feel me?"

Antaeus chuckled. "You two are well matched."

Pride swelled in Bast. They were, weren't they? God, how he wanted to spend more time with her. He wanted to show her many things. Take her places she'd only dreamed. To do that, surviving meant everything. For them both. Somehow, he'd have to find a way to convince the Council that he wasn't a threat and neither was she. He'd give them his vast fortune if necessary.

While most had been inherited, a lot had been earned. And if he'd done it once, he could do it again.

Alice grimaced, bending at the waist as if pain ricocheted through her. Bast lunged for her, holding her against him as another swell of heat rushed through her. The sweet cinnamon smell bloomed in the small room, announcing another trial of transition brightening into existence.

Over her head, he caught Antaeus's attention. With his eyes, he motioned to the bathroom, and Antaeus gave a reluctant, but curt nod. Without waiting for another prompt of approval, Bast pressed his body against hers as they shuffled together toward the private space. She was trembling by the time he closed the door.

"I promise today's the worst of it. Promise," he reassured as his mouth skimmed across hers.

She gritted her teeth. "Can't be worse than what you went through, right?" Beads of sweat popped up on her brow. "I can handle it. But how do we escape—"

"Uh-uh." He wouldn't tell her of his promise to Antaeus yet. "He can hear everything we say. Let's get you better for now." Hands on her waist, Bast lifted her onto the porcelain sink. His naked body stood nicely between her thighs. When his hand met the damp heat between her thighs, some of the fight drained from her eyes while she nodded her acquiescence. Bast watched the pleasure rise in her face as his fingers began to dance. There might not be many more moments like this for them, and by God he would enjoy every second of each one as they occurred.

In the down-times while they waited for evening to descend, Bast would call on his inner dragon. Learning it. Analyzing it. He needed this other side of himself to answer when beckoned or to leave at a moment's notice. The way things were going, no one had to tell him that Alice's life depended on it.

For now though, they would play.

THIRTY

ALICE HELD SEBASTIAN'S hand tightly as they were escorted into the long, rectangular room. The heat hadn't risen in hours, and truthfully, she didn't know which was worse: that or the fact they hadn't figured out how to get out of this mess. Anteaus and two big guys forced them to leave the motel after the sun had gone down. The drive across the city couldn't have taken more than forty-five minutes. When the town car stopped in downtown, the locale and sleek look of the high-rise had been a mild surprise.

The men she'd been introduced to, the men who served beneath Sebastian's leadership, all waited on either side of an anteroom. A few averted their eyes when they entered, as if it were too painful to watch the procession. Drew tried to give her a reassuring smile, but it seemed forced.

Now, as she stared down the large oak table surrounded on both sides by café au lait colored leather chairs, she could almost smell the opulence. Not a surprise at all.

There were seven people, both men and women, seated at the table. All of them had a clear glass of water before them; some had tea cups with saucers resting beneath. No folders or documents of any kind littered the tabletop. In fact, if she hadn't known better, she might have thought she'd been invited to Sunday brunch somewhere nice and innocent. Instead, these were the people who would decide if she and Sebastian had broken enough rules to warrant their deaths.

An involuntary shudder rippled through Alice.

She searched the people again, trying to find some hint of emotion reflected on any of their faces. She lighted upon Councilman Renner, the vampire who'd been interested in having her map the Council's history, but his lips were pressed firmly together. Something about his expression steeped in disapproval. He stared at her dispassionately, as if they'd never met before. She was an object of curiosity, not the woman he'd been willing to entrust with the Council's secrets.

"Let's get this over with, shall we?" A distinguished-looking gentleman, dark hair coiffed into perfection, rose. He walked to the end of the table where Alice and Sebastian stood. His nose tilted into the air. "I smell the newly transitioned."

Despite the eloquence with which he spoke, there was disdain beneath his words. Alice slid her hand to Sebastian's forearm and squeezed.

The man's gaze skimmed over her and went to Sebastian. "Mr. Kent, you are accused of endangering the Council, dereliction of duty and of hiding your true self, an...*abomination*, within the vampire community. It seems you compound these offenses by adding the crime of creating a new vampire without the Council's approval."

"You forgot to mention that I told a human about vampires, Councilman Sage," he responded dryly.

Sage ignored him. His tailored suit clung to him as he slid his hands behind his back. He was relaxed, despite his militant pose. "The punishments for these crimes are banishment, stripping of rank, the whim of the Council and death. In that order."

The whim of the Council. What did that mean? Although it couldn't be much worse than death.

"Then let me address the first two, Councilman. I think my response would satisfy any needs of the Council to mete out justice," Sebastian said. His chin tilted into the air. "I have served the Council loyally for more than forty years. Not once did any member of the Council get hurt or injured in any way while I was on duty. No one ever questioned my loyalty. Up until recently, I would have lain my life on the line for the Council. Without hesitation. Without regret. No matter how often the Council challenged me and my decisions, I did what was required of me. I worked hard to prove again and again that I deserved my position. That I was worthy of the Council and community attention." His gaze went around the room to each and every member. "It seems though that I may have misplaced my loyalty. At the Council's first opportunity to denounce me, it did. And I am not blind or stupid enough to ignore it. Not when I have another to consider. So it is without regret that I announce my resignation from the Council guard."

One of the men seated at the table lifted his hands above the table and began to clap. "Eloquent speech, Kent. It's the least you could have done. But how dare you accuse the Council of turning its back on you? That simply isn't possible. The Council does not issue loyalty. The Council demands it."

"No!" Sebastian shouted. "The Council has to earn it. And that is your greatest flaw and most vulnerable weak point. You rule over hundreds of thousands of vampires, yet have never earned any of their loyalty. It is why you will *fall*."

Alice watched the heated debate, immensely proud of Sebastian. It would have been easy to drop to his knees, crawl over to the men and women who held their lives in their hands and beg for forgiveness.

Another man shot to his feet. Hands pressed against the pristine table, he leaned forward, glaring at Sebastian. "How dare you—"

"How dare *you*," Sebastian returned. "I gave you my life. And this is how you reward me."

"Enough!" shouted Sage. He resumed a normal tone after clearing his throat. "We accept your resignation, despite the ridiculousness with which you reasoned yourself out of an enviable job serving us. However, that still leaves us with two very important matters. The first of which has been a very long time in coming."

"The question of your birth has finally been answered. You were never explained, and we all witnessed the reason firsthand." A blonde woman spoke in a low, soft voice. For some reason it drew Alice's attention more than the people who'd been yelling had. "Do you deny that you are a dragon? A creature not seen by anyone for more than five hundred years. A creature that once systematically killed every human, vampire or whatever life stood between it and its wealth. A creature of war. A creature brought to extinction for very good reason."

"I don't deny it. I can't. But I submit that I am as much vampire as you are. My heart has been with our community, despite its readiness to turn its back on me."

"The ability to subsist on blood does not make you

a vampire. You might be nothing more than a parasite. After what we saw, how do you expect us to call you vampire?"

Alice found her voice. "Because a parasite can't make another parasite. But a vampire can."

Gage's dark eyes burned with malice. "*You* will have your own trial shortly. I suggest you stand quietly to the side until then."

Motherfucker.

Alice took a step forward, eyes narrowed, readying herself to call down the wrath of someone who knew how to survive on the streets. Sebastian grabbed her hand, though. Squeezed.

She drew in a deep breath, almost laughing at her learned method for calming herself. Didn't need to breathe anymore, but a measured inhale and exhale still did the trick. And as with everything else Sebastian had taught her, Alice gave him her trust. He would get them both out of this. She just had to give him the chance.

"I've spent almost my entire life questioning who I am. What I am," Sebastian said after a pause. "With the help of my mate, I no longer question it. And right now, I refuse to let a bunch of men and women who don't have my best interests at heart challenge me or us."

"We don't challenge it any longer, or do you deny that you shifted into a—" a derisive snort, "—dragon not two nights ago?"

"I don't deny it," he replied. She thought he sounded rather proud.

"So you are a dragon. And now you insult us by calling this woman your mate." Sage sounded resigned. "After your envoy had been instructed to let you know that your immediate presence before us was required. Or had you not received the missive?"

"I had. And under other circumstances, I would have requested sanction to turn her before the deed was done. Your executioner knows well enough why I was delayed. Something—someone—more important than the Council needed me." Sebastian squeezed Alice's hand tighter during grumbled protests. "I also knew the Council that I'd served so faithfully and so well would not deny me this chance at happiness. That the Council wanted what's best for the warriors who put the lives of Council members before their own."

"You mean you presumed to know what was best for the Council."

"Yes, I did. That's been my job all this time. Doing what's best for the Council by analyzing every situation the Council publicly faced. This was no different."

"Then your arrogance will be the death of you. And your mate." Sage turned his back on them and slowly strolled to the empty chair he'd previously occupied. Still staring at them, he sat down, his dark eyes full of judgment. "Regardless, it seems that we are agreed on one fact. You created another vampire without the Council's approval. That, from the beginning, has been one of our primary laws. Having you break it willingly and willfully is most egregious. While every other thing about you, Sebastian Kent, could be overlooked by a merciful Council, that cannot."

Alice looked up at Sebastian, her attention snagged by the small plume of smoke drifting from his face. His gaze went to her, an apology forming in dark eyes drifting toward blood-red in coloring. Her mouth lifted in a small smile, the signs of his dragon always exciting her possibly more than they should have. He could have only done it one better by letting those gorgeous wings flap in the small room. That'd show the stupid Council. Then they'd really get to see who was arrogant.

No, not arrogant.

Justified.

THE DOOR TO the room opened and only seconds later, a cart was pushed through. He might have taken a moment to study the objects on its surface, but once he caught sight of three stakes, his heart began to flutter. When Antaeus Stavrou stepped into the room, face hardened and determined, Bast tensed. He stepped forward, putting himself between the executioner and Alice.

"Is anyone going to ask me my thoughts or opinions, or do they not matter because I'm just a human? Or I'm not quite a vampire yet," Alice amended. She was still looking at Bast, and when he glanced back to look at her, his heart swelled with so much emotion that he couldn't have pulled his gaze away from her if he tried. They stood in a quiet room, full of people who condemned him, and she took it all in stride.

He studied her blue eyes, gone brighter since she'd begun transition. Those crazy curls seemed a little tamer but framed her face as if it was a picture of sensual beauty. Which, of course, it was. Her skin seemed creamier, a little more soothed. The fatigue he'd witnessed over the past week, the underlining defeat she'd held within her, all gone now. Transition suited her well and would only enfold her tighter in its embrace over the next few days.

In his heart, he knew that the tumor, which had sent

her so close to death's door, would begin to shrink and then eradicate itself altogether. Once she survived the judgment of a council gone drunk on its own power, she would live to see many wondrous things.

"I'm afraid you are collateral damage," Councilman Renner said from across the room. Bast dragged his attention away from Alice to frown at him. "This isn't about you as a human, but the message being sent to the rest of the vampire community. Regardless if we like you, and I for one do, the idea that vampires can create vampires without consent is unfathomable. Vampires would overrun the world if left unrestrained."

"But you're deciding my fate. How can you sentence me to death when I haven't done anything wrong? I won't be punished for loving someone."

"Your crime isn't for loving someone. It's for being born," Renner said gently. "It's not a decision against you. The crime is Sebastian's, but you have to bear the brunt of it."

Alice squeezed Bast's hand, then looked up at him again. Winked.

He blinked back, confused. Did she know something that he didn't?

She turned her attention back to Sage. "We were on our way to establishing a sort of relationship, right? Was it my imagination? The Council had taken my proposal to be its historian very well, I'd thought."

Sage answered. "We would have considered it. Yes."

"I see." She released his hand to begin pacing in front of him. He almost smiled at her attorney-like demeanor in this mockery of a trial. "Would I have chronicled anything beyond the Council's members and their activities, you think?"

"I don't see how this—"

"Humor me."

Renner's eyes narrowed. "Perhaps the matters of history that pertain to the entire community, if you'd had the time for it."

"I see," she replied judiciously. "One of the things you don't know about me is that my beginnings as a genealogist are humble. Initiated because deep in my veins, the blood of royalty runs. And with that pedigree comes certain privilege. In some cultures, people believed that royalty also held sway over other creatures. Can you believe it? Just because one was born to a certain family. Knowing that, I now understand how Sebastian and I were drawn together. The affinity. It's also easy to see how others could never understand it and maybe even condemn it. But they don't know enough to make decisions about us. Not really. And let me tell you what else I know. A week ago, I didn't know anything about vampires or werewolves or even dragons. I was a simple girl living a simple life. Then I met this amazing man who introduced me to an incredible life. And one of our earliest adventures together involved a bunch of werewolves. How many of them exist, you think?"

The sudden left turn of her last question added to Bast's confusion. He had no idea where this was going.

Renner's brow furrowed. "They number in the thousands." He looked around the room for confirmation. "Not more than a few hundred thousand, I would think."

"But you don't know?"

"Not for certain. How could we?"

Alice stopped her pacing and lifted her head. The

smile that followed next gleamed. "Why don't you know?" she persisted.

"This Council is the law body for vampires. We concern ourselves with *vampire* matters. Anything we know or do pertaining to werewolves occurs when their actions affect us and only then."

"But you don't rule over them?"

"No, of course not," Sage snapped.

"I see." She resumed pacing, face cast down as if deep in thought.

Bast folded his arms across his chest, his admiration almost overriding his curiosity.

"I once heard Sebastian being called *hybride* by his own man. Ever heard that term before?" She looked up, searching faces, obviously awaiting an answer. No one spoke. Turning to Bast, she asked, "What's it mean, darling?"

Bast said between tightened lips, "Hybrid. Mongrel."

She said innocently, "But what does that have to do with…*oh!* I see. They're calling you a hybrid. A cross between two species." Alice walked over to Bast and, with the softest stroke of her hand, caressed his face. "My hybrid," she said just above a whisper. Loud enough for any vampire to hear, but the words triggered something within Bast. And he suddenly understood all of it.

With Alice's touch still centering him, he took a deep breath. Closing his eyes, he found the pool of heat at his center and focused on it. The taste of sulfur filled his throat a moment later and Bast indulged in it. His body tensed, every muscle burning with strain. He gave in to the sensation, relishing it. Willing it to spread.

He opened his eyes, allowing the members of the

Council to witness the change already forming there. The swirl of colors and reptilian elongation Alice had described to him. The world around him brightened, becoming sharper. Details in hair follicles, skin pores and fabric threads no longer secrets being kept from him. He saw it all. His mouth watered from their taste. Their smell.

Alice whirled toward the members of the Council. "If you have no right to make claims over the werewolf population…"

The pain flowed through his back, where the agony coalesced in two lateral centers. The harsh scissoring sound of fabric ripping behind him shattered the silence, and Bast simultaneously released a groan. The sweet torture would be worth it in the end.

Hands balled into fists and black scales sprouted down his arms, ripples of shining ovals unfolding like playing cards at the hands of a skilled Vegas dealer. He stretched his neck, mentally tracing where his skin hardened and changed. The heat built and rose across him in more rhythmic waves.

Bast exhaled, concentrating hard. Stopping the ascension. A quick second later, he changed focus, sending his thoughts racing to his back, where his glorious wings began to grow and spread. After a moment, he stood before the Council, wings outstretched, spanning the width of the entire room. He scanned each member, memorizing the astonished faces as smoke ascended from his nose.

Alice took a few steps back and glanced at him over her shoulder. Her gaze went straight to his wings. "So damned sexy," she muttered before turning on the Council. "If you have no rights over werewolves, if your laws are meaningless to them…" She leaned forward, glaring. "Then why the fuck do you think any of your laws apply to a dragon and its mate?"

The room erupted into shouts and the Council members began dividing—those who agreed with Alice against those who didn't. Not that it mattered to Bast. She was right. He was a dragon and he accepted what that meant. The Council was no longer a part of his life. The woman standing at his side was and forever would be.

He turned toward the doorway, finding Antaeus standing before it. The executioner dipped his head in silent agreement. He mouthed, *well matched*, and Bast almost grinned at him in reply. Antaeus turned the knob and stepped away from the door as it swung away. Freedom to be found beyond the threshold.

Taking the cue, Bast waited for Alice to lead them out. Anyone who dared stand in her way would find him or herself quickly confronted by a possessive dragon. When she didn't move though, he tilted his head over his shoulder, trying to capture her attention. "Alice?" he said gently.

No response.

Bast glided to her front, ignoring the way the Council members scrambled to get out of his way. He accidentally brushed against one of them, who shrieked as his wing made contact. His heart was pounding too hard for Bast to care. "Alice!"

Horrified, he watched as her muscles began to contract. Over and over again. The tonic-clonic seizure took her from rigid stiffness to violent activity within seconds.

"No!" he screamed.
Too late.
He'd been too fucking late.

THIRTY-ONE

PAIN RIPPLED DOWN Bast's back as he went to her, wrapping his arms around her. "No...*no*..."

Tears filled his eyes, flooding his cheeks until he could scarcely see as he lowered their bodies to the floor. He tried so hard, so incredibly hard to make her stop shaking. To get her body to stop its frantic movement. "Please, Alice. Don't do this." He looked up. Searched the room for someone—anyone—to help him. To help her. "Don't do this to me now."

He'd only just found her. Their time together too short. Too damned short.

He wanted eternity. Demanded it. If this seizure took her from him...the thought was too horrible to even complete.

Had he been too selfish by turning her into a vampire? He'd thought that with the ability to create Jasmine Gerulaitis, the crazy universe—the one that had hated him all this time, the one that made him a pariah among the only family he'd ever known—he'd thought just maybe it had figured he'd deserved a break. That they deserved a chance at love, no matter how flawed they were. He had so much and he'd give it all away. Every penny of it. Just please God, please, give him back this woman.

Turning her on the side, he tried to focus past the tears and fear. Her last seizure hadn't lasted more than a couple of minutes, although every second felt like an eternity. Protect her from injury. That's all he had to do. When she awoke, she would be fine. No matter what the doctor had said. She would be fine because she had to be.

Arm beneath her head, he leaned closer. "You're going to be fine, Alice. Are you listening to me?" He slammed his eyes shut, cleared the tears still flowing and tried again. "I love you and you will not leave me. Not now. Not ever. We have a very long life together ahead of us, and I won't do it without you. I won't."

"Kent."

His head snapped up, teeth bared as he growled at Councilman Sage. Bast called on his dragon, the one that came to him now as easily as blinking, and a ripple of scales raced down his arm again. The hand nearest to Sage stretched into a claw with lethal nails meant for shredding his enemy to pieces. And right now, Sage was enemy.

The older vampire took a step back. "I only wanted to ask if you needed anything. To help."

"Why?" rumbled from his throat.

"This isn't over, but the Council is divided. I predict that most likely she was right." His gaze went to Alice. To his surprise, Bast noted genuine concern there. "You're not truly vampire and therefore, not under our laws. You are a dragon…a rare species that we cannot afford to have against us. We hold no dominion over you, unless you choose to live as one of the vampire nation, which we of course cannot allow you to do."

Bast turned his back on the man, not caring if he lived or died right now. Not wanting to be a vampire for the first time in his life. His one focus, his only concern was the woman before him. "Did you hear that, princess? We're free." Was it his imagination, or did there seem to be less activity now? "So come back to me. Whole. Come back to me so that we can do so many things. Remember what I said? I'll give you everything you've ever dreamed. Anything at all. Just come back to me."

He gritted his teeth as stabbing pins prickled up his arm, wiping away the scales and remainder of his dragon features. Alice continued to jerk, each movement soliciting a soft moan from her. He would have loved to dream she knew what was happening to her and was on her way back, fighting and clawing her way back to him. Struggling to survive. But so far, she hadn't done anything or said a word. And he was desperate. So very desperate for one little sign. Just one.

"You figured it out, why you and I were meant to be. You're a princess, and princesses and dragons have always been together. Our true natures knew we belonged with each other. So see, you can't leave. You can't defy nature." The contractions began to slow, and Bast watched every unnatural movement, willing it to be the last. "If you love me, Alice, you'll stop now," he whispered. "Stop, please...*please.*"

And it worked. For whatever reason, and he didn't care how or why, she stopped. There was no more clenching and unclenching. No more uncoordinated jerks that rattled her entire body. Alice lay in his arms, her mouth pressed tightly together, the skin around her eyes pinched. There wasn't peace in her expression, but all of the tension he'd just witnessed from her illness settled into a single place.

She only now had to wake up.

Bast got to his feet, carrying her in his arms. He held on tightly, almost too timid to believe the seizure had stopped. Some irrational part of his brain insisted that if he took a single step, she would begin to seize again and it would be the last thing she did. That he'd never hear her laugh again. Never look into those beautiful blue eyes. Paralyzed with fear, he looked to the door, wanting with every heartbeat to take her through it and to the other side. To get her medical help. But he couldn't do it. "Alice," he groaned. *Oh, God. Please help.*

A voice called to him. "Bast."

He blinked through the blur to find Drew waiting. He stood in the doorway, watching Bast. Watching Alice.

"I—I can't. She'll die."

"She won't die," Drew reassured. "She's just sleeping. Look at her. Look at her chest. She's breathing and just sleeping."

Like he said, there was a slow rise and fall to her chest. But it wasn't enough. Not nearly. "Will she wake up?"

"I don't know, old friend. Let's take her to the hospital, and we'll wait and see, okay?"

Bast nodded and took a single step forward. Then another. And then another.

HIS EYES BURNED, but Bast forced them open, wincing as fluorescent lighting filled his vision. The monotonous *beep-beep-beep* almost didn't register anymore, but he had a feeling that if it stopped, it would have snapped him to attention, even as fatigued as he felt. His muscles, stiff from constant vigil, protested as he sat up, but Bast ignored them.

Forty-eight hours of no sleep. Forty-eight hours of waiting at her side as she slept beneath starched sheets and machines monitored her continuously from the bedside. He made sure to speak to her every hour. To make sure she knew he waited for her and had no intention of going anywhere. Not without her. Not until she woke up for him.

One more day and he'd transfer her to the care of a vampire physician, but for now, the humans seemed to be doing a commendable job. They scanned her brain, surprised that the tumor seemed to be smaller than only a few days previous. They chalked the difference up to human error, but Bast knew differently. He just hoped that the other anatomical changes she was undergoing while unconscious had occurred quickly enough. That she'd begun to transition before having a seizure could do permanent harm. There was just no way to tell until she woke up.

He turned his head to find Drew watching him. His warrior sipped on a mug of something hot. Coffee, he guessed. Bast couldn't tell the last time he'd moved from his spot against the wall, out of the way of hospital staff but close enough to be useful if needed. When this was over, Bast wouldn't have enough ways to repay him.

"I think I'm up for the night," he said through a sleep-clogged throat. Bast scanned the room for their new friend, stifling the urge to growl once found. "Any trouble?"

"None," Drew replied. "Quiet day."

The man seated in the plastic-lined chair twitched in his sleep, his fingers flexing and twitching as if he spent his time working with his hands in a respectable

trade job instead of shooting shit into his veins. Bast
tried not to see the resemblance, but he wasn't blind.
They had the same big blue eyes and bone structure.
Hell, he even recognized the untamed curls. Alice and
Richard could have almost been twins. Only now, her
"twin" looked sicker than she did, skinny and pale in
a way that would have pained him to see on Alice. But
Bast had begged Gray and the others to find him. Despite the way her brother had treated her, Alice still
loved him and if hearing his voice would help guide
her back, then Bast would have followed him to hell
and back just to get him here.

She hadn't responded to Richard's voice, but Bast
made her a promise. When she woke up, her brother
would be going to rehab. He'd foot every cent of the
bill. He told Alice that if she would only wake up to say
goodbye, Bast would send him on his way.

Something about watching him though, seeing him
here and alive while his sister lay in a hospital bed,
sent anger piping through Bast's veins. Where was the
fucking justice in the world when a sickly junkie got
to live and the woman he loved, the one who made him
proud, slowly sank further into herself? Bast flung out
an arm, striking Richard in the leg.

"Fuck, man!" He reached for his leg, rubbing the
target.

"When's the last time you talked to your sister?"
Bast asked.

"Hell, dude. I dunno. Was sleeping. You 'spect me
to be talking to her all the time? You know she don'
hear nothing no way."

Bast stood to his full height, tilting his head from
side to side, allowing the loud cracks of stiff joints

to reverberate. He flexed his fingers in full view of Richard's face, intent on letting him understand the seriousness of disobedience. They had to have this demonstration once every six hours or so and quite frankly, Bast was tired of it. He shot across the space, grabbed Richard by the shirt and stuck his face within an inch of his. "If I expect you to sing to her, you will sing. If I expect you to pray to her, you will pray. You will do any Goddamned thing—"

"Hey...no fighting..."

It was so soft, said so timidly that Bast should have missed it. But dear God, he'd been waiting more than two days to hear that voice again. Even when he'd received a cryptic message from the mysterious other dragon, promising to meet with him soon. One that spoke of unease and disquiet among the creatures of the earth. One that promised eventual war... Even then, Bast hadn't been as focused on something or someone as he was now, with full and complete attention.

He released Richard, who grunted at being dropped, managing to cross the room and be at her side with inhuman speed. "Alice?"

Her closed eyes fluttered, but slowly opened. It was the most beautiful thing he'd ever seen. "Hi," she said just above a whisper.

For a moment, Bast was riveted to the spot. He didn't know if he should touch her or what to say. He couldn't decide if he should kiss her first or tell her he loved her or any of a dozen different things. He didn't know what to do. Didn't know which way to turn. He glanced at Drew, who wore a half smile, then turned to Richard, who looked bored. The fuck.

Alice touched him first. Her fingers grazed the top

of his hand, and Bast thought his heart might jump out of his chest, it raced so hard and so fast. He swallowed reflexively. Searched for his voice. Looked for the right words.

Not knowing what else to do, he went down on one knee and kneeled next to the bed. He draped an arm across her thighs and bent his head to rest next to her side. Eyes closed, he blinked back the tears he couldn't seem to keep from forming. She let him stay there for such a long time, every once in a while stroking a hand through his hair. With every brush, some of the tension and worry eased from his body.

By the time he thought he could speak without breaking down, several minutes had passed. Bast looked up and found her watching beneath half-lidded eyes. "I love you," he said.

"I love you, too."

"I can't do that again, Alice. I cannot do that again."

"I know."

"Don't leave me like that again."

A small smile. "No. Not if I have anything to do with it." After a long pause, she said, "I heard you talking to me. I kept drifting and every time I thought I was drifting too far away, I heard you."

"I have something for you," Sebastian said. He nodded toward Drew. The vampire nudged Richard, who shuffled forward, albeit reluctantly.

Alice's mouth parted, her gaze darting from Richard to Bast and back again. "Richie?"

"Hey, girl."

Her hand flew to her face, covering her quivering lips as her eyes shimmered. Then her trembling arms extended, opening so her brother could fall into them. This time, Richard didn't need to be nudged.

"Hey, girl," he repeated softly against her hair. "Missed you."

Bast waited patiently, almost willing to let his dislike of the man outweigh his love for the woman. But as he watched them together, Alice's possessive grip and Richard's fierce hug, he reconsidered. Maybe the asshole would be less of an asshole once he got off the junk keeping him high.

After a few minutes, her tears reduced to sniffles, Alice pulled back, a sweet smile on her lips. One hand remained clasped around Richard's, but she used the other to reach for Bast. He went to her without hesitation.

"Richie, I want you to meet someone very important to me. This is Sebastian Kent, your brother-in-law, and the man who's changed my world."

EPILOGUE

One month later...

Bast lifted his gaze from the whiskey mixer to locate the two women in the other room of Corin's house. He couldn't help himself from seeking them out. Their laughter brought a smile to his lips, and once again he marveled that circumstances had brought him to this place in life.

"Thank you for bringing your mate," Corin said. "Mine is tired of my company."

Alice sat at Jasmine's swollen feet, dabbing neon green nail polish on each of her toes. Their glasses of lemonade sat untouched, the plates of cookies next to them equally ignored. Stretched out across the couch, Jasmine rubbed the sides of her protruding belly periodically, her chatter almost nonstop. While she looked happy, it was very evident that her due date galloped closer.

"I very much doubt that," Bast replied.

Corin sipped the rose-colored liquid. "Can't sleep. Heartburn. Can't get up without help. She blames me for how miserable she is."

Bast chuckled. "Well, *that* I agree with. It's the plight of fathers-to-be everywhere. Hang in there. A week to go, right?"

"Any day now."

The two men weren't fast friends the way the women had bonded, but Bast grudgingly appreciated having someone to talk to who understood being ostracized. No longer a part of the Council guard, he didn't know who else to approach with his questions and concerns. Funny how he'd never realized how much he'd made that job his entire world.

Bast rubbed his chest, still not quite used to the double thump that filled him whenever he was in Jasmine's presence.

Corin studied the motion and said, "Your animus?"

He sat back. "No, the dragon urge isn't as strong as it used to be. It's getting better. I can control it better, too."

"What of the information Jas gave you? Did it help?"

"Dribbles." Despite her diligent research, Alice could only glean bits about Aurak RithRagoth, a leader of some renown. Bast didn't know whether to attribute the dragon as merely the leader of his ancestors, or if Bast was a direct descendant of him. "It's helped me discover more about me than I used to know, about the animus, as you call it."

Additional research explained his affinity to wealth and his uncanny ability to manipulate it, apparently a prominent dragon trait. He'd also learned that every eerie sense of memory he'd experienced was another trait. Memories were inherited up to a point. It's why he remembered the taste of fire in his mouth and the glorious sensation of flying.

Dragons were additionally attracted to royalty, often in the past kidnapping their human saviors to get them through illness. That Bast had happened upon one whose bloodline offered him the succor he'd needed and more so, one *willing* to provide it without thought to herself, bordered on miraculous.

Bast continued. "Two things I'm certain of, based on what we can find. First is that I'm not alone."

Corin held up a hand and when Bast paused, the executioner tilted his head toward the direction of the women. His eyes unfocused as he eavesdropped. Seemingly satisfied over the women's discussion of the topic—something having to do with having sex to induce labor—he quirked his lips and motioned for Bast to continue.

"Sounds like Alice and I should make ourselves scarce," Bast said with a low voice.

The other man laughed softly. "That suggestion came from your mate, not mine. I think Jasmine would sooner hit up Google on how to perform a C-section on herself." Corin shrugged, but Bast wasn't fooled. If his woman would have him, Corin would have been all over that. "But continue. What do you mean that you're not alone?"

"That's just it. I don't know. I have no clue if that means my father is alive, if I have brothers or sisters. I just have some vague information about a dragon clan."

"What will you do if there are more of you?"

"At this point, I don't even know. Not even sure if it's worth pursuing. I know what I am now, and nothing's going to change it or the fact that I'm no longer welcome by the vampire community."

"Not all of the community," he replied. "Just some of them."

Sebastian snorted. Just the important ones. "I wonder who else is at the wrath of the Council?" From what he understood, Corin's situation with the Council was tenuous at best.

"More importantly, why."

"Why may not be such a hard thing to discover. I don't know if you've felt it, but it seems like there's a rippling undercurrent of discord coming from almost everywhere."

Corin remained thoughtful for a moment. The sound of the women's conversation drifted toward them, but Bast tuned it out. Let the women remain ignorant to the prospect of a storm on the horizon for a little while longer. He loved knowing that Alice remained happy. And his.

"No, that discord isn't news, but they try to keep it hidden beneath shows of power. They *are* hiding something."

Sebastian leaned forward, his voice lowering. "What have you heard?"

Corin shook his head. "Not so much heard, just a feeling. I also know that you and I aren't the only ones who are thinking this way."

"You're right, because that's the second thing I'm learning from the texts. The latest one says 'war is coming.' I'm not sure what to make of it."

"War, by itself, for men trained like us…doesn't mean much. For you, the man…that's different. You straddle the breed lines."

"I need to know war between whom before that becomes a concern."

He would not indulge in the rift between vampires and werewolves, if possible. But a full-blown war between the two groups didn't seem likely. Their animosity was centuries old, with only skirmishes to show for it. To Bast, true war meant the possible annihilation of a species.

Always, the words of Locke, the werewolf, returned to him. There were more creatures out there than he'd dreamed of. If war was expected to break out, who among the groups would rise up?

And who would rule?

Bast's attention focused at the approach of Alice. The expression on her face bordered between timid and bewildered. "What's wrong?" He could almost scent her fear.

Corin shot to his feet, and Bast followed suit. The executioner used a long stride to cross the room, almost managing to rush past Alice. She held out an arm, temporarily blocking him from going far. "She said if you acted like an idiot, I was to get Sebastian to wrestle you to the ground."

Bast's brow shot up. "Wh-what?" he choked out, barely suppressing his surprise.

Alice's cheeks pushed up in a smile. "Her water just broke. I do believe you're about to become a father." She pressed her hand against Corin's chest when he started forward again. "She means it, and I'm not about to mess with a pregnant vampire's request. To the ground if you go, as she calls it, 'all He-Man' on her."

The room tightened, with tension rolling off Corin in waves. His gaze slanted dangerously toward Alice, and Bast had the incredible, horrific feeling that things were about to get physical. Friend or no, if he took one wrong step…

Corin shuddered, as if physically shaking off his agitation, and said in a gentle voice, "I'd like to go to my wife and meet our child now."

If his tone was meant to reassure her, it did. Alice smiled even larger, then dropped her arm to the side. She went to Bast, holding him tight, and together they watched the large man go to his wife.

"Will that be us one day?" Alice asked.

Bast didn't know for certain if they'd ever have children, but he did know if Alice asked it of him, he'd be reluctant to say no. The idea of producing another generation of vampire-dragons didn't appeal to him. Not yet, not while things remained uncertain. Another year or two with his mate at his side, though? "It's quite possible, princess."

They waited for the other couple to approach. Corin had his hand behind Jasmine's back as he helped her walk toward the front door of their home. His expression mixed excitement with concern, while Jasmine couldn't have been smiling more broadly. "Showtime!" she declared.

"I'm so excited for you!"

Bast scanned Alice's face, one glance proving she would indeed want to have a baby some day.

He immediately changed his previous way of thinking. He loved her with his entire being and if she asked for a baby tomorrow, he would never turn her down. It pleased him through his toes to know she loved him that much. That she wouldn't let his mixed heritage be a hindrance for their family's ultimate happiness.

He pushed his face into her hair, snuggling against her. Needing her touch. Wanting her badly. She rubbed her hand over his chest, soothing the rising emotion.

"Call us when you're up for visitors," he said to Corin's back, plans for getting his mate alone for an hour or two taking precedence. "Oh, but wait...do you know what you're having? I don't remember you ever telling me. A boy or a girl."

Corin looked back over Jasmine's head. His smile was mischievous. "Oh, we know."

* * * * *

ABOUT THE AUTHOR

DEE CARNEY BEGAN writing short stories in middle school, but did not attempt completion of a novel until almost ten years later—which, despite good intentions, she never finished. Almost ten additional years later, she challenged herself to begin writing again, and her love for storytelling was rekindled.

Now, Dee is a bestselling, award-winning author who lives at home in Georgia with her husband and their four-legged children. When not writing, Dee is usually curled up on the couch with a good book!

To learn more about all of Dee's books, please visit her at www.deecarney.com.